The Best American Mystery Stories 2004

GUEST EDITORS OF
THE BEST AMERICAN MYSTERY STORIES

Wow! What a great collection of stories!

Otto Penzler

The Best American Mystery Stories™ 2004

Edited and with an Introduction
by **Nelson DeMille**

Otto Penzler, *Series Editor*

Best wishes —

Nelson DeMille

HOUGHTON MIFFLIN COMPANY

BOSTON · NEW YORK 2004

ISSN 1094–8384
ISBN 0–618–32968–4
ISBN 0–618–32967–6 (pbk.)

Printed in the United States of America

MP 10 9 8 7 6 5 4 3 2 1

"Bet on Red" by Jeff Abbott. First published in *High Stakes*. Copyright © 2003 by Jeff Abbott. Reprinted by permission of the author.

"Stonewalls" by Jeffrey Robert Bowman. First published in *The Chattahoochee Review*, Winter–Spring 2003. Copyright © 2003 by Jeffrey Robert Bowman. Reprinted by permission of the author.

"Height Advantage" by William J. Carroll, Jr. First published in *Alfred Hitchcock's Mystery Magazine*, November 2003. Copyright © 2003 by William J. Carroll, Jr. Reprinted by permission of the author.

"Evolution" by Benjamin Cavell. Copyright © 2003 by Benjamin Cavell. First published in *Rumble, Young Man, Rumble*. Reprinted by permission of Alfred A. Knopf, a division of Random House, Inc.

"All Through the House" by Christopher Coake. First published in *The Gettysburg Review*, Summer 2003. Copyright © 2003 by Christopher Coake. Reprinted by permission of the author.

"Where Beautiful Ladies Dance for You" by Patrick Michael Finn. First published in *Ploughshares*, Winter 2003–2004. Copyright © 2003 by Patrick Michael Finn. Reprinted by permission of the author.

Contents

Foreword

WHEN THIS SERIES, *Best American Mystery Stories*, began eight years ago, my estimable editor at Houghton Mifflin gave me no instructions, no rules, no censorious commands, no guidelines, other than that the stories must fit the definition of the title: The mystery/crime/suspense story must be by an American or Canadian and first published in the appropriate calendar year.

It was understood by us both, however, that the point of each anthology is that it contain the best writing produced that year. The reputation of the author, the subject of the story, the place in which it first appeared — none of that carried any weight. It was from the first, and remains, all about the work.

While the criteria for selecting these stories are inevitably subjective, reflecting my taste and that of each edition's guest editor, the same standards apply to this fiction as to Houghton Mifflin's legendary sister publication, *Best American Short Stories*. You know what they are: characterization, narrative drive, clarity of vision, literary style. Make me believe that the people who populate your stories are genuine, force me to wonder what will happen to them next, have interesting events befall them, say it in a way that hasn't been said a thousand times before, and you've got me in the palm of your hand.

Who writes these literary paragons, and where can their adventures be found? Oh, if only that had a brief answer. Distinguished writers produce more than their share of distinguished fiction. Joyce Carol Oates, than whom there is no more distinguished writer working today, makes her seventh appearance in this series with "Doll: A Romance of the Mississippi." John Updike's sole foray into mystery fiction made it into the 1999 volume. Elmore Leonard made it a couple of times, and so did Dennis Lehane, Jay McInerney, Walter Mosley, Michael Connelly, Russell Banks, and James Crumley.

Some lesser-known authors of — dare one say it? — equal talent have also graced these pages, sometimes to go on to bigger (if not necessarily better) things.

Tom Franklin's first book appearance was in the 1999 *Best American Mystery Stories* with the story "Poachers," from the excellent, if very little, magazine of literary distinction, *Texas Review.* It went on to become the title story of a collection published by William Morrow and was followed last year by a novel, *Hell at the Gate.*

The first time Scott Wolven appeared in a book was in the 2002 edition of *BAMS* with "The Copper Kings"; he now has a collection under contract at Scribner's with the superb editor Colin Harrison. Victor Gischler followed his debut in book form with "Hitting Rufus" with a hard-boiled novel, *Gun Monkeys,* which was nominated for an Edgar Allan Poe Award by the Mystery Writers of America.

In this edition, we may be seeing the launching of several important careers, notably that of Christopher Coake, whose "All Through the House" is one of the most stunning and memorable pieces of fiction in years.

Locating all these outstanding stories is not always easy, as many of the little magazines that publish literary fiction have fairly limited circulation. Happily, Michele Slung, my invaluable colleague, reads voraciously and intelligently and has been able to scout out hundreds of worthy stories, often from the most unlikely sources. Nat Sobel, the best agent in the world, has recommended stories since the inception of this series, and his impeccable taste has made reading none of them a waste of time. Also, many editors of literary journals have taken the time to nominate work that seems appropriate, which has been hugely helpful.

There are more stories from literary magazines in this edition of *BAMS* than ever before. That may be an anomaly, but my best guess is that more serious writers are discovering the attractiveness of the mystery, crime, or suspense story. As readers and aficionados, we can only be grateful for this fortunate turn of events, as it suggests the strength and viability of the mystery genre and gives us assurance that high-quality crime fiction will continue to be produced for years to come.

The guest editor for *BAMS 2004* is Nelson DeMille, the enormously successful author who has combined extraordinary storytelling gifts with a powerful literary style that has consistently put him on best-seller lists with such memorable thrillers as *Word of Honor, The Gold Coast, The General's Daughter,* and *The Lion's Game.*

My sincere thanks go to Mr. DeMille, who took time out from writing his own novel (which was past deadline) to read the fifty stories I submitted to him and from which he picked the twenty that comprise this volume. And I hope it is not bad form to thank again the guest editors from past years who have helped make this series as good as it is, and as successful: Robert B. Parker, Sue Grafton, Ed McBain (Evan Hunter), Donald E. Westlake, Lawrence Block, James Ellroy, and Michael Connelly.

Writers, editors, publishers, and anyone who cares about them should feel free to submit stories to me directly. Provide tear sheets or the entire publication. If the work appears in one of the two most popular mystery magazines, *Ellery Queen's Mystery Magazine* or *Alfred Hitchcock's Mystery Magazine,* save the time and postage, as they are carefully read from cover to cover. If the story initially appeared on-line, please send a hard copy together with the date on which it was published and contact information. No material will be returned, and no criticism will be offered, so please don't ask. Unpublished material, for obvious reasons, cannot be considered.

The absolute final date for submissions for the 2005 edition is December 31, 2004. Have a story published in the spring or summer and send it to me at Christmas and I'll hunt you down with an ax. The earlier I see material, the more likely I am to love it. If you send a dozen or so stories to me, I'm likely to assume your ability to tell mediocre from excellent is wanting. Please send submissions to Otto Penzler, The Mysterious Bookshop, 129 West 56th Street, New York, N.Y. 10019. Thank you.

O.P.

Introduction

As EDITOR AND INTRODUCER of *The Best American Mystery Stories 2004,* I bid you welcome.

You needn't read any further, but may now go directly to the stories.

Still here? Well, then, I won't take much of your time.

In the beginning was Otto Penzler, a legend in the field of mystery publishing, and a very persuasive gentleman. When Mr. Penzler asked me to be the editor of this anthology, I explained that I wasn't qualified to take on the task. He agreed, but in turn explained to me that his first and second choices had dropped out at the last minute, and I apparently owed him a favor.

Like many of my generation, I grew up on mystery short stories, devouring anthologies and collections as well as mystery magazines. My favorite mystery stories, and probably everyone's favorites, were Edgar Allan Poe, and Conan Doyle's Sherlock Holmes mysteries.

The short story is a deceptively simple format, and the mystery shorts seem even simpler, until you try to write one.

Two of the first things I ever had published were mystery stories: one titled "Life or Breath," in *Alfred Hitchcock's Mystery Magazine;* the other called "The Mystery at Thorn Mansion," in the now-defunct *Mystery Monthly.*

I also have a file of rejection letters and enough unpublished short stories to kindle wet logs.

It became obvious to me that short stories are not easy to write just because they are short. Which takes me back to my high school days, when I was a sprinter on the track team. Anyone can run a hundred-yard dash, but the difference between doing it in 11 seconds or 10.2 seconds is the difference between last place and first place.

Obviously, when it came to writing, I wasn't a sprinter, so I tried out for the long-distance team and became a novelist, which I found to be a lot easier.

The moral, if there is a moral, is that the short story, like the short race, needs to be close to perfect; there is no recovery from a bad start, no time to get a second wind, and no forgiveness for even one misstep.

And so, I am honored to have been chosen to pick the top twenty stories for this anthology, and to join a long and illustrious list of past editors whom I will mention here in the hope that future editors will mention me: Robert B. Parker, Sue Grafton, Ed McBain, Donald E. Westlake, Lawrence Block, James Ellroy, and Michael Connelly.

Those authors are themselves the best of the best, but I'm sure that they, like me, have trouble judging the works of others.

I am currently one of four judges for the Book-of-the-Month Club, along with Annie Proulx, Bill Bryson, and Anna Quindlen, and I can tell you that most authors would rather not be judges of other authors — I'd rather be a wine judge, or (ecstasy!) a beauty pageant judge.

So, when Otto Penzler asked me to pick the best twenty mystery stories from more than fifty entries, I was not being coy or humble when I said I was not qualified; I *am* actually qualified, I just don't like to read with the knowledge that I've got to winnow and toss.

Newsday once asked me — and Susan Isaacs and Roger Rosenblatt — to judge essays and fiction pieces sent in by hundreds of readers on the topic of Long Island history. We had to pick one nonfiction and one fiction piece, and I can tell you, these were among the worst pieces of writing any of us had ever read. Thankfully, there were two or three pieces in each category that were good, so picking the winners was not that difficult.

But here we have a different situation; without exception all fifty mystery stories that I read were very good to excellent, and the difference in quality was like the difference between the 11-second hundred-yard dash — very impressive — and the 10.2-second hundred-yard dash — exceptional.

I had great fun reading, but not so much fun picking. In fact, it was agonizing, and I suggested to Otto Penzler a bigger, fatter book of, say, *fifty* of the Best American Mystery Stories.

"Not possible," he said. "It would look like your last bloated novel."

So, I went back to the stories, this time using a single criterion: Did I really want to reread this story?

Doyle's Sherlock Holmes stories are probably the only things I've read six, eight, or ten times each. I can pick up a collection of Sherlock Holmes anytime, anyplace, open at random, and enjoy the story as much as or even more than when I first read it.

So, for better or worse, without too much further agonizing, I have picked what I hope you agree are the Best American Mystery Stories for the 2004 edition.

Enjoy.

And try to pick the best five.

NELSON DeMILLE

JEFF ABBOTT

Bet on Red

FROM *High Stakes*

"I'LL MAKE A BET WITH YOU," Bobby said. He was bourbon-drunk and he leaned close to Sean's ear to talk over the arpeggios of the piano music, the never-ending chimes of the slot machines, the high roar of gamblers who, just for a moment, were beating the odds.

"I'm listening." Sean thought it was about time to head up to his room, tired of talking to Bobby, just tired, period. Bobby was scaring off all the women with his overeager laughing, raising his glass to passing beauties like an idiot dink. It was a shame, really; this was Bobby's last night to be with a woman and the odds weren't pretty. Sean was supposed to get rid of Bobby tomorrow, take him into the desert outside of Vegas, shoot him, bury him deep in the dry earth, and then fly back to Houston with Vic's hundred grand and pretend he hadn't set foot on the Strip recently.

"I bet," Bobby gestured with his near empty glass, "I can nail that pretty little redhead at the end of the bar."

Sean looked. Pretty was an understatement. She was gorgeous, hair that soft color of auburn that made Sean's throat catch, skin flawless as a statue's, dressed tastefully in a little black number that suggested a firm, ripe figure but didn't give away too much of the show. She was sitting alone, not looking at anyone, not trying to make eye contact. Maybe a high-class hooker, maybe not. Maybe just waiting on her boyfriend to finish at the craps table. She was drinking white wine and she cradled the stem of the glass between her palms, like she was keeping a delicate bird from taking wing.

"You aim high," Sean said.

"I got the gun for it," Bobby said.

"And you could impress her with all the cash you got," Sean said. At least temporarily. Sean thought about Vic's money, neat bricks of green he would have to hide in his checked bag tomorrow morning, wishing now he was driving from Vegas to Houston, but what a dreary, endless drive it would have been. He didn't dislike Bobby, didn't like the idea of killing him, but orders were orders and when Vic gave them, you listened.

"Listen, man, that's Vegas for you. The air is thick with constant possibility. You never know which way the ball's gon' drop and then you're broke or rich, all in an instant," Bobby said. "I'm feeling like the ball's dropping my way. She's been looking at me."

"Looking ain't buying," Sean said. "And the keno screen's above your head, buddy."

"But see, that's all Vegas is about. The potential of every single moment." Bobby pulled a wad from his pants pocket, twenties rolled into a thick burrito, and Sean thought, *this is why Vic wants you dead, you dummy.*

"A thousand bucks says I get her," Bobby said.

Sean said nothing. A thousand bucks. Money in his pocket he could take and not feel guilty for taking and keeping after Bobby was dead. If he shot Bobby and then pocketed the money, that would be stealing from Vic, his boss — an unwise move. But if he won the cash from Bobby, then that was fair. Fair as could be. Plus it would be funny to watch Bobby try with the perfect redhead, and hell, if Bobby won, he'd die happier. Harmless. Sean felt an odd tug of friendship for Bobby, soon to die, with his heavy, earnest face flush with life.

"And if you do bed her, what do I have to pay?" Sean said.

"Man," Bobby said, "that happens, I'll have already won."

"That's not a fair bet," Sean said.

"Tell you what: I win," Bobby said, "and you help me straighten out this misunderstanding with Vic. You tell him I've got the deals working just the way he wants."

Vic had sent Bobby to Vegas to shut down his drug operation, sell out the remaining supplies, close the office Bobby ran the deals from three days a week, clean the last hundred grand through the Caymans, pull up stakes, and kiss Vegas good-bye. The Feds and the locals were cracking down hard and Vic didn't have enough friends in town to make dealing worthwhile. Bobby didn't want to give up

Vegas. And instead of taking three days to wrap up the project, Bobby had taken a week, living off Vic's account at the King Midas, apparently doing nothing but drinking and betting and generally not closing shop in any great hurry, keeping the money tied up. And Vic was killing mad.

"That's really between you and Vic," Sean said. "It's your business, Bobby."

"Yeah, but you got his ear more than I do. You could help me a lot. I got the feeling he was a little irritated with me the last time we talked. He doesn't get that it took me longer than I thought it would to collect all the money."

Bobby was fun but dumber than a stump. It didn't matter how long it truly took to gather funds and close shop, it mattered how long Vic gave you to get the work done. Sean finished his beer. Bobby didn't have a chance in hell with the redhead. This was betting with a dead man, and Sean was the house. "Okay," he said. "You're on."

Bobby finished his drink, motioned to the bartender for another. "Observe, grasshopper," he said, moving down toward the redhead.

"Good luck," Sean said, meaning it, being nice, ordering himself another beer for the floor show.

It took about twenty minutes. Sean watched, trying not to watch, Bobby easing onto the stool next to the woman. Sean kept waiting for her to tell Bobby to get lost, to name her price, to ask the bartender to tell Bobby to leave her alone. But instead she gave Bobby a soft, kind smile, talked with him, a little shyly at first, then laughed, let him order her another glass of wine. Once she looked toward Sean, seeing him watching them, maybe having noticed him sitting with Bobby before, knowing he was the friend watching his friend make a move. But she didn't smile at Sean and she looked right back at Bobby, who was now playing it cool, not overeager like he had been the hour before.

They finally got up when she finished her second glass of wine and headed into the acre of casino proper, Bobby giving Sean a knowing wiggle of eyebrow and a subtle thumbs-up with his hand at his side, Sean raising his beer in toast, a little surprised, the redhead never glancing Sean's way.

See you in the morning, Bobby mouthed.

Sean watched them head out into the hubbub of the slot machines and gaming tables, smiling for a minute. Well, it was one sweet way to spend your last night on earth. The angels were on Bobby's side. Sean downed his beer, went out to the roulette table, bet twice on black, watched the ball fall wrong both times, his chips vanish. He didn't really like betting. He remembered that a little too late.

Sean tried Bobby's hotel room early the next morning, about seven, figuring the guy would be sacked out, sleeping late on the last day of his life.

"Yeah?" A woman's voice, sleepy. But polite. A little smoke and purr in her voice. Bobby must have done right by her.

"Is Bobby there?"

"He's in the shower. May I have him call you?" May, not can. The redhead was a nice lady.

"No, thanks, I'll just call him later." Not wanting to leave his name.

"May I tell him who's calling —" she started, but Sean hung up. Got himself showered and dressed, fast, now wanting to get the job done, collect Bobby and the money, kill the poor guy, go home.

Sean called Bobby's room again. No answer, fifteen minutes after he first called. He didn't leave a message on the voice mail system, decided he didn't want to stop by Bobby's room, risk the redhead seeing his face again. Bobby was a breakfast eater, loving the cheap but lavish Vegas buffets, and so Sean headed down to the restaurant. It was crowded with tourist gamblers in vacation clothing, a few bored teenagers, some conventioneering high-tech geeks wearing golf shirts with corporate logos on the pockets.

No Bobby working through a fat omelette, alone or with the redhead. Sean got coffee and a plate of eggs and bacon and sat down in a corner booth, wearing his sunglasses. If Bobby came in, he could excuse himself quickly, tell Bobby to come to his room in an hour, let him enjoy his last meal.

They didn't show. Maybe Bobby'd taken the redhead out for a nicer breakfast than one might find here at the King Midas. Maybe down to Bellagio or Mandalay Bay.

Sean finished his breakfast, checked his cell phone. One message. From Vic.

"Hey, bud," Vic said. "Just calling to see if you're knocking 'em dead in Vegas." That Vic. His little code was a scream. "Hope you're winning big. Call me when you're back."

A little niggle of panic started in his stomach. Sean ignored it, finished his coffee, kept scanning the crowd for Bobby's blond hair, listening for the boom of his voice. Nothing. Tried Bobby's cell phone. No answer.

Sean waited another thirty minutes, tried Bobby's room again, got nothing. He went up to the room, used the extra key Bobby had given him when he got to Vegas yesterday. Bed a mess, Bobby's clothes still in the closet. The slightest scent of perfume was in the air — the redhead smelled like rose petals and spice. But the bathroom was clean, the shower dry, the towels in maid-hung precision.

He's in the shower. But no one had showered in this room.

"No, no, no," Sean said to himself. "Not after I was a nice guy." He ran from the room, his heart thick in his chest, and headed straight down to the lobby.

Sean drove his rental car down the Strip, then to Sahara Avenue, to the leased office Vic had rented when he and Bobby set up the Vegas operation two months ago, before Vic started feeling pressure from the Feds and decided Vegas made him overextended. The sign on the door read PRIORI CONSULTING, which Vic and Bobby had thought clever, because consulting could mean it was any kind of business, and the legal term sounded respectable and fancy.

Sean had a key and he tried the lock.

The door opened. The office was simple, just a desk and a chair and a laptop computer. A motivational poster on the wall said ACHIEVE, with some dink standing atop a mountain summit at dawn, arms raised in triumph. Like that was supposed to impress Sean or Vic, hard evidence of Bobby's absent work ethic. No Bobby. Sean locked the door behind him, set the deadbolt.

He went straight to the little vault in the back room of the office. Opened it with the combination Vic had given him, not wanting Bobby to know he knew the combo, not wanting to make a big deal about the money.

It was gone. Every last sweet brick of green was gone.

Sean sat in the King Midas bar, peeling the label off his beer in long strips, thinking *this is my skin when Vic gets hold of me.*

Bobby was gone.

Sean felt like control over his own fate had danced right out of his arms, like he was one of those losers who surrendered all to the spinning roulette ball, waiting for it to drop into red or black or a sacred number, every hope in the world wrapped up on how that damned ball fell. Now his generous act was going to screw over his life big time. Maybe the redhead would show back up here, if she was a working girl or a guest. He thought she might be a working girl; not many women came to Vegas alone. Maybe she knew where Bobby had run to. But she had lied about the shower, he believed, Bobby maybe paid her to lie. Give him a head start on his run.

Sean didn't know a soul in Vegas who could help him find Bobby, didn't know any of the street-level dealers Bobby recruited, and he had not known what else to do other than go back to the bar, cancel his flight to Houston and pray he got a lead on Bobby.

He had started to call Vic twice, hung up before finishing the number. Not knowing what he could say, almost laughing because he was afraid, scared in a way he didn't want to admit, trying to imagine the words coming from his mouth: *Bobby wanted to get laid, and it just didn't seem likely, so I let him out of my sight. We had a bet. Sorry.*

He switched to vodka martinis and was deep into his second when she came in and sat at the bar.

At first he blinked, not sure it was the same readhead. But it was, this time in leather pants and a white ruffled blouse, simple but stylish. She looked relaxed and she didn't look over at him. She ordered a glass of pinot grigio.

Sean counted to one hundred, waiting to see if Bobby trailed in behind her. Please, Jesus. But no Bobby. Sean got up from the bar stool, took his martini glass with him, eased next to her. She glanced at him.

"I'm Bobby's friend," he said in a low voice.

"I know. And you're probably a little more shaken," she said, glancing at his martini, "than stirred." Her smile was cool, not shy, not surprised. Expecting to see him, maybe even happy about it.

"Where is he?" Sean asked.

She took a dainty sip of wine. "He's resting. Comfortably."

"Where?" Trying to keep his voice calm.

"Some place you won't find him."

"I can look pretty freaking hard, honey. Tell me where he is. Right now."

She ran a fingernail along the stem of her glass and let a few heavy seconds pass before she answered. "You're not really in a position to make demands."

"Not in a crowded bar."

"Not anywhere," she said. "You need to remember that. I'm not working alone. You're being watched wherever you go."

He was silent for several seconds, thinking *what the hell is this?* "I'll remember," he said. There was nothing to be gained by threatening her. Play it cool, he decided, play along, and get her alone and then she'd talk. She was enjoying the driver's seat, relishing it a bit too much, and that was a mistake.

"So, this is the deal," the redhead said. "Bobby had a hundred grand in cash on him. You get ten grand, just to tell one little white lie. Tell Vic you took care of Bobby but he had already blown the hundred grand gambling."

"And Vic just believes me?" Sean said.

"We both know," she said, "that yes, Vic will believe you. If you want, we'll get a statement from a couple of blackjack and baccarat dealers that a guy matching Bobby's description blew through a hundred grand in the past week."

"What about the rest of the money?"

"Not your concern. But Bobby walks and gets a new life somewhere else."

"And still has every reason to tell the cops about Vic. And me. No way."

"Sean," she said. "Do you think Bobby would do jail well?"

He surprised them both by laughing. She gave him back a smile, and the intelligence was sharp in her face, she was clearly no dumb bunny–Vegas lay. "Actually, no, Bobby wouldn't do jail well at all. Be dead or someone's punk in five minutes."

"So you and I both know he's not going to run to the police or the FBI and talk about Vic."

"But he might go into WitSec, cut a deal that keeps him out of jail," Sean said.

Her smile faded. "That's a risk you take. You're not getting close to him," she said. "I've offered you the deal."

"Usually with Vic," he said, "I bring back a finger as proof." This was a lie but he wanted to see her reaction. Vic would think he was a freak if he hauled back a bloodied finger.

"In your carry-on or in your checked luggage?" Not blinking, not afraid at his announcement.

"In a little baggie, actually."

"Messy at security, and I don't believe you."

"Who are you?" he asked.

"You can call me Red."

"I'm impressed with the setup. You in with Bobby from the beginning?"

"I never met him until last night," she said.

"I think that's the first lie you've told me," he said.

"Think what you like," Red said. Her smile went crooked and she took a sip of her white wine. "Tell me. How were you going to spend the bet? The thousand bucks?"

"He told you, huh?"

"Yes." She watched the bartender approach them and she shook her head. The barkeep went back to the other end of the bar.

"Fishing gear, I guess."

"Fishing gear." She said it like she might say *urine sample*. "I am so flattered that it was my maidenly virtue versus accessorizing your bass boat."

Despite himself, he felt a blush creep up his collar.

Now Red gave him a sly sideways glance. "You want to make a bet with me, Sean?"

"No. I want to conclude our business and never see you again."

"Now you've hurt my feelings," she said with a coy pout.

"I'll bet you heal fast," Sean said.

"Bobby said you were ex-military."

"Yeah, I was a grunt once."

"I've always thought military men had a sense of honor."

"I do," Sean said.

"I have a sense of honor, too. I won't screw you over, you won't screw me and Bobby over. We're all happier. Do we have a deal?"

"Don't kid yourself that I want to cut a deal with you, honey. What if I say no?"

"Then you'll be killed," Red said. "How does that sound?"

He watched her face, chewed the last olive in his martini, swallowed the small puddle of vodka at the glass's bottom. Watched her face for a hint of bluff and didn't see any. "Bobby sure got smart since he got to town."

"This town forces you to be smarter, Sean," she said, and now she smiled at him and it seemed genuine, like they hadn't discussed big money and death.

"It hasn't worked on me yet," Sean said.

"You're plenty smart, hon," Red said. "So agree to this. Come to the Misty Moor Bar — off the Strip, near the Convention Center — in two hours. Alone and unarmed. Break either rule and you're dead. You'll get your money then. You will be expected to leave Vegas immediately; we'll even escort you to the airport."

She swung her legs off the bar stool, pulled a ten from her purse.

"I'll buy your wine," Sean said. "You can buy my drink at the other bar."

She tucked the bill back inside. "Thanks. I'll see you then," she said. "And, Sean?"

"What?"

"It's nothing personal. Bobby likes you. So do I."

Red turned and walked out, and he debated whether he should follow her. He counted to twenty, left money on the counter, got up from the barstool, headed out and hung back in the casino's crowd.

She never looked back to see if he trailed her. But if she wasn't working alone, as she said, then her partners might be watching him this very moment. He stayed back as far as he dared, weaving through the slot machines hooting at their triple cherries, past a rail-thin lady carrying a bucket of coins with all the care she would give the Holy Grail, past honeymooners nuzzling in the lobby. She headed past the bell attendants dressed like ancient Greeks. There was no taxi line at the moment, and she quickly ducked into a cab with a promo for a wireless phone service mounted on the trunk, a monkey wearing eyeglasses talking on a cellular.

As soon as her cab pulled out of the circular driveway he grabbed a taxi, told the Nigerian driver to head down the Strip, and said, "See that cab up ahead? With the monkey talking on the phone? Follow it, please."

"Excuse?"

"The ad on the back. See?" She was five cars ahead of them, her driver changing lanes, and Sean could taste his own panic in his mouth, sour and coppery. "Jesus, keep up, don't lose them, but don't get too close."

"Ah," the driver said. "No trouble is wanted."

"That's my girlfriend," he said, "and I think she's dumping me to go back to her husband. I don't want trouble, I just want to know, 'cause if she's leaving me, I'm just gonna go back to my wife."

The Nigerian made a low noise in his throat that sounded like "Americans" but said nothing more.

Screw this meeting on her turf. He wasn't about to risk Vic's rage for a measly ten grand. Let her take him straight to Bobby. He would end their little game tonight, and then get the hell out of town.

The cab took her to a small house, in an older, quiet residential area distant from all the neon and glam. Not a well-to-do neighborhood but not too scruffy. He told the driver to let him off at the corner where her cab had turned, and shoved fifty at the Nigerian, who babbled thanks and revved off. Sean sprinted away from the corner, out of her line of sight. He couldn't see Red but her cab was pulling away from a house nine homes down from where he was, marked with a decorative covered wagon mailbox.

This was, he decided, a good hideout for Bobby. Quiet neighborhood, probably not a lot of crime, older folks who kept an eye on each other. Maybe it was the woman's house, although she looked like she came from money. Or had money. The easy, unafraid confidence she had with him, the nice clothes she'd worn both nights.

He felt a lava-heat anger with Bobby; oddly, he didn't wish Red ill at the moment and his reaction surprised him. He liked her; Vic would have liked her too, but she had chosen the wrong side. She was the kind of girl he'd like to have taken back to Houston, taken out to dinner with Vic. She would have made Sean look good, would have had fun with him. Stupid Bobby, getting himself and this cool girl killed.

Sean headed for the next street, which ran parallel to the street she'd stopped on. In case she'd seen the cab, gotten suspicious. If she'd seen him, she and Bobby would run, and that might be the end of the money and of Sean.

He walked down a little street called Pelican Way — where the hell were there pelicans in Nevada? he wondered — counting houses, just giving her and Bobby time to relax, letting them start to get ready for meeting him at the bar. He counted nine houses, stopped in front of one. Brick, a one-car carport, wind chimes hanging by the front door, the trim and shutters needing a fresh coat of paint.

This ranch-style should be directly behind Red's house. He changed his plan. The house was dark, entirely so, no cars in the small driveway, old oil leaks marring the carport's concrete. The house next door was dark, too, although the house on the other side had a single light gleaming on its porch. He turned like he belonged here and walked, casually, straight up the driveway. He went through the carport, paused at the fence, listened for the rasp of dog breath, and then opened the gate and went inside.

The backyard was empty except for a swing set, an old barbecue, dusty patio furniture in need of a wash. Sean went to the fence and tiptoed onto the rail, peering into Red's backyard. Three lights on in the house. A kitchen with an old-style bay window. Then he saw Red talking on the phone, moving from the kitchen table to the counter, sipping from a water bottle, moving back again. He ducked back down under the fence. Waited a minute. Looked again.

Now the kitchen was empty. He watched, counted to two hundred. Didn't see movement in the house. Counted to two hundred again, looked. All appeared quiet.

No guards, no dogs. The thought that Red must be part of a rival drug ring in town who'd convinced Bobby to switch sides occurred to him, but then he thought not. She didn't seem the gang type. Maybe she really was just working with him, no one else, a heist by her and Bobby. He hoped. It would make his work easier.

Sean went over the fence, dropped down, sprinted for the patio. He had a Glock under his jacket and as he ran he pulled it free. He got to the patio, waited against the door. Listened to the soft buzz of the TV. Sounded like an old John Wayne movie, the distinctive rise and fall of the Duke saying, "Hell, yes, I'm back in town."

Then he heard Red's voice, gentle: "I'll be back in a little while, all right? Enjoy the movie." No answer from whoever she was talking to.

Sean moved away from the door. He heard a door open to his right, into the one-car garage. Light footsteps, just one person, heels, a woman's step. Red, alone. Then a car starting, pulling out of the driveway, headlights flickering on at the last moment. She had a car but had taken a taxi to King Midas so he couldn't follow her to a parked car in the lot. Smart girl. Sean stayed still, counted to one hundred. He went around to the carport, tried the door to the house. Locked.

He popped the glass pane in the door, and it tinkled, surely loud enough for Bobby to hear inside the house. So he worked quickly, reaching inside, fingers fumbling to unlock the door.

There was no deadbolt. Instead, there was another key lock. Bobby was locked in from both sides. Weird. He leveled his pistol through the broken glass, waiting for Bobby to barrel out at the sound of the break-in, but there was no sound in the darkened house except the melodramatic score of the Western, faint as a whisper.

Sean waited ten seconds, a tremble of panic thumping his guts, and decided standing there waiting for Bobby to charge the door wasn't bright. He went back to the patio and kicked in the glass door. Loud shattering noise. Two houses down a dog barked, sharp and hard, twice; then quiet. Sean counted to twenty. Nothing. No concerned neighbors popping a head over the fence.

Sean flicked open the door handle, slid the door open.

The room was a sunken den and the kitchen was to his right. A hallway went off at a left angle. He waited, his gun leveled at the opening, and waited some more. He could hear the sound of horses riding hard and stopping, of John Wayne mouthing a good-natured threat, of a polite man answering with an oozy official tone.

Sean inched down the hallway, the gun out like he'd learned in his days in the army. A feeble spill of light — from a television — came from a room at the end of the hall. He moved toward it, calming his breathing, listening for the sound of Bobby moving, and finally Sean charged fast into the room, going through the door, covering the room with his gun.

Bobby was there. Both hands cuffed to a bed, gagged with a cloth jammed in his mouth and duct tape masking his mouth, ribboning into his hair. One of his eyes was bruised. He was shirtless, dressed only in the khakis from last night with a wet circle of stain on the front, and he smelled like he needed a shower. A pile of pillows kept his head propped up. A little television with a VCR stood on a scruffy bureau, the John Wayne movie playing.

Sean stared for a moment, then shook his head.

Bobby groaned, made pleading noises behind the gag. Sean muted the TV, left the tape running, John Wayne swaggering across a saloon.

"Are you going to scream if I take this off?" Sean asked. "I mean, Vegas is just full of possibilities, isn't it, Bobby? So you said."

Bobby shook his head.

Sean pulled the tape and gag from Bobby's head, not worrying about the threads of hair that ripped free with the industrial tape, and Bobby said, "Oh, thank God, man. Thank God, Sean. I knew you'd find me. Get me the hell out of here."

Sean sat down on the edge of the little bed. "Tell me what's happened." Calm. Curious to hear what the story was, because this tied-up-and-bound gig was not what he expected.

"That bitch, man, she's crazy. Drugged me and tied my ass up. Christ, she's *nuts*. Untie me, man."

"Just a minute," Sean said. "You're not in with her?"

"In with her?" Bobby stared. He jerked at the handcuffs. "Do I look like it?"

"I went to your office looking for your sorry ass," Sean said. "And all of Vic's money is missing. The whole hundred grand."

Bobby's lips — chapped and blistered from the tape — turned into a frown. "Holy shit. She must've taken it."

"She was in your hotel room when I called this morning."

"Shit, man, she slipped something into my drink and knocked my ass out. I woke up here. She must've snuck me out of the hotel somehow. She's got inside help. She probably took all my keys, took the money. Unhook me, Sean. Jesus, let's get the hell out of here." An edge in his voice; Sean thought he was about to cry.

"God, you're dumb. You are so unrelentingly dumb. Did she bring the money here?"

"I don't know, I don't know — just untie me, please, before she gets back here!"

"No hurry." Sean checked his watch. "Because she's heading off to meet me at a bar. She's negotiating on your behalf, buddy, for me to tell Vic that you're dead and for you to keep all his money."

Bobby struggled against the shackles, pulling his head up from the pillows. "That's a goddamned lie. I'm not trying to steal Vic's money! She's set you up. Listen, untie me; we'll wait for her to come back and then we'll make her tell us who she's working for."

"You never saw her before?"

"No, man, I swear it. *Swear it!*"

"But she knows your business. She knows about you working for Vic. She knows my name. She knows there was a safe in the office and she got the combo. You must've seen her before."

"No, I swear."

"Then you must've blabbed to somebody, and that's who she's working with."

"No, never, never," Bobby said, but his voice dropped a notch, spurred by a little jiggle of memory, a thought of a mistake made and now wished away.

"Right, Bobby. Never would you make a mistake. You wear my ass out just listening to you."

"Listen, Sean, she's the bad guy, not me. We can get the money back. Together."

Sean said nothing for a moment, thinking it out, feeling very tired and then wired, all at once. He stood up. Went and searched the house carefully and efficiently. There was scant furniture in the house; he decided it was a rental.

"Sean?" Bobby called quietly. "Sean?"

"Just a minute. Hush," Sean said. No sign of the money anywhere. It wasn't here. He went back to the bedroom, Bobby watching him with eyes glassy with sick fear.

"Sean, you're my friend; Vic's my friend; you know I had nothing to do with this girl's scheme."

"You know, I believe you, Bobby," Sean said. "Had to chase the wrong girl, didn't you?" He nearly laughed. He had made his decision.

"Yeah, I guess," Bobby said.

"Did you get her?" Sean asked, wondering what he'd say.

"No," Bobby said after a moment.

"Then I guess I win the bet."

"Well, that was a bad bet to make," Bobby said.

"That's real true." Sean stood up, turned up John Wayne. Real loud.

Sean had thought the "Misty Moore" was maybe a bar named after the owner, some chick named Misty, but instead it was Moor without the *e* on the end, and when he went inside he noticed a silver thistle above the bar and the waitresses wore tams on their heads and snug little kilts across their asses and the wallpaper was plaid.

He spotted Red sitting in a very private back corner booth, drinking her white wine. The bar was not terribly crowded, a dozen conventioneers watching a basketball game on the big screen, a few locals. He slid into the booth, sitting next to her, not across from her.

"You take the low road," he said, "and I'll take the high road."

"Cute. Scotland was one of the few cultures not raided by Vegas," Red said. She was very calm. "Then *Braveheart* came out and they opened up this place. If you get drunk, they'll paint your face blue."

A waitress approached them and asked Sean what he would drink. "Scotch," he said. "Obviously."

"You're a few minutes late," Red said when the waitress walked off. "Fortunately I'm patient and forgiving."

"More reason to admire you," he said. "Let's get to it."

"I've got your ten thousand," she said. "You still agreeing to lie to Vic, let Bobby walk?"

"Actually, the deal has changed, Red." He kept his voice low and the waitress returned with his Scotch, set it down in front of him, walked off back to the bar.

Red was very still. "Changed?"

"You have the hundred grand. You also have a dead man in your house. You know, your house at 118 Falcon Street. Where you had the John Wayne movie marathon playing." He saw the shift in her face, saw she believed him now. "So, baby, I can call the police, from that phone right over there in the corner, and I figure they can be at your house faster than you or anybody else can be dragging Bobby's body out to your car. You'll have a lot of questions to answer."

"So will you," she said, staying calm.

"No, I won't. Because I sure don't know you, and you can't prove that I know you. Or that I knew Bobby."

"You would have been seen with him at the hotel."

"Maybe. Maybe those folks don't talk after Vic calls his friends at the casino. But Bobby-boy's dead in your house."

"I haven't shot a gun anytime recently. They have chemical tests . . ."

"I wouldn't waste a good bullet on Bobby. Smothered with a pillow, sweetheart," Sean said. "How hard they got to look for a new suspect?"

Red took a microscopic sip of her wine. She set the glass down carefully. "So. What now?"

"Who else here's with you?" he asked.

"No one."

"You had help in getting Bobby out of the King Midas. So don't lie to me. It makes me want to call 911." He smiled at her, touched her hand gently. "You're no longer running the show, sweetness."

She let two beats pass. "The guy in the windbreaker at the bar. He's my partner." Sean allowed himself a very quick glance. The guy was watching them, not threatening, but worried, and he glanced into his beer right when Sean looked at him. The guy was big but had a softness to his hands and his mouth, had a nervousness to him that made Sean feel confident.

"How'd you find out about Bobby and the money?" Sean asked.

She gestured to the waitress for another glass of wine, and he knew then she would tell him, that he had her. "My partner works for an office equipment leasing company. He delivered Bobby's office equipment when Bobby got started. Late in the day, he and Bobby got to talking. Ended up going out for a beer. Bobby doesn't like to be alone, ever, and here he was new in a big town where he didn't know anybody. They got to be drinking buddies and Bobby'd give my partner a little coke now and then when he came to town. One night Bobby drank too much, talked plenty. The safe combo — Jesus, Bobby stuck the numbers on a sticky note in his desk drawer. Not the brightest star in the sky."

"And you were the handy redhead."

"It's not natural," Red said. "I spent $250 on this hair color at a really uppity salon on the Strip after Bobby told my friend he dug redheads."

"Looks good," Sean said.

"Thank you," she said.

Sean looked back at the bar and now her partner kept his stare on Sean. "Your friend appears to be a little nervous," he said. "Are we going to have a problem?"

"No."

"He more than a friend?"

"My brother."

"Oh, please."

"No, really, he is. No joke."

"I love a family that works together," Sean said. "Okay, wave Bubba over here."

She did and at first the brother, uncool, acted like he didn't see her. But then she stood up and said, "Garry, come here, please," clear as a bell and Garry got up and came and sat across from Sean and Red. His mouth was thin. Scared, in over his head.

Sean didn't smile, didn't say hello or offer his hand. "So, the two of you thought you could screw me over."

"Not you," Red said, "Bobby and Vic. Jesus, you act like it was personal." Her smile warmed a little. "I told you it wasn't."

"Doesn't matter," Sean said. "You got a dead guy in your house. What I don't have is what I came here for, Vic's money. Now. I give you guys credit; the scheme was clever. You get rid of Bobby, get the money, and make Vic think that Bobby's on the run so he never, ever comes hunting for you."

"Thank you," Red said.

"You're welcome," Sean said. "I want that money here on this table in ten minutes or I'm calling the police and telling them that there's a funny smell coming from y'all's guest bedroom."

Garry went white as salt. Red took a calm sip of her wine.

"And if we don't cooperate, you get nothing," she said. "You get screwed over just as bad as us, because Vic'll kill you, won't he?"

"Of course not," Sean said.

"Really? You'll have failed in your errand and he's not gonna take it lightly," Red said. "Bobby told me all about him, and we did some checking on him. People piss themselves when Vic comes into a room."

"Maybe Bobby did. He's easily impressed," Sean said, and for the first time Red laughed.

"He was impressed with you, Sean. He liked you. Truly."

Sean felt a pang of regret, wanted to close his eyes, but instead put a hard stare on his face. "Don't tell me that; you'll make me feel bad."

"I'll make you feel worse," Red said. "If you send us to jail, you go home empty-handed. You'll never get your money because we'll give it to the cops, cut a deal to tell all we know about you and Vic and Bobby, and you're just as dead as we are. So call 911, Sean. We'll sit here and wait."

"For God's sake . . ." Garry said.

"Hush, now," Red said. "Sean's thinking. He needs his quiet time."

They had him by the throat just as surely as he had them. Standoff.

"So there's no way out for any of us," Red said, "unless we work together. And unless you're willing to get out from under Vic's thumb."

"I'm not under his thumb," Sean said.

"There's two types of people in this world," Red said. "Bosses and errand boys. Bobby, at least during his time in Vegas, he got to be a boss. But you're always gonna be Vic's errand boy, aren't you? He could've kept his business running in Vegas, given it to you, let you take the risk. And the reward." She leaned forward and he could smell the rose perfume he'd smelled in Bobby's hotel room with its lie-dry shower, the soft scent of wine on her breath. "Are you always going to be an errand boy, Sean?"

He said nothing, watching her.

"I mean, say Vic was out of the picture, you could take over in Vegas. There's a whole infrastructure of dealers and customers in place, ready for someone smarter than Bobby to step in. Make more money than an errand boy ever would. I could help you, Sean. We could get rid of Vic. Together. It beats sending each other to prison." And she gave him a wry grin.

"I can't just kill Vic. The rest of his organization would come after me like an army." That was all of ten guys, but it was enough.

"Not if something happened to him here. Away from them, where they couldn't know exactly what had happened. Maybe the same trouble that happened to Bobby. A rival gang, let's say. Vic dies, you take over the operation before the other gang can, you're a hero. End of story."

"What," Sean said, "are you suggesting?"

Feeling another rush of decision, of possibility, imagining a roulette ball spinning in her smile.

"Tell me," Red said, "does Vic like redheads?"

The King Midas bar, two nights later, was quieter than the first time Sean had been in here with Bobby, a different bartender, tonight a black woman with a soft Jamaican accent. Vic watched her walk to the other side of the bar. They were at a back table but with a good view of the curved teak of the bar.

"These Caribes," Vic said. "They're everywhere. If you grew up on an island, why would you want to move to a goddamned desert?" He coughed once, sipped hard at his vodka and tonic. "It's pissing me off."

"Change of pace." Sean cleared his throat. "I'm sorry this has turned into a hassle, but I'm confident we can catch the bastards that kidnapped Bobby."

"You got a lead on these assholes?" Vic took another tense swallow of vodka.

"Asians from Los Angeles, moving east," Sean said. "That's the word on the street." The lie was easy now, practiced in his mind, and it made sense.

Vic frowned. "Let 'em kill Bobby for all I care. Why should I meet with them?"

"Listen, he talks before he dies, and they've got the information to bring you down," Sean said. "They can feed it to informants, cut a deal to trade you to the cops on a platter if any of their chiefs get caught. You need Bobby back in one piece. Plus, they're being too clever, wanting to meet, wanting more money. Greed is stupid in this case. We'll kill them."

"Christ," Vic said. "You're sure this ain't a trap they're setting?"

"I'm sure," Sean said, and he saw Red walk in. Same little black dress as before but now her hair was rich coffee brown, bobbed short, like Sean knew Vic liked. "They're not that smart."

"I want them dead when we're done, you hear me?"

"I hear you," Sean said. "Listen, try to relax. This is Vegas. Have some fun. We can't do anything until the meeting tomorrow, man. Chill out. You want to go see a show?"

Vic said, "Jesus, no, sitting in a chair for two hours would drive me nuts." He finished his vodka, ordered another. Sean waited, giving him time, not wanting to force it. Finally Vic saw her.

"Check out the sweet treat at the bar," Vic said.

"Which?"

"Five stools from the right. The tasty brunette."

"She's out of your league, Vic, a little too pretty." Pushing Vic's button.

Vic raised an eyebrow but wasn't mad. Smiling at the challenge. "This from the little league."

"I'm just saying, she looks like she's happy alone," Sean said. "She wouldn't want to talk to some guy who's all stressed about his business. Not thinking about having a good time."

"Hey, I want her, I can get her," Vic said.

Sean smiled. "You think so, Vic? How about a little bet?"

JEFFREY ROBERT BOWMAN

Stonewalls

FROM *The Chattahoochee Review*

Of Historical Note: On the evening of May 3, 1863, at the battle of Chancellorsville, Confederate Lieutenant General Thomas J. "Stonewall" Jackson was shot and mortally wounded by his own troops while returning from a nighttime reconnaissance of enemy lines.

NO, I WILL TELL YOU despite the lies printed daily in Richmond newspapers, there is nothing divinely inspired to the generals of our Southern Confederacy. A rash, even harsh, judgment some might say, especially considering the recent brilliant victories they have won, and on what authority does this upstart writer sit? I confess I never spent four years on the cold Hudson cliffs of West Point, nor did I bide my time leisurely down in Lexington with Virginia's Marching Idiots, but I consider myself an adequate arbiter of talent nevertheless. First, I cite the past two years of service as an officer in the Army of Northern Virginia. Second, prior to the war, I had been forced to brood for three long University years on the writings of long-dead Romans and Greeks, Plutarch and his like, those old ones who had scratched out on papyri scrolls the campaigns of Hannibal and Alexander, and all the immortal Ancients of War emblazoned through time by their fiery laurels won at victories with names like Cannae or Issus or something equally obscure. It was in those voluminous tomes I found the military *élan* I so desired to emulate in eighteen hundred and sixty-one. With those pages in my traveling trunk, I exited the classroom and enlisted with the highest of classical ideals, to be some latter-day Southern legionnaire led by venerable gray-haired Generals into the immortal glory of battle, an Enfield in exchange for the *pilum*, a steel bayonet instead of the iron dagger. That, and like every other gentleman I knew, I very much wanted to be the first to shoot dead any invader when his foot fell on the soil of my beloved South.

Well, of wars and killing, of that I found plenty. But of Caesars, we had Lee, or perhaps foppish Stuart, benighted pathfinders stumbling their way into the ornery thickets of death. As the months went on and eighteen sixty-one became eighteen sixty-two and then onwards into eighteen sixty-three, we butchered great bunches of ignorant Yankee farm-boys and mill-workers. We killed them at Manassas (twice), at Fredericksburg, at Seven Pines, we killed them and watched them pile up in droves just about anywhere the war went in the state of Virginia, like the fallen chaff from the scythes of migrant threshers. And in these green rolling hills the tactic was always the same: march to where they weren't looking, come out of the woods on the attack, shriek like the very devil himself. I don't know who were the bigger fools, we for attempting it or the Yankees for falling for it. They ran every time, even all the way back to Washington. It was a mere matter of geography and if we had the fire to chase them long enough.

Then, after the shooting had died down and the fields were a blood stained morass of broken men and mules and metal-plowed earth, we would bury our dead and leave the Yankees out to fester and rot and turn as black in the face as a field nigger. I confess at first we found this killing to be great fun and often in camp, bottle in hand, we would joke and laugh and I became a somewhat poet laureate for the wonderful odes I had composed to these cowardly, negligent soldiers, these martinets in blue who broke their lines and skedaddled at the first rattle of musketry, the first whoop of the rebel yell.

But as time wore on, even I stilled my pen for there became evident only one truth and this was that all living things bleed and I believe about then, when we looked about and amongst our thinned ranks and saw less and less of those familiar, we all grew very tired of violence and murder. There seemed to be no rhyme or reason to death anymore and the jokes we made were the jokes told quietly at funerals by gravediggers and our laughter came from chests hollow as an empty coffin.

But out of this miasma of unease came our Caesar, our Cromwell: Stonewall Jackson. He was a general beyond pretty cap and braid, able to scan the metrics of death. He spoke no speeches, had no gift of tongue for words, but at the very sight of him atop his chestnut horse, ramrod straight in the saddle and blue eyes alight with the holy blaze of battle, we found ourselves restored into the grand tapestry of The Cause and Southern Honor. Once more I could write about hallowed fields stained by the sweet wine of Southern youth and our enemies were again dastardly foes and the past two years were elevated into something higher than mere dysentery and pellagra — we were the Three Hundred Spartans and he, Jackson, our Leonidas, the Confederacy made Thermopylae. In his stern, puritan figure we found an iron heart and will and we feasted on this like it were manna sent down by the heavens above.

Chancellorsville and all that happened there can be explained thus as malnutrition or perhaps a loss of sustenance.

At Chancellorsville we hit them so hard we could have been cavalry.

The way they ran, they could have been too.

We had marched hard all through the day and it was near night before the scouts sent out earlier by Jackson came back from their reconnaissance of Howard's camp. Major Williams led them, a bland planter's son from the Carolinas, and he came back by my company tired and bedraggled and with his bits of uniform all the more tattered from brambles and branches. He looked over my dispositions and said, "They ain't even doing nothing but sitting around and smoking and talking to each other in Dutch. That old boy Jackson's done it again." Then from somewhere behind us the attack command was passed up quietly and Williams was gone away forward in front and Jackson was there up ahead saying something to the skirmishers and as I passed I heard him say distinctly, ". . . Now I want them all dead, especially the brave ones," and then we were running through the woods, the banners dancing above our heads and the woods snatching at our legs but we ignored the slash of thorns across our faces and I looked and I saw that even some of the boys were laughing with anticipation at the whipping we were about to administer to the Army of the Potomac on this third day of May eighteen hundred and sixty-three. Then we were all yelling and I thought of plantation fields and belles of the ball and darkies and I said to myself, "South," and said to the men to my right and left, "Home boys home," and then we sprang out into a small clearing where the Dutchmen of Howard's froze like deer surprised by hounds on an autumn eve and stared with eyes gone doe-like with fear at the shrieking mass headed directly for them. We were right in the middle of their camp, all slashing steel and flying lead, screaming something fierce. The Yankees, they just about trampled one another in their mad-panicked rush to get away.

They fell like quail from a scattergun. I clearly remember Major Williams ahead of me waving a plumed hat in his hand and saying over the roar, "They Godamighty, look at them sonsofbitches run," and then he was down with what looked to be half his head shot away. I waved my sword vaguely and fired my revolver and crumpled some dim forms in the smoke about me and yelled forward in a voice so painfully hoarse I would have killed women and children for a cool, cold glass of lemonade. It was then something came out of the smoke and spun me around and knocked me to the ground and I lay there hurt and bleeding and too scared to cry out my pain lest I rupture irreparably. It was painful, crushing. I managed a scattered thought, a prayer of sorts: "Virginia my lord do not so treat your faithful," and then a great brown mass seemed to swallow me whole like the South herself was claiming her dead, justly awarded.

I dreamt, but dreams such as these are the slippery slopes to madness and I found myself unhinged from the moorings of my mind in a cornfield where the bodies of the dead lay all about in various states of decay. I alone was of one flesh and soon I began to recognize the faces of the corpses and found in each one people I had known — family, friends, acquaintances, even the women I'd had back in the districts of Richmond, all were there with death and I raised myself up from the bloody stalks and ran through the field but it only stretched wider in all directions and the bodies grew thicker like some awful harvest of offal. But on the horizon, I could make out the pale shape of a rider and I strained for my life to collapse at the horse's feet and with trembling hands grasped the hem of the rider's cloak. I turned my face to his and saw with surprise no decay there, nothing but the refined features of Jackson but Caesar there too and what I took to be Alexander the Great and a whole host of other men shimmering there underneath with a great vitality. The horseman spoke and his voice was an organ that sang out over the dead fields, "Poet, you know nothing about the workings of the heart." Before the words were complete, I thought them strange but then he drew aside his heavy gray cloak and I saw nothing inside the emptiness but a heart most hideous, a thing of sutured iron and quaking with a great turn of pistons. I longed to rip the revolting organ out of him with my hands but when I reached to do so he was already gone and I saw with a horror fathomless the arm I raised to wrest was nothing but a rotted thing of maggoted flesh and I collapsed on legs rotted through and my face was in blood and mud and I screamed the shriek which waked me to a world changed anew.

I raised my face off the ground and found the battle had moved away, at least from where I was directly, and I could hear off in the distance the harsh roar of rifle fire coming back through the woods in long discordant waves. There hung heavy over the camp a pall of gun smoke and through its fog I could make out the ground slithering around me and I thought I might still be in dreams but then saw the undulations were nothing but the wounded in their aimless wanderings for aid and succor. I remembered myself and found the pain gone in my wound and my neck and uniform front stained wet from a bottle drained to its very dregs. It sat between my legs, placed by whom or how I know not. I took a sniff from the neck and the overwhelming smell of laudanum threatened to return me back to the land from which I had just returned. I must have swooned with horror at the prospect for the pain brought my head back some clarity. With tenderness I removed a gauntlet and probed the wound for some sign of mortal death. I found nothing but a shallow groove high on the side of my head, near the part, and though the blood was all on me I could not help but think, "Life," and I rose like the dead one day will do and stood on feet none too steady and swayed.

The faintness dissipated and I noticed most of the moving forms about me had stilled their motions and now I appeared to be the only one standing among the wrecked tents and scattered provisions of a camp abruptly abandoned. The smoke continued to drift backwards from the battle lines and I began to smell burning resin and leaves from the dry bracken caught fire. Common enough occurrence on these battlefields but today it lent the gun smoke a denser opacity and as I walked towards the woods often I tripped blindly over the dead forms of enemies and allies. Finally, I gained the trees and felt a sense of relief come to my light head. But even here in the confines of the forest I grew muddled and lost in my bearings. I found myself walking in ever widening circles. At one point, there was a man ahead of me looking equally lost and I took him by the arm to ask where General Jackson's corps was but when he turned to look at me I saw he was without a nose and blood flowed freely from the rude orifice lead-gouged. I let him pass and set out again into the forest where the sounds of war echoed and rebounded among the trees.

I know not how many hours passed in my labyrinth but when I came to again out of the haze of opiates I found myself in a thinned area of the forest and the moon was a pale pearl streaming its light down cleanly from above the tree line. Somewhere deeper in the woods the flames of the fire gleamed like a jewel but the smoke here had cleared by some trick of the wind. I was halfway through the scattered grass tussocks when I heard the voice of a man cursing, harsh and strained, but in a steady monotone. I looked about but there was no one, save the dead and the wounded not expired. The cursing continued and I realized this was not the ranting of the wounded against the heavy hand of existence but a vital man struggling under some heavy load. I walked further and in the fading light, I made out the origin of the words. Beneath a tall oak, near blended in from the darkness about, a man held a dead horse by the foreleg and tugged with jerks and pulls backwards on the balls of his feet against the weight. As I came closer, I saw there was a man underneath near crushed by the beast. The person pulling had an odd medley of colors to his uniform and for the life of me I could not tell whether he was my ally or my enemy but despite the vulgarities thought he had to be at least a brother officer bereaved by the death of the man on horseback. Instinctively I came up behind him and lent a hand and together we heaved and the horse finally shifted in a great slough of dead skin, the horseman beneath freed.

"Whew!" said the other man. "Thankee kindly. I was about worn out from tugging on that thing." I looked at him and could make out little of his features, save he was of my height and weight and seemed in good health. He wore a great beard stretched down near to the middle of his chest though it was neatly barbered and smelled even pomaded, which was slathered in full evidence upon his hair. His blouse was grimy from powder stains but his coat looked newly bought. A gold watch chain gleamed dully from the pocket. He looked at me with an aspect not unfriendly and from his accent I could only conclude he was Southern and of good standing. He suddenly smiled and said, "Looks like you been wounded, friend," and he gestured with a hand towards the side of my head.

"It's nothing," I said, "I'm fine." I touched the wound and my hands came back black and clotted. My fingers felt thick and strange from the opiates but I still spoke my plan lucidly, "Well, shall we go about bringing him to the surgeons?"

The man looked confused. "Who?" he asked.

"The man, the officer," I pointed at the nearly crushed horseman, who now was beginning to mutter and move with odd, spasmodic jerks. The other man followed my finger and an expression of surprise flittered across his features. "Well, I'll be . . . I thought ye was a dead 'un . . ." he said underneath his breath and he looked about for a moment and stooped down and brought up in his hands the shattered butt-end of a Springfield rifle. He walked over to the stirring horseman and before I had a chance to shout a protest dispatched him out of this world with two swift violent chops of the club. The head made the same sound a melon did splitting open under the blade of one of the kitchen hands back home. He threw away the rifle butt and commenced to root through the pockets of the dead man. He palmed up gold coins and threw away all else into a pile behind him. My mouth was open. I closed it. I pulled my revolver from its holster, thumbed back the hammer, and leveled it at the kneeling form. The hands froze in mid-rummage at the clean click of the pistol coming back to cock.

"What in the name of God do ye think you're doing?" he asked, not daring to raise his head so it looked as though he were addressing the dead. I laid the front sight right middle below his beard.

"Halting you in the name of justice," I replied. "You'll hang for murder," I assured him. "Now stand up and turn around."

Still on his knees, the man barked a hoarse laugh, "You'll have to shoot me." He laughed. "Murder. What all do you think is going on around you, ye dumb son of a bitch." He stood and turned and walked away. "Go on and shoot me, I ain't got the time to waste on you fine-minded gentlemen."

"Very well," I murmured and squeezed on the curve of the trigger. The snap of a misfire came and quickly I cocked back and pulled again. Misfire. His high yokel laugh taunted out of the darkness. I pulled my saber and rushed after his receding form. He whirled and I saw in his arms a bayoneted rifle and I drew up like a horse tethered.

"Easy now, my pretty," he said as we began to circle each other delicately. "Don't be messing where ye going to get hurt. I'll kill ye dead I will," he said. It was a scene backlit by the forest fire and our shadows danced dark in the dirt in a ghoulish duel. My opponent continued to circle but with one hand fumbled in his pockets. I prepared myself to come in a rush and thrust but out of his grimy fingers came a percussion cap, which he stuck in beneath the pulled back hammer as he pointed the rifle at me.

"Loaded and cocked, now," he grinned, lupine. "Stick it in the dirt, son." The muzzle drooped to show me the direction.

"How come you know it's loaded?" I asked him. "Perhaps it isn't."

"Try it, son." He still grinned. "Shoot you or run you through, don't make no difference atall. Now." He jerked the muzzle downwards.

I turned the sword blade down and stuck it in the ground.

"Good," he said. "Now walk on in front of me. Get on back to where ye come from." I stepped forward and stumbled past him, each second an eternity waiting for the roar of the rifle which would announce a bullet ripping through my back and out my stomach to kill me slow and steady. It did not come but I didn't want to turn and see what he was doing. The woods loomed ahead dark and mysterious and still full of the rippling waves of gunfire and a trace of fear went through me when I thought that death awaited no matter which way I now turned. Certainly the wounded here knew these salient facts. One grasped the cuff of my trouser leg as I passed and said in a plaintive voice, "It don't look bad do it?" I never paused in my stride. I heard the man with the rifle begin to walk behind me and a few minutes later the wounded man asked him the same query. I turned and looked. The man knelt and cradled the wounded man's head. With a canteen, he gave him a drink and wiped some of the grime away from his face. "It don't look bad do it?" the wounded man repeated.

"Hey. How you?" said my opponent, and he raised up one leg. From out of his boot, he pulled a bowie knife and he stuck the knife into the man and he died. He was searching through the man's moneybag when he heard my approach and stood, knife at the ready. I held up my hands when he slashed the air in front of him as duelists do.

"Easy, boy, don't get no ideas," he told me.

"Why?" I asked him. "All I want to know is why?"

The eyes went blank for a second but then he let loose the high yokel laugh. There were gaps in between his teeth, some all but rotted away. "Goddamn," he snorted, "I tell you, you officers ain't got the brains God gave a turkey." He knelt back to his counting and finding no gold coins he threw away the purse in disgust. He turned on the balls of his feet and pulled another man, dead this one, to him with a grunt. He began the search anew.

"But why?" I asked again.

"Lord God," the man said, sighing. "To get rich, you fool! You know how much gold is out here just going to perdition and gone cause no one bothers to collect it? Least ten dollars worth, mayhap as much as fifteen."

"No, but why are you killing them?" I asked. He had moved on to yet another one, Yankee this time, groaning with the crimson slaverous froth about the mouth that comes from being lung shot. He stabbed him and held it until the quaking ceased. He looked at me with eyes baleful and red rimmed from the smoke spread everywhere on the clearing floor.

"How long you figger this feller had?" he asked. "Ten? Twelve hours? Or how about them sonsofbitches over there with they arms done shot off? Four? Lessen the sawbones gets to them and leaves them crippled for they whole lives ahead. I'm just helping them get out of this here vale of tears and into the vale of glory. It's Christian duty, pure and simple."

I looked about me and saw the men with faces contorted from hurt and their low moans seemed to be felt more than heard and the world looked a sad and blasted place indeed, metal churned and blood soaked and there seemed no flaw to his reasoning even in my addled state. But yet, I persisted.

"Some would call it murder," I said. "Courts, for instance."

The man shrugged and went back to his labors like a prophet unbowed despite the years of perpetual misunderstanding. "Let them," he said and then an explosion shook the ground from a battery firing blind into the dark and drowned out the rest of his words. When I could hear over my ringing ears, he was saying in an indifferent tone, ". . . them sonsofbitches will sit up there on high and run they mouths and tell you that what they doing is so high and mighty and if ye listened to they words you'd think God was on everybody's side in this here war. All we're doing is fighting for niggers and that means money and that means nigger money." He shook his head. "The world's come to a sorry pass when white men are killing white men over niggers." He looked at me standing in front of him as he tried to roll a big Dutchman over. "Goddamn, you could give me a hand at least," he said. I apologized and bent and helped him drag the man by the heels to where we could see his pockets in the light of the fire. I almost fainted from the exertion and sat down beside the dead.

The man continued to talk as he hefted a gold watch in his hand feeling the weight. "All a man can do," he said, "is find pleasure in what he knows is good for him. They stole me from home, give me a rifle and said, go fight. I said, All right. Said, I'll fight all you sons of bitches tooth and nail and get rich in the meantime."

He continued to gather corpses, me his earnest helper all the while. Before long, there was a stack of dead almost knee high and the purses of them had been slit open and their contents gathered in a pile which grew as we threw in a watch or gold coins and the precious metal gleamed with a weird luminescence from the silver moon light and the burnished orange glow of the fire. Before long, we both gave pause and I collapsed from weakness and he sat down beside me grinning his odd grin out of the sweat-beaded fur of his beard. He took out a pipe and put in a small white ball, lit a match and breathed in a lungful. He offered me the pipe. "Get ye some," he said kindly. I took the pipe to calm myself and breathed in and the colors of the laudanum came back to me and I felt near drunk.

"Yes indeed," said the man, "I took to ship a good bit in my younger days and the monkeys over there in Cathay got me good and drunk with that there tobaccer. I got me a New Orleans Jew doctor over in Heth's division who sells it to me for a half take on the gold. Times been where he run out and I had to go on over and be with the boys in blue and get the supply on up again. Them boys will swap ye anything long as ye got tobaccer. Especially them Irishmen, you never seen the likes of it. I stay around there and turn myself a nice profit and then come on back over. Yes sir, I drifted from one side in this war clear on over to the other one and it didn't make the slightest bit of difference in the world far as I was concerned."

I smoked the pipe again and watched the whorls and swirls of smoke come up out of my mouth and drift upwards into the black ether of the night now pinpricked by a few cold stars. I felt like taking the man's knife and cutting through my clothes to open my skin and chest until my heart was laid bare and could beat freely out into the void. "It makes a great deal of difference to me," I revealed.

The man took the pipe from me and held the match to the pipe bowl again and inhaled. "Well, more's the fool," he said in a puff of smoke. "Given time and provided death don't find ye, ye'll learn there's no difference betwixt the sides and the highest pleasure them ones, gray or blue," he pointed, "have are one and the same." I followed the finger to a group of horsemen emerging out of the forest fire as they drifted towards us in long elongations of movement, like demons from a flame.

"Cavalry?" I asked vaguely. There was a boundless lassitude to my limbs. It seemed like I were talking to the heavens above.

"No, dammit," said the pipe smoker. "Generals. They're kith and kin no matter which side they fight. I swain all they want is death. That's the only reason for them. It's the only way they get filled up, on blood, on death."

"Fulfillment?" I muttered. "No . . . No . . ."

But then suddenly the pounding of hooves on the ground was a loud and steady drumming and I heard the man beside me curse and scuttle away on all fours like a rat out into the darkness and then Jackson's face and those of his staff peered down on me from atop their horses and I realized from my cloud who I was facing and I fell off and found myself on top of a pile of dead bodies with their purses lain carelessly strewn about.

The General spoke. "How odd," he said.

"Looks like we done caught ourselves a grave robber, General," said a colonel with a handlebar mustache. His fine hand tweaked the end of one whisker.

"Now, this is a first," said the General. He looked genuinely perplexed. "I must say we can't have any of that going on in this army.

Does horrid things for discipline. I saw the effects myself down in Mexico. Have him shot tomorrow," he ordered, and then in an afterthought, "In front of the men. Where there's lice, there's filth. Be so kind to tie his hands and bring him along, Major."

I grunted some sort of protest. My head needed to clear.

"Wait," Jackson said. He raised a gloved hand. "Speak, my good man."

I wanted to beg for mercy, redress, a board of inquiry. I wanted to scream: For you! It is for you I fight! Two full long years! Stonewall! South! South!

Instead, I came out with, "I am an officer in the Confederate States Army."

"Ah," Jackson said. "A noose then. Someone make a note of it. Come along, gentlemen."

We rode back through the trees, myself bound and gagged and bouncing in the saddle behind the Major who looked as young as I was. There was nothing but the sound of horses blowing hard and the nervous sweat of their riders was a musk blended with the smell of honeysuckle newly bloomed in the month of May. The moon ran behind a cloud and even these men lost their way and we rode up and down the same path twice trying to find the single trail back into our lines. Finally, Jackson gave a whispered order and we rode back in a group in a generally Southern direction. The moon returned in a burst of silver light and right when it did one of the pickets spotted our movement, yelled a warning and loosed a single shot which hit the man riding in front of me. He stiffened, slumped and fell off the horse as other pickets joined in and a sporadic fusillade passed through our party. I twisted my bonds and managed to get a hand free and I heard the Colonel with the mustaches yell out, "Cease your fire! You're firing into your own men!"

I turned and looked and saw Jackson was hit high in the arm but alive and looking directly into my eyes with his blue ones as I tore the gag out of my mouth and yelled, "Who said that? That's a damn lie! Pour it into them, boys!"

I leapt from the horse and rolled as volleys crashed out from all sides. Horses screamed and men toppled from their saddles to the forest floor. I looked and saw pickets and officers half dressed and in disarray hurrying from out of the camps. I lay down on my

back. "Oh, Jesus, I think we just shot the General," I heard someone say. "He ain't moving," said another. Soon enough, solicitous
hands reached for me. The nervous face of an orderly peered at my
wound in the moonlight.

"How is he?" I asked. "How is the General?"

"Hush, son, shh . . ." he said and he stroked my hair. "The General's fine . . . Stretcher bearer?" he said.

I watched as the General was taken down from his horse and laid
on the ground beside me. There were two bullets in him and his
face looked wan but the eyes still burned incisively. "Across the
river . . ." he was saying to no one in particular.

"Is there your fulfillment, General?" I whispered to him.

He nodded from across the way and then was carried from me
on a litter of blankets. I saw tears in the eyes of some of the pickets.
Others looked on with morbid shock. I knew none of them would
ever come to know the mark I had made on time, nor the knowledge I had received. I was carried away from them and left them
there in their shame and anger, to fight and die or perhaps live, to
decay or marry and breed.

It was not much more than a month later that Gettysburg came but
I was not there, for midway through the march north I left and
didn't stop till I came upon my first Yankees, a troop of home
guard cavalry clopping sedately down the Hagerstown Turnpike.
Beneath their bemused stares, I got down on my knees in the
muddy country road and kissed the flag I'd come to hate and for-
swore allegiance to a country to which I no longer belonged. This
did not make a difference to them. They threw me into Elmira
prison anyway, two days after Lee got beat in the blossoming fields
and orchards of Pennsylvania.

I didn't stay long. They needed volunteers to guard the West
where the savages had begun to run amok and I wrote my name
down for Indian fighting the day I got there. They took a whole
bunch of us out West to the Dakotas and Wyoming. Most of us are
former Confederates, now in blue but with new enemies to face.
Hard-bitten, we hate the Sioux and Cheyenne with the same vitu-
perative loathing we reserve for the fighting back East. It impedes
the bread and bullets and our rosters are never full from the battles
outside Atlanta, Petersburg. Not to boast, but despite these short

supplies, we're good at what we do and we free up more land for the settlers and their metal plows every day. The newspapers in the East have taken to calling us "Galvanized Yankees" and report our deeds as one would the works of a sinner reformed.

I don't know about the Yankee part but I do know I'm galvanized. I have never commanded finer troops with such alacrity and dispatch, a beautiful synchrony of mind and body, like a well-calibrated machine.

It is autumn now in the West and every night we watch the harvest moon rise full and blood red over the Dakota foothills. The savages call this a good omen, a good season to set out for hunting before the winter cold. We agree and when we attack their villages in the frigid early morning hours, we find there is nothing but women and children in the camps, a few old men whose feeble resistance we brush aside. Then we commence the slaughter with a carnal efficiency while a few of the boys use the shots and screams as a distraction to kill the penned ponies and add to the general carnage and rape going on about. Afterwards we burn the shelters and warm by their flames as the sun crests over the hills and we watch light come to a land where the horizons stretch on endless, as do the possibilities. The other day I read in a newspaper that Sherman and Sheridan were doing much of the same to the South, my hometown in particular being mentioned as "nothing but a cinder." I felt as much for it and its inhabitants as I did for the sack of Troy, which is to say nothing.

Fulfillment. Jackson found it in his time. Few men do. I too am blessed by a cruel and righteous God for my heart is an organ of iron.

WILLIAM J. CARROLL, JR.

Height Advantage

FROM *Alfred Hitchcock's Mystery Magazine*

THE THING ON ITS SIDE at the bottom of the wooden-walled hot tub was not human. Whoever it had been, it wasn't human any longer. Just a brown, shriveled husk, lying in a foot of slimy-black water. Protein for the small animals and insects that had drawn me to look inside.

Nothing now to get upset about.

At least that's what I was force-feeding my mind to consider as I lowered the folding lid and started breathing again.

Jesus, I thought. Poor Carole . . .

I felt dizzy with shock and moved away, back toward the bench, where I started to sit, but the odor now was suddenly overwhelming. So much so, I stumbled off the porch, into the cold rain, and walked away from the cabin.

Down to the dry creek where I sat on a large rock and for a moment just breathed.

Good God, I thought. Poor Carole!

After a while, though, the rain came harder, so I moved myself back up onto the covered porch, shivering, and sat on the steps. I still felt dazed and did a bit more deep breathing, trying to focus on the rain and the thick woods that were all around me, trying to think of something other than what was lying dead only a few feet away. But it wasn't easy.

After another few minutes, I did start to feel better, and thoughts about what to do next — like calling the police — began to come to me, but I stayed sitting a while longer. There was no hurry now.

Looking up through the trees toward the mountain, lost behind the clouds, brushing my hand at the flies which buzzed my head, wondering where Dirty Hairy had got to and just how "harmless" he really was.

Finally deciding to make the call, I reached into my pocket for my cell phone, but finding the photographs there I brought those out instead and looked them over for a moment.

The photographs I'd taken the day before. Photographs of Carole's wonderful paintings, the artwork that had brought me there.

I'd first seen the paintings only the day before at Wellman's Gallery — a tiny art dealership in Pike Place Market near the bay.

I was on leave at the time — two weeks' worth taken for no reason but that I'd been feeling a little stale around the office, not myself for some reason, grouchy, maybe old. I was sick of the sight of my room at the BOQ. So I'd moved myself off-post.

Up to Seattle and a room in the condo of an out-of-town friend, where I'd been spending my leave thus far, doing not much at all — mostly walking here and there around town, spending a lot of time in coffee shops, reading some, taking pictures. Doing nothing, really — until yesterday.

I was a week into this *hard* way of life, having just stopped off at a nearby fish market where the prices were just short of astronomical, when I passed by Wellman's, which hadn't yet opened, peered inside, and saw the paintings.

Four of them. Large watercolors, prominently arranged. All of them were of various views of Mount Rainier. It was the style that caught my eye — something recognized that clicked in the back of my mind — and then as I stepped closer I saw the name of the artist on a placard in large black letters, CAROLE DORIN, and although the name didn't match, right beside the placard was the framed photograph of a face that did.

"Carole Dragnich," I said. "I'll be damned."

I stood there a few moments, then went to a phone booth, where a scan of the directory showed no Dorins nor Dragnichs at all. Then I went to a bagel stand, grabbed a coffee, and waited for Wellman's to open.

Remembering Carole Dragnich. Sergeant First Class, United States Army, Retired.

*   *   *

Short, red haired, feisty, and fun to be around. We'd been stationed and teamed together out of the same office at the 30 MI Detachment in Berlin, nearly five years earlier.

And it had been a good match, her and me, while it lasted.

At the time we'd been assigned to NATO's Counter-Terrorist Division, which in our case meant surveillance of various individuals and groups with subversive or terrorist ties — and, on occasion, long dreary hours of watching streets, doors, and windows.

Spent, in my case, brooding or dozing, but in her case sketching, filling pad after pad with renditions of whatever crossed in front of her bright eyes.

Later finishing in watercolor some of those sketches — most of which I thought, even then, were really very good.

We were friends, though never really close, which was nothing very unusual for people like us. She'd opted for early retirement after her tour in Germany, and we'd lost touch — also nothing unusual.

But we'd been partners, and close enough to make the idea of seeing her again a fun idea, so I decided to try.

Wellman's opened at nine A.M. I was in the door a minute after, giving the four paintings a close look-over — all bright and lively with color, all priced at fifteen thousand dollars.

Carole, I was thinking, was even better than I remembered.

A young woman clerk eventually approached and offered help.

"These are wonderful," I said, nodding at the watercolors.

"They certainly are," she agreed.

"I'd like to get in touch with the artist, but she's not listed in the Seattle directory. I wonder if you'd know how I might find her."

"Oh," she said, "I couldn't say, really."

I smiled at her. "Who could?"

She smiled back. "Well the fact is, I'm not sure. Ms. Dorin's husband is the one who placed these paintings with us, and we do have his number, but I'd feel funny about giving it out."

"I see."

"When Ms. Carter, the manager, comes in, she might be able to help."

"When will Ms. Carter be in?"

"After lunch."

I looked at my watch. It was 9:05.

"Maybe her agent could help you," the clerk suggested.

"And her name?"

She excused herself and went away, returning shortly with a business card and saying, "I *do* know Carole Dorin lives in Washington."

"Oh?"

"This isn't her first showing," she said. "She's really very hot right at the moment."

I looked at the card she'd handed me and saw that the office of Jess Collier, Artist Representative, was walking distance from where I was just that moment.

"Well," I told her. "Thank you."

"My pleasure," she replied. "And, if you do find her, let her know she has a big fan here."

I nodded and looked back at the paintings.

The clerk did too, saying, "I wish I had half the talent she does."

"Who wouldn't?" I agreed.

Jess Collier's office on the thirty-second floor of a very upscale building on Fourth Ave. had a large, mostly empty outer office, carefully carpeted and furnished in gray-black tones, carefully muraled with obscure black-and-white photography, and carefully receptioned by a young, leggy platinum blonde dressed in white and seated at a curved, black-tinted, glass-topped desk.

She doubtfully asked if I had an appointment and seemed relieved to find out I hadn't, then announced me on the intercom to her boss as if I'd been expected all along. After that she tentatively asked me to have a seat.

Which I took, though a few seconds later a tall woman in a severe black pants suit entered from a short hallway, looked at me, and said, "Mr. . . . ?"

"Virginiak," I said, standing.

She looked expectant. "I'm Jess Collier."

I gave her my hand to shake, which she did, briefly.

"And how can I help you?" she asked.

"Well," I told her, "I'm looking for a friend of mine — a client of yours, I think — Carole Dorin?"

She hesitated briefly. "Really?"

"Yes, we were stationed together in Germany some years ago.

Actually, I didn't even know she lived in Washington until an art dealer told me, and I'd like to get in touch with her."

She thought that over.

Collier was a good-looking woman, tall with a long, straight body that her black suit emphasized. She wore burr-cut salt-and-pepper hair on an elegantly shaped head, and had a well-arranged, make-upless face, with a pair of deeply dark blue eyes that just then seemed wary of me.

I said, "If you're being cautious, I do understand. I could leave my phone number and you could give it to Carole for me."

Collier smiled slightly. "That's not the problem," she said wryly, waving a hand toward the hall behind her. "Please," she said. "Coffee?"

I told her coffee would be good.

She led me down the short hall into her office, the sight of which once I'd entered made me stop dead in my tracks.

"Whoa," I said with a laugh.

She saw my face and smiled.

This inner office, done up with huge mirrors and floor-to-ceiling windows that looked out over downtown Seattle and most of the rest of the world, gave me the immediate impression of being airborne.

"You're not going to be sick, are you?" she asked with a laugh. "It's happened."

"It's just a little startling," I told her.

Adding to the sense of openness, the room was sparingly furnished — a large glass table for a desk, a couple of chrome-framed white leather chairs — and that was that.

"You're bothered by heights?" she asked.

"A little," I admitted.

She waved me to a chair, which I gratefully took.

"I love the sense of height," she explained. "The cleanliness of being above everything."

She could have it, I thought.

Collier took a thin cigar from a pack on her uncluttered desk, lit it, leaned against the edge, and looked at me. "Now, you say you're a friend of Carole's?"

"I am," I told her, "though we haven't been in touch for some time."

The door behind me opened then, and I got my coffee in a small china cup on a tiny glass tray.

Collier watched the receptionist quietly leave as I sipped.

"Well," Collier told me, "the problem is, I don't know how to get in touch with Carole myself."

"I see," I said.

"And frankly," she added, "I'm a bit concerned."

I put my cup on the tiny tray, put the tray on her desk, and said, "Concerned?"

She frowned a little. "How well do you know Carole?"

"Well enough to like her. Why are you concerned?"

She sat back in her chair. "A few months ago, Carole gave up her apartment in Seattle and — well — disappeared. I was surprised she hadn't contacted me because we'd become quite friendly over the past year since her divorce."

"I didn't even know she'd been married."

"Yes," she said, "for about a year before I met her, but she eventually saw her mistake and got out of it."

I nodded.

She sighed. "A month ago, her ex-husband placed four watercolors at Wellman's Gallery for sale on consignment. They comprise a project Carole called Rainier Summer."

"I saw the exhibit at Wellman's."

"Yes, and it's clearly her best work," she told me. "Carole and I had no written contract between us, and if she wanted to sell her work by the side of the road, it would be of no legal concern of mine, but my personal concern issues from the fact that it was her ex-husband who delivered the watercolors."

"I see."

"Carole's divorce last year," Collier continued, "was terribly bitter. At one point she was forced to get a restraining order against the man, so you can understand why I was surprised that she would have him deliver the watercolors."

"But she kept his name?"

"For business reasons, purely. She started selling her work as Dorin, and kept it that way."

"And where does he live?"

She frowned. "His name is Phil Dorin," she said, as if the name pained her to utter. "He has a farm near Eatonville, I think."

"That's on the way to Rainier," I pointed out. "The mountain was Carole's subject."

"I know. I called him, thinking — I don't know — that she might be living there, but he said she wasn't, and I don't think, now, she would be living there really."

"Did Dorin say he knew where Carole was living?"

"He said he didn't, but I thought he was lying." Her elegant head shook slightly. "He's a very disagreeable man."

"And you haven't heard from her, since . . . ?"

She frowned, then replied, "I haven't seen or spoken with Carole since early August."

"Three months."

"It's crossed my mind to call the police, but . . ."

"But?"

"It's also crossed my mind that I might be overdramatizing." She shrugged slightly. "I tend to do that."

"What's that?"

She smiled. "I tend to think the worst. Oh . . ." She shook her head. "Carole is probably fine. Just happy as a clam, and hopefully at work." She looked at me, as if to make her statement a question, but I didn't know the answer.

I didn't know what to think.

When I left her office a few minutes later, I still didn't know.

Collier seemed like a grown-up, responsible type, and if she thought she was overdramatizing her concern for Carole's disappearance, who was I to disagree?

But along with my disappointment at not being able to see Carole again, I felt a bit unsettled. I would have liked knowing she was all right at least, but I had no idea how to find her.

That put my thinking in a circular pattern, so I decided on a drive down to Redondo to get in some stroll-and-think time walking along the shore, which has straightened out my thoughts in the past — but not today.

After an hour's walk, I had decided only that I was hungry.

So I grabbed a sandwich at Salty's, then sat a while out in the sun on a bench at the end of the pier.

I watched an old man at the rail fishing for flounder, watched tugs out in the sound ferrying cargo up from Tacoma, watched some gulls teasing a dog on the beach — landing and waiting for the dog to chase them off, then flapping their way down the beach, waiting for the dog to chase after them again.

Until around three o'clock, when I gave up thinking and drove back to Seattle.

At a stoplight, through some trees and off in the distance, I caught a brief glimpse of Rainier — a smudge of white on the blue horizon.

And that's when I had the idea.

A kind of cart-before-the-horse idea, but it was all I could think of, so I decided to go with it.

I went back to Wellman's, where the same clerk let me take pictures of Carole's paintings and even helped me arrange them so my shots were complete.

Afterwards, I dropped them off at an overnight photo lab near my apartment and went home. I put in some phone time with a friend who had access to things not easily accessed, learning that Carole wasn't even *un*listed in the state of Washington.

Phil Dorin was, however, though his phone had been disconnected. But I did get his address.

And then I did nothing, except sit around the apartment, watch the sunset off the rear balcony, and look at a little TV. I went to bed early, but I couldn't sleep.

A small but persistent sense of anxiety — my unconscious working behind my back — having to do with Carole's disappearance, naturally, but mixed up with a vague sense of obligation — something owed — kept sleep from me.

I ended up going out for a walk, and getting back to the apartment around two in the morning, where I finally managed maybe two hours' sleep in the next six, rising around eight A.M.

Groggy, grouchy, but anxious to be on my way and glad of my big idea, which gave me, at least, some plan of action, I put myself in uniform — after a few days of civvies, I usually felt the need to be in uniform — and headed out.

I retrieved my pictures, then pointed my Bronco south and west, toward Eatonville, and made the small town around noon, under very dark, rain-heavy skies.

A coffee-shop waitress gave me uncertain directions to the address I'd written down, but after backtracking a few miles and a few wrong turns, I eventually found the farm.

It was on about five acres of cleared land divided by an unpaved road that ran up a hill to where a tiny trailer was parked. Two larger buildings stood back from the trailer, and along with a tractor and two pickups — a rust-finished old Chevy and a newer Ford Ranger — there were the rusted remains littered here and there of other unidentifiable pieces of machinery. A few cattle stood chewing in the field to one side of the drive, and on the other, a dirty white horse was doing the same.

A large mailbox that dangled from a post at the edge of the road had the name DORIN on it, so I turned in. When I got about halfway up the hill, a man emerged from one of the larger buildings and looked me over as I parked, got out, and approached him.

"Mr. Dorin?"

"Uh-huh."

"My name is Virginiak, and I'm looking for Carole, your ex-wife."

"That right?" he said with little interest.

Dorin was a big man. Very big. Six-seven, maybe six-eight, three-hundredish, big-chested, with a ponderous beer gut that hung over the top of his dirty blue jeans.

"I was told you might know where I could find her."

"Oh, yeah?" he replied with even less interest.

He had a big head, topped by sparse, curly brown hair, and his pug-nosed, thin-lipped, wind-burned face, with a couple of squinty, dark eyes peering at me, passed along an unfriendly message.

"Can't help you," he told me.

I nodded, but stayed put, watching him look me over, until he finally sneered, turned away, and walked toward the tractor.

I strolled behind him as he climbed onto a wheel, bent down over the engine, and began removing a fan-belt nut.

I said, "Her agent, Jess Collier, says she hasn't been in touch with Carole for three months."

"No kidding," he said.

I watched him slowly work the nut loose, and when he'd finished, he looked at me and asked, "What's Carole to you?"

"I'm a friend of hers," I replied. "We were stationed in Germany together."

He gave me a blank look. "Well, I can't help you, you know," he said. He started pulling at the old belt.

The dirty white horse had drifted nosily over to watch us.

"Last month," I said, "you delivered some paintings of hers to Wellman's Gallery in Seattle."

He worked the belt free, tossed it away, and began fitting the new belt over the shafts' wheels.

"Collier wonders how you came to have them," I told him.

He snorted.

"She's thought about notifying the police."

"That bitch," he muttered, struggling with the belt. "She never liked me."

He got the new belt in place, then began replacing the wheel lock, giving me a tired look. "I got work to do," he said with infinite weariness. "So, why don't you take a hike?"

I stared at him.

"Okay?" he added.

I said, "How did you get those paintings, Phil?"

He sighed, shook his head, and finished screwing down the wheel lock. "Man don't hear so good."

"How did you get those paintings, Phil?"

He paused in his work and blinked at me. "You want trouble?"

I didn't, but I could have handled some from him. I didn't like the man. I didn't say that, though. I just waited.

He stared at me a moment, then climbed up into the tractor saddle and started the engine. The horse, which had wandered close, now pranced quickly away.

I stood by the tractor.

Dorin ran the tractor a moment, then killed the engine and came down, looking at me and saying, "Still here?"

He didn't wait for an answer. Instead he started up the hill toward the trailer. I followed him.

Halfway there, he looked back at me, grunted, then walked on. I kept pace. A few yards short of the trailer, he stopped, turned, and pointed the wrench he still held toward the highway.

"Get out!" he told me. "I want you off my property — now!"

I looked toward the highway, then back at him. "Where's Carole?" I asked.

He blinked. I smiled at him.

"I said," he huffed, with labored breath, "get off my property!"

I stood where I was, watching him.

He brought the wrench he was holding up to his chest and tapped himself gently, saying, "Or maybe you end up with a permanent disability."

I kept smiling. "Knock it off, Phil."

He blinked again. "Are you hard of hearing or something? I told you to get the hell off my property!"

I waited.

He raised the wrench slightly. "So help me . . ."

"That's enough," I said.

"I'm warning you . . ."

"Enough!"

But he drew the wrench back anyway, so I grabbed it out of his hand and pushed him hard away from me, then threw the tool — as violently as I could — against the wall of the trailer, where it slammed so heavily something inside crashed.

Dorin stepped back, looking wild-eyed. A man his size wasn't used to being physically challenged by another, and it amazed him.

"I said, that's enough," I reminded him.

"Who the hell do you think you are . . ."

"Shut up," I told him, taking a step toward him.

His face had a lot of anger in it then, but all he did was breathe deep and scowl.

"Now," I said. "I'll ask you again . . ."

"I don't know where the hell she is, okay?"

"So how did you come to have those paintings?"

"I took them as payment," he snapped.

"Payment for what?"

He took a few more settling-down breaths. "Part of our divorce settlement, okay?"

I watched his eyes and knew he was lying. "When was this, Phil?"

"I don't know," he complained. "Around the first of the month, I think."

"So, she came here to give you the paintings?"

"Right."

"Even though she had to take a restraining order out on you last year?"

He snorted.

"Didn't she?"

He flicked his hand as if to wave the past away. "That was different."

"Was it?"

"She was giving me a hard time, all right?"

I waited.

"She wanted a divorce," he told me. "So fine. The hell with her, but then she gets this wise-ass lawyer, wants me to sell the farm, give her half — and I said the hell with that."

"And?"

He smiled a little evil at me. "So I went up to Seattle to see her. Straighten her out a little, that's all."

"How did you manage that?"

He shrugged.

"You bring a wrench with you?"

His smile got a bit more evil in it. "I didn't need no wrench," he told me. "I know how to straighten women out, they get out of line." He tried looking cocky. "Wasn't the first time," he added.

Right, I thought.

"Know what I mean?"

I knew. I also knew that if I hit him, I'd hit him very hard, and despite his size and height advantage, I'd only have to hit him once, but I'd be wrong no matter how right it would feel.

So I satisfied myself with coming up close, looking up into his face, putting my finger on his chest, and saying, "She better be all right, Phil."

He looked down at me and saw something in my face that kept him quiet.

"Understand me, Phil?"

I was done talking myself, so I just stood there looking at him a moment, wondering about people and the people they marry, then I turned away and walked back to my truck.

The nosy horse trotted up beside me as I neared the road, probably wanting to make friends, but he got a look at my face, saw the same thing in it that Dorin had seen, and changed his mind.

The drive to Ashford took me back through Eatonville, over an ever-narrowing stretch of highway that finally widened and became bordered by a handful of houses, a coffee shop, grocery store, and a touristy-looking thing called the Ashford Trading Post — Hair Care, Guns and Ammo Boutique.

A sign in the window read CABINS TO LET; so I pulled into the drive, parked, got out, went to the door, and found it locked. I knocked, but there was no response.

I went back to my truck, dug out a road map, and with my pictures of Carole's renditions of Rainier and with an eye up on the mountain itself, tried working out where Carole had to have been to see the view she'd rendered in paint.

If, of course, she'd worked that way at all. But this *was* my big idea after all, so I tried. Going by what I could see of the mountain from where I stood, I was, in fact, very close, but I needed help.

Which is when I noticed the man.

He was across the road from where I was standing. He'd suddenly appeared from out of the woods — a scraggly-bearded, wild-haired, dilapidated man in an army field jacket and baseball cap. He was looking at me from beside a tree.

"Hello," I called out to him.

He stared suspiciously back at me.

"I'm a little lost," I told him, starting across the road, which caused him to jerk suddenly backward, stumble, then fall hard into a ditch.

I hurried over to help him up, but as I approached he whirled around, still on the ground, and stared at me with wild fear in his eyes.

"Take it easy," I said, holding up both hands. "I just wanted to ask . . ." But he'd scrambled backward, got to his feet, and ran back up into the woods, casting worried looks over his shoulder as if I might be after him.

Right, I thought.

I went back to my truck and the photographs — still needing help — just as a sky-blue pickup skidded off the highway and into the driveway of the trading post.

A chunky young woman with punked-up red hair emerged, holding a two-year-old in one arm and a small rifle in the other. She had a big grin all over her face.

"Hi," she said, coming up to me. "You looked lost."

"Hi," I said back. "I am."

"Hi!" the toddler said.

"Dirty Hairy bother you?" the woman asked, pointing with her rifle in the direction the wild-haired man had fled.

"No," I told her. "I seemed to bother him, though."

She grinned again. "He's just curious. Harmless enough," she assured me. "How can I help you?"

"I'm looking for someone," I explained. "A friend of mine, named Carole Dorin?"

She frowned and shook her head. "Sorry," she told me.

"Sorry," the child echoed.

"She may be using her maiden name — Dragnich?"

The woman's frown became thoughtful. "Sounds vaguely familiar," she told me. "She live around here?"

"Might have moved here in the past few months. I have no address for her, and she's not listed in the phone book."

She gave it another think-over, then shrugged and shook her head again. "We get a lot of folks here let their cabins. People come and go."

I said, "My friend's an artist, and she made these watercolors of Rainier." I held up the photographs, which the two-year-old instantly grabbed. "I was wondering," I went on as they both looked them over, "if you might know where that view of the mountain could be seen."

"Brown Creek," the woman said without hesitation. "Runs — or *used* to run — down below that clear-cut up there." She pointed the rifle toward the mountain and a barren section of cleared woods. "Course the damn dam dried it up, but that's the view from the creek, all right."

"Damdam," the toddler echoed.

"Damn dam?" I said.

She smiled. "Force of habit, calling it that." She shifted the child around on her hip. "They dammed the creek up along Eatonville way for the farmers, but just about killed property values down here. Killed my business, anyway." She shrugged and nodded her head at the picture the toddler was tasting. "Creek's flowing in this picture, so it must've been done before damn dam went in, back the first of September."

"How far does the creek run?"

"I can help you better than that," the woman told me. "See that footbridge in the picture?"

"I see it."

"That's not far from here at all," she said, pointing south along the highway. "There's some cabins down along the edge, both sides. Figure you can ask after your friend there."

"Okay."

"There's a road runs down that way, but you'd have to backtrack about seven, eight miles, or you can just keep on the road you're on a ways, turn left at the little park, and you'll see that footbridge right there. You can hoof it."

"Hooffit!" the toddler told me.

"Well," I told them both, "thank you very much."

"My pleasure."

I put away my map and pictures and got inside the truck.

"Hey?" the woman said, leaning down into the window and handing me a business card. "If you need a place to stay the night, I got a great cabin with a view to die for — and a twenty percent discount for military."

"Bye-bye!" the child exclaimed.

I drove, as instructed, along the highway "a ways," then turned left at a small open area with benches and tables onto a narrow dead-end road, until I came to the footbridge, where I parked and started walking. Before I got far, I looked at the dark sky, and trotted back for my raincoat, then started out again across the footbridge spanning the rocky creek bed. Looking further southward, I could judge almost precisely where Carole had to have stood to see that particular view of Rainier, towering over me just to the north. I was just on the other side of the bridge when it began to rain.

A hard, cold rain, and my raincoat offered little protection. It crossed my mind to head back and wait the weather out, but I had a small sense of urgency building inside — planted there, probably, by Collier and cultivated a little by Dorin — so I pushed on.

But as I pushed, I began to get a sense of being observed, and after I'd made a few turns along the road, I happened to glance back and saw a dark, shambling shape, which I took to be a man, dart across the road and disappear into the woods.

Curious Dirty Hairy, I thought.

And then, a bit further on, I caught another glimpse of him, watching me from some distance beside a tree, then pulling back out of sight when he saw me looking back at him.

Harmless Dirty Hairy, I thought.

I walked on through another section of the park to another paved road, then along it, past a few ugly-looking trailers and several cabins, where I figured to ask after Carole, if I had had no luck on my own.

Then around a turn that angled close down to the dry creek, I did get lucky.

At least I found her mailbox, with the name DRAGNICH stenciled on the side, and through the rain and thick woods beyond it, I saw the cabin.

Which is when luck stopped.

I've always had a sense for things gone bad, and standing there in the rain, peering into the gloom, seeing the dark outline of the cabin through the pines, I knew nothing good was ahead. And when I checked inside the mailbox and found it stuffed with junk mail, a couple of bills, and two issues of *American Artist,* I didn't feel any better.

I made my way down a narrow, unpaved driveway, then up to the covered front stair of the large cabin. Beside the stair in a covered box were a half dozen newspapers still rolled in plastic. When I knocked, despite the empty feel of the place, my sense deepened when there was no response.

I looked through a window and saw only the dim outlines of furniture. Then I tried the door, found it locked. I stepped back into the rain and wind and went around to the rear of the cabin. A deep covered porch faced the creek bed. There was a flimsy-looking bench at one end and a large wooden hot tub at the other.

The storm around me picking up steam, I stepped onto the porch, which was a mess of leaves and animal droppings, and looked into the cabin through a sliding-glass door. I saw only the same dim outlines, but I tried the door and was surprised to find it open.

I poked my head inside.

"Hello?" I called out. "Anyone here?!"

There was no answer but the drumming of the rain on the roof.

I stepped into the darkened cabin and took a dreaded breath. There was no scent of death in the air.

"Anyone home?" I shouted. "Hello!"

Still no reply.

The section of the cabin I was in was a living room area. On the left was a compact kitchen and dining room. I found a light switch, which produced no light, but drawing back the curtain over the sliding-glass door gave me enough light to move without knocking into things.

Which I probably would have done because of the mess.

Tables and chairs overturned; drawers pulled out and dumped of their contents; the floor carpeted with various household items, books, newspaper, and assorted junk as if a small tornado had spun into the house.

Damn, I thought, feeling an adrenaline charge.

I moved to the front of the cabin and found a bedroom in the same disordered state, and another room set up as a studio with an easel smashed in a corner amid the remains of various photographic equipment, canvases — some with the start of something on them, some without — crumpled, torn sketches, and photographs of landscapes, of people, of Carole.

I checked the bathroom and all closets, where I found clothes still hanging, and I checked the pantry, which was well stocked, if turned inside out.

But no Carole.

I headed back out onto the porch, wondering what my next move should be, when I caught some movement — peripherally, back up in the thick woods to my right. When I focused I saw Dirty Hairy sitting on the root base of a large tree, looking at me.

Which is when the wind suddenly calmed around me, and flies began buzzing my head, and I heard the clatter of tiny feet scuttling somewhere to my left.

That's when I finally noticed the fresh wildflowers placed on the hot tub lid, and I smelled the smell I hated, and knew I'd found her.

And it was she — I knew — as soon as I raised the hot tub lid and saw the body. Enough was left of her face and hair to know, and because her wrists and ankles were taped together, I also knew my friend Carole Dragnich had been murdered.

I felt so suddenly tired I just sat there and watched the storm around me. The shock and lack of sleep the night before had combined to knock me out on my feet, so I just stayed put and watched the world grow dark.

Too tired to move. Too tired to think. Too tired to even grieve. I sat there like a uniformed zombie, doing nothing.

Until Dirty Hairy reappeared.

He wasn't far away at all — down, just across the creek, semi-hunkering behind a large rock, peering at me, a bunch of wildflowers clutched in his hand.

Which got me off my feet quickly.

"Hey!" I called out to him, coming off the porch. "You!"

He hunkered down further as I trotted down to the creek, but then he stood back up and started running.

"Wait a damn minute!" I shouted.

But he didn't, so I chased him.

In the rain, in the dark, across the rocky creek bed, then up into the woods.

"Wait, dammit!" I shouted. "Come back here!"

But he ran on, and he was fast and afraid and knew where he was going. After about ten minutes of stumbling around in thickening woods, I couldn't see him anymore, so I gave it up.

Gave it up and went back to the cabin — soaked to the skin, tired, dirty, and miserable — and finally made the call.

Which brought the police — sheriff's deputies from Eatonville at first, then state police investigators and a forensics crew, and finally the county sheriff himself, a morose but capable-seeming young man named Stender. I told the story of how I'd found Carole about a half dozen times to most of the officers — the rest of that day, and into the night and morning of the next day.

I told them about Carole's paintings, told them about Jess Collier and her concerns, told them about Phil Dorin and his bad attitude, told them about Dirty Hairy and the wildflowers. Told them everything — over and over — there at the cabin and later, after poor Carole's body had been removed, at the sheriff's station in Eatonville.

Until, in the early hours of the next day, they decided to let me go.

By then, around four A.M., I was past exhaustion. I'd had two hours' sleep in the past forty-eight, and I was running on fumes; so rather than drive all the way back to Seattle, I chanced driving to Ashford and the Ashford Trading Post.

It wasn't open, naturally, but a small diner was, so I had breakfast and waited.

I dozed over coffee until six, when I called the number on the card that the woman with the red hair had given me. She answered — thank God — and an hour later rented me a cabin.

Small, one room, but with food in the fridge, and a comfortable bed, where I just managed undressing before sleep overwhelmed me.

I slept the day through, dreamt of nothing, remembered waking up around two A.M. the next morning. I was stiff, sore, hungry enough to eat my shoes, and feeling like death, but after a long hot shower, a few aspirins, some coffee and muffins, I felt human again.

Moving myself and more coffee out onto the back porch, I passed a couple hours sitting on a ratty canvas chair, watching the black mountain above me, framed by a blacker sky, lord it over the world.

And I grieved, finally, at the loss of a friend.

Until dawn, when I realized I wasn't done catching up on sleep. Despairing of getting my routine to normal any time soon, I went back to bed and slept less soundly this time, with cold-sweat dreams of high places and falling — until my cell phone rang at noon.

It was Sheriff Stender. He said, "Town prosecutor wants to take your deposition tomorrow. Can you be in town?"

Rubbing my face awake, I told him I would be, then asked, "Have you located Dirty Hairy yet?"

"Not yet," he admitted, "but we got a small army out shagging the eastern foothills."

"Have you identified him?"

"Oh, sure," he said. "Name's actually McGowan — John McGowan — and he's got a minor record."

"Oh?"

"Vagrancy, trespass, attempted burglary — no crimes against persons, though. He's lived up in those woods for years."

"I see," I said, first sitting up, then getting up and moving out onto the porch. "Have you spoken with Dorin?"

"Yesterday afternoon, and he's made a statement."

"And?"

"Said he didn't kill her."

"Really."

"Well, he has a fair alibi," he told me. "Date of your friend's death has been more or less fixed as September fifteenth. There was a newspaper found with her blood on it in the cabin. Later issues were still wrapped and out by the front door."

"I saw them."

"Newspaper boy quit delivering after a week, and according to the ME, the condition of the body is consistent with that date of death."

"So what's Dorin's alibi?" I asked, not following him.

"Dorin was arrested for drunk driving by Eatonville sheriff's men on the fourteenth — a Friday. Drunk driving, resisting arrest — he was jailed and didn't make bail until Monday, the seventeenth."

"That's not ironclad," I pointed out. "She still might have been killed after that."

"That's true."

"And what did he say about those paintings?"

"Same as he told you," Stender said. "His ex-wife gave him the paintings as payment for his share of the cabin that he co-owned with her."

"So he knew where she was all along."

"He did," he agreed. "We're not ruling him out, Mr. Virginiak, he's got a record for assault against women, and the victim herself made several complaints in the past . . ."

"That figures."

". . . but right now we're focused on Dirty Hairy. He's good in these woods and it's a big area, but we've got dogs and we'll get him sooner or later."

"Sounds like you've made up your mind, Sheriff."

"We've got his prints — good sets — from inside the cabin, and he knew her body was in that hot tub — those wildflowers didn't grow on that lid — so what do you think?"

My eyes drifted up to the cloud-shrouded mountain, and I imagined the scene unfolding there.

"Listen," Stender said thickly.

I listened.

"Reason I called was to let you know," he spoke with reluctance, then stopped.

"Go on."

He sighed. "Autopsy was done and the results were leaked, and I didn't want you to just get it from TV or something —"

I waited.

"It's not good," he said.

It wouldn't be, I thought.

"Both legs and one arm were broken," he told me. "Skull was fractured. Her nose and cheeks also had fractures."

"He beat her hard," I said.

"Thing is," he went on with more hesitancy, "she went into that hot tub alive."

"What?"

"Couple of fingernails were broken off and there were deep scratches in the wood seat inside the tub, so . . . well, it's pretty much certain, that . . . you know."

"She drowned?"

He sighed, then said, "Analysis of tissue, lungs, and the condition of her brain makes it almost certain she . . . boiled."

"Jesus."

"There's a safety breaker that should have kicked in when the water temp reached a hundred five. It had been forced open . . ."

"Christ almighty!"

"I know."

"I didn't realize . . ."

"I know."

Jesus, I thought. Poor Carole.

"Anyway," he said, "the report *was* leaked. We got a call from the *Times* looking for confirmation, and I figured you should be told."

"I appreciate it."

"She had no family, apparently, except her ex-husband?" He'd made the statement a question.

"I don't know anything about any family she might have had," I told him, then I remembered. "Oh, Jess Collier, her agent, they were friends as well. She needs to be notified."

"Seattle P.D. talked with her today," he assured me. "She thinks it was Dorin, by the way."

Which, alibi or not, was what I still thought.

After hanging up, I sat on the screened porch of my cabin, drinking bad coffee and thinking hard thoughts about Carole's last minutes alive. Thoughts I didn't want to think but that came to mind anyway. Around two P.M., which is when I decided I'd need fresh clothes if I were to stay on in Ashford for the rest of the weekend, I decided to drive back up to Seattle that afternoon.

In the same way that thoughts of Carole's death came uninvited to mind, I turned my eyes toward my truck, parked only a few feet from the screen door, and there was, on the windshield, a shape that didn't belong. Something . . .

Rather damp, folded twice, and tucked under the driver's side wiper with a wildflower on the inside — a charcoal drawing of Dirty Hairy.

Unmistakably him, complete with Mets baseball cap, his eyes wide, staring out from the hair that crowded and obscured the rest of his face. The portrait was unsigned, but the style of it was definitely Carole's.

Handling it with care I took it back into the cabin, found a plastic trash bag in which to keep it, then grabbed my binoculars and went out again, where I scanned the woods around me, watching for any movement, for almost fifteen minutes.

If Dirty Hairy was near, he was too well hidden, so I gave that up and got out my cell phone to call Stender. He was out, and when I asked to speak with someone who was connected with the investigation, I got a frustrating fifteen-minute runaround. I hung up, deciding there was, after all, no hurry about reporting my find just then.

Thinking that the dampness of the paper suggested it had been left in the early morning rain and that Dirty Hairy — if he was the one who'd left it for me — would by then be long gone. And there was at least a small chance that the portrait I had was not done by Carole.

Besides, in my own mind, Dorin was a far better suspect than Dirty Hairy still, and this was evidence that might close off any other direction the investigation might take.

So for the moment I decided I would get it confirmed that the portrait had been done by Carole — and Jess Collier should be able to do that.

When I got to Seattle, and her office, and showed her the drawing, she did.

"Oh, this is Carole's, I'm sure," Collier said.

"I thought so, too."

We were in her wide-open-spaces office, standing at her desk, with the drawing of Dirty Hairy open on it.

"And he just left it for you?"

"He'd seen me the day I found Carole's body."

She sat and sighed raggedly. "It must've been horrible."

"It wasn't pleasant," I agreed.

She looked at me, her eyes red-rimmed but hard, and shook her head. "That . . . bastard!"

I knew whom she meant. "Apparently, Dorin has an alibi."

She frowned, so I explained, and she saw the problem as I had.

"That newspaper business means nothing. He could've still killed her when he got out of jail. The fact that newspapers dated later than the sixteenth hadn't been looked at may only mean Carole hadn't been home, for God's sake!"

"They haven't ruled Dorin out as a suspect, but they are focusing on Dirty Hairy."

"Well, he certainly looks like a crazed killer," she said, looking down at the drawing. "Does he have a name?"

"John McGowan," I replied. "He has a minor police record, but nothing violent."

She studied the drawing a moment longer, then tears started falling. "Charcoal was becoming Carole's forte," she told me hoarsely. "The last work she brought to me was a charcoal sketch."

"Oh?"

She nodded, dabbing her eyes with tissue, then stood and stepped over to a mirrored cabinet and pressed a corner of the door. When it opened, she slid out an unframed canvas sketch, which she stood on her desk.

"It might be the best she ever did," she said thickly.

It was a sketch of the mountain, viewed from the creek bed outside Carole's cabin, drawn on a much better day than when I had stood there. Rainier was full up and clear in the sky beyond the trees, the wooden footbridge, and the dry creek bed that lay like a rocky carpet thrown down to where Carole had to have been.

I pointed to the broad split stone at the base of the footbridge. "The detail is wonderful."

"She always knew," Collier agreed, "just what belonged and what didn't." She shook her head, adding thickly, "I'm taking this home — I'll never sell it." She faced me then, and her teary, angry eyes glittered. "I want to *kill* him, Mr. Virginiak. I really, really do."

She meant Dorin, of course, and I could understand her. Carole Dragnich had been her friend as well as her client, and wanting her killer's death was the least she could do.

I felt something along the same lines, I suppose, and after taking my sketch and leaving her, after picking up my clothes at my condo, and then on the road back to Ashford, in the driving rain and growing dark, I did what I could to see Jess Collier's wish come true.

I focused my thoughts on seeing that Carole's killer was arrested and convicted. The death penalty was alive and well in Washington State, and the arrest and conviction of such a crime would almost certainly make the killer a candidate for the hangman.

And because Carole Dragnich had been my friend, it was the least *I* could do.

But by the time I hit Eatonville — probably the result of having seen my own anger at Phil Dorin reflected in the angry eyes of Jess Collier — I had given Dorin and what I knew of him a lot of thought and decided he was probably not the killer after all.

His alibi aside, despite his brutish, bullying behavior and the fact I didn't like him, he hadn't struck me as the kind of person who would go to the lengths that were taken to perform Carole's murder.

If she'd been merely beaten to death, that would be one thing, but she was intentionally boiled alive, the act of a careful sadist or a psychotic, neither characterization consistent with the impression I had of Dorin.

By the time I'd reached Ashford, that realization turned my thoughts toward Dirty Hairy and the evidence I had of a connection between him and Carole that the police didn't know existed. As I turned down the lane to my cabin, I decided to call Stender as soon as I got inside.

But just as I came to a stop in the open area in front of my cabin, I saw a dark figure sprinting away from the screened porch and my headlights picked up the startled face of Dirty Hairy.

Getting out my cell phone and pressing 911, I used the searchlight on the side of the Bronco to follow him as he darted across the footbridge, then headed north on the paved road on the other side. I reversed my truck, spun out of the drive, and with the phone to my ear — listening to a tape giving me options — I drove south very fast to the bridge half a mile away.

Pressing 2 on the phone to report a police emergency, I sped over the bridge, squealed a right-hand turn, and fishtailed the Bronco, heading north.

Getting the speed up to seventy, my eyes scanning left and right, looking for Dirty Hairy's dark shape among all the others in the woods on either side, I listened to another taped voice tell me that my call would be answered in the order received and to please hold . . .

Which is when I spotted him, high up along a ridge to my left — just as a logging truck pulled out in front of me from the right, causing me to curse, brake, skid, and swerve off the road, then backwards, down an embankment, where I heard a loud thump, before I came to a stop in a muddy ditch.

My heart pounding in my chest, cold sweat forming inside my clothes, I was looking at a dark prostrate form lying in the gully a few feet ahead of me — the *thump* I'd heard. I got out a flashlight, finally, and stepped out of the truck into the dark on weak legs, and walked back to see what I'd hit.

I was so afraid of what I would find, I actually cried a little when I saw it. A large raccoon — dead as dead gets.

The driver of the logging truck appeared shortly. Because my cell phone was smashed and because I wanted to follow Dirty Hairy, I told him to get the state police, explained who I was and what I was doing, then I left him.

I got into my raincoat and started up the side of the steep hill, my flashlight sweeping the woods ahead.

At the top of the ridge was a thicket of black hawthorn — the point where I'd last seen him. I went down along the other side, slip-sliding over a carpet of dead, wet leaves, stopping every hundred feet or so to scan the area as far as the beam of my flashlight could illuminate, then going on.

Up and down over another ridge, into thicker woods of pine skirted by dense alder — thinking I'd lost him and starting to think of heading back to the highway — when I saw him.

He was high in the woods to my left, staring down at me until my flash picked him up, then he scampered away. I went on, coming to where I'd seen him at the base of a cliff, a dead-end triangle of rock where there was no place to go but up.

So I did. I stepped up easily at first over a natural stairway of rock, until it became steeper and I started having second thoughts. Although I couldn't see in the dark, I had to be a hundred feet or so above the base, and I really had a problem with heights.

But I went on, using my hands now, to haul myself upward over the rock face of the cliff, until I came to a narrow ledge that was just wide enough to sit on.

I rested for a moment, scanning with my flash along the ledge, seeing nothing. Then, standing on nervous knees, I started sidling along the ledge, watching carefully now and thinking I'd accidentally cornered him, which might make him suddenly brave — until I came to the cave.

It was actually more of a deep indenture under a broad overhang of rock. Stooping down from the side, I let my flashlight explore first, picking up in the light a variety of trash, bedding, clothing, boxes, et cetera, but not Dirty Hairy, as far as I could see. But this was his home.

So I went in, carefully, bent over low, watching the shadows for movement, but seeing none, coming, finally, to the deepest point, where he'd built a semi-permanent campsite. There was a stone fireplace, a large, mostly rotten mattress, various cooking items, canned food, plastic bottles of water, trash bags filled with clothing, assorted books and magazines piled here and there.

And photographs.

Spilling mostly from old yellowed envelopes onto a large, flat stone that he used as a table, on which there was also a small kerosene lamp, which I lit, then looked the photographs over.

Most of them were of people I didn't know, but in one newer envelope were a dozen or so banded together, all of Carole while she still lived — some nude, some not.

One of the photos was taken as she sat on a rock by the full flowing creek by her cabin.

Which caused me, finally, to realize something that I'd *known* already, and gave me a chill that had nothing to do with the fact that I was cold and wet.

Which is when Dirty Hairy came home.

The kind of anger I felt then, and for the rest of that night, was a rage so cold that its memory now causes a kind of nausea — as if it were a virus my body, once infected, remembers and recoils from.

A rage that was quiet, but hard as ice. A rage I held onto for nearly twelve hours, till the next morning.

When I knocked on the door to Jess Collier's apartment — on floor forty of a newish Bellevue condo — she came to the door after only a second or so, as if she'd been just on the other side expecting me, but she seemed surprised to see me.

"Mr. Virginiak?"

"Ms. Collier," I said. "I'm sorry for coming so early, but I needed to speak with you."

"You look terrible," she told me opening the door wider. "Please come in."

I stepped inside saying, "I've been up all night."

"It looks like it," she told me. "Would you like some coffee?"

"No, thank you."

She turned and led me into a large, spare, expensively furnished living room, which opened onto a large wrap-around balcony. "I was just about to get ready for work," she said, waving me to a gray leather loveseat. "Please sit down."

Which I did, looking the room over.

I'd expected artwork on her walls, but like her office there was only glass — huge sliding-glass doors, bracketed by floor-to-ceiling mirrors. With the doors open the effect was of being outside.

"Are you sure I can't get you coffee?"

I told her no.

Wearing jeans and a sweatshirt, lighting a long thin cigar, she still was a handsome woman, but she didn't look as good to me then as she had when I first met her.

I said, "I found Dirty Hairy last night."

"You did?" She perched herself on the arm of the sofa and waved a hand toward the *Times* on the coffee table between us. "There's nothing in the paper about it." She frowned at me. "Has he admitted to killing Carole?"

"No," I told her. "He didn't kill anyone."

"I see."

"He doesn't exactly play life with a full deck, but he told me that he and Carole were friends — and I believe him."

"Really?"

"He's not a bad guy, actually. He'd stolen some pictures from the cabin. Pictures of Carole, mostly nudes. He'd taken them because he'd been embarrassed for her and didn't want them to be seen by others."

"Really."

"He's a Gulf War vet and saw a little more than he could handle, and he's taking a vacation from the world, he told me."

The wind was blowing the balcony's curtains in around her, so she got up and pulled them back a bit, then reperched herself.

"He wanted to come forward with what he knew, but he's had a bad history with police, so he'd been afraid," I said. "When he saw me in uniform the other day, he figured I might listen to what he had to say, and he had a lot to tell me." I looked at my watch. "He'll be turning himself in to the state police in a few minutes," I added, "so we haven't got a lot of time."

"What do you mean?"

"Well," I told her with reluctance, "something's bothering me."

She frowned and shrugged.

I said, "Did you bring that charcoal drawing of Rainier home with you as you said?"

"Yes."

"May I see it?"

"Sure," she said, then got up, went to a desk, and from behind it, took out the drawing.

I stood and went over to look at it, saying, "And you did say that Carole delivered this drawing to you in early August, I believe?"

"Yes," she agreed, laying the drawing down and walking back to the sofa and coffee table, where she opened a briefcase that was on it and removed a small piece of paper, which she handed to me. "I brought this to the police officers who questioned me yesterday.

They asked me when it was that I last saw her, and I found this copy of the receipt I gave her."

RECEIVED FROM CAROLE DORIN, 8/5/98
A DRAWING IN CHARCOAL OF MOUNT RAINIER.

"Something wrong?" she asked.
I stared at her.
"What is it?"
"The creek is dry in the drawing."
"I beg your pardon."
I looked at her.
"Yes?"
I said, "The creek in the drawing — Brown Creek — wasn't dammed until September first."
She frowned sharply.
"That split stone at the base of the footbridge was well below the waterline, and under the footbridge itself, and could not have been seen before the creek was dammed." I frowned back at her. "She couldn't have drawn this before September first."
Her frown became thoughtful. "Carole . . ." she began, then smiled. "Carole had an artist's imagination, Mr. Virginiak. She could've done the drawing earlier. At any time, actually . . ."
"No," I told her. "There's too much detail there. I've seen that creek bed, and the rock arrangement is precisely the same as in the drawing."
Collier gave me a long look, gave her cigar a puff, then hugged herself. "So what's the problem?"
I folded the receipt I held and put it in my pocket, saying, "The creek was dry when she did the drawing, so she couldn't have given it to you in August." I watched her eyes watching me. "Which makes you a liar, Jess."
Which didn't prompt a denial.

Instead she frowned at me for a long moment, looking for some sign of stupidity in my face, which she wasn't going to find. Then finally she sighed and turned away, went back to the sofa, stubbed out her thin cigar, lit another, and smiled at me, saying, "You're very clever."

Jesus, I thought.

"So?" she said, sitting back. "Why is it that we have so little time?"

"Because," I explained, "the police will be coming for you, and I thought we needed to talk before your arrest."

"My arrest?" She affected amusement at the idea. "That receipt means nothing. In fact, I now seem to recall it was September fifth that Carole delivered the drawing to me." She shrugged easily. "I wrote an eight instead of a nine — so what?"

"But you did kill Carole," I told her.

She considered me for a moment, then said, "Take off your shirt."

I did as she asked, to show her that I was wearing no wire, then she said, "Would you care to know why?"

Collier blew smoke and began to inspect the back of her hand in a casual way. "Carole betrayed me," she said with coldness. She glanced at me. "After all that I'd done for her, she betrayed me."

She sat back easily and said, "I *found* her, you realize. Selling her artwork from a park bench, for next to nothing."

What was killing, I thought, but the ultimate betrayal?

She said, "I saw her talent, but her technique was naive. I advised her. I taught her to be all that she could be. I arranged her first showings. I became her friend. And when she finally had enough of that idiot she'd married, I was with her, giving my support every moment.

"I loved her," Collier told me, in a flat monotone.

"Did you?"

She nodded. "Carole was confused about her sexuality, but I knew, and eventually brought the true woman out of her, even though she resisted." She frowned slightly. "Then last summer she . . . went away. Said she needed space. Went to live in that cabin, didn't even call. I found her and . . . we reconciled, I thought, but then . . ." She shrugged. "She chose in the end to reject her true self — and me." She smiled ruefully. "Well, I couldn't have that, now, could I?"

I said nothing.

"It was very painful to me, Mr. Virginiak, and I don't do pain very well — I really don't."

"So," I said, finding my voice again. "You killed her."

"Oh it wasn't that simple." She puffed hard on her little cigar.

"Carole needed to be punished before dying." She blew smoke, and her mad eyes glittered at me.

Right, I thought.

"I admit that when I went there that day, I was a bit out of control. We argued and I hit her very hard with the poker, and at first I thought she was dead — until I saw she wasn't. And I'll tell you something else," she said breathlessly. "Breaking her legs gave me great pleasure, and then, after I'd put her in the tub, watching her struggle so desperately, hearing her scream as she realized what was happening" — she smiled — "I enjoyed it very much."

"Of course you did," I said.

She smiled almost impishly at me. "Does that sound strange to you, Mr. Virginiak?"

"You're not going to get away with this, Jess."

She smiled. "That receipt is hardly evidence, and I could just deny what I've told you. There's no evidence I was ever even at that cabin."

"McGowan saw you there," I told her.

Her smile flatlined.

"That's what he's telling the police now."

She thought about that, then tried, "A half-witted wild man, Mr. Virginiak?"

I shook my head at her with certainty. "He described you perfectly, Jess, and if you told the police that you'd never been to the cabin, they will know you lied."

She sighed with a sense of weary capitulation.

"And, there is the receipt," I went on, "which catches you in another lie, and if the police know what to look for — and I'll be sure they will — enough evidence will be found. Fingerprints, fiber evidence." I pointed to the newspaper and the headline: POLICE HUNT FOR HOT TUB KILLER. "You'll hang in the end, or opt for injection, or more likely, prison, forever, but you won't get away with this, Jess."

She looked then as thoughtful as she should.

I said, "You haven't really thought this through, have you?"

She said carefully, "Do you think, Mr. Virginiak, that a sane person would have done what I did?"

I didn't, but said nothing.

"I mean, I must have been insane to have done this to poor

Carole, mustn't I?" She considered her line of thought, then blew smoke, and smiled. "A hospital is more likely than prison, don't you think?"

I kept silent, watching her closely.

She only smiled that little inhuman smile at me.

And, I finally sat back, and felt all my own humanity slip away.

"That's exactly what I was thinking before I arrived here, actually," I said, watching her closely, trying to fix the right advantage. "When you say *hospital,* you do realize that means the state facility at Tillicum?"

She shrugged.

"I've seen the place," I told her. "They're very chemically oriented there."

"Are they?"

"Thorazine, Prozac, Serone, Zoloft — they'll mix you nice little cocktails, so you'll feel very little for the few years you'll be there."

"Sounds lovely," she told me, adding with a disbelieving frown, "Did you say years?"

"Oh, I'm sure we're talking years, Jess."

She looked at her watch, as if tired of me.

"You really are quite psychotic, you know, and not smart enough to hide it."

She looked doubtful.

"You boiled a woman alive," I told her. "Beat her with a poker — broke her arms and legs, then boiled her alive — and there's no remorse in you."

She looked less doubtful.

"No remorse, no regret — just a pathetic sense of having done yourself justice because another woman dumped you?" I laughed. "You are insane, Jess."

"Really."

"Yes," I said, smiling a little more inhumanity at her. "It's not what you've done, though, as much as it is what you are — so you'll be at Tillicum a long time."

She tried looking bored again, but couldn't quite pull it off.

"But the drugs will be a big help," I went on. "And what you're able to feel, you won't really mind."

She sighed and I watched again for the advantage.

"You'll barely notice waking in your bed, soaked in your own urine." I shrugged. "Happens when you're doped past caring, as you surely will be."

Her lips pressed together slightly, but that hadn't yet rocked her.

"You won't mind having no one to talk with except brain-fried drug addicts, schizophrenics, and a few psychopaths like yourself."

She brushed an ash from her sweatshirt.

"You may even get used to the hands of the guards, as they move you from one room to the next."

She only looked at me.

"Do you mind being handled, Jess?"

She stayed silent.

"Well, you'll be handled a lot, so you'll get used to it. You may even get to like it — just as you may come to enjoy the very close confinement."

Her eyes moved — fractionally — toward the opened door to the balcony.

Yes, I thought.

"You'll have your own cell," I told her. "A full eight-by-eight — very cozy."

She started to gently bite the inside of her lip, and I could almost smell her sudden fear.

My advantage, I thought.

It made me feel good.

I got up, moved to the patio door, and drew the curtain open a bit more, and looked at her. "You like high places, don't you, Jess?"

She rubbed her arm and looked away.

I smiled. "I don't mind telling you that I don't, but you like being high up — the cleanliness of being above everything? Above the corruption?" I shook my head. "You'll miss that feeling of openness and height for a while, but then . . ." I drew the curtain closed. ". . . there's a certain sense of security and comfort in being caged."

A vein began to prominently throb along her throat.

"It won't be as if you're entombed, though it may feel that way at first."

She scratched her neck idly.

"It won't be as if you were buried alive."

She looked up at me with sharp irritation.

"It won't be as bad as you think . . ."

"If you're trying to frighten me, think again."

"You're frightening yourself," I told her. "I'm just telling you how it will be."

"You're exaggerating."

"Am I?"

She put her thin cigar out and lit another.

"If I'm boring you, I could call the police now."

She swallowed and whispered, "Do what you like."

I watched her think for a moment, then I put my hands in my pockets and moved around the room, coming to rest facing a large mirror.

"The thing about being in custody, Jess, is that your options become so limited."

She was quiet.

"Yes," I said, watching myself. "Once you're in custody, you'll stay in custody — there will be no bail for you."

In the mirror I saw her looking up at me with doubt in her face.

I laughed at her. "You're insane, Jess — and it shows, right there in your face. You're a danger, to others and to yourself, and *they will not let you go.*"

And she believed me. She swallowed fear, looked away.

I looked back at my own face, and wondered who I was.

I said, "Fellow I knew once in San Diego was arrested for dealing drugs."

Something about my eyes was different, I thought.

"He knew he was facing a lot of jail time, and he knew he could never do that time, but he wasted the little time he had before he was arrested."

Something vaguely dead about them.

I turned and waited for her own dead eyes to come up to mine.

"The problem," I explained, "was that, once he had been arrested, his options were so limited."

She frowned up at me.

"He had the advantage of being sane, but they watch people closely because suicide makes cops look bad, uncaring or something, so that all he could think of in the end was to bite through the arteries in his own wrist.

"You're out of your mind, and they'll be watching you every minute, so . . ." I shrugged, letting her fill in the blanks.

The wind ruffled the balcony curtain.

I waited a moment more, then retrieved my hat and said, "McGowan will have already told the state police what he knows and what I've told him to say. It will take a while to sort out, but my guess is the Seattle police will be here shortly. If not, I'll give you an hour before I call them myself."

Her look was blank.

"I'll be across the street," I told her, nodding toward the open balcony.

She said nothing. Neither did I.

I rode the elevator down to the lobby, stopping only to ask the security guard the time — six-fifteen A.M.

I jaywalked across the highway to a coffee shop where I took a seat along the front window, which had a full view of the parking lot of Jess Collier's building, and ordered coffee and a bagel to have while I waited.

I was watching the road outside fill with morning rush-hour traffic, hoping McGowan had managed all right with the state police, wondering if the Seattle P.D. would arrive.

And thinking hard, cold, unforgiving thoughts that seem to come easier the older I get. I had no second thoughts whatsoever.

And she took nearly the full hour.

Doing what, I never knew, but at 7:05, having paid for my coffee, and thinking I'd have to call the police about Collier after all, I saw someone running.

He tore across the street from the parking lot to the front of Collier's building, where he opened the door and shouted something inside. Then the security guard came out and both ran back to the parking lot, looking up.

Which is when I left the coffee shop, and although I couldn't see the parking lot well from that vantage point, I stayed standing where I was.

I didn't see her fall.

But despite the noise of the traffic around me, the sound of her body slamming down, forty stories, through the roof of a parked car, came through to me loud and clear.

And it sounded as final as it should.

BENJAMIN CAVELL

Evolution

FROM *Rumble, Young Man, Rumble*

Part One: Sex

ON OUR FIRST DATE, Heather Gordon orders the Maryland crab cakes with red-pepper polenta and when I walk her home she asks me to take her to bed. On our second date, she has portabello and endive salad followed by veal tenderloin with poblano chiles and we make love on the swing set of an empty playground. On our third date, she tells me she is going to marry me.

For our one-month anniversary, Heather lights candles all around my bedroom and strips me naked and walks me to the bathtub, which is filled with warm water and rose petals. After three months, she takes me to Paris for the weekend. When we have been dating for six months, she asks me to kill her father.

"The first thing we have to do," Kelly says when I tell him, "is cross over."

"Cross over," I say.

"Cross over the line between the good people and the bad people."

"There's a line?"

"Sure," he says. "Actually, there are several. We'll cross them in stages. We'll work slowly. We'll keep upping the ante."

"Did you get this from a book?"

He shakes his head. "No books. This is about personal experience. We must walk the path."

"The path."

"The path to emotional detachment."

"Are you making this up?"

He shakes his head again. "It's in all the latest literature."

I stare at him. "I thought you said no books."

He frowns. "From now *on,*" he says.

We are sitting on the sofa in our apartment watching Kelly's high-definition television, which is shaped like a fish tank. The picture is so sharp that it reveals the individual pores in human faces.

Kelly says, "Everything's going cerebral these days. If we want to resist that trend, we have to master the physical world. If we want to be masters of the physical world, we have to know about life and death."

"Kel," I say, "are you sure you want to do this?"

He looks at me in silence for a while. Then he says, "This is what we've been waiting for."

The room is cavernous and blue-carpeted and honey-combed with tiny cubicles. The analysts sit in the cubicles between eighty and a hundred hours each week. The traders come in at eight-thirty and leave at five.

A green digital stock ticker rushes along the edges of the ceiling.

Kelly and I are sitting in brown leather armchairs outside a glass-walled conference room. Inside the conference room is a long cherry table with a podium at one end.

A kid about our age wearing Ferragamo lace-ups strolls past the analysts and pours himself a cup of coffee from the cart next to us.

Kelly says, "You have to come all the way over here every time you want coffee?"

The kid shrugs. "Can't put it on the trading floor. Someone would crash into it."

"You a trader?" Kelly says.

"Apprentice. You the boys from Merrill?"

Kelly shakes his head.

"We work for a start-up," I say.

The kid frowns. "But you're wearing suits."

"We're in new investment."

"You're here to pitch us?"

"Something like that," Kelly says.

The kid nods. "You guys have one of those cute tech names

where you change the first couple letters of an existing word? Like
Verizon. Or Cinergy."

"We're called eVolution," I tell him.

"Small ee, big vee?"

"That's right."

He smiles. "So what does it do?"

"The small ee, big vee?"

"The *company.*"

I look around the room at analysts hunched over keyboards and
at traders in shirtsleeves shouting into telephones. "I really don't
know," I tell him.

You can open a car door without a slimjim by bending a hanger
into a squared hook and inserting it between the window and the
weather stripping and using it to catch the lock rod. Sometimes
you can open the door by using a key from the same manufacturer.

It is possible to hot-wire the car from the inside, but to do this
you need to remove the ignition mechanism and complete the
circuit manually. This risks severe electric shock. It also damages
the car.

It is better to pop the hood and run a wire from the positive side
of the battery to the positive side of the coil wire. The coil wire is
red. Use a pair of pliers to hold the starter solenoid to the positive
battery cable. This fires the engine. To unlock the wheel, insert a
screwdriver into the steering column and use it to push the locking
pin away from the wheel.

Kelly says, before you can kill you have to know what it is like to die.

Before you can know what it is like to die, he says, you have to
know what it is to live.

"Do you know the life span of the common housefly?" he asks
me.

"One day."

"One day," he says. "Twenty-four hours in which to pack all his
loving and hating and living and dying."

I say, "I don't think a housefly does much loving and hating."

I change the channel on the high-definition television. The news
is running a feature on school shootings.

Kelly sighs. "You're missing the point."

I shrug. "His life isn't short if he doesn't know it's short."

Kelly frowns and wrinkles his forehead and then says, "He only gets one sunrise and one sunset."

"And you only get a few thousand."

"Hopefully more than a *few.*"

"Even so, "I say.

Kelly nods. "Even so."

We are in a taxi. The driver wears a green knit hat and loafers with no socks. He has a stick of incense burning on the dashboard, which makes the air smell and taste like hot soap. I am sitting in the middle, between Kelly and my boss. My boss wears a linen suit. His tan is perfectly even.

Looking out the window at skyscrapers like enormous gray wafers, I say, "I don't understand my job."

My boss says, "What's to understand?"

"Shouldn't we bring a programmer with us?"

"Didn't I explain this to you last week?"

My scalp itches. I say, "It's just that I've been thinking some more about it and I figure it couldn't hurt to have an expert along."

My boss sighs. I look at Kelly. He is shaking his head. My boss says, "Our investors didn't grow up covered with zits."

"Excuse me?" I say.

"These people made their money the old-fashioned way — they inherited it. And they'll *never* give it away to some fruitcake in clear-framed glasses who wears his jeans two sizes too small. The key is charm, not knowledge. You were born for this."

Kelly is smiling at me. I ignore him. "But what if they ask me" — I lean close to my boss and whisper — "*technical* questions?"

"Do they ever?"

"They *could.*"

He rolls his eyes. "Make something *up.* We're *salesmen,* for Chrissake."

"What are we selling? We don't make anything."

He looks at me. "We make *money,* kid. I sell experience. Kelly sells cool. You sell cheekbones and green eyes and leading-rusher-in-Ivy-League-history."

"Second-leading."

"My mistake," he says.

"It's just," I say, "that I don't know anything about computers."

He shakes his head. "This isn't about *computers*. Do you think Rockefeller knew anything about oil? Do you think Carnegie knew anything about steel? All you have to know is what people want and how to tell them they want it from you."

"But what if you don't know what people want?"

He shrugs. "Then you have to know how to tell them what they want."

When you die violently, your bowels let go. It's called involuntary-sphincter-release response and it means that you spew all the foul waste from inside you, more than you ever imagined possible.

Kelly says the next step after crossing over is the planning phase.

Really, he says, the two steps are simultaneous.

I am sitting in our living room, listening to the steam heat, and Kelly is telling me that evolution means the extinction of the weak.

"Every human and animal characteristic is the result of random genetic mutation."

"Yes," I say.

"Think of the creatures who lived before certain features developed. Think of the ones whose mutations failed to increase their fitness."

I close my eyes and picture ancient sea creatures with squat bodies and tails like embryonic alligators', bobbing on the tide, near powerless with their shrunken fins, watching one of their fellows crawl out of the surf and onto the beach. He will go on to populate the world. The rest will be prey for prehistoric sharks or else will have descendants who will be less and less suited to the sea and will eventually drown as infants or occasionally flop their way onto the sand. I wonder whether these creatures know that they are the footnotes of history while their friend on the beach is the ancestor of an entire planet. I think of all the animals not selected for a place on the ark. I think of the thieves crucified next to Jesus.

"Eyelids," Kelly says.

I open my eyes. "What?"

"Eyelids are the result of random genetic mutation."

"Yes," I say.

"You have to be able to imagine how it felt before eyelids. If you looked at the sky during the day, your retinas would burn. You'd have to walk with your face pressed into the ground, dirt in your mouth all the time. You'd have to sleep with your eyes open."

"Yes," I say.

Kelly nods. "You need to be able to imagine the time before tear ducts."

Heather's father leaves his office between 6:18 and and 6:51, Monday through Friday. On Saturday and Sunday he works noon to five. It takes him between four and seven minutes to make his way down to the garage, depending on the elevators. He drives a black Lexus sedan.

There ought to be two men in bland suits who drive Heather's father to and from work and sit all day behind Plexiglas in the hallway outside his office and shadow him wherever he goes.

This would make for more of an operation.

In that case, we might use a pipe bomb. We might use an incendiary device underneath the back seat. We might use a sniper. If the bodyguards blocked sight lines to the subject whenever they were out in the open (as they should), we might use the sniper to take out the bodyguards and use a chase man to go after the subject if he broke and ran. Of course, it is better to snipe in two-man teams. And neither of us knows how to use a rifle.

I am pressing my face into Heather's neck and smelling her perfume and her shampoo and the soap she uses, which is goat's milk and honey and costs twenty dollars a bar. Even through all of that, I can still catch the scent of her skin.

Heather is wearing a pair of my boxer shorts and a T-shirt from the gym I go to, which is called Advance.

We are watching *2001* on my DVD player.

I stop nuzzling Heather's neck and sit back into the sofa with my legs extended in front of me. Heather rests her head on my chest. The light from the television twinkles all around us.

"It's less than two thousand years since the fall of the Roman Empire."

"Is that right?" Heather says.

"That's right," I say. "Less than two thousand years after chariot races, we have airplanes and space shuttles and movie-theater popcorn."

"Amazing."

She shifts the position of her body and nestles into my chest.

I say, "We weren't even the same *species* until about twenty thousand years ago. Before that we were Cro-Magnons."

"Fascinating," Heather murmurs. Her breathing is becoming deep and slow.

"Until recently, we were carrying clubs and living in caves."

She is silent.

I watch the television. Keir Dullea has just shut down the supercomputer. This is immediately before the part I don't understand, in which he imagines himself sitting in a room that looks like the smoking room from the world's fanciest mental hospital and then sees himself as an old man and a fetus.

I say, "Kelly and I are making preparations."

Heather stirs for a moment and then relaxes back onto me. "Mmm," she says sleepily. "Preparations for what?"

"Never mind," I say. "It's all right if you don't want to talk about it."

Kelly says, "You're the bastard who gave measles to the Yanomami." He is talking to the waiter, whom he has just accused of sneezing over his Parmesan-and-onion tartlet. "These people lived in isolation for hundreds of years and then you goddamn sociobiologists and you save-the-rain-forest fairies came in and gave them a measles vaccine, except that there *were* no measles in the rain forest until you brought them. And when the vaccine made some of the people sick, you refused them treatment on the grounds that you wanted to study a society completely free from outside influence."

The waiter is trying to figure out whether Kelly is making fun of him. The men sitting next to Kelly are laughing. One of them says, "This guy is a card. A goddamn *card*."

The other one nods and says, "The genuine article."

Kelly says, "Do you have any *idea* how many germs live in the mucus inside your nose?"

We are in a restaurant called Neoterra in which each of the tables has a different shape from the others and none of them is round. Our table is shaped like a lima bean or like a slug writhing to death under a blanket of salt.

The men we are eating with all wear suspenders and Kenneth Cole glasses and have their sideburns trimmed every other day.

There are five of these men. They are venture capitalists. I cannot remember any of their names, so I have assigned names to them, at random. When I cannot remember the name that I have assigned, I say the first name I can think of. They do not seem to notice.

One of the men next to Kelly is saying, "The plain ones are always the most suggestible. The pretty ones tend to be too uppity and the ugly ones are too wary. The plain ones are up for *whatever.*"

Kelly says, "How do you know who's pretty and who's ugly?"

The man says, "You *look.*"

"But how do you assign categories? Certain features make you feel physical attraction, but these features are different from culture to culture and even, sometimes, from person to person. It is a selection-based instinct to want to combine your genes with the genes of someone physically attractive, in order that you will have attractive offspring whose appearance will make them more likely to have reproductive success. Of course, you have a chicken-and-egg problem there. Also, that does not account for differences of opinion."

The man stares at him.

Kelly says, "Do you ever try to imagine the time before dilating pupils?"

When I open my eyes, the man to my right is speaking earnestly to my boss. He is asking to see the business plan.

My boss shifts in his chair.

"You do *have* a business plan," the man says.

My boss clears his throat. "Of course we have a plan," he says. "But we're not planning to be captains of industry. This isn't industry. We're not planning to be the world's leading distributor of butt plugs. We're sure as *hell* not planning to build the world's best shuffleboard Web site so that some Daddy Warbucks can stroll up and pat us on the head and pay us twenty-five million to split twenty-four ways, so we can buy a town house and a Benz and some pussy and live god-damn upper-middle-class. Upper-middle-class means *dick.* Fuck the suburbs. Fuck commuting. Fuck neighbors. Our plan here is to be rich enough not to *have* neighbors. To be able to stand in front of your house and turn around in a circle and own everything you see. Not season tickets, not even courtside. I'm talking about owning your own team. No Internet millionaires here. Fuck that, too. I'm talking about Internet *billionaires*. What we're offering you is the opportunity to be part of that."

The man to my left, whom I have decided (I think) to refer to as Gill, looks at me and says, "So, you played halfback at Princeton?"

"Not Princeton," I tell him.

"Of course not," he says. "How tall are you? Six feet?"

"Why not?"

"You weigh around two hundred?"

"One-ninety."

He smiles. "What's your forty time?"

"My forty time."

He nods.

"I don't know these days."

He frowns.

"I'm not really an athlete anymore," I explain.

"Hmm," Gill says.

We drink in silence for a while. Suddenly Gill looks at me. I lean back toward him.

Gill says, "What's your body-fat percentage?"

We are standing at the urinals in the bathroom at Neoterra and Kelly is saying, "The difference between assault and aggravated assault is mostly about the severity of the injuries."

I say, "How bad does it have to be to be aggravated?"

"It's subjective."

We zip up. The urinals flush automatically when we walk away.

We hold our hands under the faucets, waiting for the sink to recognize that we are not just dust particles blowing in front of the electric eye.

Kelly says, "Last night I was reading about the human botfly."

"I thought you said no books."

He nods. "I think we're going to have to forget that rule."

"I already did, "I tell him.

The water begins to spray from our faucets.

He glances at me. "When?"

"From the beginning."

"Why didn't you tell me?"

I shrug. "I don't care much about it. As long as we don't say no movies."

"Of course not," he says. "That would ruin everything."

"The human botfly," I remind him.

"Right, right. Anyway, when it bites you, it raises a bump like a mosquito bite. Except that the fly has burrowed its way into your arm and the bump is covering it. It incubates for a while until it gets hungry and then it begins to consume you. You can feel it eating its way up your arm."

We take our hands from under the faucet and the water stops. We stand with our hands under the nozzles of the hand dryers.

Kelly says, "There are tiny parasitic worms that can live in drinking water. Once they're inside you, they gather in sores on your legs. The only way to get rid of them is to immerse them in water and allow them to flow out of the hole they'll open in your skin."

They are laughing when they leave the club and weaving as they walk. Both of them wear white baseball caps emblazoned with the letters of their fraternity.

Kelly says, "Are you ready for this?"

I nod.

"Deep breaths," he says. "Try to swallow."

I nod again.

The frat boys do not notice us until they are only a few feet away. Then they stop.

Kelly is wearing a long black overcoat and leather gloves with lead studs sewn into the knuckles on the inside. He says, "You boys sure you're all right to drive? You look a little under the weather."

The frat boys are silent.

Kelly says, "Is this your car?"

"Yeah," one of them says.

"This a Corvette?"

The frat boy snorts. "Try Lamborghini."

"Ah."

He narrows his eyes. "You fuck with the alarm or something?"

Kelly smiles. "Now why would you think that?"

"Should be going off with you sitting on the hood."

"Well," Kelly says, "we're not as heavy as we look. The camera adds ten pounds." He laughs.

The frat boy says, "If you get off the car by yourselves, we'll give you a running start." He spreads his hands, palms, up. He is thick through the chest and shoulders. His friend is taller than he is and wide.

Kelly slides off the car onto his feet. The frat boy smiles and turns his head to glance at his friend and when he turns back Kelly throws a straight right hand into the middle of his face. The gloved fist makes a dull-hollow slapping sound when it lands, followed immediately by the crunch of the nose breaking, and the frat boy's head disappears in red mist and then he has fallen to his knees. His friend is staring, openmouthed, and does not notice me standing up off the hood. He is reaching for Kelly when I kick him in the groin as hard as I can. He crumples next to the other one. And then we are on top of them.

I take the big one, who is curled into a ball with his hands cupped between his legs. He is dry-heaving. White lines of saliva hang from his chin. I kick him a few times in his kidneys and he rolls onto his back and I stomp his forearm with the heel of my boot and I am pretty sure I feel bones breaking. He screams. I kick him in the stomach and listen to him gasp as the air rushes out of him. Now he has no breath to scream and he is gagging. I drop onto his chest and, as I do this, I bring my elbow straight down into his mouth and feel the teeth give. He brings his arms up to cover his face and I punch the broken forearm. He screams again. When he moves the forearm, I drive my fists into him over and over. The skin splits along his eyebrows and forehead and cheekbones and blood seeps through the cracks like lava. Sweat is rolling down my face, plastering my hair to my forehead. I feel like crying.

Kelly says, "Enough."

I stand up and look at the big frat boy at my feet. His wrist is bent at a terrible angle. His mouth looks like a tomato with ripped skin. There are teeth sticking through his upper lip.

I look at Kelly, who is also standing. "Wallets?" I say, my chest heaving.

Kelly shakes his head. "This is assault, not robbery."

"Two birds, one stone?"

He chews his bottom lip and considers this. "Fuck it," he says. He reaches inside his frat boy's jacket and pulls out his wallet. The frat boy groans. Kelly kicks him in the ribs.

"We taking the car?" I say.

"No," Kelly says. He looks at the frat boy below him. "Don't take it too hard, fellas," he says. "We've just grown past you. You're the giraffes whose necks never stretched." He pulls off his gloves. "You're the elephants with short noses."

"I think we're ready for the next level," Kelly says.

I glance at him. The streetlights we pass turn his face ghostly white and run the shadow of the windshield wipers along his profile. I massage the fingers of my left hand against the knuckles of my right, which are scraped bloody and have already begun to swell.

"What's the next level?" I say.

Kelly turns his head slightly so that the wiper shadow now flows over his face asymmetrically, making a jagged line on his nose. He is smiling enough for me to see the tips of his teeth.

"It's time to shoot somebody," he says.

Heather is wearing a red dress with no back. The dress is longer on one side than the other. On the short side, it rises almost above her hip.

The skin on Heather's thighs is the color of butterscotch.

We are standing under an enormous crystal chandelier that hangs over a crimson staircase. Everywhere I look, there are men in tuxedoes. Heather has the fingers of her left hand laced through the fingers of my right.

The poster next to the theater door shows two immense eyes and, above that, the word "Gatsby" in white letters.

Heather is talking to Cynthia Lowell-Wellington and Vanessa Mather Coppedge Bryson, who are jammed up against us by the crush of people. Cynthia's boyfriend, who is taller than I am and has a dimpled chin, looms on my left, just behind Cynthia. I am fairly certain that he was on the crew team at Brown, but it is possible that he was on the lacrosse team at Penn. He shakes my hand at every opportunity.

For dinner, Heather had the New Orleans–style catfish with chipotle dipping sauce.

She is saying, "If you're going to use a bronzing agent of *any* kind, you *have* to couple it with a good moisturizer."

Cynthia says, "Should I be looking for one with sunblock in it?"

"I suppose it couldn't hurt. But really, you should be keeping yourself out of the sun completely. That's what the bronzer is for."

Vanessa leans toward Heather and says, "So, do you put it *every-where*?"

Heather nods. "No white should show."

I say, "Can you picture the time before melanin?"

Heather raises herself on the balls of her feet and kisses the side of my mouth.

The mob surges all around us, moving with tiny shuffling steps.

We are sitting in a private box on the left side above the orchestra. The house lights are down and the women onstage are singing to each other and staring into the audience. According to the program, they are singing in English, but it is impossible to understand them and my attention is focused on the seat backs of the row in front of us where a thin digital screen shows a scrolling transcription of the lyrics.

Heather is sucking my thumb.

Next to me, Cynthia's boyfriend, Clay Harrison Adams, whispers, "When's your IPO?"

I say, "We're not trying to be the world's leading distributor of butt plugs."

He says, "Oh."

The stage is darker now and the women are gone. They have been replaced by a dancing mob and bright-colored balloons. In the background a tiny green light is flashing.

Suddenly I have the urge to climb on top of my seat and throw my head back and scream. I have this urge every time I go to the theater. I believe it is a similar instinct to the one I have to turn on the engine of my car when the mechanic has his hand inside it. Or the impulse I feel on subway platforms to push the man next to me in front of the oncoming train. Or when I imagine swerving my car into a group of pedestrians and feeling the dull cracks of their heads against my windshield and gazing at the wet smears of their blood. Or when I think of diving through the plate glass of the Rainbow Room at Rockefeller Center and plunging, back arched, head up, gleaming shards of glass falling all around me, into the middle of the herd of ice-skaters circling sixty-seven stories below.

Clay says, "Johnson and Johnson?"

"What?" I say, turning to him.

"The butt plugs. Leading distributor."

I sigh. "I don't *know*, guy."

"Oh, "he says.

I think about throwing him over our balcony and watching him drop, arms and legs windmilling, into the front row.

With all these impulses, there is the idea stage, then the imagination stage, then the spine-tingle, adrenaline-shot, testicle-clench moment when you *know* that you are actually going to do whatever it is.

But you never do.

During intermission Heather and I get on one of the mirror-walled elevators and ride it until we are alone. She pushes the Run-Stop button. A voice comes over the intercom asking if everything is all right. Heather begins unbuttoning my shirt. The voice from the intercom says that if the elevator does not begin moving in the next five minutes it will call the fire department. Heather licks my chest. I put my arms around her. The voice tells us not to panic.

Heather pulls away from me and takes two steps backward, smiling slightly, and presses herself against the brass handrail. As she leans onto the handrail, her dress drifts up and I can see the thin black string of her panties. I move close to her and she kisses me hard and runs her hand along the back of my neck and along my shoulder and down my arm and then she takes my hand and puts it gently between her legs. Her underwear is already moist. I grab hold of it and pull so that the narrow strip rubs against her. She gasps. I slide my hand under the wet fabric and touch the soft, slick skin and then I ease my middle finger inside her. She tips her head back and moans. I suck on the skin of her neck. Her perfume has a bitter taste.

She says, "Oh my God."

I kneel down in front of her and grip the backs of her thighs and pull her close to me, resting my head just below her ribs.

She strokes my hair. "How much do you want me?" she whispers.

I groan against her stomach.

Back in my seat, I can smell Heather on my fingers and I can taste her when I lick my lips.

In front of us, dozens of miniature chandeliers hang on long cords from the ceiling. In the hallways behind us, the lights flash off and on and an usher closes the door to our box. The cords begin to retract and the chandeliers float toward the high ceiling.

Heather whispers, "What's wrong with you lately?"

"What do you mean?"

"You've been even more distant than usual."

I say, "I've been walking the path to emotional detachment."

She frowns. "This is Kelly's idea?"

I nod. "We're working in stages."

She opens her mouth to say something else, but the two women are singing again. They are slumped in lawn chairs. They wear straw hats and white dresses. They draw out a single note so long that I have to take a deep breath in sympathy. The urge to scream washes over me again.

The words click by in white block letters on the digital screen in front of me. IT'S HOT, says the screen. IT'S HOT.

Part Two: Violence

The man by the door is wearing a beige turtleneck and a leather jacket. He leans us against the wall and frisks us quickly.

Kelly says, "Won't you at least buy me dinner first?"

The man sighs. "Haven't heard that one yet this week."

Dexter is sitting in the far corner on a hydraulic chair that looks like a life raft. The man cutting his hair wears a long white shirt that says MECCA across the chest. The room smells of cocoa butter. The floor is covered with hair.

The man beside Dexter is almost as thick as he is and has a big jagged scar along his jaw. He wears a cream-colored suit and a silk shirt.

The only other man in the barbershop lounges on a leather sofa in the corner opposite Dexter. His entire body seems frozen, including his eyes, which are locked on mine.

Dexter raises his head and looks at me in the mirror. "Looking good, baby," he says.

I smile. "You remember Kelly?"

He shrugs. "Why not?"

"Good to see you again," Kelly says.

Dexter grunts. He jerks his head toward the window. "That your new whip?"

"Yeah."

"Whip?" Kelly whispers.

"Car," I tell him.

Dexter whistles. "Fuckin' ay. You niggers must be *flush*."

"We can't complain," I say.

"I thought you were supposed to call me before you went public."

"We will."

He frowns. "So how come you niggers are rolling Bill Gates–style all of a sudden?"

I look around at the bodyguards. "You think you have enough security?"

"Can't be too careful."

"I don't remember anyone ever taking a shot at Butkus."

Dexter grins. "He wasn't a Nubian king."

"All right, I don't remember anyone taking a shot at Willie Lanier."

"That was a different era. It's all haters out there these days. Can't stand to see a brother living the dream."

"Is *that* what you're doing?"

Dexter's barber opens a drawer in the counter in front of him and changes the guard on his clippers.

Dexter says, "You watch me in the Pro Bowl?"

I nod.

He says, "They've never seen anything like me."

The barber removes the guard from his clippers and carefully shapes Dexter's sideburns. He unsnaps Dexter's maroon smock and passes the razor over the back of his neck. He pours alcohol onto a cotton ball and runs it around Dexter's hairline. He douses him with talcum powder.

Dexter says, "That's enough. Don't give me any of that Afro-Sheen shit."

The barber nods.

Dexter shrugs out of his smock and stands. He is an inch or two taller than I am. He is wearing a white knit tank top. His body is like a clenched fist.

"Shame the way you're letting yourself go," I say.

Dexter snorts. He takes a fat wad of bills from his pocket, peels one off the top, and hands it to the barber.

The man in the corner is moving now. He is on his feet and coming toward us. I can't remember seeing him stand up.

Dexter says, "This is Wilton."

"Wilton?" I say.

Dexter smiles. "Him a yardie, y'know."

"What?" Kelly says.

"He's Jamaican," I say.

Wilton looks at Dexter. "That accent's a little Harry Belafonte."

Dexter says, "So are you."

Wilton is wearing gray wool slacks and a black ribbed turtleneck sweater.

Dexter says, "These are the boys I told you about."

Wilton nods. He does not move to shake our hands.

I say, "Dexter tells me you used to work for Mike Tyson."

He shrugs.

"You know what we're working on?"

He shrugs again.

"We're trying to reach the next stage in our development."

Wilton stares at me.

Kelly says, "For most mammals, grooming is a sign of affection. That's why I cut my own hair."

Wilton is saying, "You'd be amazed how long it takes some guys to die."

I say, "Doesn't it depend on where they get hit?"

"Not always."

We are at an outdoor shooting range, lying on our stomachs beside green T-shaped shooting benches, facing white-and-black silhouette targets set up in front of a stone wall. I am leaning on my elbows on the concrete apron, sighting down the barrel of a rifle that looks like it is made out of Legos.

I say, "I wish these things still looked like they used to."

"Why?"

"It would make me feel more real."

Wilton says, "Draw down center body mass on everybody. No head shots."

"What about bulletproof vests?"

"That's just movie shit."

"*Some*one must wear them."

"Sure. But they'll still be incapacitated if they take one in the chest, provided you have enough stopping power. Even with body armor, a heavy load can break ribs and collapse lungs."

I squint through the aperture and place my crosshairs on the center of the target.

"Raise your aim four inches at two hundred yards, ten inches at three hundred."

"Why?" I turn my head to look at him.

"Gravity," he says.

"What do I do past three hundred?"

"You miss."

I nod.

Wilton says, "How you know Dexter?"

"We went to high school together."

"You play ball with him?"

"Sure."

He frowns. "I thought he was from Cleveland."

"So?"

"So, you don't look too Cleveland to me."

I shrug, gently so as not to lose my target picture. "Near Cleveland."

"Shaker Heights?"

"Something like that."

He smiles. "Always knew that motherfucker was wannabe hard."

"Don't need to be from the ghetto to be hard."

"It helps." He looks at Kelly, who is on his stomach fifty feet to my right, sighting down the barrel of his Lego rifle. "What about the ofay?"

"Why is he an ofay and I'm not?"

He shrugs. "Ain't just about skin color."

"Mmm," I say. "We lived together in college."

Wilton nods. "He's a fuckin' fruit loop."

Sometimes, particularly when you can anticipate the precise location of your target, it is preferable to snipe at a near-flat trajectory. For countersniping, because you cannot predict your target's whereabouts and because the target will likely be concealing himself from anyone on the ground, it is vital to occupy the highest position possible.

In close quarters, the pistol is ideal because of its concealability and ease of use. However, its effectiveness drops sharply as range increases. It is very difficult to be accurate with a pistol at distances greater than fifty feet. Past a hundred, it is almost impossible.

My boss is riding in the cart in front of us with a man from Goldman who has skin like tapioca. We all wear green sweaters and brown-and-white spikes.

Kelly is driving our cart, bouncing over ruts in the dirt path. The air tastes like the dirt thrown up by the other cart. Kelly is saying, "Why doesn't he have an accent?"

"He told me he lost it."

"He talks like a goddamn Yalie."

"He's self-educated."

Kelly snorts. "You *must* know what that means."

"What?"

"Anytime a Nubian says he's self-educated, ten to one he was reading with his ass to the wall."

"Prison?"

He nods. "Probably has one of those correspondence diplomas."

"That's not fair."

He glances at me. "You two have been getting awful close lately."

"He's been *teaching* me."

"I hope you're not losing perspective."

"Perspective on what?" I say.

"Just make sure you keep in mind what it is we're doing."

The cart in front of us stops dustily. Kelly pulls in behind it.

We sit off to the side on a wooden bench while the man from Goldman sets himself over the tee.

Kelly says, "In gorilla societies, each adult male has his own position in the hierarchy. You don't look directly at anyone higher than you. Eye contact indicates provocation for all primates. No one looks at the alpha male, unless they are ready to challenge for his position. If you look him in the eye before you're ready for him, he will tear your limbs off."

I am sitting in the back seat, between Heather and her father. We are on the way to the opening of an art gallery called Cave Paintings. Heather is gazing out the window.

Her father is my size with big hands. He has a thin white scar under his right eye. I am trying not to look at him.

He is saying, "Sometimes we would wait all night and not see anyone. Some nights we would all see movement on the road and we would blow the claymores and launch flares and pour fire into the tree line and when we walked down, we wouldn't find anything except the craters we'd made."

I say, "How'd they get away?"

"Who?"

"Whoever was on the road."

He looks at me. "There *wasn't* anybody on the road. We imagined it."

"You all imagined the same thing?"

"The visions are contagious. One guy points at what he sees and you make yourself see it, too."

"So, after a while, why didn't you stop believing something was there?"

"Because sometimes something *was* there."

"What were those nights like?"

He shakes his head. "You don't want to hear about *those* nights."

"Sure I do."

He says, "Later on, I was with Recon and we did less search-and-destroy, but we still had visions."

"Does it give you nightmares?"

"Nightmares?"

"Because you hated it so much."

He frowns. "Did I say that?"

"I just assumed. I thought everybody hated it."

He says, "It was the happiest time of my life."

We are sitting in a rented van at the curb across the street from Heather's father's office building and Kelly says, "What about knives?"

Wilton looks at him. "This ain't *West Side Story.*"

"It's just that I thought we were supposed to learn these things in stages."

"You niggers want to learn knives, you can do it on your own time."

Wilton is shielding his eyes from the sun and staring up at the building, which looks like a giant milk carton. He says, "Next time we're doing reconnaissance, you ought to bring a jacket."

Kelly says, "Why not just keep the heat on?"

Wilton says, "Three guys sitting by the curb all day in a car with the motor running might as well hang out a sign that says STAKE-OUT."

"Why are we here at all? We already know his schedule."

"*You* already know it. I want to see it for myself."

"You don't trust us?"

Wilton shakes his head. "You can't learn this stuff from books."

"And you've learned it through experience."

"That's right."

"So when we have the experience we'll be as good as you."

Wilton shifts his eyes to look at Kelly. He says, "You can't have a late start."

Armor-piercing or KTW rounds can puncture steel doors and pass through bulletproof vests. Their drawback is that they make neat, surgical wounds.

Full-metal-jacketed rounds also have a better penetration value than standard loads, but they are less streamlined than the armor piercers and cause more tissue damage.

Hollowpoints carry low penetration values but expand on impact. This is also true for dum-dums.

You can create a hollowpoint effect by cutting cross-shaped grooves into the tips of your cartridges. On impact, the round will flatten out along the grooves, disintegrating muscle and bone. (Note: Handmade loads may tend to jam an automatic.)

I am kneeling by an open window on the ninth floor of the Ritz, looking past the Public Garden at Beacon Street, and Wilton says, "Blue suit with the grocery bag."

"Got it," says Kelly.

"Why him?" I say.

"I don't know," Wilton says. "Easily identifiable."

Kelly says, "It doesn't pay to stand out."

They are on their feet next to me, binoculars held to their faces. I open and close my hands against the rifle and blink my eyes and watch through the scope as the man scratches his neck, magnified ten times.

"I don't know if I can," I say.

Wilton sighs. "This is what you said you wanted."

"I know. I just wasn't expecting him to be so *alive*."

Kelly says, "I'll do it."

"Wait your turn," Wilton says.

The man stops walking and checks his watch.

I say, "Won't they be able to tell where the shots came from?"

"Who's 'they'?"

"I don't know. Somebody."

"Unlikely. The flash isn't too apparent in daylight."

"What about the sound?"

"It'll echo off the buildings. It'll seem to come from every-where."

"What if somebody sees us?"

"The chances of that increase with every second you don't take the shot."

The man is whistling now. I steady the crosshairs on the top but-ton of his suit jacket. I close my eyes and imagine the way his face will look when the bullet hits him and the noises he'll make and the way his body will come apart. I wonder whether he will drop the groceries. I open my eyes.

Wilton says, "Deep breaths. Squeeze, don't pull."

The man smiles suddenly and switches his grocery bag to the other arm. A young girl with blond hair runs into the sight picture. The man bends down and scoops her up with his free hand and spins her around in a circle. She kisses him on the cheek.

I draw back from the scope and lay the rifle on the windowsill and stand up. I shake my head. "Not in front of his daughter."

Kelly looks at me. "The fuck you care?"

"She'll never recover."

"Nobody recovers from anything. Your experiences shape who you are. You have a chance to be the defining influence in this girl's life."

I don't say anything.

"If you're so worried about it," he says, "maybe we should do her too."

"No," I say. "I won't do that."

He groans. "Have Wilton do it."

"The girl can't die."

"She can and she will. The only question is when."

"Not today."

"What difference does it make? Today, tomorrow, eighty years from now. She won't be in a position to care."

"But in eighty years, when she feels it coming, she'll be able to look at all the things she did. Now she could only think of what she didn't do."

"So what if this girl has an unpleasant last few minutes in which she imagines the life she didn't live? It'll probably be better when she imagines it than it would have been to live it. It'll be better than remembering all the things she could never quite do. Besides, it's only a few minutes at the end. And if you hit her right, she won't even have that. Like flipping off a light switch."

Wilton turns to look at him. "I don't wash anybody for free."

"We'll pay you," Kelly says.

On the street below us, the man has put the girl down and is holding her hand. Holding the girl's other hand is a pretty blond woman in a blue cardigan.

Wilton turns back to the window. The family is moving away from us. They round the corner onto Charles Street.

I say, "They'll go home tonight like they do every night and they'll never know that they just lived through the most important moments of their lives. They don't even know we exist."

Kelly says, "Goldfish have thirty-second memories. Everything that happened more than thirty seconds ago is erased to make room for the new things. That means that at the very end, when they look back, they've been dying their whole lives."

Wilton grunts. When Kelly shoots him, his body clenches and he half turns from the waist, head rigid, pupils crammed to the sides of his eyes, trying to look at Kelly behind him. Then he sags against the glass, blood spraying from the big exit wound in his chest. The sound of the handgun is much softer than I am expecting. It is the dry crack of a twig snapping over and over.

"Sorry about that," Kelly tells me.

"You're crazy," I say quietly.

He smiles. "I doubt it. It's just that I've developed a more complete understanding of our situation."

"Do you understand that Dexter's other boys will be looking for us now? Along with God-knows-who-else."

He shrugs. "I hope you see why it was necessary."

I stare at him.

He stands very close to Wilton, who is gurgling. "It's all perfectly natural. Today we're selecting for people who draw their guns on time." He smiles. "We're selecting against surly tarbabies who don't know how to watch their mouths."

We are sitting on long sofas in the dark-maple locker room at the Harvard Club and my boss is saying, "If poor people were as smart as rich people, they'd be rich by now."

The man next to him is soft everywhere and colors his hair red-brown. He netted eleven million dollars last year. He chuckles.

My boss says, "Every generation of a family has a chance to hit it big. If they keep missing, after a while you have to assume that something's wrong with the genes."

The carpet is blood-colored. The walls of the locker room are covered with lacquered plaques that show vertical columns of men's names. Kelly and I have our legs stuck out in front of us and crossed at the ankles. We are wearing white Izod shirts and gray shorts. We have long-handled rackets laid across our laps.

The television that hangs from the ceiling of the locker room shows a pretty blond woman with straight teeth and a gray-haired man, also with straight teeth, sitting at a curved desk in front of Corinthian columns and windows that show false sky. At the bottom of the screen, stock prices churn by in a blue strip.

Kelly whispers, "Ancient chieftains developed efficient methods of agriculture so that they could throw banquets to show their power."

"What?" I say.

"It wasn't to better provide for their people. For that, the old methods were sufficient."

I stare at him.

"Technology develops not to advance the species but to consolidate the power of individuals."

"Listen," I say, "I don't have any idea what you're talking about."

"I'm talking about the death of emotion and the sublimation of desire."

"I thought the death of emotion was what we wanted. I thought you said we were walking the path to emotional detachment."

He nods. "Yes. I've come to reexamine our position. At the beginning I thought we were working to evolve into things capable of murder. I thought we were trying to divorce mind from body. I thought we were trying to resist going cerebral." He sighs. "I realized recently that our problem is that we had already *gone* cerebral. We had already separated mind and body. We've been denying our instincts. For human beings to be able to kill, they don't need to evolve, they need to regress. All these computer-geek faggots live in the world of the cerebral and they've probably never been in a fight. They can't fight, they can't fuck, they have no physical *presence*. You and I have been trying to regain our instinctive behaviors. We're trying to get back to basics."

"But my instinct was to feel sorry for those frat boys and for the guy I was supposed to shoot."

"You're making the mistake of classifying compassion as a human emotion. Really, your natural instincts are to do what's best for yourself and to eliminate anything that challenges your success. You do for you, I do for me, everyone does for themselves, shake it all up and the cream rises to the top. It's mathematics."

"How can you tell me what my instincts are?"

"Because human behavior has been completely dissected. The genome is mapped. There are no more secrets."

My boss is smoothing a terry-cloth headband over his hairline. He looks at the man next to him, who is still chuckling. My boss says, "Take the Gettys, for example."

The pretty blond anchorwoman looks into the camera and says something, but I can't hear it because the sound on the television has been muted. Her words appear in a black closed-caption box below her. The black box says, "Now, the day's headlines."

I ignore the first two stories, both of which include videotape of rolling tanks. When the third story begins, a graphic appears over the anchorwoman's shoulder featuring a painting of the Ritz-Carlton Hotel splattered with enormous puddles of blood. Written over this painting in white block letters are the words "Ritz Murder."

Kelly says, "Normally they don't make so much fuss over a shine killing."

My boss says, "Location, location, location."

The man sitting with him says, "Such a waste."

Kelly says, "We don't know if it's a waste. It's not like this was some kid on the honor roll. Maybe this was just a big, mean dog who ran into a bigger, meaner dog. These things happen."

The man turns to look at him.

"Do you know any of the men on the walls?" I say quickly.

"Sure," he says. "Most of them."

"That must be hard."

He turns away from Kelly to look at me. "What must be hard?"

"To lose so many friends."

"Lose?"

"In the war."

He shakes his head. "The war dead are in the lobby, kid. These are the trustees."

"Oh," I say.

Kelly leans close to me and whispers, "Human beings have come to treat death differently than other animals do. When lions get too old, they lose their place in the pride and are forced to wander, scavenging for food, unable to hunt, until eventually they die of starvation or disease or they become immobilized by starvation or disease and are then eaten alive by hyenas. When sharks are injured, other sharks come from miles around and tear them to pieces. Human beings are the only species that tries to prolong life artificially after the subject has outlived his usefulness. We are the only creatures that mourn our dead."

"Elephants," I say.

"Elephants?"

"Elephants mourn their dead."

"That's impossible," he tells me.

We are standing in Dexter's living room, surrounded by Persian rugs and sliding glass doors and a glass-topped coffee table dusted with cocaine residue. The residue is smeared into white streaks. On the floor beside the table are three long-stemmed champagne glasses and a metal ice bucket.

On the other side of the glass doors are the floodlit patio and the swimming pool and the hot tub, both of which have underwater lights, and past all that are evergreen-covered hills that loom black in the darkness.

Dexter is in the hot tub with one of the girls. The other girl, naked and brown and smooth and gleaming, is standing on the edge of the pool and swaying in time to faint music. They are all laughing. I can't tell where the music is coming from.

Kelly motions toward the glass doors. He is dressed entirely in black. His face is covered in greasepaint.

"What if they hear?" I whisper.

"They won't," he whispers back. "And, even so, if they look back at the house they'll be looking from the light into the dark."

"It's not really *dark* in here."

"Dark enough.*"

I slide one of the doors open. It hisses on its runner. I freeze. Dexter and the girls keep laughing. I slip through the opening and onto the slate of the patio. Kelly follows me. We move slowly, crouched low, careful to keep our footfalls silent.

The dancing girl sees us first. She stops swaying and opens her mouth. Kelly shows her his gun. She does not speak.

I kneel down behind Dexter and press the barrel of my automatic into the back of his neck. His body shudders and tenses. The girl next to him gasps. She has long hair and skin the color of coffee ice cream.

I say, "Where are the roughnecks?"

"We're the only ones here," Dexter says. His voice is very steady.

"Bullshit," Kelly says.

"I swear to God."

Kelly says, "If you're lying, I'm going to slice your eyeballs open with a razor."

"I'm not lying."

"After that, I'm going to pour gasoline into your eye sockets and pull off your fingernails one by one. Then I'm going to tie your hand to the side of this pool and mash it with a cinder block. Then I'm going to take a pair of garden shears and cut your tongue in half while it's still in your mouth."

The girl in the hot tub starts to cry.

Kelly turns to her. "Is he lying?"

She shakes her head.

Kelly says, "If he is, I'm going to do the same thing to you."

She sobs more loudly. She keeps shaking her head.

Kelly looks at me. "I believe it."

I stand and walk around in front of Dexter. "It's me," I say.

He squints at my face. "Jesus Christ," he says. "You almost made me piss myself."

Kelly says, "Don't think I didn't mean what I said."

Dexter says, "What do you want?"

"We need to talk," I tell him.

Dexter is sitting on the black leather sofa in his living room and wearing a white robe that pulls very tight across his shoulders. I am seated facing him on a ceramic barstool that I dragged in from the kitchen. Kelly is on the other side of the room, leaning on a mantelpiece. The girls are upstairs in the windowless walk-in closet in Dexter's bedroom. We slid a heavy bureau in front of the closet door. We balanced a mirror between the bureau and the door. Kelly told the girls that if we heard the mirror break he was going to come upstairs and pull out their teeth with pliers and shove straightened coat hangers into their ear canals to rupture the drums.

"Where'd the hitters go?" I ask Dexter.

He says, "Wilton's disappeared. They're trying to find him."

"They have any ideas?"

He shrugs. "Not that I know of."

I glance at Kelly. He shakes his head.

"I don't believe you," I say to Dexter.

"I can't help that."

Kelly says, "The next time you lie, I'm going to shoot you in the hip. Won't be too many more Pro Bowls after that."

"Tell us," I say.

Dexter says, "They think maybe you two clipped him."

"You try to talk them out of that?"

"I tried. They weren't sure anyway."

"They have a theory?"

"They think Wilton's that thing at the Ritz."

"I thought that guy couldn't be identified."

He looks at me carefully. "Yeah, somebody put some caps in his face. Blew out his teeth and everything. Also, they took his wallet and cut off the tips of his fingers."

"So what makes them think it's Wilton?"

"It's just a guess right now. That's why you're still walking."

"How long before it's not just a guess?"

"Who knows? Depends what they find."

"Any chance you can get them off of us?"

He shakes his head. "They're looking for payback. I can't call them off."

"What are they doing now?"

"They're checking you out."

"Any prediction about what their conclusion will be?"

"Again," he says, "it depends."

"On what?"

He stares at me. "On what you've done."

"What's your instinct?"

"These guys are pros. They'll put this together in their sleep. They'll take just enough time to be certain." He takes a breath. "Then, Kelly goes for sure. I tried to tell them that *you* couldn't have been involved. They'll spend a little while thinking about that."

"And then?"

"And then I figure you go too."

"Unless?"

He shrugs. "Unless you're gone to somewhere they can't find you."

"Or they aren't good enough," Kelly says.

"They're good enough," Dexter tells him.

"Wilton wasn't."

We are silent for a while.

Dexter says, "I'll try to warn you."

"Why would you do that?" Kelly says.

Dexter jerks his head at me. "He's my friend. It isn't fair for him to get burned just because of the company he keeps."

"You're so sure it was me?"

"Sure enough."

Kelly smiles. "Then how do you know I won't do you too?"

"Because I'm your early-warning system."

"How can you warn us when you don't know where they are?"

"They still check in." He frowns. "That reminds me — how'd you get past the alarm?"

Kelly's smile widens. "I think you may need a new one," he says.

Heather comes out of the dressing room wearing blue jeans made from some kind of stretch material. She lifts the bottom of her sweater, showing a narrow strip of belly. The jeans ride low on her hips.

"What do you think?" she says.

"Great," I say.

"That's what you always say."

"I always mean it."

She examines herself in a long mirror on the wall.

"I like them," she says. "You can wear them with a blouse. You can wear them with a halter."

"You're sexy," I tell her.

She turns her head toward me and smiles. "You're sweet."

The walls of the store are lined with light brown shelves. Most of the shelves hold scented candles and kitchenware and lamps with rice-paper shades. The shelves in back hold thirty-dollar T-shirts.

Heather walks to the narrow doorframe of the dressing room and leans her head inside. She pulls her head out and says, "Still empty."

She takes my hand and leads me into a pine-smelling corridor lined with stalls. The door of one of the stalls is hanging open and Heather pulls me inside. She closes the door behind us and throws the bolt. Her jacket is lying on the gray bench in the corner. Her shoes are on the floor under the bench. Each wall, including the back of the door, is completely covered by a mirror. The mirrors reflect each other's reflections. We are surrounded by infinite versions of ourselves that extend as far as we can see in every direction. We can see ourselves from every angle.

Heather runs her tongue along the edge of my ear. She puts her palm between my legs. I feel myself stirring against the zipper of my pants. I grip her shoulders and gently push her away. She frowns at me.

I say, "I'm sorry if my behavior has been strange lately."

"I hadn't noticed."

"I've been under a lot of pressure."

"Work?"

"Not really. I've been dealing with some personal issues."

She presses me down onto the gray bench and sits across my knees with her arms around my neck. "Like what?" she says.

"Oh, I don't know. I've been working on my development."

"As a person?"

"Sort of."

She strokes my hair. "I want to get married."

"I know. You told me after our third date."

TO BOB BASON

"I mean I want to get married soon. I want to take care of you. I want you to take care of me."

"I don't have *anything*," I tell her. "At least let's wait and see what happens with the company."

"I don't like waiting. Besides, my father is practically *made* of money."

"I don't want your father to take care of us."

"No," she says, "neither do I."

Kelly's sketch has wide eyes and too much nose. Mine is a cross between Errol Flynn without the mustache and Paul Bunyan without the beard. The sketches are superimposed side by side on the blue-sky background behind the pretty blond anchorwoman with the stock ticker flowing beneath her.

We are sitting on the sofa in our living room.

Kelly says, "I don't like her as much on the HDTV. She wears too much makeup."

"Everyone wears makeup on television."

"She has bumps on her face. She looks like a pickle."

The anchor is talking to a brunette with thin lips who is standing in front of the Ritz in the rain, looking concerned. The anchor also looks concerned.

I say, "Aren't you a little bit worried?"

"About the sketches? You can't tell it's us unless you know what you're looking for. Even then, they're kind of a stretch. They made me look like Groucho, for Chrissake."

"Maybe we ought to lay low. Get out of the apartment. *Something*."

"Forget it. Those pictures could be almost anybody. The cops aren't gonna find us with these descriptions unless they're already onto us."

"And what about Dexter's boys?"

"The Jamaicans?"

"How do you know they're Jamaicans?"

He shrugs. "Wilton was."

"Fine, then," I say. "What about the Jamaicans?"

He sighs. "The important thing is for us to stay on mission."

"On mission?"

"Heather's old man."

"Are you serious?"

"We have to finish what we started."

The back of my neck is hot. "I'm not sure about that."

"You don't have to be sure. I'm telling you it's going to be done."

"I think I may have made some kind of mistake."

"Trust me," Kelly says. "This is best for everybody. This is what you said you wanted."

"I think I've changed my mind."

Kelly nods.

The sketches are gone. The anchorwoman is smiling now.

Kelly stands up from the couch and walks to the door.

"Where are you going?" I say.

He opens the door and walks into the hallway. I listen to the door click shut behind him. I turn back to the television.

When the phone rings an hour later, I pick it up immediately. "Kel?" I say.

There is no answer.

"Where are you?" I say.

I hear the ticking of the open line.

I say, "Just come back and we can talk about it."

I hold the receiver against my ear and listen to buzzing static and then Dexter's voice says, "They're coming."

Part Three: Climax

"You don't look good," my boss says.

"I had to get a hotel room last night."

He half-smiles. "You have a fight with your boyfriend?"

"We're having some work done," I say.

We are looking out the big window of the Credit Suisse luxury box at the Fleet Center, squinting at tiny players on a tiny floor hundreds of feet below us. It is almost impossible to tell what they are doing. When we want to see the game, we watch wide-screen televisions in the corners of the room.

My boss says, "I was trying to reach you. I called the cell phone."

"It didn't get reception in the hotel."

"You need to be available to me twenty-four hours. Where's Princess Grace?"

"He's not here?"

My boss shakes his head. "If you two want a job where you don't have to come in on Sundays, go work at the post office."

"I *am* in," I say.

A young trader is screaming at one of the televisions. His friends sit in front of the television in leather armchairs, Frisbeeing paper plates at the screen.

My boss says, "Any of these guys would kill for your job."

The skin on my face feels very tight. "So would I."

I imagine throwing my boss through the tinted window and watching him plummet into the middle of the court. I can see the stain of him spreading on the bleached wood.

My boss says, "Let's see some of that."

I pull my gun from inside my coat and touch the barrel to his eyebrow. "Open your mouth," I say.

"What?"

I hit him in the forehead with the side of the gun. He steps back. Blood trickles down his face.

"Get on your knees," I say.

He does.

"Open your mouth."

The traders have stopped making noise. I know that people around the room are looking at us. No one moves. My boss opens his mouth.

"Wider," I say.

I shove my gun deep into his mouth. It clatters against his teeth.

I say, "You're going to have to learn how to treat people."

He nods. He is shivering.

I say loudly, "You're a ridiculous man. You don't even understand your job. I don't know who put you in charge. I'm younger than you, I'm better than you. I don't even need this gun. I could kill you with my *hands*."

A dark patch has appeared on my boss's light gray trousers. There are tears running down his face.

I say, "You don't have the balls for this kind of work."

I take my gun out of his mouth.

Everyone stares at me uncertainly. A few of the traders applaud.

"Thank you," I say.

My boss is slumped on the floor, moaning. I smile at the room. I put my gun away and give one last wave and then walk quickly to the door.

I say, "If I see this door open while I'm still in the hallway, I'm going to come back and choose two of you at random and shoot you in the balls."

When the elevator opens, it is full of security guards. They have their guns drawn.

I say, "There's some maniac in there with a gun. He has baggies of nitroglycerin taped all over his body. He said he would detonate if he heard anyone trying to come in. If you shoot him, the whole place might go up. Can you imagine what that would be like? You'd spend days sifting through body parts. You'd have to make piles of limbs. Can you imagine an enormous pile of severed arms?"

One of the security guards says, "Get behind us."

They push past me and fan out around the entrance to the luxury box. One of them puts a finger to his lips and leans his ear against the door.

I step inside their elevator and press Lobby.

Standing on the sidewalk next to the Fleet Center, listening to the sirens approaching, I take out my cell phone and call Heather.

I say, "How soon can you be at South Station?"

"Is this a joke?" she says.

"It's not a joke. I'm leaving. Will you go with me? "

"Yes."

I cross Causeway Street. "How soon?"

"Do I have time to pack?"

"No."

"Half hour," she says.

I push the End button and put the phone back in my pocket and look over my shoulder at the Fleet Center and at the squad cars pulling up in front and that is when I see the Jamaicans.

They are on the other side of the street, half a block behind me, watching the cops pile out of their cars. One of the Jamaicans is tall and wide. The other is the one who frisked us at the barbershop. They are moving at the same speed I am. They turn away from the cops and toward me and I snap my head back around, but I am almost certain they saw me see them. I keep walking, sweat dripping down my back, feeling them behind me.

I cross Merrimac Street.

I glance over my shoulder. The Jamaicans are still matching their speed to mine. They are maintaining the same distance.

At Cambridge Street, I reach the corner just as the DON'T WALK sign stops blinking and I slow down and almost stop and then suddenly I dash into the street and hear squealing brakes and slide over the hood of a moving taxi and hear horns screaming behind me and then I am on the other side, running.

Heather's father stands up to meet me. His office is lined with black shelves that hold crystal eggs and lacquered cigar boxes.

"How did you know I'd be here?" he says.

"What do you mean?"

"It's Sunday."

"Oh." I run my tongue along the backs of my teeth. "Heather must have told me."

He looks at me. "Must have," he says.

I take a deep breath. "I need your help." I glance out the window. "By the flower cart."

Heather's father walks to the window and gazes down at the street. "Who are they?" he says.

"I don't know exactly."

"They're pros."

"Yes."

"How'd you make them?"

"I don't know. They just sort of appeared across the street from me."

"I mean, how'd they let you see them?"

"I was looking for them. I knew they were coming."

He shakes his head. "Shouldn't matter."

"But why would they want me to spot them?"

He shrugs. "Maybe they wanted to see whether you'd run. Maybe they figure only a guilty man runs."

We are silent for a while.

Seven stories below us, the big Jamaican crosses the street and walks along the sidewalk and around the far side of the building.

"Why don't they follow me in?" I say.

"They don't know which floor you're on. Also, they'd be worried about the building's security force. And they don't want to trap themselves in case things go south. If they take you in the open, they have escape routes and it's easier for them to avoid the cops. They'll cover the exits and wait to reacquire."

"You learned all this in Vietnam?"

"It's textbook," he says. He lifts his telephone receiver.

"What are you doing?"

"Cops."

I shake my head.

He puts down the receiver. "Sounds like you have something to tell me."

I don't say anything.

He steps away from the window and takes his key ring from his pants pocket and unlocks the top drawer of his desk. He brings out a heavy automatic. He pulls back on the slide and checks the cylinder.

"You keep it *loaded*?" I say.

"Doesn't do much good when it's not." He puts the gun in the waistband of his pants. "You carrying?"

I show him the pistol inside my jacket.

"You any good with that?"

I shrug.

"Who put these guys on you?"

I shrug again.

"This have anything to do with that fairy you hang around with?"

"You mean Kelly?"

"How many fairies you know?"

"But Kelly's just cool."

He snorts. "For a catamite."

"No," I say. "It's his *job*. Kelly sells cool. I sell cheekbones."

He looks at me. "I don't know what the fuck you're talking about. I don't much care. All I want to know is why there are two hard guys waiting for you outside my building."

"It's kind of a long story."

"Give me the broad strokes."

"They think Kelly took out a friend of theirs."

"Did he?"

I stare at him.

Heather's father nods. "I guess that's not too surprising."

"Will you help me?"

He frowns. "You ever do any wet work?"

I take a breath. "Not really."

"Stay close to me. When it happens, hold low and put your man down. Nothing fancy. Keep shooting until he drops."

I am having trouble breathing. "Are we going now?"

He shakes his head. "We'll wait until the game breaks. The more confusion, the better."

When it's time, Heather's father says, "Get yourself frosty. They won't go easy."

"You can tell that by watching them stand on a street corner?"

"That's right," he says. He taps his middle finger against the handle of the gun in his waistband. "Let's go have a little roughhouse."

In the lobby we fall in step with a group of gray-suited corporate lawyers and pass with them through the enormous revolving door. Outside, the street is seething. The sidewalk in front of us is a sea of bobbing heads. We move with the crowd.

I am peering over the people around me, watching the Jamaican leaning against his flower cart on the opposite sidewalk. He is staring into the crowd, trying to keep sight of the door. Heather's father is directly in front of me, crouched slightly, also watching the Jamaican.

Heather's father glances at me over his shoulder. He says, "Cross at the corner. We'll take him as soon as we hit the other side."

I nod. Everything seems far away. I no longer feel shoulders jostling against mine. I no longer feel feet scraping the backs of my heels.

I imagine what would happen if a V-shaped flight of F-4s passed over us and dropped flaming orange sheets of napalm. I see the commuters around me turn black in the heat. I see their melting faces. I imagine an earthquake in which the skyscrapers above us disintegrate into a concrete avalanche. I imagine a world without skyscrapers where we would huddle close together and wait for lions or saber-toothed cats to charge us from the underbrush. We would scatter, lungs burning, tingling-hot all over from the adrenaline burst, and the lions would go after the youngest or the sickest or the weakest and they would bring him down with airborne strikes that break his legs and they would rip him apart.

I imagine meteor showers.

We are almost to the corner when I see Kelly. He is in a second-story window across the street. I do not see his rifle. He nods to me.

I lean toward Heather's father. "We may have a problem," I say.

"You mean your boy in the window?" he says. He does not turn around.

"You saw him."

"When we got out here."

"Why didn't you say anything?"

"I didn't know it was an issue."

"He may not be a friendly," I say.

"Is he a hostile?"

"Possibly."

He turns his head now. "Is there something you're not telling me?"

We have reached the corner.

I say, "I believe there's been a series of misunderstandings and misinterpretations."

"Leading to what?"

"Kelly is probably going to try to kill you."

He stares at me. "Why would he do that?"

I don't say anything.

Heather's father says, "Because you told him to?"

The light changes and we begin moving across the street.

"I've recently come to reexamine some things," I say.

When Kelly appears next to me, Heather's father is still on his knees. The smaller Jamaican is lying next to the flower cart. There is a hole in the center of his face. His cheeks are caved in toward it. The big Jamaican is on the ground next to us. On the ground next to him are the white and gray and blue-veined coils of his guts. He has been cut nearly in half by the exit wound from Kelly's hollow-point. His face is smooth and unmarked. His eyes are wide open.

Kelly says, "Let's get what we came for."

"I don't think this is what Heather wants."

"Sure it is. You said so."

"I know that. I think I made it up."

"That's crazy."

"Yes," I say.

He shrugs. "I suppose it doesn't much matter. It was never really about her."

"What was it about?"

"Getting back to nature."

Heather's father says, "You don't have to do this."

Kelly draws his pistol. "Don't flatter yourself. It was never really about you either."

I say, "You've already made your progress. You don't need this."

"We need to finish what we started."

I shake my head. "You're being too literal."

"It's what separates us from the animals."

"I thought what separated us from the animals was that we know we're going to die."

"What separates us from the animals," he says, "is our ability to ask what separates us from the animals." He aims his pistol. Heather's father closes his eyes. "The danger," Kelly says, "is to become all talk and no action."

I close my eyes before I fire — holding low, squeezing-not-pulling — so I do not see Kelly's face when the bullet hits him. I imagine him looking at me with enormous, shocked eyes and reaching out his hand and taking a shaky step toward me and I fire again and again with my eyes closed until I hear his body fall.

He is still alive. He sounds like he is trying to clear his throat. I imagine the way he looks on the ground, flopping like a landed fish, drowning in the air.

I turn away before I open my eyes.

Heather's father is leaning against me. We are shuffling along Purchase Street, trying to seem casual. I have draped my jacket over him to hide his shoulder. Taking the jacket off revealed my gun harness, so I unstrapped it and threw it in a garbage can on Federal Street. I have the pistol in my pants pocket.

There are sirens everywhere now. The cruisers are stuck in the traffic from the Central Artery construction site. The sidewalk is full of people who do not know what has happened. We are lost in the crowd again.

Heather's father drags himself along, stepping as lightly as he can so as not to jostle his shoulder. We do not speak.

Heather is sitting in her Mercedes with the line of taxis in front of South Station.

She says, "Get in."

I open the back door and help her father inside and slide in next to him. Heather pulls away from the curb.

Her father says, "Where are we going?"

"What is he doing here?" Heather says. "What's wrong with him?"

"It's sort of a long story," I tell her. "We can't go home."

"No," her father agrees.

"We need to get out of the city for a while."

"What if they shut it down?"

"The whole city?"

"They could."

"But they don't even know what to look for. They don't know what we're driving."

"Chancy," he says.

Heather's father closes his eyes and leans against the back of the seat. We creep onto the bridge beside the Children's Museum and sit in the steaming line of stopped cars.

Heather's father is taking deep breaths.

Heather turns her head toward me. "Do it," she says.

"Do what?" I say.

"Kill him."

I feel the inside of the car begin to spin. I open my mouth but no sound comes out.

"What's wrong?" Heather says.

"I thought I imagined it."

"Imagined what?"

"That you asked for this."

"Why would you think that? This is what you wanted."

"*Me?*"

"You said you wanted to take care of me."

"I do."

"Then he's served his purpose."

"So he has to die?"

"You want me, you want money. He has both. I want a man who doesn't *ask* for everything. I want a man who *takes*."

"Are you sure you want this?"

"Really, I want it for you. I want you to feel like you can be the man in my life."

I rub my neck.

"I'm establishing my independence," she says.

Heather's father says, "You must know she's crazy." His eyes are still closed.

"Shut up," Heather says. She turns back to me. "Kill him."

"I don't know," I say.

Heather's father says, "This can't be the first time you've seen it. She used to sprinkle detergent in the birdfeeder."

"Do it," Heather tells me, "so we can start our new life."

Her father says, "She was thirteen the first time she tried to kill me."

"Why don't you stake out some territory for yourself?" Heather asks me. "Be a man. Get in the *game,* for Chrissake. You can't let people walk all over you. Let's break free. Let's set out on our own."

"Let's," I say.

"Do it, then."

"Why can't we just leave?"

She says, "We have to cut all our ties."

Her father says, "In an hour she'll love me again. She'll blame you for killing me. Every day you'll be wondering who she's going to ask to do *you.* Indecision, kid. It's what separates man from the animals."

"Regret," I say.

"That too."

I take a deep breath and unlock my door.

"Where will you go?" Heather says. "I thought you were on the run."

"I'll have to think of something."

"You're nothing," she sneers. "You always need someone else to do your work. Maybe I'll get Kelly to do it. I'm sure *he* has the balls. Maybe I'll even throw a little pussy his way."

"Good luck with that," I say. "Today we've been selecting against silk-suit thrill killers."

As I am opening the door, I hear Heather say, "I don't need you anymore."

"I love you," her father says. "I want to help you." His voice cracks.

I close the door and leave them there.

Walking back along the bridge, I imagine the beginning of the universe.

CHRISTOPHER COAKE

All Through the House

FROM *The Gettysburg Review*

Now

Here is an empty meadow, circled by bare autumn woods.

The trees of the wood — oak, maple, locust — grow through a mat of tangled scrub, rusty leaves, piles of brittle deadfall. Overhead is a rich blue sky, a few high, translucent clouds, moving quickly, but the trees are dense enough to shelter everything below, and the meadow too. And here, leading into the trees from the meadow's edge, is a gravel track, twin ruts now grown over, switching back and forth through the woods and away.

The meadow floor is overrun by tall yellow grass, thorny vines, the occasional sapling — save for at the meadow's center. Here is a wide rectangular depression. The broken remains of a concrete foundation shore up its sides. The bottom is crumbled concrete and cinder, barely visible beneath the thin netting of weeds. A blackened wooden beam angles down from the rim, its underside soft and fibrous. Two oaks lean over the foundation, charred on the sides that face it.

Sometimes deer browse in the meadow. Raccoons and rabbits are always present; they have made their own curving trails across the meadow floor. A fox, rusty and quick, lives in the nearby trees. His den, twisting among tree roots, is pressed flat and smooth by his belly.

Sometimes automobiles crawl slowly along the gravel track and park at the edge of the meadow. The people inside sometimes get out and walk into the grass. They take photographs or draw pictures or read from books. Sometimes they climb down into the old foundation. A few camp overnight, huddling close to fires.

Whenever these people come, a policeman arrives soon after, fat and gray-haired. Sometimes the people speak with him — and sometimes they shout — but always they depart, loading their cars while the policeman watches. When they depart he follows them down the track in his slow, rumbling cruiser. When he comes at night, the spinning of his red and blue lights causes the trees to jump and dance.

Sometimes the policeman arrives alone:

He stops the cruiser and climbs out. He walks slowly into the meadow. He sits on the broken concrete at the rim of the crater, looking into it, looking at the sky, closing his eyes.

When he makes noise the woods grow quiet. All the animals crouch low, flicking their ears at the man's barks and howls.

He does not stay long.

After his cruiser has rolled away down the track, the woods and the meadow remain, for a time, silent. But before long what lives there sniffs the air and, in fits and starts, emerges. Noses press to the ground and into the burrows of mice. Things eat and are eaten.

Here memories are held in muscles and bellies, not in minds. The policeman and the house and all the people who have come and gone here are not forgotten.

They are, simply, never remembered.

1987

Sheriff Larry Thompkins tucked his chin against the cold and, his back to his idling cruiser, unlocked the cattle gate that blocked access to the Sullivan woods. The gate swung inward, squealing, and the cruiser's headlights shone a little ways down the gravel track before it curled off into the trees. Larry straightened, then glanced right and left, down the paved county road behind him. He saw no other cars — not even on the distant interstate. The sky was clouded over — snow was a possibility — and the fields behind him were almost invisible in the dark.

Larry sank back behind the wheel, grateful for the warmth and the spits of static from his radio. He nosed the cruiser through the gate and onto the track, then switched to his parking lights. The trunks of trees ahead faintly glowed, turning orange as he passed. Even though the nearest living soul, old Ned Baker, lived a half mile off, he was an insomniac and often sat in front of his bedroom window watching the Sullivan woods. If Larry used his headlights, Ned would see. Ever since Patricia Pike's book had come out — three months ago now — Ned had watched the gated entrance to the woods like it was a military duty.

Larry had been chasing off trespassers from the Sullivan place ever since the murders, twelve years ago in December. He hated coming out here, but he couldn't very well refuse to do his job — no one else would do it. Almost always the trespassers were kids from the high school, out at the murder house getting drunk or high, and though Larry was always firm with them and made trouble for the bad ones, he knew most kids did stupid things and couldn't blame them that much. Larry had fallen off the roof of a barn, drunk, when he was sixteen. He'd broken his arm in two places, all because he was trying to impress a girl who, in the end, never went out with him.

But activity in the woods had picked up since the Pike woman's book came out. Larry had been out here three times in the last week alone. There were kids, still, more of them than ever — but also people from out of town, some of whom he suspected were mentally ill. Just last weekend Larry had chased off a couple in their twenties, lying on a blanket with horrible screaming music playing on their boom box. They'd told him — calmly, as though he might understand — that they practiced magic and wanted to conceive a child out there. The house, they said, was a place of energy. When they were gone Larry looked up at its empty windows, its stupid, dead house-face, and couldn't imagine anything further from the truth.

The cruiser bounced and shimmied as Larry negotiated the turns through the woods. All his extra visits had deepened the ruts in the track — he'd been cutting through mud and ice all autumn. Now and then the tires spun, and he tried not to think about having to call for a tow, the stories he'd have to make up to explain it. But each time, the cruiser roared and lurched free.

He remembered coming out here with Patricia Pike. He hadn't wanted to, but the mayor told him Pike did a good job with this kind of book, and that — while the mayor was concerned, just like Larry was, about exploiting what had happened — he didn't want the town to get any more of a bad name on account of being unco-operative. So Larry had gone to the library to read one of Pike's other books. *The Beauties and the Beast* was what the book was called, with the close-up of a cat's eye on the front cover. It was about a se-rial killer in Idaho in the sixties who murdered five women and fed them to his pet cougar. In one chapter Pike wrote that the police had hidden details of the crime from her. Larry could understand why: The killings were brutal, and he was sure the police had a hard time explaining the details to the families of the victims, let alone to ghouls all across the country looking for a thrill.

We're going to get exploited, Larry had told the mayor, waving that book at him.

Look, the mayor said. I know this is difficult for you. But would you rather she wrote it without your help? You knew Wayne better than anybody. Who knows? Maybe we'll finally get to the bottom of things.

What if there's no bottom to get to? Larry asked, but the mayor had looked at him strangely and never answered, just told him to put up with it, that it would be over before he knew it.

Larry wrestled the cruiser around the last bend and then stopped. His parking lights shone dully across what was left of the old driveway turnaround and onto the Sullivan house.

The house squatted, dim and orange. It had never been much to look at, even when new; it was small, unremarkable, square — barely more than a prefab. The garage, jutting off the back, was far too big and made the whole structure look deformed, unbalanced. Wayne had designed the house himself, not long after he and Jenny got married. Most of the paint had chipped off the siding, and the undersized windows were boarded over — the high school kids had broken out all the glass years ago.

Jenny had hated the house even when it was new. She'd told Larry so at her and Wayne's housewarming dinner.

It's bad enough I have to live out here in the middle of nowhere, she'd said under her breath while Wayne chattered to Larry's wife, Emily, in the living room. But at least he could have built us a house you can look at.

He did it because he loves you, Larry whispered. He tried.

Don't remind me, Jenny said, swallowing wine. Why did I ever agree to this?

The house?

The house, the marriage. God, Larry, you name it.

When she'd said it she hadn't sounded bitter. She looked at Larry as though he might have an answer, but he didn't — he'd never been able to see Jenny and Wayne together, from the moment they started dating in college. He remembered telling her, *It'll get better,* and feeling right away as though he'd lied, and Jenny making a face that showed she knew he had, before both of them turned to watch Wayne demonstrate the dimmer switch in the living room for Emily.

The front door, Larry saw now, was swinging open. Some folks he'd chased out two weeks ago had jimmied it, and the lock hadn't worked right afterward. The open door and the black gap behind it made the house look even meaner than it was — like a baby crying. Patricia Pike had said that, at one point. Larry wondered if she'd put it into her book.

She had sent him a copy back in July just before its release. The book was called *All Through the House;* the cover showed a Christmas tree with little skulls as ornaments. Pike had signed it for him: *To Larry, even though I know you prefer fiction. Cheers, Patricia.* He flipped to the index and saw his name with a lot of numbers by it, and then he looked at the glossy plates at the book's center. One was a map of Prescott County, showing the county road and an *X* in the Sullivan woods where the house stood. The next page showed a floor plan of the house, with bodies drawn in outline and dotted lines following Wayne's path from room to room. One plate showed a Sears portrait of the entire family smiling together, plus graduation photos of Wayne and Jenny. Pike had included a picture of Larry, too — taken on the day of the murders — that showed him pointing off to the edge of the picture while EMTs brought one of the boys out the front door, wrapped in a blanket. Larry looked like he was running — his arms were blurry — which was odd. They'd brought no one out of the house alive. He'd have had no need to rush.

The last chapter was titled "Why?" Larry had read that part all the way through. Every rumor and half-baked theory Patricia Pike had heard while in town, she'd included, worded to make it sound like she'd done thinking no one else ever had.

Wayne was in debt. Wayne was jealous because maybe Jenny was sleeping around. Wayne had been seeing a doctor about migraines. Wayne was a man who had never matured past childhood. Wayne lived in a fantasy world inhabited by the perfect family he could never have. *Once again the reluctance of the sheriff's department and the townspeople to discuss their nightmares freely hinders us from understanding a man like Wayne Sullivan, from preventing others from killing as he has killed, from beginning the healing and closure this community so badly needs.*

Larry had tossed his copy in a drawer and hoped everyone else would do the same.

But then the book was a success — all Patricia Pike's books were. And not long after that, the lunatics had started to come out to the house. And then, today, Larry had gotten a call from the mayor.

You're not going to like this, the mayor said.

Larry hadn't. The mayor told him a cable channel wanted to film a documentary based on the book. They were sending out a camera crew at the end of the month, near Christmastime — for authenticity's sake. They wanted to film in the house, and of course they wanted to talk to everybody all over again, Larry first and foremost.

Larry took a bottle of whiskey from underneath the front seat of the cruiser, and watching the Sullivan house through the windshield, he unscrewed the cap and drank a swallow. His eyes watered, but he got it down and drank another. The booze spread in his throat and belly, made him want to sit very still behind the wheel, to keep drinking. Most nights he would. But instead he opened the door and climbed out of the cruiser.

The meadow and the house were mostly blocked from the wind, but the air had a bite to it all the same. He hunched his shoulders, then opened up the trunk and took out one of the gas cans he'd filled up at the station and a few rolls of newspaper. He walked up to the open doorway of the house, his head ducked, careful with his feet in the shadows and the grass.

He smelled the house's insides even before he stepped onto the porch — a smell like the underside of a wet log. He clicked on his flashlight and shone it into the doorway, across the splotched and crumbling walls. He stepped inside. Something living scuttled immediately out of the way: a raccoon or a possum. Maybe even a fox.

Wayne had once told him the woods were full of them, but in all the times Larry had been out here, he'd never seen any.

He glanced over the walls. Some new graffiti had appeared: KILL 'EM ALL was spray-painted on the wall where, once, the Christmas tree had leaned. The older messages were still in place. One read, HEY WAYNE, DO MY HOUSE NEXT. Beside a ragged, spackled-over depression in the same wall, someone had painted an arrow and the word BRAINS. Smaller messages were written in marker — the sorts of things high school kids write: initials, graduation years, witless sex puns, pictures of genitalia. And — sitting right there in the corner — was a copy of *All Through the House,* its pages swollen with moisture.

Larry rubbed his temple. The book was as good a place to start as any.

He kicked the book to the center of the living room floor and then splashed it with gas. Nearby was a crevice where the carpet had torn and separated. He rolled the newspapers up and wedged them underneath the carpet, then doused them too. Then he drizzled gasoline in a line from both the book and the papers to the front door. From the edge of the stoop, he tossed arcs of gas onto the door and the jamb until the can was empty.

He stood on the porch, smelling the gas and gasping — he was horribly out of shape. His head was throbbing. He squeezed the lighter in his hand until the pain subsided.

Larry was not much for religion, but he tried a prayer anyway: *Lord, keep them. I know you have been. And please let this work.* But the prayer sounded pitiful in his head, so he stopped it.

He flicked the lighter under a clump of newspaper and, once that had bloomed, touched it to the base of the door.

The fire took the door right away and flickered in a curling line across the carpet to the book and the papers. He could see them burning through the doorway, before thick gray smoke obscured his view. After a few minutes the flames began to gutter. He wasn't much of an arsonist — it was wet in there. He retrieved the other gas can from the trunk and shoved a rolled-up cone of newspaper into the nozzle. He made sure he had a clear throw and then lit the paper and heaved the can inside the house. It exploded right away, with a thump, and orange light bloomed up one of the inside walls. Outside, the flames from the door flared, steadied, then began to climb upward to the siding.

Larry went back to the cruiser and pulled the bottle of whiskey from beneath his seat. He drank from it and thought about Jenny, and then about camping in the meadow as a boy, with Wayne.

Larry had seen this house being built; he'd seen it lived in and died in. He had guessed he might feel a certain joy watching it destroyed, but instead his throat caught. Somewhere down the line, this had gotten to be his house. He'd thought that for a while now: The township owned the Sullivan house, but really, Wayne had passed it on to *him*.

An image of himself drifted into his head — it had come a few times tonight. He saw himself walking into the burning house, climbing up the stairs. In his head he did this without pain, even while fire found his clothing, the bullets in his gun. He would sit upstairs in Jenny's sewing room and close his eyes, and it wouldn't take long.

He sniffled and pinched his nose. That was horseshit. He'd seen people who'd been burnt to death. He'd die, all right, but he'd go screaming and flailing. At the thought of it, his arms and legs grew heavy; his skin prickled.

Larry put the cruiser in reverse and backed it slowly away from the house, out of the drive, and onto the track. He watched for ten minutes as the fire grew and tried not to think about anything, to see only the flames. Then he got the call from dispatch.

Sheriff?

Copy, he said.

Ned called in. He says it looks like there's a fire out at the Sullivan place.

A fire?

That's what he said. He sees a fire in the woods.

My my my, Larry said. I'm on old 52 just past Mackey. I'll get out there quick as I can and take a look.

He waited another ten minutes. Flames shot out around the boards on the windows. The downstairs ceiling caught. Long shadows shifted through the trees; the woods came alive, swaying and dancing. Something alive and aflame shot out the front door — a rabbit? It zigged and zagged across the turnaround and then headed toward him. For a moment Larry thought it had shot under his car, and he put his hand on the door handle — but whatever it was cut away for the woods to his right. He saw it come to rest in a patch of scrub; smoke rose from the bush in wisps.

Dispatch? Larry said.

Copy.

I'm at the Sullivan house. It's on fire, all right. Better get the trucks out here.

Twenty minutes later two fire trucks arrived, advancing carefully down the track. The men got out and stood beside Larry, looking over the house, now brightly ablaze from top to bottom. They rolled the trucks past Larry's cruiser and sprayed the grass around the house and the trees nearby. Then all of them watched the house burn and crumble into its foundation, and no one said much of anything.

Larry left them to the rubble just before dawn. He went home and tried to wash the smell of smoke out of his hair and then lay down next to Emily, who didn't stir. He lay awake for a while, trying to convince himself he'd actually done it, and then trying to convince himself he hadn't.

When he finally slept he saw the house on fire, except that in his dream there were people still in it: Jenny Sullivan in the upstairs window, holding her youngest boy to her and shouting Larry's name, screaming it, while Larry sat in his car, tugging at the handle, unable even to shout back to her, to tell her it was locked.

1985

Patricia Pike had known from the start that Sheriff Thompkins was reluctant to work with her. Now, riding in his cruiser with him down empty back roads to the Sullivan house, she wondered if what she'd thought was reticence was actual anger. Thompkins had been civil enough when she spoke with him on the phone a month before, but since meeting him this morning in his small, cluttered office — she'd seen janitors with better quarters — he'd been scowling, sullen, rarely bothering to look her in the eye.

She was used to this treatment from policemen. A lot of them had read her books, two of which had uncovered information the police hadn't found themselves. Her second book — *On a Darkling Plain* — had overturned a conviction. Policemen hated being shown up, even the best of them, and she suspected from the look of Thompkins's office that he didn't operate on the cutting edge of law enforcement.

Thompkins was tall and hunched, perhaps muscular once but going now to fat, with a gray cop's mustache and a single thick fold under his chin. He was only forty — two years younger than she was — but he looked much older. He kept a wedding photo on his desk; in it he had the broad-shouldered, thick-necked look of an offensive lineman. Unsurprising, this; a lot of country cops she spoke to had played football. His wife was a little ghost of a woman, dark-eyed, smiling what Patricia suspected was one of her last big smiles.

Patricia had asked Thompkins a few questions in his office, chatty ones designed to put him at ease. She'd also flirted a little; she was good-looking, and sometimes that worked. But even then Thompkins answered in clipped sentences, in the sort of language police fell back on in their reports. He looked often at his watch, but she wasn't fooled. Kinslow, Indiana, had only six hundred residents, and Thompkins wasn't about to convince her he was a busy man.

Thompkins drove along the interminable gravel roads to the Sullivan woods with one hand on the wheel and the other brushing the corners of his mustache. Finally she couldn't stand it.

Do I make you uncomfortable, Sheriff?

He widened his eyes, and he shifted his shoulders then coughed. He said, Well, I'll be honest. I guess I'd rather not do this.

I can't imagine you would, she said. Best to give him the sympathy he so desperately wanted.

If the mayor wasn't such a fan of yours, I wouldn't be out here.

She smiled at him, just a little. She said, I've talked to Wayne's parents; I know you were close to Wayne and Jenny. It can't be easy to do this.

No, ma'am. That it is not.

Thompkins turned the cruiser onto a smaller paved road. On either side of them was nothing but fields, empty and stubbled with old broken cornstalks and blocky stands of woods so monochrome they could be pencil drawings.

Patricia asked, You all went to high school together, didn't you?

Abington, Class of '64. Jenny was a year behind me and Wayne.

Did you become friends in high school?

That's when I got to know Jenny. Wayne and I knew each other since we were little. Our mothers taught together at the middle school.

Thompkins glanced at Patricia. You know all this already. You drawing out the witness?

She smiled, genuinely grateful. So he had a brain in there after all. It seems I have to, she said.

He sighed — a big man's sigh, long and weary — and said, I have nothing against you personally, Ms. Pike. But I don't like the kind of books you write, and I don't like coming out here.

I do appreciate your help. I know it's hard.

Why this case? he asked her. Why us?

She tried to think of the right words, nothing that would offend him.

Well, I suppose I was just *drawn* to it. My agent sends me clippings about cases, things she thinks I might want to write about. The murders were so . . . brutal, and they happened on Christmas Eve. And since it happened in the country, it never made the news much; people don't know about it — not in the big cities, anyway. There's also kind of a — a fairy tale quality to it, the house out in the middle of the forest — you know?

Uh-huh, Thompkins said.

And then there's the mystery of *why*. There's a certain type of case I specialize in — crimes with a component of unsolved mystery. I'm intrigued that Wayne didn't leave any notes. You're the only person he gave any information to, and even then —

— He didn't say much.

No. I know, I've read the transcript already. But that's my answer, I suppose: There's a lot to write about.

Thompkins stroked his mustache and turned at a stop sign.

They were to the right of an enormous tract of woods, much larger than the other stands nearby. Patricia had seen it growing on the horizon, almost like a rain cloud, and now, close up, she saw it was at least a mile square. The sheriff slowed and turned off the road, stopping in front of a low metal gate blocking a gravel track that dipped away from the road and into the bare trees. A No Trespassing sign hung from the gate's center. It had been fired upon a number of times; some of the bullet holes had yet to rust. Thompkins said, Excuse me, and got out. He bent over a giant padlock and then swung the gate inward. He got back behind the wheel, drove the cruiser through without shutting his door, then clambered out again and locked the gate behind them.

Keeps the kids out, he told her, shifting the cruiser into gear.

Means the only way in is on foot. A lot of them won't walk it, least when it's cold like this.

This is a big woods.

Probably the biggest between Indy and Lafayette. Course no one's ever measured, but that's — that's what Wayne always told me.

Patricia watched his mouth droop when he said this, caught his drop in volume.

The car curved right, then left. The world they were in was almost a sepia-toned old film: bare winter branches, patches of old snow on the ground, pools of black muck. Patricia had grown up in Chicago, had relatives on a farm downstate. She knew what a tangle those woods would be. What a curious place for a house. She opened her notebook and wrote in shorthand.

This land belongs to Wayne's family? she asked.

It used to. Township owns it now. Wayne had put the land up as collateral for the house, and then when he died, his folks didn't pay on the loan. I don't blame them for that. The town might sell it someday, but no one really wants farmland anymore. None of the farmers around here can afford to develop it. An ag company would have to buy it. In the meantime I keep an eye on the place.

Thompkins slowed and the car jounced into and out of a deep rut. He said, Me, I'd like to see the whole thing plowed under. But I don't make those choices.

She wrote his words down.

They rounded a last bend in the track, and there in front of them was a meadow, and in the center of it the Sullivan house. Patricia had seen pictures of it, but here in person it was much smaller than she'd imagined. She pulled her camera out of her bag.

It's ugly, she said.

That's the truth, Thompkins said, and put the car into park.

The house was a two-story of some indeterminate style — closer to a Cape Cod than anything else. The roof was pitched but seemed . . . too small, too flat for the rest of the house. The face suggested by its windows and front door — flanked by faux half-columns — was that of a mongoloid: all chin and mouth, and no forehead. Or like a baby crying. It had been painted an olive color, and now the paint was flaking. The windows had been boarded over with sheets of plywood. The track continued around behind the house, where a two-car garage jutted off at right angles, too big in proportion to the house proper.

Wayne drew up the plans, Thompkins said. He wanted to do it himself.

What did Jenny think of it? Do you know?

She joked about it. Not so Wayne could hear.

Would he have been angry?

No. Sad. He'd wanted a house out here since we were kids. He loved these woods.

Thompkins undid his seat belt. Then he said, I guess he knew the house was a mess, but he . . . it's hard to say. We all pretended it was fine.

Why?

Some folks, you just want to protect their feelings. He wanted us all to be as excited as he was. It just wouldn't have occurred to us to be . . . blunt with him. You know that type of person? Kind of like a puppy?

Yes.

Well, Thompkins said, that was Wayne. You want to go in?

The interior of the house was dark. Thompkins had brought two electric lanterns; he set one just inside the door and held the other in his hand. He walked inside and then motioned for Patricia to follow.

The inside of the house stank — an old, abandoned smell of mildew and rot. The carpeting — what was left of it, anyway — seemed to be on the verge of becoming mud, or a kind of algae, and held the stink. Patricia had been in morgues and, for one of her books, had accompanied a homicide detective in Detroit to murder sites. She knew what death — dead human beings — smelled like. That smell might have been in the Sullivan house, underneath everything else, but she couldn't be sure. It *ought* to have been.

Patricia could see no furniture. Ragged holes gaped in the ceilings where light fixtures might have been. Behind the sheriff was a staircase, rising up into darkness, and to the right of it an entrance into what seemed to be the kitchen.

Shit, Thompkins said.

What?

He held the lantern close to a wall in the room to the right of the foyer. There was a spot on the wall, a ragged, spackled patch. Someone had spray-painted an arrow pointing at it, and the word BRAINS.

Thompkins turned a circle with the lantern held out. He was looking down, and she followed his gaze. She saw cigarette butts, beer cans.

Kids come in here from Abington, Thompkins said. I run them off every now and then. Sometimes it's adults, even. Have to come out and see for themselves, I guess. Already the kids say it's haunted.

That happens in a lot of places, Patricia said.

Huh, Thompkins said.

She took photos of the rooms, the flashbulb's light dazzling in the dark.

I guess you want the tour, Thompkins said.

I do. She put a hand on his arm, and his eyes widened. She said, as cheerfully as she could, Do you mind if I tape our conversation?

Do you have to? Thompkins asked, looking up from her hand.

It will help me quote you better.

Well. I suppose.

Patricia put a tape into her hand-held recorder, then nodded at him.

Thompkins held the lantern up. The light gleamed off his dark eyes. His mouth hung open, just a little, and when he breathed out it made a thin line of steam in front of the lantern. He looked different — not sad, not anymore. Maybe, Patricia thought, she saw in him what she was feeling, which was a thrill, what a teenaged girl feels in front of a campfire, knowing a scary story is coming. She reminded herself that actual people had died here, that she was in a place of tremendous sadness, but all the same she couldn't help herself. Her books sold well because she wrote them well, with fervency, and she wrote that way because she loved to be in forbidden places like this, she loved learning the secrets no one wanted to say. Just as, she suspected, Sheriff Thompkins wanted deep in his heart to tell them to her. Secrets were too big for people to hold — that was what she found in her research, time after time. Secrets had their own agendas.

Patricia looked at Thompkins, turning a smile into a quick nod.

All right then, the sheriff said. This way.

Here's the kitchen.

Wayne shot Jenny first, in here. But that first shot didn't kill her. You can't tell because of the boards, but the kitchen window looks out over the driveway, just outside the garage. Wayne shot her through the window. Jenny was looking out at Wayne, we know that, because the bullet went in through the front of her right shoulder and out the back, and we know he was outside because the glass was broken and because his footprints were still in the snow when we got there — there was no wind that night. The car was outside the garage. What he did was, he got out of the driver's side door and went around to the trunk and opened it — best guess is the gun was in there; he'd purchased it that night, up at a shop in Muncie. Then he went around to the passenger door and stood there for a while; the snow was all tramped down. We think he was loading the gun. Or maybe he was talking himself into doing it. I don't know.

We figure he braced on the top of the car and shot her from where he stood. The security light over the garage was burnt out when we got here, so from inside, looking out, with the kitchen lights on, Jenny wouldn't have been able to see what he was doing — not very clearly, if at all. I don't know why she was turned around looking out the window at him. Maybe he honked the horn. I also don't know if he aimed to kill her or wound her, but my feeling is he went for a wounding shot. It's about twenty feet from where he stood to where she stood, so it wasn't that hard a shot for him to make, and he made most of his others that night. Now down here —

[The sheriff's pointing to a spot on the linoleum, slightly stained, see photos.]

Excuse me?

[Don't mind me, Sheriff. Just keep talking.]

Oh. All right then.

Well, Jenny — once she was shot, she fell and struggled. There was a lot of blood; we think she probably bled out for seven or eight minutes while Wayne . . . while Wayne killed the others. She tried to pull herself to the living room; there were . . . ah, smears on the floor consistent with her doing that.

[We're back in the living room; we're facing the front door.]

After he'd shot Jenny, he walked around the east side of the house to the front door here. He could have come in the garage into the kitchen, but he didn't. I'm not sure what happened from there exactly. But here's what I think: The grandmother — Mrs. Murray — and Danny, the four-year-old, were in the living room — in here — next to the tree. She was reading to him; he liked to be read to, and a book of nursery rhymes was open face down on the couch. The grandmother was infirm — she had diabetes and couldn't walk so well. She was sitting on the couch still when we found her. He shot her once through the head, probably from the doorway.

[We're looking at the graffiti wall, see photos.]

But by this time Jenny would have been . . . she would have been scream-ing, so we know Wayne didn't catch the rest of them unawares. Jenny might have called out that Daddy was home before Wayne shot her; hell, this place is in the middle of nowhere, and it was nighttime, so they all knew a car had pulled up. What I'm saying is, I'm guessing there was a lot of confusion at this juncture, a lot of shouting. There's a bullet hole at waist height on the wall opposite the front door. My best guess is that Danny ran to the door and was in front of it when Wayne opened it. He could have been looking into the kitchen at his, at his mother, or at the door. I think Wayne took a shot at him from the doorway and missed. Danny ran into the living room, and since Mrs. Murray hadn't tried to struggle to her feet, Wayne shot her next. He took one shot and hit her. Then he shot Danny. Danny was behind the Christmas tree; he probably ran there to hide. Wayne took three shots into the tree, and one of them, or I guess Danny's struggles, knocked it sideways off its base. But he got Danny, shot his own boy in the head just over his left ear.

[We're looking through a door off the dining room; inside is a small room maybe ten by nine, see photos.]

This was a playroom. Mr. Murray and Alex, the two-year-old, were in it. Mr. Murray reacted pretty quick to the shots, for a guy his age, but he was a vet, and he hunted, so he probably would have been moving at the sound of the first gunshot. He opened that window —

[A boarded window on the rear of the house, see photos.]

— which, ah, used to look out behind the garage, and he dropped Alex through it into the snowdrift beneath. Then he got himself through. Though not without some trouble. The autopsy showed he had a broken wrist, which we figure he broke getting out. But it's still a remarkable thing. I hope you write that. Sam Murray tried his best to save Alex.

[I'll certainly note it. Wayne's parents also mentioned him.]

Well, good. Good.

Sam and Alex got about fifty yards away, toward the woods. Wayne prob-ably went to the doorway of the playroom and saw the window open. He ran back outside, around the west corner of the house, and shot Sam in the back right about where the garden was. There wasn't a lot of light, but the house lights were all on, and if I remember right, the bodies were just about at the limit of what you could see from that corner. So Sam almost made it out of range. But I don't know if he could have got very far once he was in the trees. He was strong for a guy his age, but it was snowy and neither he nor the boy had coats, and it was about ten degrees out that night. Plus Wayne meant to kill everybody, and I think he would have tracked them.

Sam died instantly. Wayne got him in the heart. He fell, and the boy didn't go any farther. Wayne walked about fifty feet out and fired a few shots, and one of them got Alex through the neck. Wayne never went any closer. Either he knew he'd killed them both, or he figured the cold would finish the job for him if he hadn't. Maybe he couldn't look. I don't know.

[We're in the living room again, at the foot of the stairs.]

He went back inside and shut the door behind him. I think he was confronted by the dog, Kodiak, on the stairs, there on the landing. He shot the dog, probably from where you're standing. Then —

[We're looking into the kitchen again.]

Wayne went to the kitchen and shot — he shot Jenny a second time. The killing shot. We found her facedown. Wayne stood over her and fired from a distance of less than an inch. The bullet went in the back of her head just above the neck. He held her down with his boot on her shoulder. We know because she was wearing a white sweater, and he left a bloodstain on it that held the imprint of his boot sole.

He called my house at nine-sixteen. You've seen the transcript.

[How did he sound? On the phone?]

Oh, Jesus. I'd say upset but not hysterical. Like he was out of breath, I guess.

[Will you tell me again what he said?]

Hell. Do you really need me to repeat it?

[If you can.]

. . . Well, he said, Larry, it's Wayne. I said, Hey Wayne, Merry Christmas, or something like that. And then he said, No time, Larry, this is a business call. And I said, What's wrong? And he said, Larry, I killed Jenny and the kids and my in-laws, and as soon as I hang up, I'm going to kill myself. And I said something like, Are you joking? And then he hung up. That's it. I got in the cruiser and drove up here as fast as I could.

[You were first on the scene?]

Yeah. Yeah, I was. I called it in on the way; it took me a while to — to remember. I saw blood through the front windows, and I called for backup as soon as I did. I went inside. I looked around . . . and saw . . . everyone but Sam and Alex. It took me . . .

[Sheriff?]

No, it's all right. I wasn't . . . I wasn't in great shape, which I guess you can imagine, but after a couple of minutes, I found the window open in the playroom. I was out with — with Sam and Alex when the deputies arrived.

[But you found Wayne first?]

Yes. I looked for him right off. For all I knew he was still alive.
[Where was he?]
Down in here.
[We're looking into a door opening off the kitchen; it looks like
— the basement?]
*Yeah. Wayne killed himself in his workroom. That was his favorite place,
where he went for privacy. We used to drink down there, play darts. He sat
in a corner and shot himself with a small handgun, which he also purchased that night. It was the only shot he fired from it. He'd shut the basement door behind him.*
. . . You want to see down there?

They sat for a while in the cruiser afterward. Thompkins had
brought a thermos of coffee, which touched her; the coffee was terrible, but at least it was warm. She held the cup in her hands in
front of the dashboard heaters. Thompkins chewed his thumbnail
and looked at the house.

Why did he do it? she asked him.

Hm?

Why did Wayne do it?

I don't know.

You don't have any theories?

No.

He said it quickly, an obvious lie. Patricia watched his face and
said, I called around after talking with his parents. Wayne was
twenty grand behind on his loan payments. If he hadn't worked at
the bank already, this place would have been repossessed.

Maybe, Thompkins said and sipped his coffee. But half the farms
you see out here are twenty grand in the hole, and no one's slaughtered their entire family over it.

Patricia watched him while he said this. Thompkins kept his big
face neutral, but he didn't look at her. His ears were pink with cold.

Wayne's mother, she said, told me she thought that Jenny might
have had affairs.

Yeah. I heard that too.

Any truth to it?

Adultery's not against the law. So I don't concern myself with it.

But surely you've heard something.

Well, Ms. Pike, I have the same answer as before. People have been sleeping around on each other out here for a lot longer than I've had this job, and no one ever killed their family over it.

Thompkins put on his seat belt.

Besides, he said, if you were a man who'd slept with Jenny Sullivan, would *you* say anything about it? You wouldn't, not now. So no, I don't know for sure. And frankly, I wouldn't tell you if I did.

Why?

Because I knew Jenny, and she was a good woman. She was my prom date, for Christ's sake. I stood up at her and Wayne's wedding. Jenny was always straight, and she was smart. If she had an affair, that was her business. But it's not mine, now, and it's not yours.

It would be motive, Patricia said softly.

I took the bodies out of that house, Thompkins said, putting the cruiser into reverse. I took my friends out. I felt their necks to see if they were alive. I saw what Wayne did. There's no reason good enough. No one could have wronged him enough to make him do what he did. I don't care what it was.

He turned the cruiser around; the trees rushed by, and Patricia put both hands around her coffee to keep it from spilling. She'd heard speeches like this before. Someone's brains get opened up, and there's always some backcountry cop who puts his hand to his heart and pretends the poor soul still has any privacy.

There's always a reason, she said.

Thompkins smirked without humor; the cruiser bounced up and down.

Then I'm sure you'll come up with something, he said.

December 25, 1975

In the evening, just past sundown, Larry went out again to the Sullivan house. He and the staties had finished with the scene earlier in the day. There hadn't been much to investigate, really; Wayne had confessed in his phone call, yet Larry had told his deputies to take pictures anyway, to collect what evidence they could. And then all day reporters had come out for pictures, and some of the townspeople had stopped by to gawk or to ask if anything needed to be done, so Larry decided to keep the house under guard. Truth be told, he and the men needed something to do; watching the house was better than fielding questions in town.

When Larry pulled up in front of the house, his deputy, Troy Bowen, was sitting in his cruiser by the garage, reading a paperback behind the wheel. Larry flashed his lights, and Bowen got out and ambled over to Larry's car, hands in his armpits.

Hey Larry, he said. What're you doing out here?

Slow night, Larry said, which was true enough. He said, I'll take over. Go get dinner. I'll cover until Albie gets here.

That's not till midnight, Bowen said, but his face was open and grateful.

I might as well be out here. It's all I'm thinking about anyway.

Yeah, that's what I thought. But I don't mind saying it gives me the willies. You're welcome to it.

When Bowen's cruiser was gone, Larry stood for a moment on the front stoop, hands in his pockets. Crime scene tape was strung over the doorway in a big haphazard X; Bowen had done it after the bodies were removed, still sniffling and red-eyed. It had been his first murder scene. The electricity was still on; the little fake lantern hanging over the door was shining. Larry took a couple of breaths and then fumbled out a copy of the house key. He unlocked the door, ducked under the caution tape, and went inside.

He turned on the living room light, and there everything was, as he'd left it this afternoon. His heart thumped. What else had he expected? That it would all be gone? That it hadn't really happened? It had. Here were the outlines. The bloodstains on the living room carpet and on the landing. The light from the living room just shone into the kitchen; he could see the dark swirls on the linoleum, too. Already a smell was in the air. The furnace was still on, and the blood and the smaller pieces of remains were starting to turn. The place would go bad if Wayne's folks didn't have the house cleaned up soon. Larry didn't want to have that talk with them, but he'd call them tomorrow. He knew a service in Indianapolis that took care of things like this. All the same he turned off the thermostat.

He asked himself why he cared. Surely no one would ever live in this place again. What did it matter?

But it did, somehow.

He walked into the family room. The tree was still canted sideways, knocked partway out of its base. He went to the wall behind it, stepping over stains, careful not to disturb anything. The lights on the tree were still plugged into the wall outlet. He squatted, straddling a collapsing pile of presents, then leaned forward and pulled the cord. The tree might go up, especially with the trunk out of its water.

Larry looked up at the wall and put his hand over his mouth; he'd been trying to avoid looking right at anything, but he'd done it now. Just a few inches in front of him, on the wall, was the spot where Danny had been shot. The bullet had gone right through his head. He'd given Danny a couple of rides in the cruiser, and now here the boy was: matted blood, strands of hair —

He breathed through his fingers and looked down at the presents. He'd seen blood before; he'd seen all kinds of deaths, mostly on the sides of highways, but twice because of bullets to the head. He told himself, *Pretend it's no different.* He tried to focus and made himself pick out words on the presents' tags.

No help there. Wayne had bought them all presents. *To Danny, From Daddy. To Mommy, From Daddy.* All written in Wayne's blocky letters. Jesus H.

Larry knew he should go, just go out and sit in his cruiser until midnight, but he couldn't help it. He took one of Jenny's presents, a small one that had slid almost completely under the couch, and sat down in the dining room with the box on his lap. He shouldn't do this, it was wrong, but really — who was left to know that a present was gone? Larry wasn't family, but he was close enough — he had some rights here. Who, besides him, would ever unwrap them? The presents belonged to Wayne's parents now. Would they? Would they want to see what their son had bought for the family he'd butchered? Not if they had any sense at all.

Larry went into the kitchen, looking down only to step where the rusty smears weren't. Under the sink he found garbage bags; he took one.

He sat back down in the dining room. The gift was only a few inches square, wrapped in gold foil paper. Larry slid a finger under a taped seam. He carefully tore the paper away. Inside was a small, light cardboard box, also taped. He could see Wayne's fingerprint caught in the tape glue before he cut it with a thumbnail. He held the lid lightly between his palms and shook out the container onto his lap.

Wayne had bought Jenny lingerie. A silk camisole and matching panty, in red, folded small.

Jenny liked red. Her skin took to it somehow; she was always a little pink. The bust of the camisole was transparent, lacy. She would look impossible in it. That was Jenny, though. She could slip on a T-shirt and look like your best pal. Or she could put on a little lipstick and do her hair and wear a dress, and she'd look like she ought to be up on a movie screen someplace. Larry ran his fingers over the silk. He wondered if Wayne had touched the lingerie this way, too, and what he might have been thinking when he did. Did he know, when he bought it? When had he found out?

Don't be coy with me, Wayne had said on the phone. He'd called Larry at his house; Emily would have picked up if her hands weren't soapy with dishwater. Larry watched his wife while he listened. I know, Wayne said. I followed you to the motel. I just shot her, Larry. I shot her in the head.

Larry dumped the lingerie and the wrappings into the garbage bag.

He took the bag upstairs with him, turning off the living room light behind him and turning on the one in the stairwell. He had to cling tight to the banister to get past the spot where Wayne had shot the dog, a big husky named Kodiak, rheumy-eyed and arthritic. Kodiak didn't care much for the children, who tried to uncurl his tail, so most of the time he slept in a giant basket in the sewing room upstairs. He must have jumped awake at the sound of gunshots. He would have smelled what was wrong right away. Jenny had gotten him as a puppy during high school. Larry had been dating her then; he remembered sitting on the kitchen floor with her at her parents' house, the dog skidding happily back and forth between them. Kodiak had grown old loving her. He must have stood on the landing and growled and barked at Wayne, and Wayne shot him from the foot of the stairs. Through the head, just like everyone else. Larry had seen dogs driven vicious by bloodshed; it turned on switches in their heads. He hoped Kodiak had at least made a lunge for Wayne before getting shot.

Larry walked into Wayne and Jenny's bedroom. He'd been in it before. Just once. Wayne had gone up to Chicago on business, and the kids were at school, and Jenny called Larry — at the station; she told dispatch she thought she saw someone in the woods, maybe a hunter, and would the sheriff swing by and run him off?

That was smart of her. Larry could go in broad daylight and smoke in the living room and drink a cup of coffee, and no one would say boo.

And, as it turned out, Jenny could set his coffee down on the dining room table and then waggle her fingers at him from the foot of the stairs. And he could get hard just at the sight of her doing it, Jenny Sullivan smiling at him in sweatpants and an old T-shirt.

And upstairs she could say, Not the bed.

They'd stood together in front of the mirror over the low bureau, Jenny bent forward, both of them with their pants pulled down mid-thigh, and Larry gritting his teeth just to last a few minutes. Halfway through he took his hat from the bureau top — he'd brought it upstairs with them and couldn't remember why — and set it on her head, and she'd looked up and met his eyes in the mirror, and both of them were laughing when they came. Jenny's laugh turned into something like a shriek. He said, I never heard you sound like that before, and Jenny said, I've never sounded like that before. Not in this room. She said, This house has never heard anything like it. And when she said it, it was like the house was Wayne, like somehow he'd walked in. They both turned serious and sheepish — Jenny's mouth got small and grim — and they'd separated, pulled their clothes up, pulled themselves together.

Now he went through the drawers of the bureau, trying to remember what Jenny wore that day. The blue sweatpants. The Butler Bulldogs shirt. Bright pink socks — he remembered her stumbling around, trying to pull one off. He found a pair that seemed right, rolled tight together. Silk panties, robin's egg blue. He found a fluffy red thing that she used to keep her ponytail together. Little fake ruby earrings in a ceramic seashell. He smelled through the perfumes next to her vanity, found one he liked and remembered, and sprayed it on the clothes, heavily . . . it would fade over time, and if it was too strong now, in ten years it wouldn't be.

He packed all of it into the plastic bag from the kitchen.

Then he sat at the foot of the bed, eyes closed, for a long few minutes. He could hear his own breath. His eyes stung. He looked at the backs of his hands and concentrated on keeping steady. He thought about the sound of Wayne's voice when he called. *I left her sexy for you, Larry.*

That made him feel like doing something other than weeping.

When he was composed he looked through the desks in the bedroom and the drawers of all the bed tables. He glanced at his watch. It was only eight.

He walked down the hall into the sewing room and sat at Jenny's sewing table. The room smelled like Kodiak: an old dog smell, a mixture of the animal and the drops he had to have in his ears. Pictures of the children and Jenny's parents dotted the walls. Wayne's bespectacled head peeped out of a few, too — but not very many, when you looked hard. Larry opened a drawer under the table and rooted through. Then he opened Jenny's sewing box.

He hadn't known what he was looking for, but in the sewing box he found it. He opened a little pillowed silk box full of spare buttons, and inside, pinned to the lid, was a slip of paper. He knew it right away from the green embossment — it was from a stationery pad he'd found at the hotel he and Jenny had sometimes used in Lebanon. He unfolded it. His hands shook, and he was crying now — she'd kept it, she'd kept something.

This was from a year ago, on a Thursday afternoon; Wayne had taken the boys up to see his folks. Larry met Jenny at the hotel after she was done at the school. Jenny wanted to sleep for an hour or two after they made love, but Larry was due home, and it was better for them to come and go separately anyway, so he dressed quietly while she dozed. He'd looked at her asleep for a long time, and then he'd written a note. He remembered thinking at the time: *evidence*. But he couldn't help it. Some things needed to be put down in writing; some things you had to put your name to, if they were going to mean anything at all.

So Larry found the stationery pad and wrote, *My sweet Jenny,* and got teary when he did. He sat on the bed next to her and leaned over and kissed her warm ear. She stirred and murmured without opening her eyes. He finished the note and left it by her hand.

A week later he asked her, Did you get my note?

She said, No. But then she kissed him and smiled and put her warm, small hands on his cheeks. Of course I did, you dummy.

He'd been able to remember the words on the note — he'd run them over and over in his head — but now he opened the folded paper and read them again: *My sweet Jenny, I have trouble with these things but I wouldn't do this if I didn't love you.*

And then he read on. He dropped the note onto the tabletop and stared at it, his hand clamped over his mouth.

He'd signed it *Yours, Larry* — but his name had been crossed out. And over it had been written, in shaky block letters: *Wayne.*

December 24, 1975

If Jenny ever had to tell someone — a stranger, the sympathetic man she imagined coming to the door sometimes, kind of a traveling psychologist and granter of divorces all wrapped up in one — about what it was like to be married to Wayne Sullivan, she would have told him about tonight. She'd say, *Wayne called me at six, after my parents got here for dinner, after I'd gotten the boys into their good clothes for the Christmas picture, to tell me he wouldn't be home for another couple of hours. He had some last-minute shopping, he said.*

Jenny was washing dishes. The leftovers from the turkey had already been sealed in Tupperware and put into the refrigerator. From the living room she could hear Danny with her mother; her father was playing with Alex in the playroom. She could hear Alex squealing every few minutes or shouting nonsense in his two-year-old singsong. It was 8:40. *Almost three hours later,* she told the man in her head, *and no sign of him. And that's Wayne. There's a living room full of presents. All anyone wants of him now is his presence at the table. And he thinks he hasn't done enough, and so our dinner is ruined. It couldn't be more typical.*

Her mother was reading to Danny; she was a schoolteacher too, and Jenny could hear the careful cadences, the little emphasis that meant she was acting out the story with her voice. Her mother had been heroic tonight. She was a master of keeping up appearances, and here, by God, was a time when her gifts were needed. Jenny's father had started to bluster when Jenny announced Wayne was going to be late — Jennifer, I swear to you I think that man does this on purpose — but her mother had gotten up on her cane and gone to her father, put a hand on his shoulder, and said, He's being sweet, dear, he's buying presents. He's doing the best he knows.

Danny of course had asked after his father, and she told him, Daddy will be a little late, and he whined, and Alex picked up on it, and then her mother called both of them over to the couch and let them pick the channel on the television, and for the most part they forgot. Just before dinner was served, her mother hobbled into the kitchen, and Jenny kissed her on the forehead. Thank you, she said.

He's an odd man, her mother said.

You're not telling me anything new.

But loving. He is loving.

Her mother stirred the gravy, a firm smile on her face.

They ate slowly, eyes on the clock — Jenny waited a long time to announce dessert — and at eight o'clock she gave up and cleared the dishes. She put a plate of turkey and potatoes — Wayne wouldn't eat anything else — into the oven.

Jenny scrubbed at the dishes, the same china they'd had since their wedding, even the plates they'd glued together after their first anniversary dinner. She thought, for the hundredth time, what her life would be like if she were in Larry's kitchen now instead of Wayne's.

Larry and Emily had bought a new house the previous spring, on the other side of the county, to celebrate Larry's election as sheriff. Of course Jenny had gone to see it with Wayne and the boys, but she'd been by on her own a couple of times, too. Emily spent two weekends a month visiting her grandmother at a nursing home in Michigan. Jenny had made her visits in summer, when she didn't teach, while Wayne was at work. She dropped the boys at her folks' and parked her car out of sight from the road. It was a nice house, big and bright, with beautiful bay windows that let in the evening sun, filtering it through the leaves of two big maples in the front yard. Larry wouldn't use his and Emily's bed — God, it wouldn't be right, even if I don't love her — so they made love on the guest bed, narrow and squeaky, the same bed Larry had slept on in high school, which gave things a nice nostalgic feel; this was the bed where Larry had first touched her breasts, way back in the mists of time, when she was sixteen. Now she and Larry lay in the guest room all afternoon. They laughed and chattered; when Larry came — with a bellow she would have found funny if it hadn't turned her on so much — it was like a cork popped out from his throat, and he'd talk for hours about the misadventures of the citizens of Kinslow. All the while he'd touch her with his big hands.

I should have slept with you in high school, she told him during one of those afternoons. I would never have gone on to anyone else.

Well, I told you so.

She laughed. But sometimes this was because she tried very hard not to cry in front of Larry. He worried after her constantly, and she wanted him to think as many good thoughts about her as he could.

I married the wrong guy was what she wanted to tell him, but she couldn't. They had just, in a shy way, admitted they were in love, but neither one had been brave enough to bring up what they were going to do about it. Larry had just been elected; even though he was doing what his father had done, he was the youngest sheriff anyone had ever heard of, and a scandal and a divorce would probably torpedo another term. And being sheriff was a job Larry wanted — the only job he'd wanted, why he'd gone into the police force instead of going off to college like her and Wayne. If only he had! She and Wayne had never been friends in high school, but in college they got to know each other because they had Larry in common, because she pined for Larry, and Wayne was good at making her laugh, at making her seem not so lonely.

And then Larry met Emily at church. He called Jenny one night during her sophomore year to tell her he was in love, that he was happy, and that he hoped Jenny would be happy for him, too.

I'm seeing Wayne, she said, blurting it out, relieved she could finally say it.

Really? Larry had paused. *Our* Wayne?

But as much as Jenny now daydreamed about being Larry's wife (which, these days, was often) she knew such a thing was unlikely at best. She could only stand here waiting for the husband she did have — who might as well be a third son — to figure out it was family time, and think of Larry sitting in his living room with Emily. They probably weren't talking, either. Emily would be watching television, Larry sitting in his den, his nose buried in a Civil War book. Or thinking of her. Jenny's stomach thrilled.

But what was she thinking? It was Christmastime at the Thompkins's house, too, and Larry's parents were over; her mother was good friends with Mrs. Thompkins and had said something about it earlier. Larry's house would be a lot like hers, except maybe even happier. Larry and his father and brother would be knocking back a special eggnog recipe, and Emily and Mrs. Thompkins, who got along better than Emily and Larry did, would be gossiping over cookie dough in the kitchen. The thought of all that activity and noise made her sad. It was better to think of Larry's house as unhappy; better to think of it as an empty place, too big for Larry, needing her and the children —

She was drying her hands when she heard the car grumbling in the trees. Wayne had been putting off a new muffler. She sighed, then called out: Daddy's home!

Daddy! Danny called. Gramma, finally!

She wished Wayne could hear that.

She looked out the kitchen window and saw Wayne's car pull up in front of the garage, the wide white circles of his headlights getting smaller and more specific on the garage door. He pulled up too close. Jenny had asked him time and time again to give her room to pull the Vega out of the garage if she needed to. She could see Wayne behind the wheel, his Impala's orange dash lights shining onto his face. He had his glasses on; she could see the reflections, little match lights.

She imagined Larry coming home, outside a different kitchen window, climbing out of his cruiser. She imagined her sons calling him Daddy, and the thought made her blush. The fantasy was almost blasphemous, but it made her tingle at the same time. Larry loved the boys, and they loved him; she sometimes stopped at the station house, and Larry would take them for a ride in his cruiser. His marriage to Emily might be different if they could have children of their own. Jenny wasn't supposed to know — no one did — but Emily was infertile. They'd found out just before moving into the new house.

Wayne shut off the engine. The light was out over the garage, and Jenny couldn't see him any longer; the image of the car was replaced by a curved piece of her own reflection in the window. She turned again to putting away the dishes. I think he's bringing presents, she heard her mother say. Danny answered this with shouts, and Alex answered him with a yodel.

Jenny thought about Wayne coming in the front door, forgetting to stamp the snow from his boots. She was going to have to go up and kiss him, pretend she didn't taste the cigarettes on his breath. He would sulk if she didn't. This was what infuriated her most; she could explain and explain (later, when they put the kids to bed), but he wouldn't understand what he'd done wrong. He'd brought the kids presents — he'd probably bought her a present. He'd been moody lately (working long hours was what he'd told her), and — she knew — this was his apology for it. In his head he'd worked it all out; he would make a gesture that far outshone any grumpiness, any silence at the dinner table. He'd come through the door like Santa Claus. She could tell him, *The only gift I wanted was a normal family dinner,* and he'd look hurt, he'd look like she slapped him. *But,* he'd say, and the corners of his mouth would turn down, *I was just trying to* — and then he'd launch into the same story he'd be telling himself right now —

They had done this before, a number of times. Too many times. This was how the rest of the night was going to go. And the thought of it all playing out so predictably —

Jenny set a plate down on the counter. She blinked; her throat stung. The thought of him made her feel ill. Her husband was coming into his house on Christmas Eve, and she couldn't bear it.

About a month ago she'd called in a trespasser while Wayne had the kids at a movie in Indy. This was risky, she knew, but she had gotten weepy like this, and she and Larry wouldn't be able to see each other for weeks yet. She'd asked if the sheriff could come out to the house, and the sheriff came. He looked so happy when she opened the door to him, when he realized Wayne was gone. She took him upstairs, and they did it, and then afterward she said, Now you surprise me, and so he took her out in the cruiser, to a nearby stretch of road, empty for a mile ahead and behind, and he said, Hang on, and floored it. The cruiser seemed almost happy to oblige him. She had her hands on the dashboard, and the road — slightly hilly — lifted her up off the seat, dropped her down again, made her feel like a girl. You're doing one-twenty, Larry said, calm as ever, in between her shrieks. Unfortunately, we're out of road.

At the house she hugged him, kissed his chin. He'd already told her, in a way, but now she told him: I love you. He'd blushed to his ears.

She was going to leave Wayne.

Of course she'd thought about it; she'd been over the possibilities, idly, on and off for the last four years, and certainly since taking up with Larry. But now she knew; she'd crossed some point of balance. She'd been waiting for something to happen with Larry, but she would have to act even sooner. The planning would take a

few months at most. She'd have to have a place lined up somewhere else. A job — maybe in Indy, but certainly out of Kinslow.
And then she would tell Larry — she'd have to break it to him
gently, but she would tell him, once and for all, that she was his for
the taking, if he could manage it.

This was it: She didn't love her husband — in fact she didn't
much like him — and was never going to feel anything for him
again. It had to be done. Larry or no Larry, it had to be done.

Something out the window caught her eye. Wayne had the passenger door of the Impala open and was bent inside; she could see
his back under the dome lamp. What was he doing? Maybe he'd
spilled his ashtray. She went to the window and put her face close to
the glass.

He backed out of the car and stood straight. He stood looking at
her for a moment in front of the open car door. He wiped his nose
with his gloved hand. Was he crying? She felt a flicker of guilt, as
though somehow he'd heard her thoughts. But then he smiled and
lifted a finger: *Just a second.*

She did a quick beckon with her hand — *Get your ass in here* —
and made a face, eyeballs rolled toward the rest of the house. *Now.*

He shook his head, held the finger up again.

Jenny crossed her arms. She'd see Larry next week; Emily was going to Michigan. She could begin to tell him then.

Wayne bent into the car, then straightened up again. He
grinned.

She held her hands out at her sides, palms up: *What? I'm waiting.*

1970

When Wayne had first told her he wanted to blindfold her, Jenny's
fear was that he was trying out some kind of sex game, some spice-
up-your-love-life idea he'd gotten out of the advice column in *Play-
boy.* But he promised her otherwise and led her to the car. After fifteen minutes there, arms folded across her chest, and then the discovery that he was serious about guiding her, still blindfolded,
through waist-high weeds and clinging spiderwebs, she began to
wish sex was on his mind after all.

Wayne, she said, either tell me where we're going or I'm taking
this thing off.

It's not far, honey, he said; she could tell from his voice he was grinning. Just bear with me. I'm watching your feet for you.

They were in a woods; that was easy enough to guess. She heard the leaves overhead, and birdcalls; she smelled the thick and cloying smells of the undergrowth. Twice she stumbled, and her hands scraped across tree trunks, furred vines, before Wayne tightened his grip on her arm. They were probably on a path; even blind she knew the going was too easy for them to be headed directly through the bushes. So they were in Wayne's woods, the one his parents owned. Simple enough to figure out; he talked about this place constantly. He'd driven her past it a number of times, but to her it looked like any other stand of trees out in this part of the country: solid green in summertime and dull gray-brown in winter, so thick you couldn't see light shining through from the other side.

I know where we are, she told him.

He gripped her hand and laughed. Maybe, he said, but you don't know *why*.

He had her there. She snagged her skirt on a bush and was tugged briefly between its thorns and Wayne's hand. The skirt ripped and gave. She cursed.

Sorry! Wayne said. Sorry, sorry — not much longer now.

Sunlight flickered over the top of the blindfold, and the sounds around her opened up. She was willing to bet they were in a clearing. A breeze blew past them, smelling of springtime: budding leaves and manure.

Okay, Wayne said. Are you ready?

I'm not sure, she said.

Do you love me?

Of course I love you, she said. She reached a hand out in front of her and found he was suddenly absent. Okay, she said, enough. Give me your hand or the blindfold's off.

She heard odd sounds — was that metal? Glass?

All right, almost there, he said. Sit down.

On the ground?

No. Just sit.

She sat, his hands on her shoulders, and found, shockingly, a chair underneath her behind. A smooth metal folding chair.

Wayne then unknotted the blindfold. He whipped it away. Happy anniversary! he said.

Jenny squinted in the revealed light, but only for a moment. She opened her eyes wide and saw she was sitting, as she'd thought, in a meadow, maybe fifty yards across, surrounded on all sides by tall green trees, all of them rippling in the wind. In front of her was a card table covered with a red-and-white checked tablecloth. The table was set with dishes — their good china, the plates at least — and two wine glasses, all wedding presents they'd only used once, on her birthday. Wayne sat in a chair opposite her, grinning, eyebrows arched. The wind blew his hair straight up off his head.

A picnic, she said. Wayne, that's lovely, thank you.

She reached her hand across the table and grasped his. He was exasperating sometimes, but no other man she'd met could reach this level of sweetness. He'd lugged all this stuff out into the middle of nowhere for her — *that's* where he must have been all afternoon.

You're welcome, he said. The red spots on his cheeks spread and deepened. He lifted her hand and kissed her knuckles, then her wedding ring. He rubbed the places where he'd kissed with his thumb.

He said, I'm sorry that dinner won't be as fancy as the plates, but I really couldn't get anything but sandwiches out here.

That's fine. She laughed. I've eaten your cooking, and we're better off with sandwiches.

Ouch, he said. He faked a European accent: This kitten, she has the claws. But I have the milk that will tame her.

He bent and rummaged through a paper bag near his chair and produced a bottle of red with a flourish and a cocked eyebrow. She couldn't help but laugh.

Not entirely chilled, he said, but good enough. He uncorked it and poured her a glass.

A toast.

To what?

To the first part of the surprise.

There's more?

He smiled slyly, lifted his glass, then said, After dinner.

He'd won her over; she didn't question it. Jenny lifted her glass, clinked rims with her husband's, and sat back with her legs crossed at the knee. Wayne bent and dug in the bag again, and then came up with sliced wheat bread and cheese and a package of carved roast beef in deli paper. He made her a sandwich, even slicing up a fresh tomato. They ate in the pleasant breeze.

After dinner he leaned back in his chair and rubbed his stomach. When they'd first started dating, she thought he did it to be funny; but really, he did it after eating anything larger than a candy bar. She was willing to bet he'd been doing it since he was a toddler. It meant all was well in the land of Wayne. The gesture made her smile, and she looked away. Since they'd married he'd developed a small wedge of belly; she wondered — not unhappily, not here — if in twenty years he'd have a giant stomach to rub, like his father's.

So I was right? she asked. This is your parents' woods?

Nope, he said, smiling.

It's not?

It was. They don't own it anymore.

They sold it? When? To who?

Yesterday. He was grinning broadly, now. To me. To us.

She sat forward, then back. He glanced around at the trees, his hair tufting in a sudden gust of the wind.

You're serious, she said. Her stomach tightened. This was a feeling she'd had a few times since their wedding — she was learning that the more complicated Wayne's ideas were, the less likely they were to be good ones. A picnic in the woods? Fine. But this?

I'm serious, Wayne said. This is my favorite place in the world — second favorite, I mean. He winked at her, then went on: But either way. Both my favorite places are mine, now. Ours.

She touched a napkin to her lips. So, she said. How much did — did we pay for our woods?

A dollar. He laughed and said, Can you believe it? Dad wanted to give it to us, but I told him, No Pop, I want to buy it. We ended up compromising.

She could only stare at him. He squeezed her hand and said, We're landowners now, honey. One square mile.

That's —

Dad wanted to sell it off, and I couldn't bear the thought of it going to somebody who was going to plow it all under.

We need to pay your parents more than a dollar, Wayne. That's absurd.

That's what *I* told them. But Dad said no, we needed the money more. But honey — there's something else. That's only part of the surprise.

Jenny twined her fingers together in front of her mouth. A suspicion had formed, and she hoped he wasn't about to do what she guessed. Wayne was digging beside his chair again. He came up with a long roll of paper, blueprint paper, held with a rubber band. He put it on the table between them.

Our paper anniversary, he said.

What is this?

Go ahead. Look at it.

Jenny knew what the plans would show. She rolled the rubber band off the blueprints, her mouth dry. Wayne stood, his hands quick and eager, and spread the prints flat on the tabletop. They were upside down; she went around the table and stood next to him. He put a hand on the small of her back.

The blueprints were for a house. A simple two-story house — the ugliest thing she had ever seen.

I didn't want to tell you too soon, he said, but I got a raise at the bank. Plus, now that I've been there three years, I get a terrific deal on home loans. I got approval three days ago.

A house, she said.

They were living in an apartment in Kinslow, nice enough but bland, sharing a wall with an old woman who complained if they spoke above a whisper or if they played rock 'n' roll records. Jenny put a hand to her hair. Wayne, she said, where is this house going to be?

Here, he said and grinned again. He held his arms out. Right here. The table is on the exact spot. The contractors start digging on Monday. The timing's perfect. It'll be done by the end of summer.

Here . . . in the woods.

Yep.

He laughed, watching her face, and said, We're only three miles from town. The interstate's just on the other side of the field to the south. The county road is paved. All we have to do is have them expand the path in and we'll have a driveway. It'll be our hideaway. Honey?

She sat down in the chair he'd been sitting in. She could barely speak. They had talked about buying a house soon — but one in town. They'd also talked about moving to Indianapolis, about leaving Kinslow — maybe not right away, but within five years.

Wayne, she said. Doesn't this all feel kind of . . . permanent?

Well, he said, it's a house. It's supposed to.

We just talked last month. You wanted to get a job in the city. I want to live in the city. A five-year plan, remember?

Yeah. I do.

He knelt next to her chair and put his arm across her shoulders.

But I've been thinking, he said. The bank is nice, really nice, and the money just got better, and then Dad was talking about getting rid of the land, and I couldn't bear to hear it, and —

And so you went ahead and did it without asking me.

Um, Wayne said, it seemed like such a great deal that —

Okay, she told him. Okay. It *is* a great deal. If it was just buying the woods, that would be wonderful. But the house is different. What it means is that you're building your dream house right in the spot I want to move away from. I hate to break it to you, but that means it's not quite my dream house.

Wayne removed his hand from her shoulders and clasped his fingers in front of his mouth. She knew that gesture, too.

Wayne —

I really thought this would make you happy, he said.

A house *does* make me happy. But one in Kinslow. One we can sell later and not feel bad about when we move —

She wasn't sure what happened next. Wayne told her it was an accident, that he stood up too fast and hit his shoulder on the table. And it looked that way, sometimes, when she thought back on it. But when it happened she was sure he flung his arm out, that he knocked the table aside, that he did it on purpose. The wineglasses and china plates flew out and disappeared into the clumps of yellow grass; she heard a crash. The blueprints caught in a tangle with the tablecloth and the other folding chair.

Goddammit! Wayne shouted. He walked a quick circle, holding his hand close to his chest.

Jenny was too stunned to move, but after a minute she said Wayne's name.

He shook his head and kept walking the circle. Jenny saw he was crying, and when he saw her looking, he turned his face away. She sat still in her chair, not certain what to say or do. Finally she knelt and tried to assemble the pieces of the broken dishes.

After a minute he said, I think I'm bleeding.

She stood and walked to him and saw that he was. He'd torn a gash in his hand on the meaty outside of his palm. A big one — it would need stitches. His shirt was soaked with blood where he'd cradled his hand.

Come on, she said. We need to get you to the hospital.

No, he said. His voice was low and miserable.

Wayne, don't be silly. This isn't a time to sulk. You're hurt.

No. Hear me out. Okay? You always say what you want, and you make me sound stupid for saying what I want. This time I just want to *say* it.

She grabbed some napkins and pressed them against his hand. Jesus, Wayne, she said, seeing blood well up from the cut, across her fingers. Okay, okay, say what you need to.

This is my favorite place, he said. I've loved it since I was a kid. I used to come out here with Larry. He and I used to imagine we had a house out here. A hideaway.

Well —

Be quiet. I'm not done yet. His lip quivered, and he said, I know we talked, I know you want to go to Indy. Well, we can. But it looks like we're going to be successful. It looks like I'm going to do well, and you can get a job teaching anywhere. I'll just work hard, and in five years maybe we can have two houses —

Oh, Wayne —

Listen! We can have a house in Indy and then this — this can be our getaway. He sniffled and said, But I want to keep it. Besides you, this is the only thing I want. This house, right out here.

We can talk about it later. You're going to bleed to death if we don't get you to the emergency room.

I wanted you to love it, he said. I wanted you to love it because *I* love it. Is that too much to ask from your wife? I wanted to give you something *special*. I —

It was awful watching him try to talk about this. The spots of red in his cheeks were burning now, and the rims of his eyes were almost the same color. The corners of his mouth turned down in little curls.

Don't worry, she said. We'll talk about it. Okay? Wayne? We'll talk. We'll take the blueprints with us to the emergency room. But you need stitches. Let's go.

I love you, he said.

She stopped fussing around his hand. He was looking down at her, tilting his head.

Jenny, just tell me you love me and none of it will matter.

She laughed in spite of herself, shaking her head. Of course, she said. Of course I do.

Say it. I need to hear it.

She kissed his cheek. Wayne, I love you with all my heart. You're my husband. Now move your behind, okay?

He kissed her, dipping his head. Jenny was bending away to pick up the blueprints, and his lips, wet, just grazed her cheek. She smiled at him and gathered their things; Wayne stood and watched her, moist eyed.

She finally took his good hand, and they walked back toward the car, and his kiss, dried slowly by the breeze, felt cool on her cheek. It lingered for a while, and despite everything, she was glad for it.

Then

The boys were first audible only as distant shrieks between the trees.

They were young enough that any time they raised their voices they sounded as though they were in terror. They were chasing each other, their only sounds loud calls, denials, laughter. When they appeared in the meadow — one charging out from a break in a dense thicket of thorned shrubs, the other close behind — they were almost indistinguishable from one another in their squeals, in their red jackets and caps. Late afternoon was shifting into dusky evening. Earlier they had hunted squirrels, unaware of how the sounds of their voices and the pops of their BB guns had traveled ahead of them, sending hundreds of beasts into their dens.

In the center of the meadow, the trailing boy caught up with the fleeing first; he pounced and they wrestled. Caps came off. One boy was blond, the other was mousy brown. The brown-haired boy was smaller. Stop it, he called from the bottom of the pile. Larry! Stop it! I mean it!

Larry laughed and said with a shudder: Wayne, you pussy.

Don't call me that!

Don't be one, pussy!

They flailed and punched until they lay squirming and helpless with laughter.

Later they pitched a tent in the center of the meadow. They had done this before. Near their tent was an old circle of charred stones, ringing a pile of damp ashes and cinders. Wayne wandered out of the meadow and gathered armfuls of deadwood while Larry secured the tent into the soft and unstable earth. They squatted down around the gathered wood and worked at setting it alight. Darkness was coming; beneath the gray overcast sky, light was diffuse anyway, and now it seemed as though the shadows came not from above but from below, shadows pooling and deepening as though they welled up from underground springs. Larry was the first to look nervously into the shadowed trees while Wayne threw matches into the wood. Wayne worked at the fire with his face twisted, mouth pursed. When the fire caught at last, the boys grinned at each other.

I wouldn't want to be out here when it's dark, Larry said, experimentally.

It's dark now.

No, I mean with no fire. Pitch dark.

I have, Wayne said.

No you haven't.

Sure I have. Sometimes I forget what time it is and get back to my bike late. Once it got totally dark. If I wasn't on the path, I would have got lost.

Wayne poked at the fire with a long stick. His parents owned the woods, but their house was two miles away. Larry looked around him, impressed.

Were you scared?

Shit, yeah. Wayne giggled. It was dark. I'm not *dumb*.

Larry looked at him for a while, then said, Sorry I called you a pussy.

Wayne shrugged and said, I should have shot that squirrel.

They'd seen one in a tree, somehow oblivious to them. Wayne was the better shot, and they'd crouched together behind a nearby log, Wayne's BB gun steadied in the crotch of a dead branch. He'd looked at the squirrel for a long time before finally lifting his cheek from the gun. I can't, he'd said.

What do you mean, you can't?

I can't. That's all.

He handed the gun to Larry, and Larry took aim, too fast, and missed.

It's all right, Larry said now, at the fire. Squirrel tastes like shit.

So does baloney, Wayne said, grim.

They pulled sandwiches from their packs. Both took the meat from between the bread, speared it with sticks, and held it over the fire until it charred and sizzled. Then they put it back into the sandwiches. Wayne took a bite first, then squealed and held a hand to his mouth. He spit a hot chunk of meat into his hand, then fumbled it into the fire.

It's *hot*, he said.

Larry looked at him for a long time. Pussy, he said and couldn't hold in his laughter. Wayne ducked his eyes and felt inside his mouth with his fingers.

Later, the fire dimmed. They sat sleepily beside it, talking in low voices. Wayne rubbed his stomach. Things unseen moved in the trees — mostly small animals, from the sound of it, but once or twice larger things.

Deer, probably, Wayne said.

What about wildcats?

No wildcats live around here. I've seen foxes, though.

Foxes aren't that big.

They spread out their sleeping bags inside the tent and opened the flap a bit so they could see the fire.

This is my favorite place, Wayne said, when they zipped into the bags.

The tent?

No. The meadow. I've been thinking about it. I want to have a house here someday.

A house?

Yeah.

What kind of house?

I don't know. Like mine, I guess, but out here. I could come out onto the porch at night, and it would be just like this. But you wouldn't have to pitch a tent. You know what? We could both have it. We'd each get half of the house to do whatever we want in. We wouldn't have to go home before it gets dark, because we'd already be there.

Larry smiled but said, That's dumb. We'll both be married by then. You won't want me in your house all the time.

That's not true.

You won't get married?

No — I mean, yeah, I will. Sure. But you can always come over.

It's not like that, Larry said, laughing.

How do you know?

Because it isn't. Jesus Christ, Wayne. Sometimes I wonder what planet you live on.

You always make my ideas sound dumb.

So don't have dumb ideas.

It isn't a dumb idea to have my friends in my house.

Larry sighed and said, No, it isn't. But marriage is different. You get married, and then the girl you marry is your best friend. That's what being in love is.

My dad has best friends.

Mine too. But who does your dad spend more time with — them or your mom?

Wayne thought for a minute. Oh.

They looked out the tent flap at the fire.

Wayne said, You'll come over when you can, though, right?

Sure, Larry said. You bet.

They lay on their stomachs, and Wayne talked about the house he wanted to build. It would have a tower. It would have a secret hallway built into the walls. It would have a pool table in the basement, better than the one at Vic's Pizza King in town. It would have a garage big enough for three cars.

Four, Larry said. We'll each have two. A sports car and a truck.

Four, Wayne said, A four-car garage. And a pinball machine. I'll have one in the living room, rigged so you don't have to put money in it.

After a while, Wayne heard Larry's breathing soften. He looked out the tent flap at the orange coals of the fire. He was sleepy, but he didn't want to sleep, not yet. He thought about his house and watched the fire fade.

He wished for the house to be here in the meadow now. Larry could have half, Wayne the other. He imagined empty rooms, then rooms full of toys. But that wasn't the way it would be. They'd be grown-ups. He imagined a long mirror in the bedroom and tried to see himself in it: older, as a man. He'd have rifles, not BB guns. He tried to imagine the rooms full of the things a man would have and a boy wouldn't: bookshelves, closets full of suits and ties.

Then he saw a woman at the kitchen table, wearing a blue dress. Her face kept changing — he couldn't quite see it. But he knew she was pretty. He saw himself open the kitchen door, swinging a briefcase that he put down at his feet. He held out his arms, and the woman stood to welcome him, making a happy girlish sound, and held out her arms too. Then she was close. He smelled her perfume, and she said — in a woman's voice, warm and honeyed — *Wayne,* and he felt a leaping excitement, like he'd just been scared — but better, much better — and he laughed and squeezed her and said into her soft neck and hair, his voice deep: *I'm home.*

PATRICK MICHAEL FINN

Where Beautiful Ladies Dance for You

FROM *Ploughshares*

BY THE TIME HE'D TURNED TWENTY, Ray Dwyer looked like a movie gangster's bodyguard, and was either feared or adored by everyone who knew him. He drove trucks on a local route for Tamco, one of the many quarries in South Joliet, and when he wasn't working, Ray Dwyer liked to dress up in nice shirts and slacks from Baskin's on Roosevelt Avenue and take pretty girls to elegant dinners and shows. There was never a shortage of pretty girls who wanted to accompany Ray Dwyer, for not only was he naturally muscular with green eyes and handsome black hair he combed slick with Royal Crown hairdress, but he was always a perfect gentleman who didn't force or even expect anything beyond a kiss at the end of the date, no matter how much he'd spent on the evening.

And even though this angered the other men who knew Ray Dwyer, an impossible act to follow when it came to pretty girls (most guys tried to hike a girl's skirt after bowling, burgers, and maybe a beer or two at Stone City or Andy and Sophie's), who among them had the balls to say anything to him? Everyone knew about the quarry strikes a few years back, when Ray Dwyer, five months out of high school and unarmed, beat the living Christ out of three cops who'd tried to pull him away from the quarry gate he was blocking with the rest of the truckers and heavy machinists. Three cops. With his bare hands. Ten more patrolmen had to eventually bring him down, and Ray Dwyer had a smooth, deep scar from one of their billy clubs hidden under his handsome black hair to prove it, which he never did, since Ray Dwyer was never one to boast about his own strength, no matter how hammered he was.

And everyone also knew Ray Dwyer's secret when it came to his ease and virtue with the pretty girls: Ray Dwyer was raised in a home where pretty girls outnumbered him four to one. His father, James Dwyer, a quarry machinist who'd loved Camel cigarettes and corned beef hash, died of a heart attack when Ray was still a boy, which left Ray Dwyer the little man of the house surrounded by his mother and three younger sisters: Mary, Katie, and Maureen. Like most men Ray's age, he still lived at home, and would continue to do so until he fell in love with the right pretty girl whom he would marry and have a family with.

The Dwyer girls were seventeen, eighteen, and nineteen years old, and whenever a fellow wanted to take one of them out, he'd usually be intimidated enough to ask her big brother, Ray, for permission beforehand, something Ray Dwyer found incredibly dumb and unmanly.

"Aw, come off it," Ray would tell the fellow between swigs of Old Style at the Stone City tavern. "You don't need my okay, but thanks," Ray would say, then offer a friendly squeeze of the fellow's trembling, relieved shoulder.

Hell, it was only natural that the guys wanted to take Ray's sisters out, and he had no problem with it, as long as the guys behaved themselves. And the guys sure as shit did behave when it came to the Dwyer girls; any guy who even *thought* of getting fast with one of them would have been out of his goddamn gourd.

So Ray Dwyer didn't think twice when John Lucas, a hillbilly from Georgia or some damn place who'd just started driving for the GAF quarry, took Katie Dwyer to the movies on a Saturday night without asking for Ray's approval. As a matter of fact, Ray Dwyer was so happy with his own plans for the night that his sister's date with John Lucas never once crossed his mind. Ray was so happy because he was on his own date with Samantha Baskin, an absolutely *beautiful* girl with black hair and perfect skin she somehow kept tan even in the middle of winter, whose father owned the very clothing store where Ray had purchased the crisp white shirt and charcoal slacks he wore that night. First they had dinner at a small French restaurant downtown (Ray wasn't much for that frog food, but Samantha was crazy about it, and if Samantha had wanted Ray to eat dog chow, he would have gladly asked for seconds — thirds, even), and then Ray took Samantha to a Jerry Lewis movie she wanted to see. Ray's first choice would have been a Western, but he laughed at all the scenes Samantha laughed at even though he found the movie pretty silly, because Ray was deeply in love with Samantha Baskin, and as far as he was concerned, Samantha Baskin was the only girl on Earth he wanted to marry. But there was a problem: Samantha Baskin was Jewish, and Ray Dwyer wasn't, and though Ray never once even hinted to Samantha that he wanted to marry her (how the hell could he say that?), she'd told him how bent her parents were on making sure she married someone who was Jewish, too. Ray didn't care what church Samantha went to, and he knew the problem was Samantha's parents, and not Samantha. Hell, Samantha only went to her church two or three times a year, anyway. But Ray wasn't thinking about the problem too much that night, since Samantha was sitting right next to him and holding his hand and having a good time — a hell of a good time.

When Ray took Samantha home (this had been their tenth date, and Samantha had agreed to go out with Ray again the following weekend), she invited him into her house, since her parents had driven up to Milwaukee for the weekend to visit relatives. Then Samantha took him into her bedroom, where Ray lost his virginity. They stayed in Samantha's bed for a couple of hours, kissed and watched each other without saying a word, even though Ray was *dying* to ask her if she'd consider running away with him someday real soon.

But Ray Dwyer never did ask Samantha that question, since he was afraid of ruining what he considered the greatest moment of his life, a moment that lifted and dizzied him for the rest of the weekend. Until he got to work Monday morning.

Ray Dwyer had actually been whistling to himself as he walked from the clock room to his truck when his friend Bob Placher took him aside. He'd been whistling because he'd never before felt so lucky and swell on a Monday morning. "Listen, Ray," Bob Placher told him; he was whispering and gently gesturing with both hands. Ray noticed that the other drivers and machinists who walked past didn't nod hello to him like they usually did, but tossed quick glances his way that were either sympathetic or fearful; they were obviously in on what Bob was about to tell him, and Ray Dwyer was afraid the news had something to do with his job. "Now take it easy,

Ray," Bob Placher said, then went on to tell him about John Lucas — how, on Saturday night, after John Lucas dropped Ray's sister Katie off, he'd driven over to the Stone City tavern and, as he slammed boilermakers, went on to brag at the top of his hillbilly lungs about how he'd just fucked the sweet singing hell out of Katie Dwyer, and how Katie Dwyer was the tightest piece of ass he'd ever had, and that if he'd known the pussy was this good around here, he would have moved up north ten years ago. "Now take it easy, buddy," Bob Placher said again, and that's exactly what Ray Dwyer did; he simply nodded, thanked Bob for keeping him informed, then climbed into his truck, which was loaded for delivery to Collins Headstone up in Lockport.

Only as Ray Dwyer sat in his cab waiting behind the other trucks to pass through the gate did he realize the significance of how quiet and strange his sister Katie had been acting the day before, how she hadn't gone to Mass because she felt sick, how she'd stayed in her room all day. Ray Dwyer hadn't thought twice about it, since everyone gets sick sometimes.

Ray Dwyer was about to turn left onto Patterson Road, since that was the route he'd follow to Lockport, but he turned right instead. Then Ray Dwyer drove half a mile to the GAF quarry, left his truck on the side of Patterson Road, marched through the gate, and found John Lucas leaning against his own truck, sipping coffee and smoking.

"What," John Lucas said, a tired, empty drawl that didn't sound like a question.

And then Ray Dwyer murdered John Lucas — grabbed his head and slammed it into the side of his truck over and again, until it came apart in his huge, bare hands.

By the time Ray Dwyer got out of prison, his mother had died, the quarries had closed, and all three of his sisters had married and moved far away — Mary to Texas, Katie to southern California, and Maureen to Florida. Who knew what became of Samantha Baskin? She'd never visited Ray, never written, and Ray couldn't blame her. Ray's sisters, on the other hand, had always been great about keeping in touch with him through phone calls and letters, but Ray was shamefully thankful none of them were close enough to see him now — gray, inmate pale, living like a bum in a rooming house thirty miles from the neighborhood where he'd been raised, looking for any kind of work he could find. Sure, Ray could have moved back to his old stomping grounds, and sure, Ray could have probably found *some* kind of work there with ease, but he was terrified of running into anyone he knew, ashamed of shuffling back with his empty hands outstretched, begging for a chance to sweep floors.

Ray had been looking for a job for over a month without even a hint of luck; he'd filled out applications until his fingers hurt, forced phony smiles at interviews to show how happy and eager he was, walked and walked and walked from bus stop to bus stop to bus stop until his legs and feet swelled with a strange, new half-numb kind of pain. He'd covered Blue Island, Midlothian, Harvey, Calumet City, Robbins, Marionette Park, Alsip, Homewood-Flossmoor, South Holland, and *nothing* had turned up. But Ray didn't blame anyone for not wanting to give him work. How could he? Why would anyone want to give *him* a job? During interviews he'd learned to tell when the person on the other side of the desk had gotten to the part of the application that asked: Have you ever been convicted of a felony? At that point, the person's eyes would blink, and the concentration would immediately shift, rising for one second from the application to the big, dumb criminal sitting right there who'd filled it out.

"Thank you. Thank you for your time," Ray Dwyer would say, shaking their apprehensive and weak and reluctant hands before he walked back onto the street, sometimes holding back tears that came from nowhere, but never, ever blaming them for sending him away.

To make matters worse, there was an awful recession, and times were tough all over. Business had been especially bad for George Kariotis, who had immigrated to Chicago from Greece ten years before and opened his own restaurant in Tinley Park. The restaurant was simply called Kariotis's, and was renowned for an authentic cuisine of lamb served fifteen different ways with vegetables most people hadn't ever heard of, on special blue and white china that had belonged to his family for three generations, George always said, though he'd actually gotten the plates wholesale at the Merchandise Mart downtown. And though the menu wasn't cheap, George Kariotis always made sure there were some reasonably priced plates so that even young men could impress dates with a dimly lit amber privacy where scratchy antique records of Rembetica baglamas ballads played from hidden speakers George Kariotis had installed himself.

There were two cooks and three busboys employed at Kariotis's, all of whom were Greek like George and, like George, could speak perfect English accompanied by a strong, yet unobtrusive accent. But George never allowed his cooks and busboys to speak English at work; instead, he told them to speak their native Greek in the kitchen as loud as they could so the patrons could actually hear how good and authentic their food was going to taste when it arrived, steaming, to their tables. When times were better, these particulars paid off. Customers would often wait for over an hour to get a table, even on weeknights. Both the *Tribune* and the *Sun-Times* food sections had written glowing articles about Kariotis's, the "Little Tinley Park Gem with Old World Flavor and Style," this "Delicious Hellenic Dining Experience." George Kariotis had proudly and carefully clipped these articles from the papers and framed them on the wall above the cash register, right between the travel poster of the Parthenon and the stoic, yellowed photograph of his great-grandfather Yiorgios.

But the recession was on, and few could afford even this simple elegance anymore. Some nights, even on the weekends, the restaurant was completely empty, and on most weeknights, Kariotis's was closed by eight. George Kariotis eventually had to fire one of the cooks and all three busboys. The fired cook, whose name was Teddy Dendrinos, got drunk on wine and tried to start a fight with George in the kitchen, yelling awful, hurtful things and cursing in the native Greek George had encouraged him to speak for all those years. Then Teddy wept and, in accented English, apologized for being so disrespectful.

"What do I do now?" he said.

George had his arm around him. "I don't know," he said. "I don't know, Teddy."

Teddy Dendrinos moved back to Greece and luckily got a high-paying position in a five-star Athens hotel. He sent postcards with this good news, postcards George Kariotis tacked on the wall above the cash register, right below the framed newspaper articles that made George sad to think how quickly success and prosperous times could be taken away.

In his final attempt to save his business, George Kariotis emptied his savings account — *all of it*. And with this money he hired two belly dancers, put an employment advertisement in the papers for "Lot Security," since "Bouncer" might have scared off what few patrons he had left, and ordered a big expensive sign surrounded with blue and white lights that he hung on the front of his restaurant. The sign read: *Where Beautiful Ladies Dance for You,* and this was the first thing Ray Dwyer noticed when he got off the bus that Monday afternoon to apply for the security position he read about in the paper, a job he was sure he wouldn't get.

But this fellow who owned the restaurant, George Kariotis, this expressive, tough-looking little man with peppery hair who shook Ray Dwyer's hand and looked him in the eyes when he spoke, took one look at him and hired him on the spot.

"Isn't there an application?" Ray Dwyer asked; he thought this good luck might be some kind of mean trick.

"You want an application? Okay. Make a muscle."

Ray Dwyer flexed his biceps; George Kariotis couldn't even fit both hands around it. He whistled once and laughed. "Holy moly! You passed the application. What is it, Ray? You been to prison or something?" George laughed again and winked, and when Ray Dwyer paused, swallowed, then admitted that he actually had been to prison, George's smile slipped away behind a wisp of cigar smoke, and he offered a sincere apology. "I'm sorry, Ray," he said. "I didn't know. I didn't mean to make a joke. That's not my business. But this is," George Kariotis said and, with his cigar, motioned toward the darkened restaurant, the empty tables and chairs. "This is my business," he said.

And then George Kariotis gave Ray Dwyer a cigar and, over the course of two hours, told him *everything* there was to tell about his restaurant, his business, the many things big and small he'd done to make it the place it once was. He showed Ray Dwyer the speakers, the records, the plates he'd bought downtown, the kitchen where the cooks and busboys argued in Greek, the newspaper articles, and the postcards from Teddy Dendrinos.

"You know it made me sick to have to fire that man," George explained. "It even made me sick to let the busboys go." Then George Kariotis got quiet for the first time since Ray had accepted his handshake; he got quiet and stared at the empty tables and chairs. And then he looked at Ray and said:

"I can't make any promises, Ray. My new idea, these dancers. Well, it might work, and it might not work. I may have to let you go, too. Maybe next week, next month, I don't know. Or maybe you'll work here forever. Okay?"

"Yes," Ray said. "I understand."

The two men shook hands on it, and Ray Dwyer agreed to start that night.

It was hard for Ray to believe he was actually getting paid to do what he did: stand around with his arms crossed and make sure none of the men tried to touch the beautiful ladies, the belly dancers, as men sometimes did, especially when they had too much to drink.

And it was hard for George Kariotis to believe he hadn't thought of bringing in these dancers six months earlier. Within a week of hanging up his new sign, George's restaurant had a steady, nightly stream of men who came to see the dancers, and who, more importantly, came to spend money on appetizers and drinks — lots and lots of drinks. Some men came in small groups, but most came by themselves, and the reason they kept coming was because there was no other place in Tinley Park, Orland Park, or anywhere else nearby where men could sit and eat and drink and watch beautiful ladies dance — *no other place.*

"I can't believe it," George said to Ray one night, beaming. "So they can't afford to take their wives and children to dinner, but they can afford to look at *her,*" he said, and nodded toward Rita, the older, larger dancer who wore dangerously revealing purple silks and captivated her audience with a series of slow, flowing movements, an arrogant, hesitant half smile, and a stare that would linger only for a moment's contact before vanishing in a betrayal of suggestion.

Karima, on the other hand, was much younger, and moved quickly with a wide, teasing smile she shared with each man for longer than he probably deserved. Ray always had to be on his toes when it was Karima's turn to dance, once every hour for fifteen to twenty minutes. The men seemed to believe Karima truly wanted them, and this often provoked them to stand when she came by, to grab her when she came by, to offer catcalls and whistles and large tips when she came by. And when a man did grab Karima, Ray only needed to appear from a corner of darkness, shake his finger, and the man would sit back down and behave himself for the rest of the night.

Ray didn't know too much about the dancers. They were foreign and dark like George, but Ray had no idea what countries they came from. They might have been Greek, but since they always spoke to George in English, Ray decided that didn't make too much sense. He'd tried briefly to talk to the dancers, and, for some reason, they'd ignored him.

"Hey, that was real good," he'd said to Rita after the first time he'd watched her dance, but she only blinked and walked right past him and into the kitchen, where she stayed between sets.

And when Ray had complimented Karima's silver-sequined outfit as she left the floor followed by whistles and claps, and holding a fistful of bills, Karima only glanced at him with a look of disgust and marched into the ladies' room, where she usually stayed between sets.

Sometimes the two dancers seemed to hate each other, and sometimes they talked and laughed like sisters. Ray decided they were impossible to figure out, and that he wouldn't waste any time trying. Who cared? He had a good job, a good boss, and had been able to buy some fancy new clothes that he wrote about in letters to his three sisters, all of whom had invited Ray to live with them when he first got out of prison.

I can't tell you how much I appreciated your invitation to come and stay with your family, Ray wrote to each of them. *But I wanted to prove to myself, and to all of you, that I could get back on my feet by myself. And that's what I'm starting to do. My boss treats me real good, and I get to dress up in a tie when I go to work. Imagine that. Me working at a tie job!*

Ray didn't tell his sisters about the rat droppings he'd often find in his room, or the roaches, or his crazy old woman neighbor who pissed in the hallway. He didn't tell anyone about these things, and nobody knew Ray Dwyer was living in such a shithole, until George gave Ray a ride home one night about a month after he'd started working for him.

"Oh, Ray." George squinted through the windshield. "You can't live here. This place is a dump."

Ray wanted to say that he couldn't afford anything better, and this was true, but he was so grateful and happy with his job that he didn't want George to think he had to pay him any more. So Ray shrugged and lied. "It's fine, George. I don't mind it at all."

"Hell," George told him. "You shouldn't be living in a goddamn dump like this. Tomorrow, I'm coming by in the morning. I'll pick you up at nine o'clock. Pack your things tonight. You can live at my place."

"No, no, no," Ray said. "I couldn't, George."

"I have an extra bedroom, and I live by myself, one block from the restaurant, and there's no reason why you should live in a dump like this when I have so much room."

Ray continued to protest, and George finally said, "Look, Ray. I know how proud you are. You're a proud, proud man, and I respect your pride. I'm not trying to give you something for free. You can pay me rent. We'll talk about it tomorrow."

"Okay," Ray finally said. "Tomorrow."

The two men shook hands on this arrangement as well, and Ray Dwyer agreed to move in the next day.

For a few months it seemed as though business at Kariotis's couldn't possibly get any better. The place was busy seven nights a week, usually from eight until midnight, with men who came to watch Rita's waving silks and sly, fleeting smiles, to see Karima's young, attentive eyes that nurtured a most impossible wanting.

Most nights after closing, Ray and George would go home and, at the small kitchen table, look over the total sheets that made George whistle and say, "Holy moly!" Then they'd drink wine and smoke and tell stories until the sun was about to come up. George, who always did most of the talking, would often talk about women, especially the dancers.

"Rita, my *God!*" he'd say. "Sometimes, Ray, I have to leave the floor because I know I can't have her. I have to go to the kitchen and stand in the freezer to forget about trying to have this woman."

George had explained why having these dancers was impossible: "No man can ever truly have a woman like that, Ray. How can any man impress a woman who lives on the power of dismissing every other man who looks at her? *How?*"

"They don't pay any attention to me," Ray said. "They ignore me."

"So you see what I mean. The hell with them!"

Other nights, George and Ray would look at the big map of the world that hung on the kitchen wall, and George would point to all the different cities and countries he'd visited before moving to the States. George had been on many adventures all over the world, and even though he sometimes drank too much wine and repeated stories Ray had already heard, Ray always listened attentively and acted surprised and amazed, as if hearing the tale for the first time.

"Here, right here, this is Albania," George said. "I sold American cigarettes and chocolate on the black market there, *like a pirate.*"

"And this is Istanbul," George said. "I got arrested for trying to smuggle hashish across the border. But the goddamn Turks had sold me dirt wrapped in plastic! Dirt! The police had to let me go because there is no law against smuggling dirt. I was goddamn lucky to get ripped off in Istanbul, Ray!"

"And this is Rome," George said. "Where my heart was broken."

No matter what places George pointed to on the map, Morocco, Egypt, France, Russia, or Corsica, he always ended on Rome with the same quiet words, "Where my heart was broken," without ever elaborating on what exactly had happened there. He'd just end his story, get more wine, change the subject, or simply say good night and go to bed. Of course Ray was curious to hear the details, but knew it was rude to pry. He imagined this incident in Rome was the reason George had never married, even though George had explained why he was single:

"A family is too difficult for men in my business, Ray. Too many hours of work, and not enough time to spend with the wife and babies. They get lonely, see? No, my restaurant is my wife, and the people I employ are my children."

George did have lovers; Ray was sure of this. Some nights after closing George would shower and change and splash on nice cologne, and then tell Ray, "I'm going out for a while." Those nights were, for Ray, difficult to get through. He couldn't stand being by himself in such a quiet house with all that room to roam, and since he and George had been up so late the night before, he could never simply go to sleep. For some reason, it had been much easier for Ray to be by himself in the rooming house, where he'd only had a bed, a dresser, four walls, and a window. But alone at George's house, Ray found himself moving from room to room, smoking too much, pacing. He'd turn on the kitchen radio, shut it off, then turn it on again; he'd drink a glass of George's wine, another, and another, trying to wear himself down into drunken slumber, which, alone in that house with all that room, seemed impossible. Television only made things worse, with its pictures and music and awful noise. Ray had never liked looking at television anyhow.

Eventually, usually at dawn, George would come home. "You still up?" he'd ask, and Ray, relieved, would casually yawn and say, "Yeah, George. I was just about to turn in."

But thankfully George only went out once or twice a week. Most of the time Ray enjoyed living at George's house. Like on Greek Easter Sunday, which, for whatever reason, was a week later than the regular one. George closed the restaurant and had a party at the house with friends and relatives, all of whom treated Ray like they'd known him for a lifetime. Everyone was happy for George since his business was doing so well, and George, after having lots of wine, kept telling everyone the belly dancers had been Ray's idea: "He's the brains in my business!" George announced, and everyone applauded and toasted Ray, who blushed and laughed and shook his head, since he knew in his heart that he was just a dumb bouncer who wouldn't have come up with an idea like that in a million years.

Summer brought even more business to the restaurant, so much more that George had to order more tables and chairs and glasses and ashtrays. There was a new cook named Alex, too, and two new busboys. George even had a new informal slogan for his place: Kariotis's is Greek for standing room only. This was true; George had to start turning people away because the dancers were running out of room to perform.

"Holy moly!" George said. "We're going to have to knock down that wall. And that one, too. We'll sell tickets, Ray. Then we'll be outside, like a goddamn carnival!"

The place was jammed on weeknights, on weekends, and the place was jammed the night Ray Dwyer actually had to throw somebody out.

Ray hadn't noticed the fellow when he first came in because, quite simply, the fellow wasn't remarkable. He wasn't big, small, ugly, or anything. He didn't even order booze, but nursed a few Cokes over the course of an hour. And when Karima came out for her number, this fellow, this sober, unremarkable fellow who'd shown up by himself, started grabbing Karima's ass. For some reason, Ray decided wagging his finger wouldn't be enough to calm the man, so he walked right up to the table and said, "You're going to have to stop that, sir," and the fellow smiled and said, "Sure, okay. Sorry about that."

But the fellow obviously wasn't sorry about that or anything else, because as soon as Ray turned his back, the man started grabbing Karima even more — not only her ass, but her belly and hips. Some of the other patrons laughed, and a couple of them started grabbing Karima as well.

"Throw him out," George said. "Throw this son of a bitch out, Ray."

So Ray grabbed the guy's collar, lifted him from his seat, then dragged him right out the front door. George was right behind them.

"Don't ever come back here to my place," George told the man, who stood in the parking lot glaring back at them, staggering a bit as if Ray's hands had shaken something loose.

"You fuckers are through," the man said, and since he wasn't drunk, the words had a strange, serious weight behind them. "You hear me? Through."

"Go home," George told him. "Go on!"

Then the fellow cleared his throat and spat right on the blue-and-white-lit sign that George had ordered when he hired the dancers. George made a bolt to charge the guy, his fist cocked, and Ray grabbed him and held him back. "Forget it, George," Ray told him, and then they watched the man get in his car and speed away.

The fellow never returned. But long after this incident, George and Ray would wonder about him, who he was and whom he knew, because a few days after they kicked him out, his departing words came true when two men in suits from the city showed up to inquire about the dancers. They came at noon when the restaurant was closed; Ray was helping George unload the new tables and chairs his cousin had delivered in a big truck.

"Where beautiful ladies dance for you?" the first suited man asked. "You have strippers here?"

"Strippers? No, no," George explained, laughing as if this was a huge misunderstanding that would get cleared up as soon as he said, "Dancers. We have belly dancers every night. You know, for the men to see."

"Strippers," the second man said. "According to the zoning agreement, and as far as the city's concerned, you have strippers."

"But they don't strip," George said. "They keep their clothes *on*."

"So men come here to watch fully clothed women dance?"

"Well, the dancers have outfits, you know? Like bathing suits, I suppose."

"Look," the first man said. "I don't care if they're wearing bathing suits or holy black habits. You can't have dancing girls in Tinley Park, and that's that."

The second man handed George a fine for five hundred dollars. "Next time it's a grand," he told George.

"Then two grand," the first man said. "And then you'll lose your business license. You hear me? You're going to get shut down if this keeps up."

Before they left, they made George and Ray take down the big sign; and when the city men did leave, George and Ray put it right back up.

"Are you sure we should do this, George?"

"Fuck them!" he barked. "Fucking animals. This is *my* business," he said. "And if I want to have dancers in *my* business, I'll goddamn well have them!"

Any way he looked at it, Ray Dwyer was in danger of losing his job. He knew the city meant business when the suited men had warned George about closing him down, and even if George had listened and fired the dancers, there'd be no reason to have a bouncer, and no more packed, busy nights to bring in the kind of money George needed to stay on top; he'd have to get rid of the busboys, he'd have to get rid of the cooks, and even if George kept Ray Dwyer on to clean the parking lot, he'd have to get rid of him, too.

But George hadn't listened to the suited city men; he kept the dancers and refused to pay the fines that had increased to the two-grand maximum within a few weeks. "Fuck them!" he'd say, then rip the fines into shreds and toss them in the trash.

There was no reasoning with George; Ray had tried to offer suggestions, possible solutions: "Why don't you write a letter to the alderman? Or go to the city council and try to make some kind of deal. You're smart, George. I'm sure you can come up with something."

"No, no, no," George said. "Why should I crawl to them like a goddamn beggar?"

"Then how about if you get all the customers to sign a petition?"

"No," George said. "I won't do it. The city's just a bunch of fucking criminal animals. They won't listen."

So Ray made a petition himself on a yellow legal pad he'd found in George's office, and that night he went around the restaurant and explained the situation to the patrons, all of whom were eager to sign. He'd gotten thirty names when George marched up and snatched the pad from his hands. "What the hell is this?" he asked.

"A petition!" Ray announced. He was smiling, and sure George would be at least thankful that he cared. "Look at all the names."

"Who the hell put you in charge?" George said. "I said no petitions, and I mean no petitions. This is my goddamn place! Now quit this nonsense and do your job," George said, then threw the pad in the trash and locked himself in his office. He didn't speak to Ray for three days.

There were no more late nights at the house with George's wine and stories, since George never wanted to leave the restaurant, even after closing. He'd stay up most nights pacing the empty floor, staring out the windows, blaring the Rembetica albums while he drank heavily and made mumbled proclamations to Ray or to himself or to some invisible jury he might have imagined sitting at the empty tables, slurring his words in both English and Greek. Ray could hardly stand to listen to him anymore.

One night after closing, Karima asked George if he could give her a ride home, since her car was in the shop. George, who was already drunk and angry, told Ray to borrow his car and take her home.

"I can't leave," George told him. "Who knows when the bastards will come to burn me down."

Karima lived in Midlothian, twenty minutes away. She didn't seem to like the fact that Ray was driving, because for most of the trip she kept her arms crossed and didn't say anything beyond ordered directions. "Turn here," she said. "Go left on the next street," she said.

Sometimes, because of her accent, Ray couldn't understand what

she said. "Pardon me?" he asked, and each time he did, Karima was
visibly annoyed with both sound and movement:

"I *said* two more blocks!"

"I'm sorry," Ray said. "Sorry."

Karima didn't even look at Ray until he pulled up to her apartment and parked the car. "Here you go," Ray said, but Karima
didn't get out of the car.

"Have you always been the bouncer?" she asked.

"No," Ray told her; he was suddenly uncomfortable with himself,
as if probed by a board of strange enemies, since this was the first
time he'd been completely alone with a woman in well over thirty
years. "I used to drive trucks," he said.

"Trucks," Karima repeated. Then she was staring at him, silent.

"Turn off the car," she finally said, and with his moist, trembling
fingers, Ray reached for the key and cut the engine. Something
warm and numb had taken over his body, controlled his breath, his
movement, his speech.

"And then what?" Karima asked, and Ray answered, "Prison. I
was in prison for a long time."

"Prison! Oh, my, what for?" Karima asked. "What did you do to
get sent to prison?"

"I got sent to prison because I killed a man."

Karima gasped, covered her mouth, then let out a sickeningly
childish laugh that bothered Ray, since he didn't find anything
funny about prison or murder. "A killer," she said. "A killer drove
me home tonight."

Ray should have despised being called a killer, and part of him
did, but for some reason he only smiled and said, "Yeah. I guess so,"
and waited for Karima to leave.

But Karima stayed right where she was, then reached up and ran
her fingernails along the back of Ray's neck. Ray involuntarily
closed his eyes and sighed, because he'd never truly forgotten what
it was like to be touched by a beautiful girl, and though not a *single
day* had passed without his thinking about her at least once, Ray
Dwyer was strongly and sadly reminded of Samantha Baskin, the
only beautiful girl he'd ever loved. And, as if reading his mind,
Karima asked, "Do you love a special girl?"

Ray, his eyes still closed, said, "Yes. Samantha Baskin." He hadn't
wanted to say this or anything else, since he knew in his heart that

Karima, this dancer who usually ignored him, didn't really deserve to know whom he loved; she was toying with him, but the words had still fallen from his lips, and there was nothing he could do about it.

"Samantha Baskin," Karima said. "And if I let you make love to me, Mister Killer, would you call me Samantha Baskin?"

With this, Ray opened his eyes, closed his lips, and glared across the seat at Karima, who was not, he realized, a beautiful, pretty, or even nice girl; she was none of these things, and Ray regretted telling her so much. "No," he said; her game had made him almost furious, and empty of little else but sadness. "I wouldn't call you anything," he said. "Now please get out."

Karima called Ray a faggot, told him to go fuck himself, then got out of the car and slammed the door behind her. Ray drove away, but he had to pull over when tears came to his eyes, tears he tried to push back into his head by squeezing the bridge of his nose.

The next morning, Ray woke up when he sensed someone standing over his bed. He opened his eyes and saw George — bloodshot, puffy, bearded George — brandishing a brand-new pair of industrial-strength bolt cutters.

"Wake up," George hissed. "Come on, wake up! I need your help."

The city had finally pulled George's business license and closed him down for good. There was an order posted on the restaurant's front door, right above the thick chains that were wrapped and locked around the handles.

"I can't do this," Ray said, holding the bolt cutters George had shoved in his hands. "Read that. I'll get put in jail if I monkey with the lock."

"Hell!" George said. "Nobody's looking. And if anyone asks, I'll say *I* did it!"

Ray looked over both shoulders before he fastened the cutters around the thick lock. He closed his eyes and squeezed the handles until he felt the metallic burst of the lock as it snapped in two. George pushed Ray out of the way, pulled the chains off the door, then unlocked it and hurried inside.

Ray didn't want to follow George, but he watched him from the open doorway and thought he should try to at least talk him back outside. He watched George scurry around the empty restaurant, muttering to himself as he counted the empty tables and chairs. And though Ray knew there was little he could do, he quietly stepped inside and said, "George, please come back out. It's over. This has gone too far."

"We are *still* open, goddammit," George said.

"Please," Ray told him. "We'll wait until things simmer down. Let's just go home."

George dismissed the idea with a quick, backhanded wave as he continued pacing the floor, taking this unnecessary inventory of what he still believed was his. Ray, unable to feel pity for George, left the bolt cutters by the door and turned to leave George by himself.

"Ray," George said, and Ray stopped. "You will be here tonight. You will be here to work."

And Ray, knowing he had no other choice, said, "Sure, George. I'll be here."

That night, Ray Dwyer put on a crisp white shirt and charcoal slacks, and carefully groomed his hair with two fingertips of Royal Crown pomade. And though he'd just polished his black leather shoes the day before, he decided to polish them again. He stood before the bathroom mirror and admired how handsome he still looked after all these years. Sure, his hair was gray, and his green eyes, though still clear and strong, had bags under them, but for a fifty-year-old man, Ray knew he could do a lot worse. Ray Dwyer also knew he didn't have much, and that he was probably only hours away from having less than that, which is why he didn't feel too proud or full of himself for enjoying the few simple things that still belonged to him: his fancy clothes, his muscles, and his good looks.

The many regulars who showed up to see the dancers that night didn't know they were trespassing, and, actually, neither did the dancers. Still, the patrons were a little rowdier than usual when Karima danced; occasionally, one of the men pinched her, and lots of the men whistled and cheered like a bunch of bachelor party drunks. Ray, on his toes as usual, wagged his finger to calm them down.

George seemed to be encouraging this disorder by whistling at Karima as well. At one point he even pinched her hip, then held out a bill she took in her teeth. Before that, George had marched around the restaurant, shaking the patrons' hands and bellowing, "Welcome to *my* place! You can come here to see these beautiful dancers every goddamn night of the week, and you'll always be welcome!"

Ray could see that even the patrons found George's behavior more than strange; many gave one another sidelong glances once George left their tables, yet they still ordered their drinks and cheered when Karima sauntered onto the floor.

Everyone, however, seemed to settle once Rita was well into her number, as everyone usually did while she was on. The audience didn't cheer, whistle, or grab at her, but only stared with a marked and sluggish attention common to those under the influence of narcotics. Her watery movement even relaxed Ray, who leaned against the wall by the men's room and closed his eyes, slightly happy and thankful he'd at least had a chance to work in such a special place, even if it had only been for a handful of months. And then something happened.

First a bunch of men said, "Hey!" and "What the hell?" and when Ray opened his eyes, he saw nothing but darkness, and realized Rita's music had stopped; the power had been shut off. He heard George call his name, but couldn't move from the spot where he leaned. Before Ray knew it, the lights were back on, the music was playing again, and the front door was pushed open by an army of what looked like twenty-five Tinley Park cops.

"Show's over!" one of the cops said. "Everyone out!"

Then someone threw a glass, another yelled, "Fuck you!" and that's when all hell broke loose. The cops charged in with their flashlights and nightsticks, swinging at men who'd overturned tables, tossed chairs, and they even swung at the men who weren't too drunk and only trying to leave. Ray was frozen, petrified beyond movement, and when he heard George yelling for him, calling his name over and over, Ray only became more frightened, and he slid into the bathroom and closed the door.

The first two cops who burst in would have probably only slugged Ray Dwyer a few times if he'd simply listened when they said, "Come on, fucko. Let's go. Come on," but he didn't really hear what the cops said; he only stood there, petrified, hearing threats, and not orders, shooting from their mouths.

The last time he'd had a run-in with the police — when Ray

Dwyer had fought them, that is — was when he was a proud, fresh, eighteen-year-old union quarry trucker who was blocking the Tamco entrance gate, on strike with the other drivers and machinists who were up against a greedy, no-good management staff that was trying to yank the food right out of their goddamn mouths; he'd fought the cops who'd tried to pull them away so the dirty goddamn scabs could get through, and had been a hero. He'd been bailed out of jail by the president of the local, who bought him a drink that afternoon at the Stone City tavern, right there on Patterson Road. Loads of guys bought Ray drinks that afternoon, so many drinks that they eventually had to carry him home to his mother and three younger sisters. And for weeks after that, loads of guys slapped his back and told him how proud his old man would have been, seeing his boy, Ray, stand up to them cops like that. A real Dwyer, they'd called him. An honest-to-God fucking Dwyer.

But this time, Ray Dwyer wasn't on strike against anyone; he was simply confused and scared, as were the five, ten, then fifteen cops who beat and dragged him out of the bathroom when he wouldn't come out on his own. Later, these cops would say Ray Dwyer swung at them, but he honestly couldn't remember.

And once they had Ray Dwyer on the floor, the very same floor where Rita, only moments earlier, had relaxed a roomful of drunken men with mature, calculated beauty, the police officers swung their nightsticks and flashlights high above their heads, and beat Ray Dwyer within a stifled breath of his life.

Ray's body didn't take the beating as well as it had thirty years earlier. This time, the cops left much more than a smooth scar under his hair. One of his lungs was collapsed, one of his arms broken, and the doctors were quite sure Ray Dwyer would never see out of his left eye again.

But when Ray Dwyer came to in the hospital, his good eye saw George, who was kneeling next to the bed, his eyes red from crying.

"My friend," George said. "Lord Christ, I'm sorry. This is all my fault."

And though Ray Dwyer couldn't speak because his lips were too busted up and sore to even smile, he forgave his boss, George, since he certainly knew what it was to make a mistake, to live with regret over doing something remarkably stupid. He winked with his good eye, stuck his thumb up, and these gestures made George Kariotis smile.

Ray really wished he could talk, and he wished that he and George were in the kitchen drinking wine, smoking, telling stories. Because if they had been, Ray would have assured George that everything was going to be all right, even if the city did close his place down. He imagined taking George by the arm and showing him the big map of the world, then pointing to three places on it, the places where his three sisters lived: Mary in Texas, Katie in southern California, and Maureen in Florida. "See?" Ray imagined telling him. "We can leave this old dump and open a new place. Down here, or here. Or hell, even here. I've never been there, but my sisters tell me it's warm. So what do you say, George?"

And though George Kariotis didn't yet know the reason for the occasion, Ray Dwyer raised his good arm, and the two men shook hands on this, one hell of a good idea, and Ray Dwyer promised himself to tell George all about it as soon as he was well enough to speak.

ROB KANTNER

How Wendy Tudhope Was Saved from Sure and Certain Death

FROM *Alfred Hitchcock's Mystery Magazine*

Had Officer Nick Bolthouse not rolled up her street at just the right moment, Wendy Tudhope would now be dead, shot to pieces by an ex-husband who finally snapped.

It was a miracle, Wendy now tells one and all — a miracle that a most opportune radio call sent Officer Bolthouse to her home at just the right time.

But Wendy, God bless her, doesn't know the half of it.

1. Brian

The vanity license plate on the big gold Lexus read SUE. But this was not the driver's name; it was business promotion. For Brian was a lawyer, an "attorney-at-law." Also, according to his business card: counselor, adviser, advocate, and litigator.

The most accurate label did not, however, appear on his card. For truth be told, which when the topic is a lawyer can be problematic, Brian Dobozy was above all else an awesome earner. Last year he admitted to the IRS net income well in excess of half a million. Clients paid him this as a result of time sheets, which if totaled would have posited for that year 5,333 hours of work performed by him on behalf of innumerable divorcées and drunks. Which, it follows, left him with just 9.4 hours during each of that non–leap year's 365 solar days to do all other non-cash-generating activities, such as eating, sleeping, and playing.

Thus, Brian M. Dobozy's law practice was the juridic equivalent of stack 'em deep and sell 'em cheap. Herein the principles are: 1. When considering a new case, what matters is not current caseload or legal merit, but client pocket-depth. 2. Give priority to the client screaming loudest. 3. When in doubt, delay. 4. Bill for everything, tangible and non. 5. Always get paid. Success as an earner came partly from sticking to these principles, which made up for his being an indifferent legal mind, a so-so writer, and not quite the world's greatest strategist. With even an iota of self-awareness, Brian Marcellus Dobozy could also have attributed his prosperity to a vivid courtroom presence, strong manipulation skills, fast footwork, blithe willingness to be detested, inurement to embarrassment, and unparalleled ability to keep twirling a dozen plates at once.

Which makes for one heck of a hectic 14.6-hour workday. That's why, on this sunny autumn morning, Brian Marcellus Dobozy, J.D., simultaneously drove his big gold Lexus at twenty over the limit on Detroit's Lodge Freeway, talked on his cell phone, and scribbled notes on a pad braced to his steering wheel. He was, of course, late on this occasion for a show-cause hearing in a divorce matter. But that was all right. The client was tame, the judge was a poodle. Brian Marcellus Dobozy, *Juris Doctor*, was sure he could get the hearing dismissed for a few weeks.

He had no clue who Wendy Tudhope was.

He did not know the impact he would have on her today.

And never would.

2. *Brian, Donna, and Dario*

Dario Giannetti also knew nothing about Wendy Tudhope. And even if he had, Dario would have dismissed her out of hand. Happy, contented women were of no use to him.

This is why, on this particular sunny autumn morning, Dario Giannetti sat on a hallway bench outside Judge Popcorn's courtroom, chatting up one Donna Nenno, whom he had just met. Though quite heavy and showing more than her fair share of middle-aged wear, Donna was not uncomely. But Dario was not picky about size, age, or looks; he had other criteria that Donna met to a

T. She was female. She was embroiled in a messy divorce. Her soon-to-be-ex had dumped her for another. She was hurting for money. She was filled with fear at the bleak alone-years she saw ahead, and though she tried hard to hide it, she was almost giddy with disbelief at the unexpected attentions of a handsome, well-spoken, obviously professional man.

Having flashed her and distracted her and lathered on the chatter, Dario Giannetti proceeded to work her expertly, fielding her tentative questions with smiles, direct eye contact, and occasional humor. *What do you do?* Law enforcement, he answered. That pleased her. He not only obeyed rules, but enforced them too. He knew she was thinking, he probably carries a gun, giving him the tangy odor of danger. *Where do you live?* Plymouth, he told her. Really good. Upscale community with a veneer of class. *Do you have kids?* All grown, he replied. Perfect, he saw in her eyes. He brought to the table the weary experience of parenthood without inflicting on the impending Donna-Dario relationship (for that, he knew, was the head-movie she was watching) the burden of having to deal with them. Plus, he knew that to her he looked yummy. Lithe and slight, exotically dark complexion, great cologne, and that perfectly coiffed, very thick, brilliantly white hair. Women like Donna, he knew from experience, yearned to wear him like an emblem.

Oh yes, for Dario Giannetti things were moving well there in that busy courthouse hallway, as Donna Nenno shifted herself a bit closer on the bench, gave him an occasional casual touch, furtively adjusted strands of her blond hair, tittered at his jokes. He'd passed her screening questions with flying colors, and ta-da! all without lying. The one question she had not asked was how his own divorce was going. To that question he would, without blinking, have lied. Not only was his divorce not in fact "going," it had in fact been over and done with for five years already. It was during that experience that he'd learned firsthand that these courthouse hallways teemed with many a Donna Nenno — shell-shocked by her marital train wreck and for this one time in her otherwise average, proper, and wholesome life unlikely to resist the almost visceral urge to smear a man like Dario "Mister Right Now" Giannetti onto her emotional wounds like a big old salve stick.

Having regular professional courthouse business, Dario trolled this hallway once or twice a month, "to pick the low-hanging fruit," as he thought of it. Mostly nothing happened, but eight times it had, and quite tastily too. Feeling Donna's warmth, Dario had her toe-tagged for Number Nine. Excellent, he thought. He didn't want to work today, anyway. He'd wait for her here and have a tasty itinerary to present to her after her court business. Probably lunch at Très Vite, then a drive around Belle Isle. Afterward, drinks at Half Past Three, and then they'd head up to the St. Clair Inn where the wine and romance would flow in the candlelight.

"Wait a minute, hon," Donna said, touching his hand as she threw a look over her shoulder. "Here comes my lawyer. We're going in. Can you stick around?"

"Sure," he said casually. He glanced past her to see who she was eyeing, and the sight of the tall, handsome man in a gray suit bustling toward them made him flinch. Damn. Why him? Why now?

Donna stood; he followed suit. "It's just a quickie," Donna said nervously as the lawyer cruised up, smiling sardonically at them. "Morning, Brian," she said.

"Hi," he said, squinting down. "Who's your friend, Donna?"

"This is Dario," she answered, beaming.

"Hi-ya, Counselor," Dario said, with a wink Donna could not see.

Brian's eyes, aware but unimpressed, shifted to Donna. "Let's go," he gestured.

"Okay," she said. "Wait for me," she told Dario, squeezing his hand.

"I think not," Brian said casually.

"What?" she asked.

"Dario has someplace else he needs to be." Brian smiled. "Isn't that right, Mister Dario Giannetti."

Dario's inward sigh was sullen. "Yeah, come to think of it."

Round face pale, Donna's blue eyes glanced back and forth between the two men. "You know each other? What's this about?"

Brian had a large hand steady on her elbow. "Tell you later. Let's go," he murmured, guiding her toward Judge Popcorn's door. Over his shoulder he threw lightly at Dario: "Buzz off."

Grim, vexed, Dario Giannetti marched down the hall toward the elevator. Donna or no, he had not planned to work today. But now, denied Donna by the evil appearance of Dirtbag Dobozy, one of the few men in the world who had ever whipped him, he had steam to blow off. The best therapy was to collar a few rascals. He owed himself a return visit to the Bide-a-Wee. He knew the big bust last Monday hadn't bagged them all. The remaining rascals would have their guards down, never expecting him to strike again so soon.

Just as Wendy Tudhope, a whole state away, did not expect the visitor who was preparing to hit the road.

3. Dario, Hua, and Roger

Qian Hua, on the other hand, fully expected the impending visit. She did not know who it would be, or when they would come, but it was certainly on its way. For *ren shi* like her — the term translates roughly as "human snakes" — life is a constantly watchful, vigilant, and tense business, characterized by close calls and narrow escapes. As with last Monday's raid, during which the agents — plainclothes men with guns, supported by uniformed police with more guns — had blocked the Bide-a-Wee Motel exits and then overrun the place. Hauled off had been several of Hua's coworkers who, like her, had no papers. Cited again was Mr. Max. Hua herself had been showering at the time, preparing for her night job at Humphrey's. The agents had overlooked her.

That time. But they would be back. The certainty did not scare Hua. She had been at this too long, been through too much, to let what was wholly out of her control distract her from the job at hand. Which was, on this bright, sunny autumn noontime, making up the ground-floor rooms of the Bide-a-Wee Motel. She had two to do before going to her afternoon/evening job. Hard work, but she was very good at it, and she knew her good work pleased the generally unpleaseable Mr. Max.

He was certainly one of the better people she had met since leaving Guangdong Province last year. As Hua scrubbed the tub with brisk, efficient movements, she let a slide show of faces parade through her mind. The loan sharks who took the equivalent of ten thousand dollars of her parents' money as down payment, and required Hua to sign a *renqing* for the other two-thirds, with her family literally held as collateral. The *shetou* (snake heads), the smugglers whom she paid for her seagoing escape. The Vietnamese gangsters who, after bringing her ashore in California, informed her that for this "service" she owed them a thousand dollars, which she clearly did not have. The thugs who ran the "safe house" — what a contradiction in terms that was — where Hua, treated less than kindly by men without souls, worked off her debt under sweatshop conditions. Until one glorious day she saw her chance and escaped.

Sure that if caught by the INS she would be jailed in American dungeons for many years, and anxious to avoid recapture by the Vietnamese thugs, Hua had stayed on the move. From city to city on a zigzag course east, she hooked up and split off, worked jobs good and bad, dodged trouble sometimes through luck but usually by pluck and daring, worked on her English, applied her formidable intelligence learning all she could about being an American, and in all ways and at all times did what had to be done.

Metro Detroit, with more varieties of non-Caucasians in larger numbers than just about anywhere else, seemed like a safe haven for now. Here Hua went from simply surviving to starting really to live, perhaps even to thrive. Certainly the Bide-a-Wee housekeeping job was grueling work with its disgusting moments. And no question her exhausting work on the stage at Humphrey's, with its raucous music, fetid smells, and usually intoxicated and often grabby customers, was a trial for one as fastidious and proper as she. But the jobs brought in the cash she needed. Especially the dancing. With her exoticness and flair, Hua earned more cash in one night than her housekeeping job brought her in a full week. All of which she parceled out, every Saturday: a portion for the loan shark, some to her family back in China, the rest to pay for her tiny room and books and food.

Today, Hua thought as she wiped down the bathroom mirror, she was tired. Two rooms to go here, then she would have liked nothing better than to go home and collapse and sleep till dawn. But she knew she would do her shift at Humphrey's anyway. Because every day she went there, she told herself, was one day less that she'd have to. Things would get better. Things always got better. This was America.

According to the clock, she had spent twelve minutes in room 322. Just enough. Hoisting the full plastic garbage bag, she stepped out onto the sidewalk. To her right she saw a plain blue sedan pull past. It was driven by a man with brilliantly white hair and seemed to be headed for the motel office. The sight piqued her curiosity as she walked with the heavy garbage bag past her housekeeping cart and other motel room doors and toward the end of the courtyard. Rounding the corner into the shorter driveway she passed a few more rooms and a white Buick on her way to the garbage dumpster. She disposed of her bag and had started back the way she'd come when she noticed a middle-aged man just finishing changing the tire on the white Buick. Obviously rushed, he was throwing tools back into the trunk.

She wondered why she suddenly felt so edgy.

As Hua approached room 322, two things happened. First, she remembered what she'd heard about the INS agent who'd led Monday's raid: "bright white hair." Second, she saw him again. It was *him*, she was sure, down at the end, walking straight at her.

Without thinking, Hua turned and skipped quickly back the way she'd come. She was certain the agent had seen her and was picking up his pace. She had to hide, but where? Rounding the corner, for the moment out of his sight, she saw the white Buick. Its owner was absent, and the trunk lid was still up. Flying on her lithe dancer's legs, Hua raced for the car and leapt lightly into the trunk, at once bending down and pulling the lid shut atop her.

Inside was close, warm, and very dark, like the container in which she'd ridden over from China. Hua measured her breathing and forced herself into a relaxed stillness as one minute grew into two, three, four. The thud against the car almost made her jump, and for an instant she thought she was done for. But then the engine started and the car lurched backward, and Qian Hua knew that she had slipped through their fingers yet again.

But to where? And for what?

4. Hua, Roger, and Eric

Roger Twine was an unhappy man.

As such, he was just like another man who at that moment was driving his Ford Expedition south, bound for the Cincinnati home of Wendy Tudhope. Both the Expedition driver and Roger Twine, who were wholly unaware of each other, wore the stern, tight-lipped scowl that Wendy would have recognized. She was just now greeting her twin daughters as they returned home from junior high; for the record, she did not know and would never meet Roger Twine.

Unhappy Roger Twine, standing in a long, shuffling line of boarding passengers in the humid jetway of Gate A56 at Detroit Metropolitan Airport, was cheesed off to be standing in the long shuffling line of boarding passengers. For one thing, Roger Twine was a PacLantic Airways Gold Club member. Gold Club members do not stand in lines — long, shuffling, or otherwise. Gold Club members are not limited to just one carry-on bag. Gold Club members are not assigned a middle seat on the starboard side of a DC–9, only to be injection-molded, Roger expected, between a couple of linebackers. Gold Club members do not board planes by row, thereby losing first shot at overhead compartment space for the one carry-on that Roger was allowed today by the snotty gate agent, thank you so much, you really earned your six bucks an hour today, butthead.

Roger Twine was also cheesed off because he wasn't supposed to be on this 4:05 flight in the first place. Roger had been ticketed on a 2:00 flight. Had he taken it, Roger would, as carefully planned, have rolled into his driveway by five-thirty, safe and sound, clean and green, his wife no wiser.

Now, he had to figure out a cover story, which would be tricky. Ellen clearly had her dark suspicions about him, especially after that cell-phone episode last month.

Those damned security people! Roger shuffled ahead a step or two. It was all their fault. Sure, he'd been running late anyway. That flat tire — who'd have predicted that? Of the hundreds of cars he'd rented over two decades of travel, he'd never had a flat. Not till today at the Bide-a-Wee, forcing Roger, who was, as usual, cutting things close getting to the airport, to change the tire himself. He didn't dare call his road service: Ellen opened all the mail.

Even with that delay, he'd have made the 2:00 were it not for the Gestapo Checkpoint Charlie that now "guarded" the airport rental car plaza. Security was one thing, but wasn't it overkill to search every returning rental car? Why, Roger seethed, couldn't they use a little commonsense judgment? Did Roger Twine, tall, middle-aged, gray-haired, distinguished-looking, casually dressed in pricey polo and Dockers, toting an expensive laptop computer and rolling a leather wheel bag, fit the profile of a terrorist?

Yet, common sense notwithstanding, the guards — no kids, these; he wouldn't have been surprised if they'd starred in the old *Adam-12* TV show — approached both sides of Roger's car and peered in. And then asked him to pop the trunk release. Which of course he did.

Oops.

A long time later, the cops of various flavors — Roger never did get straight how many agencies were represented in the airport security office, but it seemed like everybody showed up but Tom Ridge — grudgingly decided that Roger was telling the truth when he insisted that he had NO idea, *none* whatsoever, why the trunk lid of his rental car had swung open to reveal a young Asian woman.

Luckily, she was alive and unhurt. Even more helpfully, the very young woman, though obviously scared and lacking English language skills, had attested to the cops that Roger had not known she'd secreted herself in his trunk.

And so, after taking down all Roger's information and grimly assuring him they'd contact him again if needed, the cops had turned him loose. Clearly late for his 2:00, barely in time for his sardine-can center seat on the 4:05, with an hour in the air to eke out an alibi for Ellen. She had paged him twice and left a message on his cell-phone voice mail and was already ear-pricked and sniffing the wind and lying in wait.

With excruciating slowness Roger shuffled through the DC–9 door. Peeking around the corner, Roger saw that first class, where he *should* have been, was indeed full. Damn it to hell, he thought. Probably not a one among them with the miles Roger had!

What to tell her? By now Ellen had certainly called the post and learned he had not been there at all today.

Inching down the first-class aisle, dragging his roll bag, Roger bobbed and weaved, trying to get a glimpse of the overhead storage compartments back in coach. He could see that the rear compartments were full already. Above row 12, where Roger had (freakin' *middle)* seat D, there was still space in the overhead compartment. Maybe enough for his roll bag.

It was hot on the plane, and Roger was sweating. His face felt like it was burning up. From somewhere ahead a baby was screaming. Making things worse, it occurred to Roger that Ted probably had the duty today. Ted had been told that Roger was spending the day at a conference at the Carlisle. Roger's stomach wrenched.

Almost out of first class now and into coach. Ahead, Roger could see people stuffing the overhead compartments full. Space was running out. The girl behind him turned for some reason, giving him the backpack-smack, without so much as a glance of apology. Roger flinched and tensed for an instant, brimming with harsh words.

If by evil chance Ellen had gotten to Ted, and Ted had mentioned the Carlisle to her, and Ellen had checked for Roger at the Carlisle, then Katie bar the door. Through Roger's mind kaleidoscoped scratchy audio and video samples of Ellen screeching questions, demands, and accusations; lawyers and judges and accountants; e-mails and chat logs and AmEx invoices; testimony by Darlene and Carol and (ohmyGod no) Jenny; exposure of the funny business with Roger's retirement fund. Not to mention the permanent loss of Ellen's fat inheritance.

Up ahead, a blond man in glasses and sport coat thrust a big silver steel box into the compartment above row 12. And then moved on to his seat in row 15.

"Hey!" Roger shouted. "You! Get that out of there!"

Faces turned. The man looked at Roger, puzzled.

"That's *my* row!" Roger yelled. "You get that piece of junk out of there!"

The man smirked, like this was some kind of put-on. "Take it easy, man. First come, first served."

Roger was almost to 12 now. His middle seat was empty, the flanking ones occupied. Above, the steel case hogged half the compartment. Clearly there was no room for Roger's roll bag too. "Are you taking it out?" Roger demanded. "Or do I do it for you?"

Murmurs bubbled all around Roger in the hot aircraft, with the uncomfortable shuffling of people politely pretending they weren't paying attention. The row-15 snotnose, who had obviously never flown before and did not know the rules, said calmly, "Please leave it alone and find your own space."

"We'll see about that," Roger said. Hovering over the passenger seated at the aisle, Roger reached into the compartment for the steel case. It was heavy and seemed to be stuck. Grunting and cursing, Roger tugged at it, as protesting voices echoed around him. The case shifted and then came loose. Triumphantly Roger pulled at it hard, freeing it from the compartment.

But the steel case, being heavier than he expected, and awkward and slippery, tumbled loose from his hands.

And fell.

And landed with a sickening smack.

5. *Eric and Missy*

"Can you tell me his condition?" Eric asked, cupping his cell phone to his ear as he swung shut the door of his car. Listening intently, he ambled up to the tinted glass door of Suite 300 on which was stenciled FEDDERSPILL BROS. ENGINEERING SERVICE. "That's good," he said into his phone as he sauntered through the door and past the receptionist with a wave and wink. "No," he said presently, "just, uh, I saw the incident, just wanted to be sure he was all right. Thanks for the update."

Eric clicked his phone shut as he passed a well-dressed woman seated in a visitor chair. She looked expectantly at him, sizing him up; Eric smiled back. In the sprawling open-plan offices, the air was hissing slowly out of yet another very hectic day. Eric knew, because he'd checked before leaving for the airport, that the Visteon team would be burning midnight oil on a rush RFP, but otherwise most employees left by five-thirty or so. Unlike many in his position, Eric did not believe in routine overtime, voluntary or otherwise. Work people too many hours and the law of diminishing returns kicks in. Besides, he believed, people needed and deserved lives outside the job. Even employees.

As was his habit, Eric first breezed into the corner office, to find Jerry, as almost always, on his feet and on the phone. The younger man wore a dress shirt and tie and sported a buzz cut, the opposite of Eric not only in job function but also in apparel, appearance, and attitude. Creative friction was one secret of a well-run business and Fedderspill Brothers was well run indeed, as attested to by their growing list of tier-one automotive clients. What Eric and Jerry shared, besides some DNA, was white-hot intellect. And fierce loyalty.

Jerry dropped his phone on the hook without a goodbye. "What happened? Miss the flight?"

Eric shrugged lazily, dropping into a visitor chair. "Got canceled.

Some air-rage yay-hoo wigged out, dropped a suitcase on another guy's head."

Staring bug-eyed, Jerry exhaled in disbelief, but stayed on message. "But what about Monaghan? When you going to see them now?"

"Fortunately, the guy wasn't hurt bad," Eric said. "He'll be all right."

"What about Monaghan?" Jerry pressed.

Eric shrugged again. "I'll run out there tomorrow instead. Lainie was fine with it."

"She can afford to be," Jerry answered, fussing with something atop the pile of papers on his desk. "She's not the one needs something from us, it's the other way around."

"I'm sure we'll work something out," Eric replied.

"You realize," Jerry fussed, "we need them inside the tent with us, peeing out. You'll have to hit a home run for us, Ricky."

"So," Eric said patiently, "instead of meeting Lainie and Tom tomorrow, I'll see them the day after. It'll be all right." The two eyed each other, Jerry tense under the weight of a thousand details and innumerable eventualities, Eric living more in each moment, calmly taking things as they came. "Any fires for me to fight? I've got tee-ball tonight."

"Nothin'," Jerry fussed, fluttering fingers. "Go on, take off, I'll lock up." Eric rose. "Oh, wait a minute," Jerry rushed on, "there's one more second interview —"

"Sitting out there?"

"Her, yeah," Jerry grumped. "I was supposed to see her a half-hour ago, I've been jammed. But now that you're here —"

"I'll take it," Eric said easily. "No problem. For which slot?"

"The marketing," Jerry said, handing the file to him.

"If I like her," Eric grinned, "I might give her a friendly warning to steer clear of that jinx job."

"If you like her," Jerry said darkly, "and she's willing to work for what we're willing to pay, you handcuff her to a desk."

Laughing, Eric eased out and up the hall with his languid way of walking. In contrast to Jerry's, his own office was a riot of papers and drawings on a U-shaped work surface, dominated by a boxy CAD terminal and two wide-format printers at one end, and a conference table at the other. Several prints from Goya's *Los Caprichos*

lined the walls. Above his cluttered desk a framed sign read, TO
THE OPTIMIST, THE GLASS IS HALF FULL / TO THE PESSI-
MIST, THE GLASS IS HALF EMPTY / TO THE ENGINEER, THE
GLASS IS TWICE AS BIG AS IT NEEDS TO BE. Eric leaned
against his desk, glancing over the resumé as the woman came in.
"Mr. Fedderspill?"

He smiled at her. "Eric. Have a seat, Ms. . . . Bowmer?"

"Melissa," she acknowledged and seated herself stiffly in a visitor
chair. She was Eric's age, about, but seemed more ground down by
the years. Full face and figure, been-around eyes squinting through
tinted lenses, dark hair pulled back indifferently into a loose tail.
She wore a navy single-breasted suit over what looked like a white
tank top. Her ears and fingers were ringless; she sported no jewelry
at all save an anklet chain above a stain that appeared to be a tattoo. Eric thought she worked overly hard at her smile and sensed
that her dynamism — what little she had — was forced, especially
for one of the marketing persuasion, for whom perkiness was the
default demeanor. He wondered what her problem was. The late
hour? Quiet desperation caused by who knew what? Bad spot in the
meds cycle? At first take she seemed not terribly likable, but that
neither surprised Eric nor ruled her out for the job. People who
were good at marketing, he had learned, were not for him the likable sort. But this wasn't just that. With her there was something
more. He felt it almost at once. Something way back, just beyond
reach in the fog.

Skimming the résumé, Eric realized he had seated himself on his
drafting stool, with his big work desk between him and the appli-
cant. He was surprised at himself; usually he conducted interviews
at the conference table to foster a more relaxed atmosphere. Oh
well, he thought, here we are. With a smile, he started the interview, as usual, with the present, working his way back.

She answered questions by rote, reeling off well-oiled set pieces
with all the verve of an actor at a long run's end. To Eric she looked
blurry, her features not quite in sync. For a man who earned his
bread with his ability to see clearly and render tangible the most
obtuse concepts, Eric found that his eyes and his perceptions kept
trying to stretch Melissa Bowmer into someone else entirely. Even
her name was all wrong.

Gradually one particular smile of hers emerged that seemed

right. In earlier days that one particular smile had played many minutes per period. Now it just flickered from time to time, suggesting that three decades of intervening life had not disabused her of her self-image of privilege and entitlement. Eric began to hear from an echoing distance the clatter of a manual typewriter and the *chugga-chugga* of the Associated Press teletype. In his mind's eye he saw Melissa Bowmer, or whoever she was, sitting cross-legged in jeans on the city room table. Never pretty, just young, she cradled a bottle of red pop, smiled that one particular smile, and was most pleased to be giving Eric his "reality adjustment."

At this point in the interview they had worked their way back to her college career. Eric set the résumé down. "Ever get back there?"

"Where?"

"The *Daily.*"

Melissa Bowmer sat stock still. Several times, unwillingly, her lips pressed, as if trying to hold something in. "So you do remember," she said steadily. "I couldn't tell."

"But it wasn't Melissa," Eric said vaguely, looking past her. "You were Missy. Missy . . . Schrupp."

"I'm flattered," she said.

"Why?"

"Because you remember me." Again with that one particular smile.

"Why wouldn't I?"

Vacating the smile, she released a long long breath. "Okay."

Eric watched her and said nothing. Outwardly composed, inwardly he was stunned to find himself face to face with someone he had not encountered in nearly thirty years.

"Sometimes, you know, sometimes" — Melissa said, nervously swiping her hair — "decisions are — well, they're hard."

"I know," Eric said. "I've made a few myself." Sitting there, he realized the shock he was juicing in wasn't from meeting Missy again. The shock came from being forcibly brought face to face with someone he'd thought long gone, the long-ago Eric who was insecure, sensitive, scared.

"Then you understand."

"Oh, I do indeed." Which was true. He understood that Missy Schrupp, simply by appearing, had the power to take him back to that place and hurt him, quite profoundly, once again.

She looked away. "I do wish I'd handled it better. I was just a kid."
"Whatever."

"Well." She eyed him. "Any point in continuing?" she ventured.

Because he was a kind man, Eric's instinct was to fog. Instead he told the truth: "None."

She blinked once and looked away. "Okay. Thanks for your time." She rose. He did too, and out of innate politeness walked her to his office door. There she looked up into his eyes, her confidence and balance gone. "I really need this job."

"Sorry it didn't work out," he said, putting her back in the past where she belonged. Despite the gentleness of tone, his words felt terse and vindictive in his mouth. But, he reasoned, he was showing her far more mercy than she had shown him, there at the end.

"I could do a hell of a job for you here," she said quietly. "If you'd just let go of what happened."

"Let go?" Eric repeated softly. After a moment she realized he would not — or could not — say more. Stonily, she ducked her head and turned and walked down the hall. "Good luck," he forced himself to say, well out of her earshot.

Strolling back into his office, tired from the long day, the airport calamity, and the emotions that had just swept through him, Eric found the words he'd groped for before: I can let go of what you said, and I can let go of what you did. What I can't let go of is how you made me feel.

6. Missy, Ty, and Sam

By now, on that bright autumn day, Len Schooley was passing Wapakoneta, his black Ford Expedition cruising steadily at the speed limit in the center lane of southbound I-75. Wendy Tudhope sat at her iMac in the library of her suburban Cincinnati home, surfing the Net for an article on the translation of relics. And, some two hundred and fifty miles north, Missy Bowmer drove west on the boulevard, passing the GM Poletown plant at the Detroit–Hamtramck line. Sitting stiffly at the wheel of her red Chevy Celebrity, she drove by instinct, in a place all too grimly familiar: dead numb.

She wanted a drink, but what else was new. Since the age of thirteen, when she'd stolen her first taste of her grandma's home-made raisin-jack from a big jug in the cellar, she'd wanted a drink. During and after each day of high school and before every piano recital. Before each date and after having sex. Before both weddings, throughout the marriages, and especially during the divorces. She'd wanted a drink to celebrate and to grieve, in crowds and alone, by the glass or out of the bottle, fully engaged and utterly blacked out. She'd especially wanted a drink since her most recent one, twenty-two wretchedly white-knuckled days ago, when Evan issued his ultimatum and underlined it by abandoning her.

"I'm not going anywhere," the son of a bitch had insisted, even while packing his PlayStation 2 (a sign of how serious he was). "Just over to Merle's." This paintball pal and NASCAR nut lived, Missy believed, somewhere in Detroit's Boston–Edison section. She remembered, vaguely, visiting his place once. His big house was across from a park where she thought she recollected Evan saying Ty Cobb used to hit baseballs in for the neighborhood kids, way back when. She thought about going there now. She was pretty sure she could find it. She needed to see Evan. To tell him about her twenty-two sober days; to tell him how badly she needed him; to tell him about Fedderspill.

Another hard knock, and like all the others hardly her fault. Who could have predicted it? Oddly, she did remember Eric. He was a cute puke a year behind her, bespectacled and earnest as could be. She was pretty sure they'd had a flinglet, and why not, in those liberal pre-AIDS seventies; it was just something to do, like trying on different skates. To dally carnally with someone who worked for her was probably not the wisest thing, but rules were looser back then, too.

Let's see, she thought, checking street signs. Boston–Edison, that was northwest of here. Maybe she'd take Woodward. If she could find that park, she could find Evan's house . . .

Oh, those had been grand times. Missy was the university paper's first female managing editor. What a glorious and long overdue switcheroo to have all these males working for her for a change. Each vying for position, currying her favor, waiting on her hand and foot, and hoping for that single nod from Missy that would put his skinny fanny in an editor's chair. Missy had enjoyed that courtship routine, especially with the most ambitious ones. They'd do anything to please her. She gave them extra work assignments, she made them take her to lunch, she played them off each other, she'd get them backbiting and gossiping about and against each other — always exciting.

Missy slowed up at the old GM World Headquarters building for the light at Woodward. North, that's right, and then west on — what would it be? Virginia Park? She'd try that. She was a little vague on exactly where this Ty Cobb park was.

Eric had paid her court, as she remembered things, but in a more businesslike way. Thinking about it now, she thought he never seemed to like her very much. He did precisely what she asked, and he seemed pleased at her hints that an editor's chair would be his. Of course there had never been a chance of that, ever; his application was dead on arrival. As a junior, he should have known that! Juniors never got to be editors. Missy had been amused that he'd taken seriously her double-talk and empty hints, trailing after her like a donkey stretching its neck for a carrot. After Missy had finally, and with quiet satisfaction, given him his reality adjustment, she had been surprised (but only briefly) that he quit the newspaper entirely. What a waste, she thought. He'd have made a great reporter someday, he really would — if he ever quit acting like a baby.

The Woodward red lights were not synchronized. Missy plugged north, barely getting into second gear. At Seward another light stopped her. Thinking about Eric was upsetting, but why, she could not have said. Presently she discerned, from the drill-down deep into the sludge of her memory, that those days had not been so great after all. Moreover, Missy realized with dull certainty that she had never slept with Eric at all. He had been engaged to be married, she remembered now, to a mousy English teaching fellow. He had never had the eye for Missy that others had had back then — *way* back then.

Focusing, Missy realized she was staring at a bar sign. Below the bar's name and a neon beer ad was a poster that said PITCHER NIGHT! With instant and brutal clarity Missy's fertile imagination conjured a large glass pitcher brimming with thick, golden, ice-cold Sam Adams beer, foam slopping richly over the edges, condensation misting the crystalline sides. Ty Cobb's park and Evan's house were a few blocks away yet. And Eric, Eric Fedderspill, damn him. Why not? Why the hell not?

After two beers, Missy started to leave. Then she decided to have just one more.

7. Sam and Fern

The electric hole saw whirred and whined with a piercing scream as it cut its cylindrical path through the thick wood of the Christian panel door. Fern Kluska, braced and intent, leaned on the saw till it cut all the way through, then shut off the saw and set it, spooling to silence, on the plastic sheet on the carpet. Beside it lay in meticulous order the twinkling brass pieces of the deadbolt lock set. Scooping the clear plastic safety glasses up on her forehead, Fern picked up the instruction sheet and strolled out to the big bay window in the living room.

In theory, Fern was pausing to review the instructions — she had, after all, never before installed a deadbolt lock. But the real reason for her pause was to check Avril's driveway yet again. Sure enough, the Expedition had not returned.

Question was: Why had it been over there in the first place?

All day Fern had wondered. After all, Avril's personal protection order barred Len from coming within a hundred yards of her. Yet late this morning there it was, his black Ford Expedition, sitting in the driveway of the home he and Avril had shared till last month. Fern's first notion, upon spotting it while leaving for work, had been to call the cops. Her second thought had been to ring Avril to be sure she was all right. Her third option, and the one she had actually acted on, had been to do nothing and await developments.

Fern was, after all, no busybody. And she and Avril had never been *friends* friends. Fern had learned long ago not to get too chummy too quickly with newcomers. Many, especially much younger ones like Len and Wendy, bought into Boston–Edison on a pink cloud of infatuation with the neighborhood's rich history. Celebrities, even dead ones, are a draw, and Boston–Edison had been home to names like Dodge and Fisher, Ford and Gordy. Why, the Georgia Peach himself, Ty Cobb, once lived beside Voight Park, three doors down from where Fern now stood. Decades later, people bought in, and having discovered in due course how much TLC (time, labor, and cash) it took to restore and maintain these dilapidated homes and how maddening it was dealing with the City of Detroit's turgid bureaucracy, they often gave up and moved away.

So Fern never got too close too quickly to newcomers. She did make a point of taking them fresh bread and introducing herself (with Jathan, when he was younger, but never Latroy, who was too self-conscious). The house across from hers had gotten two loaves: one when Len and Wendy had arrived ten years ago, and the second when Avril had moved in with the freshly divorced Len. The departed (and, Fern knew, remarried) Wendy had become a chum; Len, some sort of businessman, was always brusque and on the go with no time to talk. Avril, however, fell somewhere in the middle: a front-porch chatmate.

Like Wendy before her, Avril had confided in Fern the play-by-play of the decline of her marriage to Len. Fern knew about the affairs, she was aware of the fights, she had read the personal protection order, and through it all she patiently provided a thin, reedy shoulder for Avril to cry on. Avril was annoyed that Len had built Wendy a swimming pool, but refused to install a hot tub for her. She was angry at the increasing amount of time and money Len spent in Detroit's topless bars and new casinos. Most of all, she was terrified of Len's stony silences and hair-trigger, fist-swinging rages. When the PPO was issued Avril swore, fluently and convincingly, that she would never speak to Len again. Even so, Fern knew that, PPO notwithstanding, Len had spent several nights with Avril across the street. Evidently, Fern reflected, the "fun" part of their dysfunctional relationship still worked pretty well.

Which was the main reason why Fern had done nothing when she saw Len's Expedition in the driveway this morning. It had had no dew on it, so he must have come by after breakfast. By late afternoon, when Fern returned from her part-time job, it was gone.

Rousing herself, Fern went back to the master bedroom door. She had to finish the lock job quickly. Jathan would be home from school (or wherever, Fern reminded herself glumly) soon, and Fern needed no repeat of yesterday. Popping the hole cutter out of the saw, Fern inserted the spade bit into the chuck. The lock was half the business; the other half was the necessary sit-down with Latroy. Jathan was, after all, his son.

From out front came a piercing screech, a rapid series of loud thumps, and then a ripping metallic crash. Dropping her tools, Fern raced to the bay window. Across the street, the peacefulness of

Avril Schooley's property had been marred by a car, a red sedan, that had jumped the curb, plowed through a hedge, mangled several sections of wrought iron fence, and smacked dead center into a utility pole, where it now sat steaming.

Fern ran, throat-clenched, out the door, down her sidewalk, and across the street. Dead silence from Avril's house; ditto from the other neighbors. The only action was a man obliviously walking his dog in Voight Park up the way. Digging in her pocket, Fern pulled her cell phone and called 911 while walking tentatively toward the hissing car. Its driver door gaped open and a woman Fern did not recognize slumped halfway out, immobile in her shoulder strap. Fern trotted over and bent down, checking vital signs. The woman was alive, semiconscious, and moaning softly, "Evan," it sounded like, over and over. She reeked of alcohol, but Fern had seen and smelled much worse. Finishing her call, she situated the woman comfortably on the front seat and waited for the sound of the sirens.

Like prairie dogs popping from their holes, neighbors started to appear. But still there was no sign of Avril, no movement or sound from her house. Fern peered past the car and the demolished fence into the backyard, looking for signs of life. Nothing except wilting plants, a weedy patio, tipped-over lawn furniture, and the swimming pool showing the sheen of green.

And on the pool surface floated something else, something darkish. Fern squinted and stepped closer. Indistinctness gave way to a set of shapes that presently became a whole. It was a dog, a small spaniel. Not moving, dead still, floating there, a big dark wound gaping. Avril's dog Sasha.

Frozen, Fern stared, then whirled around as a police car pulled up. In a flash Fern connected one dot after another: the violence, the PPO, the black Expedition in the driveway, the silent Schooley house.

Oh my God, Fern thought frantically, running toward the cop car. Avril!

8. Fern and Nick

Officer Nick Bolthouse was just getting out of his squad car when his radio crackled: "Patrol One Ten."

Easing back into the driver's seat, he pressed the shoulder mike: "Go."

"What's your ten-three, over."

Bolthouse had not yet signed out for dinner. "Beechmont at Eight, over."

"Roll on a potential ten-seventy-two at one eight oh oh nine, Loiswood, acknowledge."

"Patrol One Ten," Bolthouse said, pulling his door shut, wondering: potential domestic disturbance?

"Be further advised that a black Ford Expedition with Michigan plates may be on site or nearby. If so, obtain backup and detain the driver on a wanted-for-questioning out of Michigan."

"Roger," Bolthouse acknowledged, starting the engine. The big Police Interceptor engine roared as he goosed the black-and-white Crown Vic onto Beechmont, swinging left immediately on Eight Mile. Driving with one hand, he switched frequencies with the other and said, "Watch Commander, Patrol One Ten, over."

"Watch Commander," crackled the radio. "What's up, Nick?"

"That's my question," Bolthouse said, racing north on the two-lane.

"Probably nothing," the watch commander said. "Detroit P.D. had a ten-eighty-nine up there today. Suspect is one Schooley, Leonard Aitch: Caucasian, fifty-one, two hundred, black on brown. Victim was his second wife. Detroit got intelligence from a neighbor lady that Schooley's first wife lives down here now. Name of Tudhope, Wendy. Thought is that Schooley may be heading our way to visit her."

"Maybe looking for a clean sweep?"

"That's the thought."

"Roger," Bolthouse said, running the light onto Clough Pike east.

"We tried to call her but her line's busy," the watch commander added.

"I'm two minutes out," Bolthouse reported.

"Probably nothing."

"Patrol One Ten."

The entrance to the Anderson Hills subdivision came up fast. The patrolman rolled right and then left onto Loiswood. He knew this to be a dead-end street, and 18009 was at the end, driveway empty, two young teenaged girls playing badminton in the front yard. Bolthouse eased into the cul-de-sac and around, eyeing the house; the girls ignored him. Thumbing his mike he said, "Patrol One Ten, show me ninety-eight at one eight zero zero niner Loiswood. All's calm. Intend to make inquiries. Please advise, over."

"Patrol One Ten, stand by," came the dispatcher. Bolthouse completed his U-turn and was facing out on Loiswood, barely moving now. Ahead of him, coming into the street, was a large boxy vehicle, an SUV, black. As it drew closer, Bolthouse saw that it was a Ford Expedition, and it had no front plate, which meant it was not from Ohio. Abruptly the Expedition slowed, then swerved sharply into a driveway.

"Got him," Bolthouse reported without emotion, hitting the lights. "Now effecting traffic stop." He shot toward the Expedition, which backed out in front of him and took off the way it had come. "Correction," Bolthouse said, punching the gas. "Now ten-thirty-eight, eastbound toward Clough Pike, of a black Ford Expedition, Michigan plate Norma Michael Norma Two Six . . ."

After leading police from several jurisdictions on a high-speed chase, Leonard Herman Schooley, cornered in a pasture just east of Lexington, Kentucky, took his own life.

The others, whose lives intersected just once in the chain-reaction that saved Wendy Tudhope, met fates various, sundry, and wholly unconnected:

Officer Nick Bolthouse continues to patrol Cincinnati's eastern zones. He just passed the sergeant's exam.

Fern Kluska still lives with her husband, Latroy, in Detroit's Boston–Edison community. Son Jathan is away at school.

Eric Fedderspill flew without incident for his Monaghan visit, where he hit the "home run" hoped for by his brother. They're building a new headquarters.

Roger Twine's marriage and career came to a rather abrupt end. For the time being he works the counter at an alternator shop in Westland.

Qian Hua now lives in Philadelphia. She is two days away from meeting the lawyer who will help her gain American political asylum as a member of Falun Gong.

Dario Giannetti unfortunately believed his most recent honey when she told him her soon-to-be-ex was not the jealous type.

Donna Nenno is happily single and steadily dating a man who worships the ground she walks on.

In Cincinnati, with her husband and daughters, Wendy Wilton Schooley Tudhope lives.

9. As for the Others

Missy Bowmer lurched upright at the sound of her name. Her vision clearing, she saw an officer leaning in the cell door. "Let's go," he said.

"Where's my lawyer?" Missy asked, stumbling to her feet. Her head pounded and her vision wobbled. God, I stink, she thought morosely.

"Meet you in the courtroom. Come on." Taking her by the arm, the officer led her out of the cell and put the cuffs on her. Then he led her up the corridor, around a couple of corners, through two or three doors, and into the teeming courtroom. "Stand right there," he said, taking off her handcuffs. "They'll call you."

Amid the courtroom clamor, a hearing seemed to be going on. Penned in behind a wood railing, Missy stood with several other people. After a moment she spotted her lawyer in the spectator area. He gave her a single nod. She waited, dry-mouthed. Brian had told her what to expect, but still she was scared.

"People versus Bowmer," boomed a voice. "Step forward."

Brian strode to a podium and beckoned her. Going to him, she turned and faced the judge, a stern-faced blonde woman wearing a black robe up high behind the bench. Papers ruffled, the microphone squeaked, and the clerk rattled, "Melissa Schrupp Bowmer, you are charged with driving while intoxicated, first offense. Reckless driving, property damage under five thousand dollars."

"Your plea?" Judge Somers asked.

"Guilty," Brian Dobozy said.

The judge issued the sentence — word for word as Brian had predicted. Then the next case was called. With a large hand on Missy's back, Brian guided her out of the courtroom. As they reached the lobby, she heard him say, "I was brilliant in there, wasn't I?"

JONATHON KING

Snake Eyes

FROM *High Stakes*

HE SAW THEM COMING. Over the high grass a swirl of dust spun
up on the horizon, rising on the midday heat. He squinted into
hard sunlight and timed the movement. *Car,* he thought. *Maybe
two.* Behind him, to the west, towering clouds with anvil-flat bot-
toms moved across the sky from the Everglades toward the ocean,
soaking up moisture and turning bruised and dark as they came. In
his hand was the twisted neck of a burlap sack and he could feel the
writhing of thick animal muscle inside of it.

He pulled the wide-brimmed hat from his head and wiped the
sweat from his eyes and then looked down, refocusing on the shadows of a saw palmetto clumped up beside him. The snakes were not
forgiving of a man's inattention. And contrary to legend, diamond-
backs did not always sound their dry rattle before they struck. He
stood watching both the trailing dust of approaching men and the
half-hidden maw of a gopher hole, where the rattlers in this open
ridge country liked to nest. He'd been in this part of south Florida
long enough to know either one could bring trouble. And as in all
gambles, anticipation and assessment are always key.

Four days earlier, on a dirt street in Miami, he had arrived on a
corner at the edge of town with a handbill: "Wanted: Men Not
Afraid of Snakes and Reptiles. Cash Money!" He'd joined two dozen
others at the printed address. Most of the men who showed up
were in their twenties and thirties, anxious and fidgety, their feet
shuffling and hands busy around cigarettes and small packages of
chew. Some wore their tweed suits, the color faded from the sun,
the collars and cuffs rubbed soft at the edges. Others were in sus-

penders and caps but still scuffed about in stitched, hard-leather shoes. Street shoes. City shoes.

O'Hanlon had been in Miami less than a week, fresh off the train from his Brooklyn neighborhood, and he could already spot the "binder boys." They were the young, slick-talking hustlers from the city who'd come to the land boom of Florida. They'd heard on cold northern sidewalks that there were fortunes to be made in the sun. Packing their cardboard suitcases and carrying a roll of savings or a stake gathered from family and friends, they'd come south. In a place gone real-estate mad they'd buy a chunk of unseen land and then sell it for profit days later, long before they ever had to make a payment. The "binder" on the property would change hands ten times until the last fool left holding it was stuck with the inflated bill, unable to find another buyer.

It was high-stakes gambling, not high finance. O'Hanlon had learned the scam from the shoeshine boy outside his flophouse hotel. He also learned that by this late fall of 1925, the boom was going bust. It had been a cleanout for the ones who had arrived early and who had money to begin with. No doubt some nameless butter-and-egg man from Yonkers fell into luck and came out sharp. But by this time the binder boys had fallen to O'Hanlon's level, scrounging after any odd job they could just to buy a meal.

At the morning gathering he watched the group, scrutinizing each man's hands, reading their eyes when they turned to speak to one another and especially when the conversation went quiet.

"You can always measure a man by his hands and eyes," O'Hanlon's father had taught him. "Don't even need to see 'em get into the ring. If they're scared, it's in their eyes, son. If they're weak, it's in their hands."

He had heard it hundreds of times in his father's boxing gym on Delacourt. He had grown up in that gym, watching men bring their dreams in off the street, watching the ones whose ambition or determination or desperation drove them. He'd also seen the ones who let that same motivation leak away and watched others have it beaten out of them. The many who were without talent or were just plain lazy left without scars, their pride put in its proper place before the real fighting started. The few with skill labored and learned and could raise a dozen expectations with their potential. But he had only witnessed one champion, then seen him fall under the thumb of promoters and handlers and gamblers. The rich got richer, the rest of us worked and watched.

His father's lessons were still with him that morning when a battered Model T truck pulled to the corner. A gray-bearded man with red suspenders climbed out of the cab and then swung himself up into the truck bed. With a voice scratched with age and handrolled tobacco, he introduced himself as Rattlesnake Pete. O'Hanlon took in the old man's hands, the fingers knurled and twisted, two of them missing half their length. He could see that despite their damage, they were not weak hands.

"Any you all boys ever catched you a snake?" he said, his drawl coming straight out of Alabama. The group of men had started to gather, but no one offered an answer. The man called Pete did not bother to look up for any nods of assent or bragging. His attention was on the truck-bed floor where he'd bent to hoist a burlap bag.

"Ya'll work with me an' we got ten acres of brush land to clear outta rattlers," he went on while untwisting the neck of the bag. A half dozen of the men narrowed their eyes on the movement of Mr. Pete's hands and another half dozen, most of the binder boys, took a subtle step back.

"I pay you fifty cent a snake and that'll beat pickin' beans any day, boys," he said, still looking into the hole of the bag opening and then suddenly stabbing his hand in.

"Course, this ain't no bean neither," he said as his fist came out with a slick, writhing ribbon of flesh.

Six more men stepped two full steps back. A few stayed rooted. They were not necessarily brave men. The promise of fifty cents a snake was the glue. Mr. Pete now focused his attention back on the group, looking each of them in the eyes, going face to face. Then, without a word of embellishment or warning, he flung the snake down into the dirt, and two more of the men jumped back while the beast coiled itself in the shadow of the truck bumper and began to vibrate.

"All right, boys," the snakeman said, climbing down from the bed and moving more smoothly and surely than a man his age should have. "Ain't no danger if ya'll do what I learn ya."

O'Hanlon and three others who'd stayed close cut their eyes to old Pete's movements, O'Hanlon studying the footwork, watching the body parts closest to the snake. The old man eased in, bending at the knee and never letting his eyes leave the rattler's head.

"Oncet ya'll know where he's at, just keep his attention. They's just stupid animals, boys. Ain't got nothin' in they heads but meanness and belly hunger and they already know ya'll too big to eat."

Now on his knee only a yard from the snake, the old man raised one hand and the reptile's unblinking eyes locked onto the movement and rotated its head to match its slow path. O'Hanlon could hear the heavy breathing of the man next to him and the scuffle of feet farther back of the onlookers now trying to gain a view. With the animal's head now focused on his left hand, the old snake man drifted his right hand more slowly to circle back behind the floating head.

"Ain't a magician nor card player don't know how to git you lookin' at the one thing whilst they trickin' you with the other," old Pete said, staring intently at the snake's head and sliding his left hand to further distract it. If the beast did not follow his left, the snake man kept his right hand still and waited for the snake's attention to return to the movement before closing the gap. The breath sound next to O'Hanlon had stopped. Or maybe it was his own.

"Ya'll old enough to know THAT!" old Pete suddenly yelped, simultaneously flicking his right hand across ten inches of space and snatching up the snake just behind its spade-shaped head. "Ain't ya'll?"

The man called Pete stood up and extended his arm. From his fist the rattler hung, curling its body frantically into a series of desperate S-shapes, its unhinged mouth glistening wide and white and angry.

The man beside O'Hanlon was shaking his head in appreciation and the group behind began to mumble.

"Fifty cent for five minutes of work, boys," Pete said, now with a teasing light in his eye. "Anybody that's game, climb on up into the truck."

Three of them made it into the field. Rattlesnake Pete was not nearly as dramatic when showing the newcomers how to flush a gopher hole with kerosene to bring the snakes writhing and blind out into the sunlight. He'd armed them with long-handled, close-tined pitchforks if they wanted. The old man had been hired, he said, to clear the scrub just north and west of Miami of all its rattlers. The buyer of the land was to begin construction on what he promised would be the finest horseracing track and paddock south of Lexington, and just the thought of snakes and thorough-bred horses together would not do.

With an early morning sun already burning deep into his shoulders and the exposed angles of his nose and cheeks and forehead, O'Hanlon had spent his first day in the field watching. The more experienced snake hunters moved quickly away from the recruits, knowing the terrain and the gopher holes — which actually belonged to a large kind of land tortoise — where easy catches could be made. O'Hanlon quickly discarded their lies about the snake's habit of staying in the shade to avoid the heat of the sun. The logic seemed right; the semitropical sun was raw and unmerciful. But O'Hanlon soon recognized that the cold-blooded species needed the sun to stay warm and he'd found his first catch half curled on a gray-white slab of limestone, the sun full on its distinctive, diamond-patterned skin. By watching the others, he'd stolen the idea of a hook at the end of the pitchfork handle fashioned from a length of stiff wire. Moving slowly, he eased the wire under the snake as it rattled its tail at him and then lifted it off the rock. By suspending the beast in air he robbed it of a solid foundation from which to launch a strike. Then, while carefully watching the movement of the head, he stuffed it into the open gunnysack and earned his first legitimate fifty cents since arriving in Florida.

By the third day he had snared ten of the animals, as many as even the more experienced men of the dozen who stayed on. At noontime old Pete fed them all lunch under any nearby shade oak. From the bed of his truck he handed out day-old loaves of hard bread, chunks of cheese cut from huge disks, and all the oranges a man could eat. It was during the breaks that O'Hanlon heard that Pete collected one dollar from the land developer for each of the snakes they all caught. The old man tallied the number on his own count, though he did offer the sacks to the rich owner to count for himself. Several of the men smiled knowingly when one suggested that Pete was not beyond overstating the catch or releasing a few of the undamaged snakes to be caught and paid for again.

"That ole rich man, he'll stick his hand down your pocket to take ya'll money but he ain't gone take a chance puttin' his finger on that snake for countin'," said one, raising smiles and nods from the others.

"He don't have to when he has fools like us to do it for him," said another.

That statement put a damp silence over the group. But when the foreman called them up they all still stretched out their legs and took to the field. O'Hanlon rose with them, the five dollars he'd earned tucked deep under the leather of his boot.

O'Hanlon kept his head down, eyes up at the brim of his hat, watching and assessing the arrival of the now close vehicles as they jounced across the open field through the brush. Within minutes he recognized the cough and clatter of old Pete's truck, but not the cream-colored touring car. He did not look up fully until they stopped ten yards away, next to an outcropping of cabbage palms. Pete's foreman, the man they called McGahee, was driving the truck and got out first, his hands in his pockets and his porkpie hat tipped back.

"Any luck, Irish?"

"Just the one so far," O'Hanlon answered, raising the bag ever so slightly.

But O'Hanlon's eyes were on the Pierce-Arrow convertible, the Florida sun flashing off its chrome and somehow melting into the glowing enamel of its polished hood. The driver got out. O'Hanlon measured him at just over six feet and 190 pounds, which he carried well. He was wearing the same shoes as the binder boys, but his were new and polished. His dark suit was equally new but made of a rough cloth, and he unbuttoned his jacket as he assessed O'Hanlon from a distance. Their eyes met and neither looked away until the passenger of the car stood up in the back seat and the driver turned to open the door.

The colonel was dressed in a white linen suit complete with a vest stretched tight across his substantial belly and a straw boater with a yellow and black ribbon. He did not move to step out, but instead stood erect, surveying the land from a height, his large head turning slowly. The sun made the cloth of his suit seem luminous and he raised a large cigar to his lips and posed as if he knew it.

"How is the drainage here, Mr. Pete?" he said as the snakeman walked round the back of his truck.

"She's pretty dry here 'cause of the ridge, Colonel. Even in the rainy season she'll drain without too much help."

The colonel did not answer and the rest could only stand and wait. The only sound was the ticking of the cooling engines. "Too damn hot for horses in October," the colonel finally said, and moved to the doorway, which his driver now opened. On the ground his height was diminished but O'Hanlon noted that the man carried his girth with considerable grace. A starched collar pinched at the folds of flesh in his neck and a carefully trimmed walrus mustache gave him a look of old English. He seemed to be studying the sandy soil with the toe of his polished boot; then he stepped forward to where O'Hanlon was standing.

"How many snakes do you see a day out here, son?"

O'Hanlon looked up into the colonel's eyes and marked their clear grayness, a pale color that reflected nothing. His fingers were thick and blunt at the ends, the flat, squared nails carefully clipped and buffed. They were not the hands of a man easily ignored.

"The number goes up, sir, when you get better at spotting them," he answered.

"I suppose that's so," the colonel said, turning to Mr. Pete. The snakeman took his hat off and scratched at his balding head. McGahee turned away, shaking his.

The colonel toed the ground again and the afternoon silence enveloped them all. The tall driver moved up next to his boss without a word and O'Hanlon could feel the heat on his shoulders. A single rivulet of sweat ran down between his shoulder blades. He watched as the colonel bent to brush a burred sticker from his spotless pants leg. O'Hanlon was waiting for the gentleman to speak when he heard the dry rattle. At first he thought it was coming from his bag but quickly realized it was unmuffled and too sharp and just to his right. The volume increased and froze all five men. O'Hanlon cut his eyes to the shade of the cabbage palm and caught the movement, the angle of the snake's strike, the sound of scaled skin on rock.

The jaws of the rattler were less than a foot from the flesh of the colonel's outstretched arm when O'Hanlon's hand snapped out in a blur and stopped it. His fist closed just behind the snake's head and twisted the body up and away, but the momentum of the animal caused its tail to snap against the colonel's pants leg. At the exact same moment an explosion sounded from O'Hanlon's left. His eyes blinked at the sound of the report but then refocused just as the snake's head disintegrated.

For a moment, all five men could only stare. O'Hanlon first

looked at the shredded gristle in his fist and the blood spattered across his arm. Then he turned to see the smoking barrel of a handgun held by the colonel's driver. The tall man's arm was still locked at the elbow, his eye still sighting down the weapon. The heavy crack of the gunshot seemed to have sucked all other sound out of the air, no bird or breeze or rustle of palm fronds. Even the heat seemed to have stopped at the level around their heads, robbing them all of a single breath.

"Gotdamn, boys!" Mr. Pete finally said, breaking the silence.

The colonel stood, looking first at the red knot in O'Hanlon's hand and then at his driver's .45. He cleared his substantial throat and placed two fingers into his right ear but could only reiterate the old snakeman's reaction.

"Goddamn, gentlemen."

O'Hanlon put the palm of his hand over the tureen of soup, guarding it each time a car or truck rolled down the city street, raising a yellow film of dust that would drift with the ocean breeze and threaten his meal. He had splurged and spent twelve cents on the large pail, the extra for the chunks of beef stirred in. It was the first time he'd eaten meat since he'd come south. It was, he guessed, a celebration of sorts. He was sharing the soup with the shoeshine boy in front of his hotel, sitting up in the customer's chair while the black boy, whose name he did not know, squatted on his box.

"Colonel Bradford just give you a job," the shoeshine said again, repeating the line, and then putting another spoonful into his mouth, savoring both the taste and the idea.

After the gunshot and the cussing, the colonel had relighted his cigar and taken a more careful measure of O'Hanlon, assessing him as one might a prospective horse purchase. He was only a couple of inches shorter than the colonel's driver and several pounds lighter, though it was difficult to gauge with the ropy muscle of his forearms and the wide, coat-hanger look of his shoulders. His dark hair and nearly black eyes only gave a suggestion of immigrant. The colonel noted O'Hanlon's hands, one still loosely gripping the neck of the burlap bag, the other, blood-spattered, holding what was left of the snake. Neither of them showed even the slightest flutter.

"I could use a handsome young man up at the club," the colonel suddenly announced, turning his big head slightly to Mr. Pete's direction.

The snakeman stepped up and looked at O'Hanlon, winking as he did.

"He's the best man I got out here, Colonel. You seen how quick he is. Be a shame to lose him."

The colonel let a grin come into his face.

"I'm sure he is, Mr. Pete. But I will pay him twenty-five dollars a week and he won't have to stand out in this godforsaken sun all day." He brought a card out from his vest pocket and handed it to O'Hanlon before turning to climb back into his car. "Be at this address day after tomorrow, son. Seven A.M. sharp."

O'Hanlon finished out the day with Mr. Pete. He was paid for three more snakes caught before twilight and his pay included fifty cents for the rattler missing its head. When Pete dropped the crew of men off on the street corner at dusk, he caught O'Hanlon's attention and called him to the opened window of the truck. He lowered his voice even though their faces were drawn near.

"You got somethin' in your eye, boy, though I cain't say what," the old man said, trying to look under the brim of O'Hanlon's hat "You best think on it hard when you're up to the colonel's, 'cause if you're 'spectin' to outsmart somebody for they money with that quick hand and brain of yours, that ain't the place to do it. Ain't nobody took nothin' off the colonel and walked away with it."

O'Hanlon tilted his head up from the shadow of its brim, exposing a bemused look on his face. He squinted into the old man's eyes, challenged by the thought that they might hold the same power to glimpse a man's soul as his own.

"Thank you, sir," he finally said, the first time in the days he'd spent with the old man that he'd spoken directly to him. "I will appreciate the advice, sir, I'm sure."

Danny O'Hanlon's father didn't need to tell his son that he would never make it as a fighter. He knew himself by the time he was seventeen that his near-photographic memory of technique and tactics, his ability at assessing an opponent and the undeniable quickness of his hands and feet were not enough. He could pound the heavy bag for hours, rattle the speed bag until it sang like a snare drum, and work endlessly in the ring with a seemingly limitless endurance. But the desire was missing. He was not like the desperate ones who melded hunger and meanness together with a physical talent to satisfy both. He had done well in amateur bouts, but when he worked the corners with his father at the professional matches he could see the hearts in men who knew and wanted nothing more than the fight. He also saw the men with money in the third row, watching intently, not guffawing or shaking their fists in elation or rage, but watching. The rich got richer without pain. They only watched, while the fighters let their hearts bleed.

"It's off limits, son," his father would say when he caught Danny staring at the fine suits and glossy women in row three. "They're born to it, lad; forget about it." And Danny O'Hanlon would turn back to watch men at war, but he would not forget. On his twentieth birthday he left New York, left this father's corner as the cut man and took the train south. Now he'd met a rich man, and seen his eyes and hands.

"I got me a cousin works the Breakers Hotel up to Palm Beach," said the shoeshine, still working his soup. "Been tryin' to get me a job in that place almost a year now. Says that's where all the rich folk are."

O'Hanlon knew of the talk. The railroad and tourist hotel Henry Flagler built on the island of Palm Beach was well known. He had overheard locker-room talk by fighters and their hangers-on who knew when certain people left the city and "the dollars went south for the winter."

Both he and the shoeshine boy had gone quiet with the thought of it, both looking out into the growing twilight, chewing softly on the bits of beef and their own image of money.

"My cousin says the colonel own the finest gamblin' joint in Florida, right there on Palm Beach island," said the shoeshine.

"I thought gambling was illegal in Florida," O'Hanlon said, though he'd seen plenty of it since his arrival.

"Hell, Irish. Ain't nothin' illegal you got that kind of money. My cousin say one a his favorite customers go to the colonel's every night but Sunday when he in the Poinciana Hotel. Get his shoes all shined every single time like a routine and give my cousin a silver dollar. Says it's lucky. You believe that, Irish?"

O'Hanlon scraped up the final spoonful of soup, the sound of metal on metal making a soft, screeching sound.

"How would I know about lucky?"

"What you mean, 'How would you know'? You got you a job wit' the colonel, Irish! You done got you some lucky."

That night O'Hanlon swam in the ocean again. He took a bus to A1A and made his way down to the beach well past dark. It was a windless night and the small breakers made only a hissing sound when they washed up and for a moment made a new dark border in the sand. He stripped to his shorts and eased himself step by step into the black water up to his shoulders and then turned to mark a beachfront light as a bearing. The current was pulling softly north and he began stroking straight out, a metronome in his head, a beat built with routine. Every three hundred strokes he would stop and turn, treading water long enough to find the high beach light and then adjust his course. His muscles were tight in the first two sets but then loosened with the action. The taste of salt water in his mouth again reminded him of summers on Coney Island, his father frantic with his six-year-old son's ludicrous ability to swim in the Atlantic without a single lesson or practice. After ten three-hundred-stroke turns, the light had disappeared in the distance, and O'Hanlon kept on. He had heard once from a lifeguard on Coney Island that no man would swim too far out in the ocean to get back, simply because he would have no choice but to get back. At the twenty-first turn O'Hanlon stopped swimming and flipped over on his back, his lungs aching, his eyes looking up at a black bowl of stars. There was nothing to hear but the beat of his heart in his ears. Nothing to feel but the gentle movement of the swells, raising him first, only inches, and then settling him back. He never thought of what was below the surface. Never let his imagination hold sharks or hungry bluefish eyeing his floating white flesh. Out here he could just drift and focus and plan. With his ears in the water he could track out a plan in the stars and let it roll or start it all over again until he could see it. Then, when the vision was clear, he would turn to land and begin stroking again, watching for the light, timing his endurance until he would finally stagger back up the sand, confident that he could make it again.

The eastern sky was still dusky gray when the train slowed for the West Palm Beach station. O'Hanlon timed an oncoming patch of dark brush and jumped. He let his knees take the shock of the landing and rolled onto one shoulder, his arms wrapped around the waterproof canvas bag stuffed with all his possessions.

He waited in the groundcover, the smell of cinder and dry grass in his nose. No shouts or whistles, only the same clack of metal and shiver of hinged wood that had drowned out his noise when he'd jumped the freight car after midnight back in Miami. In time he gained his feet and moved away toward the streets, brushing the dirt and sticker seeds from his pants legs. At first he used the alleys and the walls of wooden storage shacks and warehouses for cover until he was several blocks to the east. Only then did he step out into the wide expanse of a city street and try to take his bearings.

The shoeshine had given him directions, told him to look for the tall, white-stucco building rising above town and use it as a landmark. From that tower the bridge across the lake would be due east. It was the shoeshine who also convinced O'Hanlon to jump the night train north.

"Ya'll still gonna have some walkin' to do. Best get there early, Irish. Ya'll don't want ta keep the Colonel waitin'."

O'Hanlon kept moving east toward a lightening sky. The street was lined with small cottages set back off the roadway, the lean of their rooflines their only distinction. An occasional lantern light could be seen coming through a window. Working people, up in the predawn to start their day. Farther on, the working-class houses were replaced by small shop fronts and automobile repair bays, and then the paved streets of a true business section began. A milk delivery truck passed him. A man dressed in a suit coat walked a dog. Along the way O'Hanlon noted the same interruption in construction that he'd seen in Miami. Lots with foundations already set, but unfinished walls left ragged. Piles of fill dirt were sprouting weeds from sitting too long undisturbed. They were projects started and then abruptly stopped by worried investors. By the time he reached the lakefront, the top five floors of the ten-story building were glowing in the early rays of sunrise. It was the only thing that seemed beyond pedestrian on this side of the lake. But on the opposite shore, even in the early shadows, O'Hanlon could see Henry Flagler's Royal Poinciana Hotel, stretched out in white like some languorous, highly bred woman. Even from here one could see the distinction. Even from here one knew where the clean ocean breezes stopped first. On the island was where the untroubled money was.

The tender at the western end of the bridge took a full minute to judge O'Hanlon before allowing him to pass, the man's rheumy eyes jumping from the colonel's card to O'Hanlon's face, worn clothes and the bag he carried.

"Working for the colonel, eh?"

O'Hanlon nodded. The tender looked once more at the bag and then tipped his head to the east.

"Just north of the hotel, son. And nowhere else."

O'Hanlon retrieved the card and started his walk, counting his steps over the length of the span, looking down into the clear water, judging its depth and the pull of its currents.

By the time he reached the eastern end the sun was streaming through the fronds of the few planted palm trees and his shirt was pasted to his back with an early sweat.

Carpets of thick-leafed grass and a military-like line of royal palms banked the lane that led past the hotel to the colonel's. O'Hanlon could see glimpses of the new mansions set back off the roadway and done in the Mediterranean revival style of white-stucco arches and terra-cotta tiles.

The colonel's was more modest. It was a white-framed, two-story affair on the lakefront with striped canvas overhangs and a pyramid-shaped shingled roof at the entrance. Several louvered cupolas were situated on the shingled roof to vent the heat. On the street side a five-foot-tall cement wall guarded the front of the club. There was no movement at the front so O'Hanlon followed the sound of a truck engine and voices around to a side alley and approached a group of three men unloading cases of fresh produce and cartons of dry goods. He was about to ask for the colonel when the driver's voice sounded from a porch above.

"Well, if it isn't snake boy come to work an honest day."

O'Hanlon looked up to see the man he would now always consider "the gunman" in his internal file of new faces and then back to the workers. Their heads had snapped up at the sound of the voice but then quickly turned back to their lifting and carrying once they knew it was not their duty to respond.

"I came for the colonel," O'Hanlon said.

"No. You came to work, snake boy. So quit standing around and work," the gunman said. "Next wagon's comin' round the corner, boys. Let's get to it."

O'Hanlon dropped his bag near the picket fence and joined the brigade line, passing food cartons and cases of illegal liquor hand to hand in through the kitchen door. No one said a word to him. The occasional grunts and exhalations of the men remained the only sound as the sun rose, the alley warmed, and the next truck pulled in.

O'Hanlon spent his first three days working the trucks, digging out rooted palms on the property and replanting tropical ferns. At night he would walk back over the bridge where he'd found a cheap room with the other workers. After a week he'd figured out that the driver, who'd become Mr. Brasher, was also the security captain of sorts. The four quiet men who reported to the house after dinnertime dressed in plain black suits gave deferential nods to the workers and then disappeared into the building, only to be seen later, walking the upstairs porches or peering from high railings. Another man stayed close to Brasher at all times, agreeing when spoken to, occasionally scratching down an instruction on a small pad.

One morning O'Hanlon and the work crew were breaking up a coral outcrop to run a waterline to the main house when a slab of rock slipped from its lashings and fell from the back of a truck. The sharp coral sliced through the lower leg of an older worker called Mauricio, crushing his ankle. His scream brought Brasher and his assistant running from the house. When the group lifted away the boulder, Mauricio's leather boot lay at a sickening right angle to his leg. While the others simply stared, O'Hanlon quickly went to work, carefully ripping away the man's blood-soaked trouser. The glisten of wet, white bone shown through the cleaved and reddening meat of muscle. Brasher's assistant, a man called Dimmett, drew a sharp breath and even Brasher took a slight step back. O'Hanlon checked their reactions and then used his left hand to squeeze shut the fleshy wound, and as blood flowed between his fingers he called out for supplies.

"Towels! Clean towels!" he yelled at no one in particular, but it was one of his crew that went running.

"Do you have a first-aid kit?" he said, this time looking up to Brasher, who seemed to be confused by the question. "Some bandages? Some iodine? You don't want this getting infected, boss. It's way too deep for that."

Brasher shook his head, then looked up to the porch where one of his men was standing, the metal barrel of a rifle in his hands, watching the commotion.

"In the casino!" Brasher called up to him. "Get that first-aid pouch from behind the coat-check counter." The man hurried off. The laborer scrambled back with an armload of kitchen towels and O'Hanlon pressed one flat to the wound and wrapped it with another.

"I need your belt, boss," O'Hanlon said. Brasher's hand went to his buckle but stopped. He looked at Dimmett and flicked a finger. The other security man pulled his belt off and had to grab at the Colt revolver that he carried in a holster at the small of his back. O'Hanlon watched the man fumble with the weapon and then took the belt and tied it tight around the reddening wrap of towels. He looked into Mauricio's eyes and watched the pupils dilate and roll with oncoming shock.

"Let's get him over to the doc's at the hotel," O'Hanlon said, looking up at Brasher, who hesitated. "Come on!" he said. "If that artery in his calf is split, he's going to lose a lot of blood."

Brasher looked down again at the towels.

"You'll have to take him over the bridge. There's a doctor's right on Clematis by the drugstore."

"Brasher, the doc from the hotel was here in five minutes last night when that lady fainted inside," O'Hanlon said. "Hell, it'll take us near thirty to bounce him over to West Palm."

The other laborers didn't look up to see Brasher's face and instead moved to lay the rest of the towels as a mat in the bed of the truck.

"Then you better get moving, snake boy," Brasher said, and motioned the other security man to help gather up Mauricio. "The help don't get treated at the hotel."

O'Hanlon held Brasher's eyes longer than he wanted to, then moved to Mauricio's legs while the others hooked under his arms. Once they had him settled in the truck Dimmett climbed in to drive and O'Hanlon watched through the back window as the security man carelessly put the handgun on the seat beside him.

It was after five when they returned from the mainland. Brasher was waiting.

"Colonel wants you out front, parking cars," he said, handing

O'Hanlon a suit complete with new shoes. "You do know how to drive?"

"Not a problem," O'Hanlon said.

"Good. Get cleaned up and get something to eat and be out on the front porch at seven."

Throughout the night he politely greeted the colonel's guests, ladies in fine summer fashions, men in dark, conservative suits. The autos were all expensive sedans and touring cars. They all smelled of fine perfume and hair tonic. O'Hanlon only ground the gears of one, for which he received a smirk from the other valets.

When the evening was through, the colonel, with Brasher two steps behind, escorted the last of the guests to the street. O'Hanlon was sent scurrying for the car and returned with the Collingsworths' Chrysler B70. The colonel held the passenger door for the lady and O'Hanlon the driver's side for Mr. Collingsworth. When the car rumbled off, the colonel, dressed in a tuxedo, waited until O'Hanlon gained the sidewalk before speaking.

"I understand you may have saved a man's leg today Mr., uh —"

"O'Hanlon, sir. Danny O'Hanlon."

"Irish?"

"Yes, sir."

"From New York City?"

"Chicago," O'Hanlon lied, cutting his eyes to Brasher.

"You're too young to have been in the war. Where did you learn your medical skills?"

"My father, sir. I was a corner man with my father in the fight game," O'Hanlon said, going back to the truth.

"Fight game," said the colonel, the taste of disapproval on his voice. He took a draw from his Cuban cigar. "A nasty business."

O'Hanlon said nothing. Then the colonel extended his arm and slipped a ten-dollar bill into his hand. He stared at the bill a moment, unsure what the philanthropy might cost him.

"Thank you, sir."

"You earned it, lad. Report here for the rest of the week. Mr. Brasher will look after you."

The colonel took another deep draw of smoke and looked up through the palm fronds at a waxing moon.

"Another beautiful night in paradise," he said, perhaps to himself. "But duty calls. Let us do the count and see how much they left behind tonight."

O'Hanlon stood unmoving but caught Brasher's final look as he held the door for the colonel and then shut it. The distinct snap of a metal lock sounded. Only then did he leave, heading south to the bridge and then walking its span, watching the water and marking the lights of the West Palm high-rise in the distance.

It was another week before he saw the inside of the casino itself. An arriving guest had bashed into the rear bumper of another guest's automobile. The valet behind the wheel of the damaged car said he did not recall the name of the owner. O'Hanlon's perfect memory had "Mr. Reed" instantly on his tongue and Brasher sent him inside to give the news to the man. Inside he approached a man he knew to be the floor manager.

Reed was pointed out, standing at one of the English hazard tables. The room was tastefully decorated; brocaded sofas, tall-stemmed lamps and polished wood. Around the roulette, faro, and other gaming tables the men stood exchanging polite conversation. They seemed to be only mildly distracted by the play of the cards or the spin of the wheel, and when they became too animated, their wives' faces turned chilly with reproach. O'Hanlon had not expected the kind of raucous backslapping and cussing he'd been a part of in locker-room poker games, but the quiet, controlled atmosphere unsettled him at first. His discomfort subsided as he moved through the room, working his way to the side of Mr. Reed, and he realized that no one seemed to notice him, or if they did, they were trying mightily to ignore his presence. When he got to Reed's elbow he stood for a few extra seconds, watching the route of money moving from tables to drawers. He scanned the room for office doors or the presence of the quiet security men he knew were somewhere on duty. Then he excused himself and sought Reed's attention. The man turned to him and listened to the message and then dismissed O'Hanlon with a wave of limp fingers as if an errant mosquito had pestered him. "Park it, boy. We'll see to it tomorrow."

O'Hanlon kept his hands clasped behind his back, nodded, and in a low voice said, "She's a beauty, sir. We're very sorry."

Reed looked at him again, this time with more interest. "And she will be again, son. With a bit of luck," he said, turning back to his game.

O'Hanlon excused himself and walked away, again taking in the layout, the length of hallways, and the single staircase in view. "Bit of luck," he whispered to himself.

He picked a particularly busy Friday night, one with a clear sky and no moon. An easy southeasterly breeze was blowing in from the Atlantic. He'd counted and timed the retiring guests so that the final car was his to fetch. The others were gone when he returned with the car and the front of the club went quiet as it pulled away. O'Hanlon waited several minutes at the wall, giving the colonel and Brasher time to gather the money from the drawers and retire to the colonel's office to count it. While he waited he picked the lock on the front door and then stepped back out to see Dimmett making his final rounds on the balcony. The security man would be in the hallway in between thirty and thirty-five seconds at O'Hanlon's count, like every night before. Under the lamplight O'Hanlon extracted a flask and poured a pint of pig's blood that he'd bottled from a West Palm butcher shop onto his pants leg from the thigh down, smeared the thick red fluid with his hands, and added a smear across his cheek.

At his count of twenty-eight he staggered into the hallway and cut his eyes to the top of the stairs where Dimmett's footsteps were just falling. He groaned and stumbled into the bottom two risers and heard the security man catch his breath and say, "Christ!"

"Hit! By the B70," O'Hanlon spat out between his teeth, clutching his leg with both hands, the blood oozing between his fingers. Dimmett bent and started to reach down but recoiled at the sight and froze.

"Your belt, man! It's a cut artery," O'Hanlon hissed through his teeth, urgent but not too loud. Dimmett was panicky. He undid his buckle, stripped the belt out, and ignored the sound of the revolver as it tumbled onto the wooden step behind him. When he bent forward to wrap the belt around the leg, O'Hanlon arched back, picked up the Colt, and came down hard on the back of Dimmett's skull with the butt. He cradled the unconscious body and waited a full minute, listening. The club remained silent. His first assessment? True to form.

Gaining his feet, O'Hanlon put the Colt in his waistband at the small of his back and then slung Dimmett's arm over his shoulder and hefted him. He now knew the way down the hall to the colonel's office. With the security man propped up against the doorframe, he banged the oak door with the heel of his hand, hoping to move the people inside but not arouse others still in the club. He heard footsteps and then Brasher's voice.

"Who is it?"

"It's Dimmett," said O'Hanlon. "He's been hit by a car."

"O'Hanlon? You know the damn rules, O'Hanlon. Nobody's allowed in here after closing."

"Christ, Brasher! The man's hurt bad. It was a customer who hit him for Christ's sake!"

O'Hanlon heard the colonel's muffled baritone voice, too soft to make out the words. A metal lock snapped open from the inside. Brasher opened the door a few inches and looked squarely into Dimmett's slack face and then at O'Hanlon's blood-smeared cheek. "The hell?" Brasher said, letting the door swing wider.

O'Hanlon timed the movement, like a good fighter using his opponent's own body momentum to set him up. When Brasher stepped back, O'Hanlon pushed Dimmett's dead weight up and into Brasher's left hand, which was already holding the .45. Brasher hooked his gun arm under the falling man to support him and O'Hanlon instantly snapped down on the barrel of the gun, twisting it up against the falling weight of Dimmet's body. A muffled snap sounded as Brasher's trigger finger broke at the knuckle and by the time his knee hit the floor O'Hanlon had the .45 pointed at his face while the Colt in his other hand was trained across the room on the colonel's chest. Both of the men froze.

"Well, goddamn, gentlemen," O'Hanlon said quietly. "This — is a robbery."

With the .45 at the colonel's temple, it took only five minutes for Brasher to tie both his employer and Dimmett with lengths of wet rawhide O'Hanlon had brought with him in his waterproof bag. O'Hanlon only let the colonel call him a common thief and a fool once before gagging the old man with a satin handkerchief from his own suit pocket. There was no comment from Brasher, only a smoldering, animal stare as O'Hanlon finally lashed him to a fine and sturdy straight-backed chair.

The office safe behind the colonel's desk had not yet been opened, or had perhaps been slammed shut at the initial knock on the door. But O'Hanlon was not a greedy man. The three hundred thousand dollars in cash still in partially counted stacks on the colonel's desk was enough. He pushed the bills into his waterproof bag and closed it.

"Nobody steals from the colonel and gets away with it. We'll hunt you down, snake boy," Brasher finally said.

O'Hanlon shook his head, gagged Brasher, and then moved to the door and listened for any movement out in the hall.

"Tough to find much cooperation with the law when you explain that the stolen cash came from an illegal gambling operation?" he said, leaving the rhetorical question in the air. "Snake eyes, Brasher. It's all a gamble."

O'Hanlon could hear the scrape of the chair the second he closed the door. He knew the route through the club to the back and marched out, moving fast, but not running. At the open kitchen door he saw the chef, carving at something on the counter, and two of the security men on the other side, waiting for the food. He ducked by without being seen, crossed the slate patio outside, and slipped into the dense wall of palm fronds and sea grape leaves to the rear gate. Sharp voices and a scuffling of feet sounded as he latched the door and headed into a neighbor's yard. Floodlights came on behind him and he moved into the alley. He did not look back, did not panic, and never stopped moving east until he felt water.

He could feel the body of the swells below him, rising and falling, working against him, but not hard enough. He kept a rhythm with his feet, flutter kicking at a pace he could keep forever. On the darkened beach, O'Hanlon had filled two bicycle tires and positioned them inside the bag and next to the money. He tucked his clothes inside, then sealed the duffel shut and pushed off onto the sea. That was the beauty of the island, the security that the rich felt knowing they were on an island with only one entrance across the bridge. The better to keep the riffraff away. O'Hanlon knew Brasher would shut that route first. He knew he'd work the lake shorelines. Maybe they would get to the beach, figure out the ocean escape eventually. But the flow from the southeast would keep him moving up the coast. He could make three or four miles by sunup.

When he finished his third three-hundred-stroke turn he rolled over and hooked his arms over the bag. His muscles were warm from the work. The taste of salt water was in his mouth again and he watched the lights of the Breakers Hotel on the beach disappear in the distance. There was nothing to hear but the beat of his heart in his ears. Nothing to feel but the gentle movement of the swells, raising him first, only inches, and then settling him back. In the stars he tracked a plan, and when the vision was clear, he would turn to land and begin stroking. No man goes out too far to make it back, simply because he has no other choice.

STEPHEN KING

Harvey's Dream

FROM *The New Yorker*

JANET TURNS FROM THE SINK and, boom, all at once her husband of nearly thirty years is sitting at the kitchen table in a white T-
shirt and a pair of Big Dog boxers, watching her.

More and more often she has found this weekday commodore of
Wall Street in just this place and dressed in just this fashion come
Saturday morning: slumped at the shoulder and blank in the eye, a
white scruff showing on his cheeks, man-tits sagging out the front
of his T, hair standing up in back like Alfalfa of the Little Rascals
grown old and stupid. Janet and her friend Hannah have frightened each other lately (like little girls telling ghost stories during a
sleepover) by swapping Alzheimer's tales: who can no longer recognize his wife, who can no longer remember the names of her
children.

But she doesn't really believe these silent Saturday-morning appearances have anything to do with early-onset Alzheimer's; on any
given weekday morning Harvey Stevens is ready and raring to go by
six-forty-five, a man of sixty who looks fifty (well, fifty-four) in either
of his best suits, and who can still cut a trade, buy on margin, or sell
short with the best of them.

No, she thinks, this is merely practicing to be old, and she hates
it. She's afraid that when he retires it will be this way every morning, at least until she gives him a glass of orange juice and asks him
(with an increasing impatience she won't be able to help) if he
wants cereal or just toast. She's afraid she'll turn from whatever
she's doing and see him sitting there in a bar of far too brilliant
morning sun, Harvey in the morning, Harvey in his T-shirt and his

boxer shorts, legs spread apart so she can view the meager bulge of his basket (should she care to) and see the yellow calluses on his great toes, which always make her think of Wallace Stevens having on about the Emperor of Ice Cream. Sitting there silent and dopily contemplative instead of ready and raring, psyching himself up for the day. God, she hopes she's wrong. It makes life seem so thin, so stupid somehow. She can't help wondering if this is what they fought through for, raised and married off their three girls for, got past his inevitable middle-aged affair for, worked for, and sometimes (let's face it) grabbed for. If this is where you come out of the deep dark woods, Janet thinks, this . . . this parking lot . . . then why does anyone do it?

But the answer is easy. Because you didn't know. You discarded most of the lies along the way but held on to the one that said life *mattered*. You kept a scrapbook devoted to the girls, and in it they were still young and still interesting in their possibilities: Trisha, the eldest, wearing a top hat and waving a tinfoil wand over Tim, the cocker spaniel; Jenna, frozen in mid-jump halfway through the lawn sprinkler, her taste for dope, credit cards, and older men still far over the horizon; Stephanie, the youngest, at the county spelling bee, where "cantaloupe" turned out to be her Waterloo. Somewhere in most of these pictures (usually in the background) were Janet and the man she had married, always smiling, as if it were against the law to do anything else.

Then one day you made the mistake of looking over your shoulder and discovered that the girls were grown and that the man you had struggled to stay married to was sitting with his legs apart, his fish-white legs, staring into a bar of sun, and by God maybe he looked fifty-four in either of his best suits, but sitting there at the kitchen table like that he looked seventy. Hell, seventy-five. He looked like what the goons on *The Sopranos* called a mope.

She turns back to the sink and sneezes delicately, once, twice, a third time.

"How are they this morning?" he asks, meaning her sinuses, meaning her allergies. The answer is not very good, but, like a surprising number of bad things, her summer allergies have their sunny side. She no longer has to sleep with him and fight for her share of the covers in the middle of the night; no longer has to listen to the occasional muffled fart as Harvey soldiers ever deeper into sleep. Most nights during the summer she gets six, even seven hours, and that's more than enough. When fall comes and he moves back in from the guest room, it will drop to four, and much of that will be troubled.

One year, she knows, he won't move back in. And although she doesn't tell him so — it would hurt his feelings, and she still doesn't like to hurt his feelings; this is what now passes for love between them, at least going from her direction to his — she will be glad.

She sighs and reaches into the pot of water in the sink. Gropes around in it. "Not so bad," she says.

And then, just when she is thinking (and not for the first time) about how this life holds no more surprises, no unplumbed marital depths, he says in a strangely casual voice, "It's a good thing you weren't sleeping with me last night, Jax. I had a bad dream. I actually screamed myself awake."

She's startled. How long has it been since he called her Jax instead of Janet or Jan? The last is a nickname she secretly hates. It makes her think of that syrupy-sweet actress on *Lassie* when she was a kid, the little boy (Timmy, his name was Timmy) always fell down a well or got bitten by a snake or trapped under a rock, and what kind of parents put a kid's life in the hands of a fucking collie?

She turns to him again, forgetting the pot with the last egg still in it, the water now long enough off the boil to be lukewarm. He had a bad dream? Harvey? She tries to remember when Harvey has mentioned having had any kind of dream and has no luck. All that comes is a vague memory of their courtship days, Harvey saying something like "I dream of you," she herself young enough to think it sweet instead of lame.

"You what?"

"Screamed myself awake," he says. "Did you not hear me?"

"No." Still looking at him. Wondering if he's kidding her. If it's some kind of bizarre morning joke. But Harvey is not a joking man. His idea of humor is telling anecdotes at dinner about his Army days. She has heard all of them at least a hundred times.

"I was screaming words, but I wasn't really able to say them. It was like . . . I don't know . . . I couldn't close my mouth around them. I sounded like I'd had a stroke. And my voice was lower. Not like my own voice at all." He pauses. "I heard myself, and made myself stop.

But I was shaking all over, and I had to turn on the light for a little while. I tried to pee, and I couldn't. These days it seems like I can always pee — a little, anyway — but not this morning at two-forty-seven." He pauses, sitting there in his bar of sun. She can see dust motes dancing in it. They seem to give him a halo.

"What was your dream?" she asks, and here is an odd thing: For the first time in maybe five years, since they stayed up until midnight discussing whether to hold the Motorola stock or sell it (they wound up selling), she's interested in something he has to say.

"I don't know if I want to tell you," he says, sounding uncharacteristically shy. He turns, picks up the pepper mill, and begins to toss it from hand to hand.

"They say if you tell your dreams they won't come true," she says to him, and here is Odd Thing No. 2: all at once Harvey looks there, in a way he hasn't looked to her in years. Even his shadow on the wall above the toaster oven looks somehow more there. She thinks, He looks as though he matters, and why should that be? Why, when I was just thinking that life is thin, should it seem thick? This is a summer morning in late June. We are in Connecticut. When June comes we are always in Connecticut. Soon one of us will get the newspaper, which will be divided into three parts, like Gaul.

"Do they say so?" He considers the idea, eyebrows raised (she needs to pluck them again, they are getting that wild look, and he never knows), tossing the pepper mill from hand to hand. She would like to tell him to stop doing that, it's making her nervous (like the exclamatory blackness of his shadow on the wall, like her very beating heart, which has suddenly begun to accelerate its rhythm for no reason at all), but she doesn't want to distract him from whatever is going on in his Saturday-morning head. And then he puts the pepper mill down anyway, which should be all right but somehow isn't, because it has its own shadow — it runs out long on the table like the shadow of an oversized chess piece, even the toast crumbs lying there have shadows, and she has no idea why that should frighten her but it does. She thinks of the Cheshire Cat telling Alice, "We're all mad here," and suddenly she doesn't want to hear Harvey's stupid dream, the one from which he awakened himself screaming and sounding like a man who has had a stroke. Suddenly she doesn't want life to be anything but thin. Thin is okay, thin is good, just look at the actresses in the movies if you doubt it.

Nothing must announce itself, she thinks feverishly. Yes, fever-ishly; it's as if she's having a hot flash, although she could have sworn all that nonsense ended two or three years ago. Nothing must announce itself, it's Saturday morning and nothing must an-nounce itself.

She opens her mouth to tell him she got it backward, what they really say is that if you tell your dreams they will come true, but it's too late, he's already talking, and it occurs to her that this is her punishment for dismissing life as thin. Life is actually like a Jethro Tull song, thick as a brick, how could she have ever thought other-wise?

"I dreamed it was morning and I came down to the kitchen," he says. "Saturday morning, just like this, only you weren't up yet."

"I'm always up before you on Saturday morning," she says.

"I know, but this was a dream," he says patiently, and she can see the white hairs on the insides of his thighs, where the muscles are wasted and starved. Once he played tennis, but those days are done. She thinks, with a viciousness that is entirely unlike her, You will have a heart attack, white man, that's what will finish you, and maybe they'll discuss giving you an obit in the *Times,* but if a B-movie actress from the fifties died that day, or a semi-famous balle-rina from the forties, you won't even get that.

"But it was like this," he says. "I mean, the sun was shining in." He raises a hand and stirs the dust motes into lively life around his head and she wants to scream at him not to do that, not to disturb the universe like that.

"I could see my shadow on the floor and it never looked so bright or so thick." He pauses, then smiles, and she sees how cracked his lips are. "Bright's a funny word to use for a shadow, isn't it? Thick, too."

"Harvey —"

"I crossed to the window," he says, "and I looked out, and I saw there was a dent in the side of the Friedmans' Volvo, and I knew — somehow — that Frank had been out drinking and that the dent happened coming home."

She suddenly feels that she will faint. She saw the dent in the side of Frank Friedman's Volvo herself, when she went to the door to see if the newspaper had come (it hadn't), and she thought the same thing, that Frank had been out at the Gourd and scraped something in the parking lot. How does the other guy look? had been her exact thought.

The idea that Harvey has also seen this comes to her, that he is goofing with her for some strange reason of his own. Certainly it's possible; the guest room where he sleeps on summer nights has an angle on the street. Only Harvey isn't that sort of man. "Goofing" is not Harvey Stevens's "thing."

There is sweat on her cheeks and brow and neck, she can feel it, and her heart is beating faster than ever. There really is a sense of something looming, and why should this be happening now? Now, when the world is quiet, when prospects are tranquil? If I asked for this, I'm sorry, she thinks . . . or maybe she's actually praying. Take it back, please take it back.

"I went to the refrigerator," Harvey is saying, "and I looked inside, and I saw a plate of devilled eggs with a piece of Saran wrap over them. I was delighted — I wanted lunch at seven in the morning!"

He laughs. Janet — Jax that was — looks down into the pot sitting in the sink. At the one hard-boiled egg left in it. The others have been shelled and neatly sliced in two, the yolks scooped out. They are in a bowl beside the drying rack. Beside the bowl is the jar of mayonnaise. She has been planning to serve the devilled eggs for lunch, along with a green salad.

"I don't want to hear the rest," she says, but in a voice so low she can barely hear it herself. Once she was in the Dramatics Club and now she can't even project across the kitchen. The muscles in her chest feel all loose, the way Harvey's legs would if he tried to play tennis.

"I thought I would have just one," Harvey says, "and then I thought, No, if I do that she'll yell at me. And then the phone rang. I dashed for it because I didn't want it to wake you up, and here comes the scary part. Do you want to hear the scary part?"

No, she thinks from her place by the sink. I don't want to hear the scary part. But at the same time she does want to hear the scary part, everyone wants to hear the scary part, we're all mad here, and her mother really did say that if you told your dreams they wouldn't come true, which meant you were supposed to tell the nightmares and save the good ones for yourself, hide them like a tooth under the pillow. They have three girls. One of them lives just down the road, Jenna the gay divorcée, same name as one of the Bush twins, and doesn't Jenna hate that; these days she insists that people call her Jen. Three girls, which meant a lot of teeth under a lot of pillows, a lot of worries about strangers in cars offering rides and candy, which had meant a lot of precautions, and oh how she hopes her mother was right, that telling a bad dream is like putting a stake in a vampire's heart.

"I picked up the phone," Harvey says, "and it was Trisha." Trisha is their oldest daughter, who idolized Houdini and Blackstone before discovering boys. "She only said one word at first, just 'Dad,' but I knew it was Trisha. You know how you always know?"

Yes. She knows how you always know. How you always know your own, from the very first word, at least until they grow up and become someone else's.

"I said, 'Hi, Trish, why you calling so early, hon? Your mom's still in the sack.' And at first there was no answer. I thought we'd been cut off, and then I heard these whispering whimpering sounds. Not words but half-words. Like she was trying to talk but hardly anything could come out because she wasn't able to muster any strength or get her breath. And that was when I started being afraid."

Well, then, he's pretty slow, isn't he? Because Janet — who was Jax at Sarah Lawrence, Jax in the Dramatics Club, Jax the truly excellent French-kisser, Jax who smoked Gitanes and affected enjoyment of tequila shooters — Janet has been scared for quite some time now, was scared even before Harvey mentioned the dent in the side of Frank Friedman's Volvo. And thinking of that makes her think of the phone conversation she had with her friend Hannah not even a week ago, the one that eventually progressed to Alzheimer's ghost stories. Hannah in the city, Janet curled up on the window seat in the living room and looking out at their one-acre share of Westport, at all the beautiful growing things that make her sneeze and water at the eyes, and before the conversation turned to Alzheimer's they had discussed first Lucy Friedman and then Frank, and which one of them had said it? Which one of them had said, "If he doesn't do something about his drinking and driving, he's eventually going to kill somebody"?

"And then Trish said what sounded like 'lees' or 'least,' but in the dream I knew she was . . . eliding? . . . is that the word? Eliding the first syllable, and that what she was really saying was 'police.' I asked her what about the police, what was she trying to say about the police, and I sat down. Right there." He points to the chair in what they call the telephone nook. "There was some more silence, then a few more of those half-words, those whispered half-words. She was making me so mad doing that, I thought, Drama queen, same as it ever was, but then she said, 'number,' just as clear as a bell. And I knew — the way I knew she was trying to say 'police' — that she was trying to tell me the police had called her because they didn't have our number."

Janet nods numbly. They decided to unlist their number two years ago because reporters kept calling Harvey about the Enron mess. Usually at dinnertime. Not because he'd had anything to do with Enron per se but because those big energy companies were sort of a specialty of his. He'd even served on a presidential commission a few years earlier, when Clinton had been the big kahuna and the world had been (in her humble opinion, at least) a slightly better, slightly safer place. And while there were a lot of things about Harvey she no longer liked, one thing she knew perfectly well was that he had more integrity in his little finger than all those Enron sleazebags put together. She might sometimes be bored by integrity, but she knows what it is.

But don't the police have a way of getting unlisted numbers? Well, maybe not if they're in a hurry to find something out or tell somebody something. Plus, dreams don't have to be logical, do they? Dreams are poems from the subconscious.

And now, because she can no longer bear to stand still, she goes to the kitchen door and looks out into the bright June day, looks out at Sewing Lane, which is their little version of what she supposes is the American dream. How quiet this morning lies, with a trillion drops of dew still sparkling on the grass! And still her heart hammers in her chest and the sweat rolls down her face and she wants to tell him he must stop, he must not tell this dream, this terrible dream. She must remind him that Jenna lives right down the road — Jen, that is, Jen who works at the Video Stop in the village and spends all too many weekend nights drinking at the Gourd with the likes of Frank Friedman, who is old enough to be her father. Which is undoubtedly part of the attraction.

"All these whispered little half-words," Harvey is saying, "and she would not speak up. Then I heard 'killed,' and I knew that one of the girls was dead. I just knew it. Not Trisha, because it was Trisha on the phone, but either Jenna or Stephanie. And I was so scared. I actually sat there wondering which one I wanted it to be, like Sophie's fucking Choice. I started to shout at her. 'Tell me which one! Tell me which one! For God's sake, Trish, tell me which one!' Only then the real world started to bleed through . . . always assuming there is such a thing. . . ."

Harvey utters a little laugh, and in the bright morning light Janet sees there is a red stain in the middle of the dent on the side of Frank Friedman's Volvo, and in the middle of the stain is a dark smutch that might be dirt or even hair. She can see Frank pulling up crooked to the curb at two in the morning, too drunk even to try the driveway, let alone the garage — strait is the gate, and all that. She can see him stumbling to the house with his head down, breathing hard through his nose. Viva ze bool.

"By then I knew I was in bed, but I could hear this low voice that didn't sound like mine at all, it sounded like some stranger's voice, and it couldn't put corners on any of the words it was saying. 'Ell-ee itch-un, ell-ee itch-un,' that's what it sounded like. 'Ell-ee itch-un, Ish!'"

Tell me which one. Tell me which one, Trish.

Harvey falls silent, thinking. Considering. The dust motes dance around his face. The sun makes his T-shirt almost too dazzling to look at; it is a T-shirt from a laundry-detergent ad.

"I lay there waiting for you to run in and see what was wrong," he finally says. "I lay there all over goosebumps, and trembling, telling myself it was just a dream, the way you do, of course, but also thinking how real it was. How marvelous, in a horrible way."

He stops again, thinking how to say what comes next, unaware that his wife is no longer listening to him. Jax-that-was is now employing all her mind, all her considerable powers of thought, to make herself believe that what she is seeing is not blood but just the Volvo's undercoating where the paint has been scraped away. "Undercoating" is a word her subconscious has been more than eager to cast up.

"It's amazing, isn't it, how deep imagination goes?" he says finally. "A dream like that is how a poet — one of the really great ones — must see his poem. Every detail so clear and so bright."

He falls silent and the kitchen belongs to the sun and the dancing motes; outside, the world is on hold. Janet looks at the Volvo across the street; it seems to pulse in her eyes, thick as a brick. When the phone rings, she would scream if she could draw breath, cover her ears if she could lift her hands. She hears Harvey get up and cross to the nook as it rings again, and then a third time.

It is a wrong number, she thinks. It has to be, because if you tell your dreams they don't come true.

Harvey says, "Hello?"

MICHAEL KNIGHT

Smash and Grab

FROM *StoryQuarterly*

AT THE LAST HOUSE ON THE LEFT, the one with no security system signs staked on the lawn, no dog in the backyard, Cash-dollar elbowed out a pane of glass in the kitchen door and reached through to unlock it from the inside. Though he was 99 percent certain that the house was empty — he'd watched the owners leave himself — he paused a moment just across the threshold, listened carefully, heard nothing. Satisfied, he padded through an archway into the dining room where he found a chest of silverware and emptied its contents into the pillowcase he'd brought. He was headed down the hall, looking for the master bedroom, hoping that, in the rush to make some New Year's Eve soiree, the lady of the house had left her jewelry in plain sight, when he saw a flash of white and his head snapped back on his neck, the bones in his face suddenly aflame. He wobbled, dropped to his knees. Then a girlish grunt and another burst of pain and all he knew was darkness.

He came to with his wrists and ankles bound with duct tape to the arms and legs of a ladderback chair. His cheeks throbbed. His nose felt huge with ache. Opposite him, in an identical chair, a teenage girl was blowing lightly on the fingers of her left hand. There was a porcelain toilet tank lid, flecked with blood, across her lap. On it was arrayed a pair of cuticle scissors, a bottle of clear pol-ish, cotton balls, and a nail file. The girl glanced up at him now and he would have sworn she was pleased to find him awake.

"How's your face?" she said.

She was long-limbed, lean but not skinny, wearing a sweatshirt with the words *Saint Bridget's Volleyball* across the front in pastel plaids. Her hair was pulled into pigtails. She wore flannel boxers and pink wool socks.

"It hurts like hell." His nostrils were plugged with blood, his voice buzzing like bad wiring in his head.

The girl did a sympathetic wince.

"I didn't think anyone was home," he said.

"I guess you cased the house?" she said. "Is that the word — cased?"

Cashdollar nodded and she gave him a look, like she was sorry for spoiling his plans.

"I'm at boarding school. I just flew in this afternoon."

"I didn't see a light," he said.

"I keep foil over the windows," she said. "I need total darkness when I sleep. There's weather stripping under the door and everything."

"Have you called the police?"

"Right after I knocked you out. You scared me so bad I practically just shouted my address into the phone and hung up. I was afraid you'd wake up and kill me. That's why the tape. I'll call again if they aren't here soon." This last she delivered as if she regretted having to make him wait. She waggled her fingers at him. "I was on my right pinky when I heard the window break."

Cashdollar estimated at least ten minutes for the girl to drag him down the hall and truss him up, which meant that the police would be arriving momentarily. He had robbed houses in seven states, had surprised his share of homeowners, but he'd never once had a run-in with the law. He was too fast on his feet for that, strictly smash and grab, never got greedy, never resorted to violence. Neither, however, had a teenage girl ever bashed him unconscious with a toilet lid and duct-taped him to a chair.

"This boarding school," he said, "they don't send you home for Christmas?"

"I do Christmas with my mom," she said.

Cashdollar waited a moment for her to elaborate but she was quiet and he wondered if he hadn't hit on the beginnings of an angle here, wondered if he had time enough to work it. When it was clear that she wasn't going to continue, he prompted her. "Divorce is hard," he said.

The girl shrugged. "Everybody's divorced."

"So the woman I saw before —" He let the words trail off into a question.

"My father's girlfriend," she said. "One of." She rolled her eyes. Her eyes were a curious, almost fluorescent shade of green. "My father is the last of the big-time swingers."

"Do you like her?" he said. "Is she nice?"

"I hardly know her. She's a nurse. She works for him." She waved her hand before her face as if swiping at an insect. "I think it's tacky if you want to know the truth."

They were in the dining room, though Cashdollar hadn't bothered to take it in when he was loading up the silverware. He saw crown molding. He saw paintings on the walls, dogs and dead birds done in oils, expensive but without resale value. This was a doctor's house, he thought. It made him angry that he'd misread the presence of the woman, angrier even than the fact that he'd let himself get caught. He was thirty-six years old. That seemed to him just then like a long time to be alive.

"I'm surprised you don't have a date tonight," he said. "Pretty girl like you home alone on New Year's Eve."

He had his doubts about flattery — the girl seemed too sharp for that — but she took his remark in stride.

"Like I said, I just got in today and I'm away at school most of the year. Plus, I spend more time with my mother in California than my father so I don't really know anybody here."

"What's your name?" he said.

The girl hesitated. "I'm not sure I should tell you that."

"I just figured if you told me your name and I told you mine then you'd know somebody here."

"I don't think so," she said.

Cashdollar closed his eyes. He was glad that he wasn't wearing some kind of burglar costume, the black sweatsuit, the ski mask. He felt less obvious in street clothes. Tonight, he'd chosen a hunter green car coat, a navy turtleneck, khaki pants, and boat shoes. He didn't bother wearing gloves. He wasn't so scary-looking this way, he thought, and when he asked the question that was on his mind, it might seem like one regular person asking a favor of another.

"Listen, I'm just going to come right out and say this, okay? I'm wondering what are the chances you'd consider letting me go?"

The girl opened her mouth but Cashdollar pressed ahead before she could refuse and she settled back into her chair to let him finish. "Because the police will be here soon and I don't want to go to prison and I promise, if you let me, I'll leave the way I came in and vanish from your life forever."

The girl was quiet for a moment, her face patient and composed, as if waiting to be sure he'd said his piece. He could hear the refrigerator humming in the kitchen. A moth plinked against the chandelier over their heads. He wondered if it hadn't slipped in through the broken pane. The girl capped the bottle of nail polish, lifted the toilet lid from her lap without disturbing the contents, and set it on the floor beside her chair.

"I'm sorry," she said. "I really am but you did break into the house and you put my father's silverware in your pillowcase and I'm sure you would have taken other things if I hadn't hit you on the head. If you want, I'll tell the police that you've been very nice, but I don't think it's right for me to let you go."

In spite — or because — of her genial demeanor, Cashdollar was beginning to feel like his heart was on the blink; it felt as thick and rubbery as a hot water bottle in his chest. He held his breath and strained against his bonds, hard enough to hop his chair, once, twice, but the tape held fast. He sat there, panting.

The girl said, "Let me ask you something. Let's say I was asleep or watching TV or whatever and I didn't hear the window break. Let's say you saw me first — what would you have done?"

He didn't have to think about his reply. "I would have turned around and left the house. I've never hurt anyone in my whole life."

The girl stared at him for a long moment then dropped her eyes and fanned her fingers, studied her handiwork. She didn't look altogether pleased. To the backs of her hands, she said, "I believe you."

As if to punctuate her sentence, the doorbell rang, followed by four sharp knocks, announcing the arrival of the police.

While he waited, Cashdollar thought about prison. The possibility of incarceration loomed forever on the periphery of his life but he'd never allowed himself to waste a lot of time considering the specifics. He told himself that at least he wasn't leaving anyone behind, wasn't ruining anyone else's life, though even as he filled his head with reassurances, he understood that they were false and his pulse was roaring in his ears, his lungs constricting. He remembered this one break-in down in Pensacola when some sound he made — a rusty hinge, a creaking floorboard — startled the owner of the house from sleep. The bedroom was dark and the man couldn't see Cashdollar standing at the door. "Joyce?" he said. "Please. Is that you, Joyce?" There was such sadness, such longing in his voice that Cashdollar knew Joyce was never coming back. He pitied the man, of course, but at the same time, he felt as if he was watching him through a window, felt outside the world looking in rather than in the middle of things with the world pressing down around him. He crept out of the house feeling sorry for himself. He hadn't thought about that man in years. Now, he could hear voices in the next room but he couldn't make out what they were saying. It struck him that they were taking too long and he wondered if this wasn't what people meant when they described time bogging down at desperate moments.

The girl rounded the corner into the dining room trailing a pair of uniformed police officers, the first a white guy, straight out of central casting, big and pudgy, his tunic crumpled into his slacks, his belt slung low under his belly; the second, a black woman, small with broad shoulders, her hair twisted into braids under her cap. "My friend —" The girl paused, shot a significant look at Cashdollar. "— Patrick, surprised him in the dining room and the burglar hit him with the toilet thingy and taped him up. Patrick, these are Officers Hildebran and Pruitt." She tipped her head right, then left to indicate the man and the woman respectively.

Officer Pruitt circled around behind Cashdollar's chair.

"What was the burglar doing with a toilet lid?"

"That's a mystery," the girl said.

"Why haven't you cut him loose?"

"We didn't know what to do for sure," the girl said. "He didn't seem to be hurt too bad and we didn't want to disturb the crime scene. On TV, they always make a big deal out of leaving everything just so."

"I see," said Officer Pruitt, exactly as if she didn't see at all. "And you did your nails to pass the time?" She pointed at the manicure paraphernalia.

The girl made a goofy, self-deprecating face, all eyebrows and lips, twirled her finger in the air beside her ear. Officer Hildebran wandered over to the window. Without facing the room, he said, "I'll be completely honest with you, Miss Schnell —"

"Daphne," the girl said and Cashdollar had the sense that her interjection was meant for him.

Officer Hildebran turned, smiled. "I'll be honest, Daphne, we sometimes recover some of the stolen property —"

"He didn't take anything," the girl said.

Officer Hildebran raised his eyebrows. "No?"

"He must have panicked," Daphne said.

Cashdollar wondered what had become of his pillowcase, figured it was still in the hall where the girl had ambushed him, hoped the police didn't decide to poke around back there. Officer Pruitt crouched at his knees to take a closer look at the duct tape.

"You all right?" she said.

He nodded, cleared his throat.

"Where'd the tape come from?"

"I don't know," he said. "I was out cold."

"Regardless," Officer Hildebran was saying to Daphne, "unless there's a reliable eyewitness —"

Officer Pruitt sighed. "There is an eyewitness." She raised her eyes, regarded Cashdollar's battered face.

"Oh," Officer Hildebran said. "Right. You think you could pick him out of a line-up?"

"It all happened pretty fast," Cashdollar said.

And so it went, as strange and vivid as a fever dream, their questions, his answers, their questions, Daphne's answers — he supposed that she was not the kind of girl likely to arouse suspicion, not the kind of girl people were inclined to disbelieve — until Officers Hildebran and Pruitt were satisfied, more or less. They seemed placated by the fact that his injuries weren't severe and that nothing had actually been stolen. Officer Pruitt cut the tape with a utility knife and Cashdollar walked them to the door like he was welcome in this house. He invented contact information, assured them that he'd be down in the morning to look at mugshots. He didn't know what had changed Daphne's mind and, watching the police make their way down the sidewalk and out of his life, he didn't care. He shut the door and said, "Is Daphne your real name?" He was just turning to face her when she clubbed him with the toilet lid again.

Once more, he woke in the ladderback chair, wrists and ankles bound, but this time Daphne was seated cross-legged on the floor, leaned back, her weight on her hands. He saw her as if through a haze, as if looking through a smudgy lens, noticed her long neck, the smooth skin on the insides of her thighs.

"Yes," Daphne said.

"What?"

"Yes, my name is Daphne."

"Oh," he said.

His skull felt full of sand.

"I'm sorry for conking you again," she said. "I don't know what happened. I mean, it was such a snap decision to lie to the police and then that woman cut the tape and I realized I don't know the first thing about you and I freaked." She paused. "What's your name?" she said.

Cashdollar felt as if he were being lowered back into himself from a great height, gradually remembering how it was to live in his body. Before he was fully aware of what he was saying, he'd given her an honest answer.

"Leonard," he said.

Daphne laughed. "I wasn't expecting that," she said. "I didn't think anybody named anybody Leonard anymore."

"I'm much older than you."

"You're not so old. What are you, forty?"

"Thirty-six."

Daphne said, "Oops."

"I think I have a concussion," Cashdollar said.

Daphne wrinkled her nose apologetically and pushed to her feet and brushed her hands together. "Be right back," she said. She ducked into the kitchen, returned with a highball glass, which she held under his chin. He smelled Scotch, let her bring it to his mouth. It tasted expensive.

"Better?" Daphne said.

Cashdollar didn't answer. He'd been inclined to feel grateful but hadn't the vaguest idea where this was going now. She sat on the floor and he watched her sip from the glass. She made a retching face, shuddered, regrouped.

"At school one time, I drank two entire bottles of Robitussin cough syrup. I hallucinated that my Klimt poster was coming to life. It was very sexual. My roommate called the paramedics."

"Is that right?" Cashdollar said.

"My father was in Aruba when it happened," she said. "He was with an AMA rep named Farina Hoyle. I mean, what kind of a name is Farina Hoyle? He left her there and flew all the way back to make sure I was all right."

"That's nice, I guess," Cashdollar said.

Daphne nodded and smiled, half sly, half something else. Cashdollar couldn't put his finger on what he was seeing in her face. "It isn't true," she said. "Farina Hoyle's true. Aruba's true."

"What are you going to do with me?" Cashdollar said.

Daphne peered into the glass.

"I don't know," she said.

They were quiet for a minute. Daphne swirled the whisky. Cashdollar's back itched and he rubbed it on the chair. When Daphne saw what he was doing, she moved behind the chair to scratch it for him and he tipped forward to give her better access. Her touch raised goosebumps, made his skin jump like horseflesh.

"Are you married?" she said.

He told her, "No."

"Divorced?"

He shook his head. Her hand went still between his shoulder blades. He heard her teeth click on the glass.

"You poor thing," she said. "Haven't you ever been in love?"

"I think you should cut me loose," Cashdollar said.

Daphne came around the chair and sat on his knee, draped her arm over his shoulder.

"How often do you do this? Rob houses, I mean."

"I do it when I need the money," he said.

"When was the last time?" Her face was close enough that he could smell the liquor on her breath.

"A while ago," he said. "Could I have another sip of that?" She helped him with the glass. He felt the Scotch behind his eyes. "It's been a coupla months," he said. The truth was he'd done an apartment house last week, waited at the door for somebody to buzz him up, then broke the locks on the places where no one was home. He was in and out in less than an hour. Just now, however, he didn't see the percentage in the truth. He said, "I did this mansion over by the country club. I only ever do rich people and I give half my take to Jerry's Kids."

Daphne socked him in the chest.

"Ha, ha," she said.

"Isn't that what you want to hear?" he said. "Right? You're looking for a reason to let me go?"

"I don't know," she said.

He shrugged. "Who's to say it isn't true?"

"Jerry's Kids," she said.

She was smiling and he smiled back. He couldn't help liking this girl. He liked that she was smart and that she wasn't too afraid of him. He liked that she had the guts to bullshit the police.

"Ha, ha," he said.

Daphne knocked back the last of the Scotch, then skated her socks over the hardwood floor, headed for the bay window.

"Do you have a car?" she said, parting the curtains. "I don't see a car."

"I'm around the block," he said.

"What do you drive?"

"Honda Civic."

Daphne raised her eyebrows.

"It's inconspicuous," he said.

She skated back over to his chair and slipped her hand into his pocket and rooted for his keys. Cashdollar flinched. There were only two keys on the ring, his car and his apartment. For some reason, this embarrassed him.

"It really is a Honda," Daphne said.

There was a grandfather clock in the corner but it had died at half past eight who knew how long ago and his watch was out of sight beneath the duct tape and Cashdollar was beginning to worry about the time. He guessed Daphne had been gone for twenty minutes, figured he was safe until after midnight, figured her father and his lady friend would at least ring in the new year before calling it a night. He put the hour around eleven o'clock but he couldn't be sure and for all he knew, Daphne was out there joyriding in his car and you couldn't tell what might happen at a party on New Year's Eve. Somebody might get angry. Somebody might have too much to drink. Somebody might be so crushed with love they can't wait another minute to get home. He went on thinking like this until he heard what sounded like a garage door rumbling open and his mind went blank and every ounce of his perception funneled down into his ears. For a minute, he heard nothing — he wasn't going to mistake silence for safety a second time — then a door opened in the kitchen and Daphne breezed into the room.

"Took me a while to find your car," she said. She had changed clothes for her foray into the world. Now, she was wearing an electric blue parka with fur inside the hood and white leggings and knee-high alpine boots.

"What time is it?" he said.

But she passed through without stopping, disappeared into the next room.

"You need to let me go," he said.

When she reappeared, she was carrying a stereo speaker, her back arched under its weight. He watched her into the kitchen. She returned a minute later, breathing hard. She braced her hands on the table, waited for her wind to come back.

"That was a mistake," she said. "I should've started small."

He looked at her. "I don't understand."

"It's a good thing you've got a hatchback," Daphne said.

For the next half-hour, she shuttled between the house and the garage, bearing valuables each trip, first the rest of the stereo, then the TV and the VCR, then his pillowcase of silverware, then an armload of expensive-looking suits and on and on until Cashdollar was certain that his car would hold no more. Still she kept it up. Barbells, golf clubs, a calfskin luggage set. A pair of antique pistols. A dusty classical guitar. A baseball signed by someone dead and famous. With each passing minute, Cashdollar could feel his stomach tightening and it was all he could do to keep his mouth shut but he had the sense that he should leave her be, that this didn't have anything to do with him. He pictured his little Honda bulging with the accumulated property of another man's life, flashed to his apartment in his mind, unmade bed, lawn chairs in the living room, coffee mug in the sink. He made a point of never holding on to anything anybody else might want to steal. There was not a single thing in his apartment that it would hurt to lose, nothing he couldn't live without. Daphne swung back into the room, looking frazzled and exhausted, her face glazed with perspiration.

"There." She huffed at a wisp of stray hair that had fallen across her eyes, lowered her parka hood.

"You're crazy," Cashdollar said.

Daphne dismissed him with a wave.

"You're out of touch," she said. "I'm your average sophomore."

"What'll you tell the cops?"

"I like Stockholm Syndrome but I think they're more likely to believe you made me lie under threat of death." She took the parka off, draped it on a chair, lifted the hem of her sweatshirt to wipe her face, exposing her belly, the curve of her ribs, pressed it first against her right eye, then her left as if dabbing tears.

"Ha, ha," he said.

Daphne said, "I'll get the scissors."

She went out again, came back again. The tape fell away like something dead. Cashdollar rubbed his wrists a second, pushed to his feet and they stood there looking at each other. Her eyes, he decided, were the color of a jade pendant he had stolen years ago. That pendant pawned for $700. It flicked through his mind that he should kiss her and that she would let him but he restrained himself. He had no business kissing teenage girls. Then, as if she could read his thoughts, Daphne slapped him across the face. Cashdollar palmed his cheek, blinked the sting away, watched her doing a girlish bob and weave, her thumbs tucked inside her fists.

"Let me have it," she said.

"Quit," he said.

"Wimp," she said. "I dropped you twice."

"I'm gone," he said.

Right then, she poked him in the nose. It wouldn't have hurt so much if she hadn't already hit him with the toilet lid but as it was, his eyes watered up, his vision filled with tiny sparkles. Without thinking, he balled his hand and punched her in the mouth, not too hard, a reflex, just enough to sit her down, but right away he felt sick at what he'd done. He held his palms out, like he was trying to stop traffic.

"I didn't mean that," he said. "That was an accident. I've never hit a girl. I've never hurt anyone in my whole life."

Daphne touched her bottom lip, smudging her fingertip with blood.

"This will break his heart," she said.

She smiled at Cashdollar and he could see blood in the spaces between her teeth. The sight of her dizzied him with sadness. He thought how closely linked were love and pain. Daphne extended a hand, limp-wristed, ladylike. Her nails were perfect.

"Now tape me to the chair," she said.

RICHARD LANGE

Bank of America

FROM *StoryQuarterly*

AFTER WE TAKE CONTROL of a bank and subdue the security guard, it's my job to watch the customers while Moriarty slides over the counter and empties the tills. I'm not sure why this task fell to me. Even after all this time, I'm not the most convincing bad guy. I've worked on my posture and stuff in the mirror, practiced evil glares and unnerving twitches, but I still worry that someone is going to see through me.

The gun I carry helps. A big, ugly, silver thing, it's fairly undeniable. I'm careful not to abuse the upper hand it gives me, though. You see psychos playing those games in movies, and you're always glad when they get theirs. And I've been on the other end of it too, shortly after I moved to LA. I know what it feels like. As I left a liquor store one night, a couple of peewees rushed me and flashed a piece. My wallet practically flew out of my pocket and into their hands. It took me weeks to stop shaking. I vomited right there on the sidewalk. I keep that in mind when we're doing our thing. No need to push it.

It's a special day. We're gathered in the cramped little office that Moriarty peddles pagers and cell phones out of, to review his plans for our final job. Moriarty, because he's the mastermind of our crew. Under his direction, we've pulled off twenty-seven successful bank robberies in three years — more than Jesse James — and in all that time we've never been caught, never had the cops on our trail, never even fired our weapons.

It must be a thousand degrees outside. Even with two fans whirring and all the windows open, the air just lies there, hot and thick as bacon grease. One story below, down on Hollywood, an old Armenian woman is crying. She sits on a bus bench, rocking back and forth, a black scarf wrapped around her head. Her sobs distract me from Moriarty's presentation. He asks a question, and I don't even hear him.

"Hey, man," he scolds. "Come on. Really."

"I'm with you, I'm with you." I get up off the windowsill and go to the Coke machine he keeps stocked with beer. The can I extract glistens with cold sweat, and I press it to the back of my neck and motion for him to continue.

It's the same scenario as the last job, and the one before. There's not much finesse at our level. We're not blowing vaults or breaching high-tech security systems. Basically, it's hit-and-run stuff. We grab as much cash as we can before someone activates an alarm, then run like hell to our stolen getaway car. Moriarty has always wanted us to look like amateurs. He has a theory that the cops will pay less attention to us that way. We've taken other precautions as well. No two jobs are ever less than twenty miles apart, and we vary our disguises: ski masks, nylons, wigs, and fake beards. We wore alien heads once, grays, and once we went in turbans and shoe polish, trying to have a little fun with it.

Moriarty has me trace our route in and out with my finger, then crumples the map and burns it in an ashtray. I admire his thoroughness. It makes me proud to be his partner. And the control he exerts over himself — my God! He has mastered the messy business of life. Every day he eats a banana for breakfast and a tuna sandwich for lunch. Every day! And his whole week is similarly cast in stone. Thursday nights: pool at the Smog Cutter from nine to eleven, and two beers — no more, no less. Saturdays, a movie, target practice, an hour of meditation, and the evening spent studying history. Sundays he's up at six to read the *New York* and *LA Times* from cover to cover. I believe him when he says that living this way gives him time to think. It makes perfect sense: He's a speeding train, and his routine is the track; all he has to concentrate on is moving forward. That doesn't mean he's perfect — he still lives with his mother, gets a little too spitty when he talks about guns, and seriously believes Waco was just a taste of things to come — but that will of his!

"So everybody's clear?" he asks. "No muss, no fuss?"

"Clear, *mon commandant.*" This from Belushi, the third member of our crew, who's lying on the couch, smoking another cigarette.

Moriarty steps out from behind his desk and opens the office re-frigerator. He tosses a Popsicle to Belushi and one to me, and we sit sucking them in silence. The Armenian woman is still crying down-stairs, and it starts to get to all of us. Belushi snaps first, growling, "For fuck's sake, put on some music or something." Moriarty slips a cassette into the boom box, and "Whole Lotta Rosie" blasts out of the speakers.

"Maybe we should go down and see what's wrong," I suggest.

"I'll tell you what's wrong," Belushi says, a chuckle rattling the phlegm coating his throat. "It's too hot, the air's for shit, and the world is run by evil old men. You could rip your eyeballs out, and the tears would keep right on coming."

He's one of those hard-core doomsayers, Belushi, and a junkie too — hence the nickname — but he also understands money like nobody I've ever met before. Rumor has it he comes from a rich family, so maybe it's in his blood. He's been the driver on all our jobs, and our accountant. Our goal when we started this thing was a quarter million each — serious fuck-you money — and today the balance of my Swiss bank account stands at $248,320. You'd never guess it, seeing him sprawled out like he is now, grinning that yel-low, broken-toothed grin, but Belushi has taken all of our booty and, through some serious offshore hanky-panky, more than tri-pled it. That's why this is our last gig. It'll be little more than a for-mality, but we have to stick to the plan, because sticking to the plan is what brought us this far.

Moriarty plugs in his vintage Ms. Pac-Man machine, and it comes to life with a barrage of beeps and whines. A sticky drop from his rapidly melting Popsicle falls onto the screen, and he wipes it away with his thumb.

"So how's your love life?" he asks Belushi. Here they go again.

"None of your business."

"There's nothing wrong with paying for it, you know. It's a vic-timless crime."

"Not according to the women who end up with you."

"Is your mom bad-mouthing me again?"

Belushi fakes a belly laugh and draws his long, thin arms and legs in to push himself up off the couch. The hottest day of the year, and he's dressed all in black. "I'll see you bastards Thursday," he says.

When the door closes behind him, Moriarty shakes his head.

"My man's a trip, ain't he?" he says.

"He's something," I reply.

A sheet of paper with the current scores of our never-ending tournament is taped to the side of the Ms. Pac-Man machine. Moriarty checks it, then starts his game. I move back to the windowsill to drink my beer and try to catch a breeze. From there, I watch Belushi exit the building and approach the Armenian woman, who's still crying, even though I can't hear her over the music. I can't hear what Belushi says to her, either, but whatever it is stops her frenzied rocking. He reaches into his pocket for some money and gives it to her. She takes his hand in both of hers and kisses it, and he pats her on the back before scuttling down the street.

Yes, my man is definitely a trip.

Belushi and Moriarty call me John Doe because I'm the normal one, which means I've got the wife and kid, and I hit the floor running every morning, looking for some way to scrape together the cash it takes to keep my family afloat. When we reach our goal after this last job and finally, by mutual consent, get access to our money, Belushi is splitting for Amsterdam where he's going to register as an addict so he can receive free government-issue heroin, and Moriarty's finally moving out on his own, to Idaho, the last free place in America or something like that. Me, I just want a Subway franchise somewhere quiet, with good schools. A three-bedroom Kaufman & Broad and a decent car. Bank robbery is a hell of a way to get a little boost up the ladder, I know, but aren't they always saying to go where the money is? You can make anything mean anything if you try.

When I get home, Maria's in the kitchen peeling potatoes for her famous French fries, to go with the burgers I'll throw on the barbecue. I told her I was going out to bid on a painting job. She asks me how it went.

"Looks good," I say. "It's a big place. Might keep me busy for a month or so."

"Hooray for our team, huh?"

"We'll see, we'll see."

She picks up a knife and slices the potatoes into long, thin strips, which she places in a bowl of water.

"Someone broke into the apartment next door and stole their television," she says.

"You're kidding."

"They were asleep when it happened. Didn't hear a thing."

"Man, oh man."

"I know. Scary."

She's not trying to make me feel bad, but I do. I should have pulled her and Sam out of this neighborhood years ago, when the graffiti first sprouted, the first time the car was broken into. I kept thinking things would turn around. I was like that back then, all silver linings and never say die. Now, though, I acknowledge the impossible. And after Thursday — the Hole in the Wall Gang's last ride — we're saying good-bye to bad luck.

"Let's start looking for another place," I say, moving up behind Maria to wrap my arms around her and bury my face in her hair. I love her hair. I have always loved her hair.

"Maybe over in Glendale," she says.

"How about farther? How about the mountains? Completely the hell away from here."

"Don't be a joker."

"Baby, I'm serious. It's time."

She turns to kiss me. Her wet hands on my face smell of potatoes and dirt. She's Cuban, brown and smooth-skinned. Her parents begged her not to marry me. They had a friend of the family lined up, a medical student, but she was as stubborn then as she is now.

"Okay, the mountains," she says.

"The mountains."

We rest against each other for a second, then she laughs and pushes me away. "Ahh, you're crazy. I brought some quizzes home to correct. Go check on Sam and let me work."

I pause in the doorway and watch as she sits at the table and takes up her pen. The curtains billow in the window behind her, dance in the evening breeze, and the shadows of the refrigerator and the toaster grow longer and cooler by the minute. She rests her forehead in her hand and smiles, and I finally understand why people are so afraid of dying. I want to be with her forever.

"Papi," Sam says. "Hey, Papi, look."

I jerk back out of a deep and dreamless catnap, and the sudden return of sight stings my eyes. One minute I was contemplating the brittle droop of the fronds of the palm tree outside our living-room window, and the next I was gone. I hate being tired all the time.

"Papi!"

Sam is almost five. He told me last week that he wants to be a doctor when he grows up so he can fix broken hearts. This evening he's busy pulling apart his collection of action figures and recombining the pieces to create new forms of life. He slides one across the coffee table for me to look at.

"This is the man who found out he was a robot," he explains. "He watched in the mirror and took off his face, and there was a robot head underneath. Now he drinks oil and is very, very sad. He gets mad sometimes and breaks things."

"Does he have any friends?" I ask.

Sam purses his lips, thinking. "He's too scary and too sad. He cries too much. If he had some money, he would buy a new head, but he doesn't."

"How much would a new head cost?"

"Around ten dollars, I think."

"Here," I say, pretending to hand the little man something. "Here's ten dollars. Go buy yourself a new head."

"He can't hear you," Sam says. "He's got robot ears too."

Sam splashes in his inflatable wading pool while I set up the grill and start the briquettes. Some of the people who live in the other bungalows in our complex are cooking outside, too, and we wave at each other across the courtyard that all of our doors open onto. There's plenty of shade now. The sun is low on the horizon, coating every leaf of every tree with honey, and the birds are deep into their happy hour. The air is filled with raucous screeches as they swarm a freshly seeded patch of lawn.

"Look, Papi."

Sam lies on his stomach and drops his face beneath the water. Bubbles fizz around his head. He rises up and waits for my smile and nod, then goes under again. One of the neighbors turns on a radio and Mexican music competes with the chatter of the birds. When we move to the mountains, I'll build our house myself. One of those wooden dome jobbies you can order plans for, kind of a futuristic log cabin kind of a thing. I picture myself sawing boards and pounding nails. It seems entirely possible.

We eat on the porch, citronella candles pushing back the bugs

and the darkening night. Burgers, Maria's fries, and a salad of avo-
cados and sliced ripe tomatoes dressed with oil and vinegar and
lots of pepper. Sam's damp hair clings to his forehead, and the
towel Maria dried him with is still draped around his shoulders.
Maria scolds him when he burps, but then I burp too. She wrinkles
her nose in disgust and pours more iced tea. The birds have qui-
eted, and in the distance there is the faint *pop pop pop* of gunfire. I
glance at Maria and Sam, but neither reacts, and I tell myself that
it's because they haven't heard the shots, not that they've grown
used to the sound.

Later we watch an old monster movie together, that one about
the giant tarantula running amok in the desert. I switch from iced
tea to beer. Sam is curled around a pillow on the floor in front of
the television, and Maria lies with me on the couch. The weight of
the day presses down upon me, and my eyelids grow unbearably
heavy. I fall asleep to the sound of a woman screaming. When I
awaken after midnight, Maria has moved to the floor, next to Sam,
and they've both sacked out. I pick Sam up and carry him to bed,
then gently rouse Maria, who wobbles into the bathroom.

Someone famous is selling something cheap on TV. "Fuck you,"
I whisper, and shut it off. A rustling outside the front door tightens
everything in me like a knot. I turn out the light and edge over to
the window. Pulling the curtains aside just a bit, I peek out at the
porch, but there's nothing there, just a napkin we missed when we
cleaned up. Maria returns in her bathrobe and wants to know
what's wrong. I tell her not to worry, that I'm just paranoid after
what happened next door. We share a glass of ice water and go
to bed.

In the morning, Sam's wading pool is gone.

Moriarty has me meet him up at Lake Hollywood. They call it a
lake, but it's actually a reservoir tucked into the hills where the
movie stars live, a concrete-lined hole surrounded by a chain-link
fence. Pretty enough, if you squint. Moriarty does six miles a day on
the road that circles it, round and round, rain or shine. He makes
me feel like a slob.

I park where he instructed me to and walk over to the fence. The
still, black water is covered with a layer of dust that sparkles in the
sunlight, and the smog is so thick, the trees on the far shore are
barely visible. Above me, a big house juts out from a hill, propped

up by a few spindly wooden supports. The view from the deck must be terrific in October or November, when the air clears; you can probably see all the way to the ocean, and I bet the people who live there step out every evening to lean on the railing and watch the sun set.

Moriarty pounds past me in a flat-out sprint and continues for another hundred yards or so before turning around. He returns at a jog, throwing punches.

"Hey," he huffs. "How you doing?"

"I'm good," I reply.

He lifts his T-shirt and wipes away the sweat on his face with it. Another runner passes by, and they exchange nods.

"Wait at your truck," he says to me.

I walk across the road and lean against my Nissan. Fingers intertwined behind my head, I stare out at the reservoir and contemplate the golden film of dust that floats upon it. It doesn't seem very sanitary, this storage system. Maria's been after me to spring for bottled water, and I'm beginning to see her point. If the stuff that comes out of our tap originates here, who knows what kind of deadly crap it's laced with.

Moriarty is parked a short distance up the road. He pulls a duffel bag out of his trunk, then slams it shut. I know the song he's whistling as he approaches. It's a Sousa march my dad had a set of dirty lyrics for:

> *Oh, the monkey wrapped his tail*
> *around the flagpole*
> *To watch the grass grow*
> *Right up his asshole.*

Something like that. Used to crack me up when I was a kid.

Moriarty sets the bag in the bed of my truck and unzips it to show me the sawed-off shotgun inside.

"There's a box of shells too," he says.

"Thanks."

"Lock it away where the kid can't get at it. Don't be stupid."

"Come on, man."

"Do you know how to use it? You probably won't have to, because the sound of the shells sliding into the chamber will send your average burglar packing with a pant load, but just in case?"

"I can't imagine it's too difficult."

Moriarty grins and closes the bag. "Just point and shoot."

An old lady steps out of his car and shouts, "Stuart, I don't want to be late."

"Yeah, Ma, okay," Moriarty shouts back. "Church," he says to me with rolling eyes. "See you Thursday."

"You betcha."

We shake hands, and he jogs to his car. I take another look at the big house above me, and I can't help it. Call it jealousy, whatever you want, but I can't help picturing the Big One hitting, and the surprise and terror on the owners' faces when those supports snap like toothpicks, and they end up riding that fancy sonofabitch down the hill and through the fence and straight to the bottom of poisonous goddamn Lake Hollywood.

I was a wreck when Moriarty happened upon me, so twisted inside that at times I couldn't even breathe deeply enough to fill my lungs. Driving along the freeway or standing in line at the supermarket I'd find myself gasping for air like an astronaut unmasked on Mars. A year earlier, after my third paycheck in a row had bounced, I'd told the contractor I'd been working for to get fucked, and drawn out all of our savings to set myself up as an independent. I didn't love painting houses, but I figured that in a short while I'd have enough capital to move into buying and renovating neglected properties and reselling them at a profit. Twelve months later, though, I'd only had four jobs, and to get those I had to bid so low that I barely broke even. One beer in the evening turned into three, then six. "What kind of idiot did you marry?" I'd ask Maria, and she'd say something nice, but that's not what I wanted to hear, so I'd ask again, "What kind of idiot did you marry?" I'd keep asking until I brought her to tears.

Moriarty found me at the unemployment office in Hollywood. I ignored him on his first approach, because everybody there seemed so strung out and crazy, and who knew what this blond bastard with the crooked smile was up to. *Just let me fill out my forms and be on my way* was my philosophy that morning, but he kept at me, asking to borrow some of my newspaper and following me outside to the catering truck parked at the curb, where we stood eyeing each other through the steam rising from our coffees.

He says he could tell right then that I was the one, but I don't know how. That first conversation, as I recall it, was nothing more than your standard two strangers shooting the shit kind of thing: a little sports, a little music, and each of us maybe trying a little too hard to convince the other that we were worth more than the two hundred bucks a week we were waiting in line for. In my version it wasn't until later — when we retreated to a bar to wash the shame of the morning from our craws — that the truth began to come out. When Moriarty wrapped his hands around his beer like he was praying and sighed, "I'll tell you what, getting by is killing me," that's when I first thought we might have something in common.

Turned out we lived in the same part of Hollywood, so we started getting together for drinks once a week or so. Bank robbery was a running joke from the beginning, or at least I took it as a joke. Moriarty would say, "I'm serious," and I'd laugh and say, "I know you are." To me it was like, "Hey, let's make a movie," or, "Let's open a pizza place," one of those shared pipe dreams guys sometimes use as an excuse to keep meeting when they're too shy or uptight to admit they enjoy each other's company. You know, "This isn't just drinking; we've got business to discuss." You get to fantasize together, share your plans for all the money you're going to make, act a little foolish.

Even when Belushi came into the picture — an old college buddy of Moriarty's — and Moriarty got into the pager racket, thanks to a loan from his mom, and we started meeting at his office instead of the bar because he decided we shouldn't be seen together in public anymore, I still didn't take it seriously. And how could I? I mean, the three of us — us! — sitting around, hefting pistols, and discussing timing while studying maps Moriarty had drawn of the various banks he'd cased — it was hilarious. I remember laughing to myself the first time we actually drove out to scout an escape route, because I knew an hour later I was going to be home playing Crazy Eights with Sam and helping Maria clean the bathroom. That was real life. My life.

So how, then, do I explain what happened next? I don't. I can't. *BOOM!* There I am, standing in one of those same banks on legs that are shaking like a pair of Slinkys. I've got a gun in my hand and pantyhose pulled over my head, and when I yell, "Get down on the floor!" you'd think it was the voice of God rumbling out of a thundercloud, the way the customers throw themselves at my feet. I'd always imagined that when you crossed the line you saw it coming, but it turned out to be more like gliding over the equator on the open sea. Don't let them kid you, it's nothing momentous, going from that to this.

El Jefe phones early Monday morning with an offer of a few days' work on a house in Los Feliz. He was a bigwig in the Nicaraguan army until they ran his ass out on a rail after the revolution. Now he's got a rinky-dink painting business here, with most of his jobs coming through fliers he leaves in mailboxes and under windshield wipers. When white people hire him, he calls me in, because he jacks up his prices for Caucasians and figures they won't complain as much if some of it is going to a fellow gringo. Besides that, white women feel more comfortable with one of their own around, he says, "to keep an eye on us thieves and rapists." It's a hundred tax-free bucks a day, and it'll keep my mind off the heist.

The house is a big, two-story Spanish-style that we're taking from dull tan to something slightly darker. It's me and a couple of short, silent Guatemalan Indians doing the labor, with El Jefe supervising between cigars and chats on his cell phone. The best thing about painting is that it has a rhythm that allows you to drift away. On this morning I run through our first Christmas in the mountains, tweaking the vision bit by bit until it snaps into perfect focus, right down to the broken-glass sparkle of the new snow, the pop and hiss of the logs burning in the fireplace, and the smell of the tree that Sam and I cut down and drag home through the wintry woods. It's such a pretty picture that the sun chewing on the back of my neck doesn't bother me at all, and I'm almost reluctant to put down my brush and descend the ladder when lunch rolls around.

I get the sandwiches and thermos of lemonade that Maria made for me out of the cooler in the bed of my truck and settle against the shady side of one of the palm trees planted in the strip of grass between the street and the sidewalk. The Guatemalans sit on the curb some distance away, talking quietly as they peel back the foil from their burritos. We haven't exchanged two words all morning, but that's the way it goes on these jobs. I think they know why El Jefe brings me around, and I'm not about to stroll over and plop myself down beside them and give them a "we're all in the same boat" speech, because we're not, and they know that, too.

El Jefe pulls himself out of his dented BMW, where he's been sitting with the air-conditioner blasting for the last half-hour. He mutters something to the Guatemalans, who bow their heads and nod, reluctant to meet his gaze, then he marches across the yard to check our progress. Out of habit, I guess, he still carries himself like a military man — back straight, shoulders squared, one hand always resting on his hip, where his side arm would be if he were in uniform. It's funny seeing him strut around like this now that he's gone soft and sprouted a belly, but I don't dare laugh, not with those crazy eyes of his and his history.

He walks into the backyard and then returns a few minutes later and motions with a quick snap of his wrist for me to join him. We step softly along a stone path that leads to a covered patio where we can look down onto the swimming pool, which sits at a lower elevation than the house. Two nude men are sunning themselves, side by side on chaise longues. As we watch, one of them stands and kisses the other before diving into the water.

"Fucking *maricones*," El Jefe whispers. He raises an imaginary rifle to his shoulder and aims it at the men.

"What's the big deal?" I ask.

"It makes me sick, those *putos*." He removes his mirrored sunglasses and wipes the sweat from his eyes with the palm of his hand. "We flushed our shit in Managua."

I shrug and say, "Free country and all that."

"And this is freedom, to fuck another man?"

"To fuck whoever you want, I guess. Who cares?"

"What?" he says, staring at me with disgust.

I don't want to get into it, so I return to the front yard and prepare to go back to work. El Jefe's all fired up, though, and won't leave it alone. He hovers behind me and says, "This country has lost its way."

"Yeah, yeah," I snap. "And you used to be hell with a cattle prod and a pair of pliers. I'm busy here, okay?"

I've never popped off to him like this before, and I'm afraid to look up to see what effect it's had on him. Sweat is running down my forehead, my nose, my cheeks, and a few drops fall into the can of paint I'm stirring. After a while his shadow slides away, and I hear him walking across the lawn. When he reaches his BMW, he calls to me.

"Hey, gringo."

I try to strike a defiant pose as I stand to face him.

"You think I am a bad man?"

He looks almost sad now, almost ashamed, but I'm not about to back down. "I think you've done bad things," I reply.

An unripe date drops from a palm tree above his car and bounces off the hood with a loud bang. He stiffens at the sound, a slight flinch, then relaxes again and says, "So it's lucky that only God will be the judge of both of us."

Before I can fish up a response, he gives me a quick salute and slides into his car and drives away. At quitting time he returns with liquor on his breath and hands each of us our pay sealed inside an envelope, as is his usual custom. I open mine at a stop sign on the way home and find an extra fifty-dollar bill tucked among the twenties. You might not believe it, but I swear, I give it to the stinky old bum who's always hanging out in front of the 7-Eleven.

The bedroom is dark; darker still the figure filling the doorway. I strain my arms and legs, try to sit, roll to the floor, yell, but nothing works. He walks slowly to the side of the bed and jams the barrel of a pistol into my mouth, twists it past my lips and teeth, pulls the trigger. An awful goddamn dream. I awaken with ringing ears, my heart heaving against my ribs like an animal struggling to escape a trap. I taste gunpowder and oiled metal, and even before the world has fully congealed, I'm on my feet. The shotgun and shells Moriarty loaned me are hidden on the top shelf of the closet, inside an old gym bag. I carry them out to the living room and sit on the couch.

The porch light stains the curtains orange. A moth's shadow flashes huge across them. It's bright enough in the room for me to make out the TV, the VCR, the stereo, everything where it should be. I've never been out here naked before. My balls feel funny, resting on the cool vinyl of the couch. I raise the gun to my nose, and the smell brings back my nightmare. A shudder runs through me.

There's something sharp beneath my bare foot. I reach down to pick up whatever it is, one of Sam's toys, the man who found out he was a robot. It seems important that I help the little guy by giving him the new head he wants. I'll fix him and leave him for Sam to find in the morning, a kind of miracle. Thinking there must be more of the figures scattered about, I slide to the floor and lie on my stomach. I sweep my hand through the dark and dusty cavern beneath the couch, but find nothing except an old soda straw and a penny.

"Honey?"

Maria startles me. I roll over and grab the shotgun and point it at her, and then lower it just as quickly when I realize what I've done. *My God.* My fucking God.

"What's going on?" she asks.

"Nothing."

"Is that a gun?"

The refrigerator grumbles under its breath in the kitchen while I nod stupidly and say, "I had a dream," as if that explains everything.

I pull myself back onto the sofa, upsetting the box of shells. They fall to the floor one by one, clank and roll, clank and roll. Maria slips into the orange glow, arms crossed over the front of her robe, her worried face conflicted with a nervous smile. My shame only burns more intensely when she sits beside me and reaches out, probably afraid, to lay a hand on my shoulder. Her lips touch my cheek, and I feel as soft and black as a piece of wormy fruit. I squeeze the man who found out he was a robot so hard, he cuts into my palm. How do normal people live with all the mistakes they've made?

After work on Wednesday I stop off at the supermarket to pick up milk and eggs, and whom do I spot but Belushi. He's slouched near ketchup in the condiment aisle, brow furrowed, rubbing his temples with his index fingers. His black-clad frame sways like a tree rocked by the wind.

I know he lives in the neighborhood, but our paths have never crossed before, and I marvel at how strange he looks compared to the other shoppers. Big bubble sunglasses hide his eyes, and tattooed leopard spots tumble out of the sleeve of his T-shirt, which advertises five-cent mustache rides.

I don't have it in me, the guts it takes to set yourself apart like that. I had my ear pierced once, but it only lasted a week, until a carpenter on the job where I was working at the time made a smart remark.

"Boo," I say to Belushi when I finally sidle up next to him.

He glances over at me and smiles like we do this every day.

"Twenty-five kinds of barbecue sauce," he says. "And all that mustard, man." His speech is slurred, and thick strings of saliva stretch between his lips.

"You shopping?" I ask.

"Nah, nah. I came in for cigarettes and got distracted."

He loses his balance and almost topples over. A security guard at the end of the aisle pays close attention.

"Truthfully, I'm pretty fucked up. Could you give me a ride home?"

His apartment is only a couple of blocks away, in a nice building, much nicer than mine. It must be true what Moriarty says about him coming from money. He invites me in for a beer, and I say sure, because it looks like he might need help getting to his door.

The walls and ceiling of the elevator are covered with a mosaic of tiny mirrors. I crouch and make a monkey face, and it's like watching myself on thousands of little TVs. Belushi staggers into the kitchen when we reach his apartment. He's got a computer and a big-screen, and there are two or three electric guitars lying about. Instead of a couch, fat pillows surround a low table covered with those religious candles they sell in Mexican stores.

Belushi returns with a bottle of Heineken and hands it to me, then drops onto one of the pillows. It feels a little hippy-dippy, but I join him. I wish he'd open a window or at least twist the blinds to let some sun through. It's like an animal's den in here, or the end of some dark road. I imagine bones in the shadows, jagged rocks, old burned wood. He takes a noisy hit from a purple bong and asks in a high, choking voice whether I'm nervous about tomorrow's job.

"Sure," I reply. "You?"

"I'm a fucking mess," he says with a smile. "Your old lady doesn't know what's up, does she?"

"No way. No. She'd flip."

"How are you going to explain coming into money?"

I shrug to avoid answering. I've given the matter a lot of thought, but he doesn't need to know that. He's got plenty of other things to laugh at me about.

"You and Moriarty have been friends for a long time, huh?" I say.

Belushi lights a cigarette. The ashtray is a coiled rattlesnake with red rhinestone eyes.

"Yep. Me and the buttfucker go way back. He's my favorite Martian. The same spaceship stranded both of us on this prison planet, and we've been looking for a way off ever since."

"Is that right?" I reply.

"It is," he snaps.

"Can you do this?" I ask, flashing him the Vulcan salute from *Star Trek.*

He laughs and says, "Make it so." Picking up the remote, he turns on the stereo. Strange music fills the apartment, layer upon layer of squealing guitars over a flat *chunk chunk* drumbeat. It sounds like a factory coming apart in a hurricane. Belushi's fist keeps time, pounding against his knee. There's a poster on the wall of the Pope marching with Nazis.

"I know what you're thinking," Belushi says, gesturing at the TV and guitars and everything, "but I need this money as much as you."

"I understand," I reply, and I guess I do. There's more than one kind of miserable.

"I'm going to miss you when this is over," he says.

This blindsides me, but I nod and say, "And me, you."

I carry Maria's coffee in to her, set the cup on the dresser where she's getting ready for work. She smiles at me in the mirror when I crouch beside her and rest my chin on her shoulder. I run my hands up under her nightgown and cup her breasts. Turning my face to her neck, I tongue the beauty mark there and inhale deeply. I need to memorize it all in case something goes wrong.

"You have dark circles," she says. "Still not sleeping?"

"I'm fine. Don't worry."

The big day is finally here. I could be rich by nightfall, or dead. What a wide-open feeling. I can't put my finger on it.

Sam is sitting on the living room floor in front of the TV, a bowl of cereal in his lap. His eyes are locked onto the screen, where a cartoon spaceship goes down in flames.

"Invader X neutralized," he declares, imitating the voice of some hero in a visored helmet.

I remember the joy of losing myself like that as a child. What a gift it seems now. I resist the urge to pick him up, to intrude, and instead sit on the couch and love him from afar.

The three of us leave the apartment together, and I walk Maria and Sam to the Sentra. She'll drop him off at kindergarten on her way to school. I kiss them both and wait to make sure the car starts, because the battery hasn't been holding a charge lately. It's hard to let them go this morning. Tears sting my eyes as the car crests the hill in front of our house and pops out of the shadows and into the ravenous sunlight.

The plan is to meet at three o'clock in the parking lot of a mini-mall a few blocks from the bank. Until then, it's business as usual. The Guatemalans are already up on their ladders when I arrive at the house in Los Feliz. El Jefe steps out of his BMW and watches me unload my truck. He's smoking a cigar and drinking from a quart carton of orange juice.

I'm painting up under the eaves this morning, which is nice because it keeps me out of reach of the sun, but hell because of the spiders. If this was my job, I'd have sprayed the webs down with a garden hose yesterday and let the wall dry overnight, but El Jefe's not much for prepping, so I have to use a brush to sweep the webs away. They're as thick as cotton in places, and studded with dried-out flies that jump and crackle. The webs wrap around me when they fall, cling to my face with ghostly tautness, and slither into my lungs on the current of my breath. And the monsters that spun them! Fat, black spiders drop like poison rain. I swat them away when they scrabble over my arms, my neck, but it's too much. I have to take a break, sit on the lawn with my head between my knees.

After lunch I begin to work myself up to sticking my finger down my throat. That's how I'll get away, by vomiting and telling El Jefe I'm too sick to keep going, maybe blame it on a spider bite. I'm prying open a new can of paint when my pager goes off. I bought it when I went into business for myself. After that fell apart, we decided to keep it active in case of emergencies. The readout shows Maria's number at school, followed by 9 1 1.

"Jefe!" I yell, approaching his car at a run. "I need to use your phone."

He rolls down the window. Chilled air breaks over me like a wave. "It's expensive, you know."

"It's my wife. Something's wrong."

"You pay for the call?"

I snatch the phone from his hand, dial, and Maria answers. There's worry in her voice. Sam has fallen at kindergarten and may have broken his leg. She can't leave school right now and wonders if I can pick him up and drive him to the hospital. No problem, I say. Relax. Everything'll be okay.

"Gotta go," I tell El Jefe. "I'll pick my shit up later." I throw the phone into his lap and run for my truck. It's not until I'm driving away that I think to look at my watch. Quarter after one. I'm supposed to have a gun in my hand and a bulletproof soul in less than two hours.

Sam is lying on his back on a cot in the school nurse's office. He stares at the ceiling, afraid to move, his face pale and sweaty.

"I'm hurt," he says, "but not bleeding."

He whimpers when I scoop him up, cries for his shoes, which the nurse has removed. She gives them to him, and he twines his fingers through the laces, clutching them tightly. I shield his eyes from the sun as I carry him across the parking lot. A bell rings behind us, doors open with a *whoosh*, and hordes of screaming children run for the playground.

He lies across the seat of the truck. The top of his head rests against my thigh. He looks up at me as I drive, his bottom lip held between his teeth. I know he's in pain, but he doesn't complain once, though every block seems to have a pothole that makes the truck shake like an unwatered drunk.

"Want to play music?" I ask. He's not usually allowed, but I need to see him smile. I turn on the radio and say, "Go ahead."

He reaches out tentatively, as if this might be a trick, and pushes one of the buttons, changing stations. When no scolding follows, he sets to work in earnest. We listen to snatches of some rapper, the Eagles, news, a Mexican station, and back again, and he laughs at the cacophony he's creating. I feel awful for ever depriving him this pleasure, for ever slapping his hand and shouting, *knock it off.*

Meanwhile my partners are waiting, and the ticking of my watch grows louder with each passing second. If I don't show up, they'll call the job off, but I know Moriarty and his completion principle. He'll just plan another, and that's unacceptable. I want this to be over now. I want to be a citizen again. I want to spend my fucking money.

I lay my hand on Sam's chest. His heart is beating as fast as mine.

"I'll teach you a song," I say. *"Oh, the monkey wrapped his tail around the flagpole . . ."*

When they wheel Sam off for his X-rays, I use a pay phone to call Maria at school. The secretary puts me on hold, then comes back on to ask if I'd like to leave a message, because Mrs. Blackburn is unavailable at the moment.

"This is her husband. Tell her I've got our son here at Kaiser in Hollywood."

"Let me write it down," she says. "You're her husband?"

I don't have time for this, so I hang up on her and dial Moriarty's pager, the only way I have to get in touch with him. There's a sign over the phone that says no incoming calls, but I leave the number anyway. Then I try the school again. The same woman answers, and I slam the receiver down.

I'm clenching my jaw so tight, my teeth hurt. Any minute something inside me is going to burst. I lean against the wall, close my eyes, and breathe deeply, which only makes me feel worse, because the air in the corridor reeks of shit and medicine. There's a TV on somewhere. A woman on it asks, "Do you love me?" and a man answers, "I don't know right now." "Do you love me?" the woman screams. I begin to pace, ten steps up the hall and ten steps back. The world narrows into a strip of snot-green linoleum over which I have complete control. It should always be this easy.

Maria arrives, flushed and sweaty-palmed. Another teacher took over her class, allowing her to leave school early. The doctor informs us that Sam has a hairline fracture of the tibia. Nothing serious, but he'll need a cast. It's two-thirty. I can still make my rendezvous with Moriarty and Belushi if I go now.

"Hey, I left my stuff at the site," I tell Maria. "I should probably pick it up before they quit for the day."

"Okay. Go ahead."

"You'll be fine here by yourself?"

"See you at home."

I kiss her on the cheek and force myself to walk until I'm out of her sight.

BOOM! Here we go, rolling in out of the heat and noise and destroying the silky air-conditioned calm of the bank. Today it's Mexi-

can wrestling masks and happy-face T-shirts, party clothes to com-
memorate our final heist. "Get down," I yell, "down on the floor,"
showing my gun. There are one, two, three customers, and they
drop like trapdoors have opened beneath them. Moriarty bee-
lines for the security guard, who meekly holds out his hands to be
cuffed. One, two, three customers, all secure. I wonder if the plants
standing in the corners are real or made of plastic. Something tick-
les my neck. I reach up and snag it, a long black hair, Maria's. I raise
it to my lips as Moriarty hurdles the counter and makes his way
down the line of tellers. No trouble there. They've been trained
not to resist. Just push the silent alarm and back off. Well, supposedly silent. The signal zips up my spine like a thimble on a wash-
board, and all of my pores are screaming. One, two, three, old lady,
fat man, *vato*. Each second is disconnected from the one that came
before it, so that they bounce around like pearls cut loose from a
necklace. Moriarty's finished. He heads for the door, the bag slung
over his shoulder. I follow him out to the car, dive inside, and
Belushi slams his hand against the steering wheel and screams *Yes!*
He swings out into traffic and we're gobbled up into the steaming
maw of the city, where we disappear for good.

If it's true that the same God will judge both El Jefe and me, I want
this added to the record: In the end, I didn't lie to my wife. When
she wondered about the money, I came clean. I hadn't planned to,
but I did.

"Where did it you get it?" she asked.

"I robbed a bank. Lots of banks."

She stiffened in my arms — we were in bed at the time — then
rolled over to watch my face.

"Will they catch you?"

"No."

It took the rest of the night to work through it. Maria felt I'd put
the family's future in jeopardy and wanted answers to a lot of questions I hadn't dared ask myself before for fear that the answers
would have pulled me up short, destroying the ruthless momentum that had enabled me to do what had to be done. I explained as
best I could while she waffled between tears and outrage. Dawn
found us silent and drained at the kitchen table, sharing a pot of
coffee. The walls of the apartment ticked and popped in the gathering heat, and the fresh light of the new day stumbled over the

cracks in the plaster left by the last earthquake. Her decision was conveyed by a simple gesture. She reached across the table and took my hands into hers: We would go on.

I'm sitting on the couch, using a Magic Marker to draw a spaceman on Sam's cast. He keeps leaning forward to monitor my efforts, and isn't pleased with how it's turning out.

"No, Papi, his body's not right."

The phone rings, and Maria picks it up in the kitchen. Another real estate agent. We're driving up to Big Bear on Saturday to look at houses. Only a week has passed since the robbery, and already things are changing. So many options, so many decisions. To tell you the truth, it leaves me a little dizzy. I'm like a dog that's finally managed to jump the fence, and, rather than running like hell, sits in front of the gate, waiting for his master to let him back in.

Sam asks me to give him the pen so that he can finish the space-man himself. I leave him to his work and walk into the kitchen where Maria is making notes on a legal pad, the phone's receiver pressed to her ear with her shoulder. I'm too big for the apartment tonight. If I move too quickly, I'll break something.

"I'm going out," I whisper, motioning to the door.

Maria frowns and holds up her hand to indicate that I should wait for her to finish. When I come out of the bedroom after putting on a clean shirt, she's still on the phone, so I just wave and go. Sam is busy with his drawing. He doesn't hear me when I say good-bye.

I stop in at the Smog Cutter. There's a country song playing on the karaoke machine, and old Fred is singing. I grab a stool and settle in to see if Moriarty will show up for his regular Thursday night session at the pool table. We haven't seen each other since the robbery, since Belushi presented us with our account numbers and the partnership was dissolved. For security reasons we agreed to go our separate ways from that moment on, but I just want to say *Hey* and find out how he's doing.

Because I can, I buy a round for the house, and I'm everybody's best friend for five minutes. It makes me laugh to see how easy it is, and how quickly it fades.

Nine comes and goes, then ten, and still no Moriarty. He must have changed his routine. Hell, he may already be in Idaho. And

Belushi's not home, either, or at least he doesn't answer when I push the button for his apartment on the intercom downstairs. Well, fuck it then. "Here's to us, fellas," I say, raising a pint of bourbon in the parking lot of a liquor store. The only good thing about the moment is that I'm pretty sure that as long as I live I'll never feel this lonely again.

The shotgun Moriarty loaned me is locked in the toolbox in the bed of my truck, where I put it when Maria told me to get it out of the apartment. I've been meaning to dispose of it, and this seems as good a time as any.

I drive up to Lake Hollywood. The lights from the mansions in the hills circling the reservoir are reflected in its inky blackness. I press my face against the chain-link fence, then turn to gaze up at the stilt house that caught my attention on my earlier visit. Someone inside is playing a piano. Another belt of bourbon, and I swing the shotgun up and fire twice into the air. The blasts roll across the reservoir and back.

I toss the shotgun over the fence, where it plops into the water and sinks from sight. The piano is silent, and a shadowy figure crouches on the deck of the house, watching me. I stare up at him and tip the bottle again, hoping to spook him even more, but when I slink away, it's with darkened headlights, so that he can't make out my license plates.

On my way home I pass one of the banks we took off, and something wild bucks inside me. *BOOM!* The full moon is rising over the mountains, all orange and smiley, and without even thinking I lift my trigger finger and trace its shape against the sky.

TOM LARSEN

Lids

FROM *New Millennium Writings*

TIMOTHY "LIDS" PICONE has always been partial to the smell, but this guy is too much. Eight, ten times a day he hears him hacking his lungs out. Minutes later he can smell it, right through the fucking wall. Stanley calls him the pothead or sometimes just "the pot." Picone doesn't see how the guy can function. But he does function.

The walls are so thin he can pick up everything with his stethoscope. He's heard some things he'd like to forget. The pothead really plays the role. Flashy clothes, flashy car. His sound system could do serious structural damage. Sometimes Picone has to plug his ears to sleep at night.

It's been three weeks since he moved in. Stanley put up the deposit but the rent came out of Picone's pocket. It should be well worth it. Every Friday night the pothead checks out with an empty duffel bag and when he comes home the bag is full. The rest of the week is traffic, all hours of the day and night. Mostly yuppies and college kids. Funny how dopers look like everyone else these days. Except for Maurice. The dreadlocks and gangster shades are a dead giveaway. Droopy eyelids just like Picone's. The droopy lids make Maurice look dangerous. Picone's just make him look sleepy. All things considered, it's better that way.

Maurice usually arrives with an entourage and a lizard skin attaché case. Might as well have "Drug Dealer" stenciled on the side. Picone can hear the snap of latches through the wall. The pothead's door and windows are wired and he has a wall safe in his bedroom. He's heard the tumblers clicking.

According to Stanley, the pothead and Maurice are planning a major transaction — cocaine by the kilo. Picone wishes they'd get on with it.

He eats the rest of the tuna salad while working on the Matterhorn. Seven completed puzzles are spaced over the living room floor, separated by pathways. As he works Picone listens to classical music on the radio. His attention is perfectly divided.

He got into the puzzles while he was at Rahway. For a time he had them all over his cell but the guards broke them up in a roust and then the cons started stealing pieces just to aggravate him. Funny, he had to wait until he got out of the joint to do his puzzles in peace.

He knows them by heart and each one triggers a different response. Childhood memories that refuse to focus. Love affairs that never happened. He studies the pattern of bark on the pine tree in the foreground. The mountain and the lilting strains of a violin combine to bring tears to his eyes. Anymore he can cry at the drop of a hat.

Sometimes he dreams about taking a trip around the world, to visit the actual sites of his puzzles. The farthest Picone's ever been from New Jersey is Las Vegas, two years ago on a job. He saw a Vegas puzzle in a casino gift shop — an aerial view of the Strip at night. But it was an old one. Sammy Davis was still at the Sands.

His favorite is the one of the Golden Gate Bridge towers poking up through the fog. He can stare at it for hours. The fog so thick you could scoop out a hunk and stick it in your pocket. He used to wonder how the photographer knew it would be that way, but then Stanley told him the fog rolls in like that all the time in Frisco. Stanley's been around. Picone and Stanley met in prison. In fact, Stanley was one of the cons who would steal his puzzle pieces. He claimed the puzzles were making Picone crazy. Stanley ought to see this.

The pothead turns his television on. The tinkly piano of *The Young and the Restless* comes through the wall and in less than a minute he smells the reefer. Like clockwork, this one. An hour later the fat girl with the jangly bracelets shows up and then three yuppies in business suits. The doorman must be on the payroll.

In the afternoon Picone walks down to play his number. On his way back he runs into the pothead coming out of the building. They smile and exchange nods.

"You're the new guy in 312," the pothead says.

"That's right."

"Jack Mercer." He reaches for Picone's hand. "I'm your next door neighbor."

"Lou . . . Lou Dorsey."

"Listen Lou, I've been meaning to tell you. If it gets too loud in my place just give a thump on the wall. I know how thin those walls are. The guy before you had parrots. It was like living in the goddamn Amazon."

"No problem. I don't hear so good."

"Great! I mean for me. Hey, why don't you stop over some time? Have a beer."

"Thanks, maybe I'll take you up on that."

"Okay. Look Lou, I gotta run. If you need anything just let me know." He reaches again for Picone's hand.

"Will do."

Mozart and the Matterhorn. Picone imagines himself living in a cabin with a view of the mountain. Not that he's much of an outdoorsman. The one time he camped out he slipped a disk and ended up in traction. He drops a section of the tree in place and takes a deep drag on his cigarette. The box advertises other mountain puzzles, including Mt. Rushmore in South Dakota. Picone tries to place South Dakota on his mental map but the middle states just run together. When he was a kid his family moved to Ohio for a few months after his old man jumped bail. He can never remember the name of the town but it always seemed to be raining there.

He turns off the radio during the daily Sousa program. Minutes later he hears the elevator door open and the jangle of keys next door. It takes a while for the pothead to unlock all the locks. When he's inside Picone hears him latching latches and turning deadbolts. What a joke! You could put your fist right through the door.

This morning he took the old name off his mailbox and replaced it with Lou Dorsey. No sense giving the guy a reason to be suspicious.

The moaner drops by and for the rest of the afternoon he is forced to listen to the pothead hammer her into the headboards. He likes to think she's faking it. During a break in the action he makes a pot of tea and slips a pizza into the microwave. Hanging around an empty apartment would drive most people crazy but Picone doesn't mind. He admires the sociability of others, the pothead for instance, but he doesn't envy them. Stanley's the closest friend he's got and Picone can't stand the sight of him.

He eats the pizza standing at the kitchen window. The shadows of the buildings stretch across the street and he can hear the traffic light switch above the intersection. He watches the Asian woman from the grocery store arrange bulbs of garlic in the window. This part of town used to be Italian but the Koreans and Vietnamese have taken over. The old paisanos piss and moan but Picone figures if they wanted it, they never should have sold it.

Up the hill he hears the bells from St. Anthony's chime four o'clock. Further up he can see the old bleachery water tower. When they were kids Petey Falcone dared him to climb the tower. He can remember Petey sprawled in the grass below, growing smaller as he pulled himself up the ladder. From the top Picone could see the whole city and he was startled by how shabby it looked. A place where nothing good ever happened. Even the trees looked dirty. He circled the narrow catwalk for nearly an hour. When he finally climbed down Petey was gone. Picone never went back there and in thirty years nothing good ever happened.

A sudden knock on the door scatters his thoughts. It's the pothead, looking casual in linen pants and a silk shirt.

"Howdy neighbor. Mind if I come in?"

"I'm uh, kind of busy right now. Can we make it another time?"

"Hey, no problem. Listen Lou, I'm having some friends over later. Maybe you'd like to stop by?"

"Tell you the truth I haven't been feeling well lately. The doctor says I need some rest."

"Gee I'm sorry to hear that." The pothead tries to see inside but Picone blocks his view. "Tell you what, I'll see if I can switch this thing to another location. Give you some peace and quiet for a change."

"Ah hey, you don't have to do that. I'm one of those guys who can sleep through anything."

"I insist. Really, it's no problem. It's about time somebody else cleaned up the mess."

"I appreciate the offer but don't bother. It won't make any difference to me."

The pothead heaves a sigh. "To tell you the truth Lou, I'd give anything just to sack out in front of the tube for an evening. Sometimes I get sick of the whole business."

For a moment he really does look sick of the whole business, but then something shakes him out of it. He tells Picone a Polish joke and a story about someone named Bernie on the seventh floor. Picone feels foolish standing in the hallway. The pothead is making an overture of some kind, but Picone can't figure it out. Is he queer? Does he suspect something?

"Lou Dorsey . . . that's a great name. A movie star name. My real name is — get this — Angus. Can you believe it? Parents are cruel, man. I mean life is hard enough, right?"

"You don't look like an Angus," Picone assures him. The guy must suspect something, but what? Picone hasn't left the apartment for days except to lay in supplies. Maybe that's it. A world beater like the pothead would find that strange. It is strange.

"You know, you do look a little under the weather, Lou. Ever try vitamins? I've been taking them all winter and haven't had a sniffle."

"I guess I've been a little shaky since the operation."

"Jesus Lou! You should have said something. Now I'm definitely moving the party to Greta's place."

"Seriously, you don't have to brother."

"It's no problem. She lives three blocks away. Believe me, I know what it's like to be laid up. I broke my leg skiing last year. Nearly went crazy stumbling around my apartment for three months."

Picone steps back inside hoping to cut him off, but the pothead just keeps rambling. He pushes the door halfway but the pothead moves in closer.

"Give this a try, Lou." He hands Picone a thin joint. "Might not cure what ails you but you'll be too blitzed to care."

Picone waves him off but the pothead reaches over and drops it in his shirt pocket.

"Maybe you'll change your mind later. If nothing else it will help you sleep. Plus you can watch almost anything on TV." He gives a wink. "Just don't try to program your VCR."

Picone stands with his hand on the doorknob, looking down at the twisted end of the joint in his pocket.

"Thanks. Listen . . . I'll talk to you later, okay?" He steps inside and quickly shuts the door.

Stanley calls.

"We're on for Friday evening, Lids. The Kellehers will be at their daughter's for the weekend so you won't have to worry about them. After the deal, Mercer and the nigger should be celebrating at the Club Cabana until the wee hours."

"How do you know they'll leave the money here?"

"We're talking fifty grand at least! What do you think — they'll have it on them?"

"What if they take it to Maurice's?"

"The nigger lives in the badlands. Besides, Mercer went to the trouble of having a safe installed. He'll want to use it."

"He wants me to come over and have a beer."

"You talked to him?"

"He stopped me in the parking lot and introduced himself. What could I do?"

"That's terrific. Did you tell him you were gonna rob him?"

"I told him I was Lou Dorscy. I just had an operation."

"Jesus, I don't believe this! Look, I don't wanna know, okay? Just remember, Friday night. The Kellehers will be away. You should have most of the night."

"Tell me Stan, where do you get your information? All of a sudden you're like the fucking CIA."

"I know somebody. You gotta know people, Lids."

Martha Kelleher is carrying groceries in from a waiting cab when Picone returns from the diner. He tries to slip past but the old girl stumbles into him at the door.

"Need a hand with those, ma'am?" he offers.

"Why thank you, young man. I declare that doorman hides when he sees me coming." Her voice is warm and grandmotherly. Picone balances a bag in each arm and follows her into the elevator.

"I live on the third floor," she tells him.

"I know. I'm your new neighbor, Lou Dorsey."

"So *you're* the Wagner aficionado." She taps his wrist. "I can't tell you what a relief it is to be rid of the last one. Tell me, Mr. Dorsey, you're not a bird lover are you?"

"Not me." He struggles to push the button. "I don't think my Dobermans would go for it."

Mrs. Kelleher stiffens.

"Just kidding." He grins.

What's with the charming routine? For weeks he didn't speak to anyone but the waitress at the diner and now he's hobnobbing with the neighbors. Stanley would frown on this.

"My husband loathes Wagner. I must admit I find him a bit bombastic myself." Mrs. Kelleher's smile gives a hint of former beauty.

"It's just the radio," he confesses. "I'm afraid I'm not much of a music buff."

They step off the elevator into a cloud of marijuana smoke.

"This is an outrage!" Mrs. Kelleher waves a hand in front of her face. "My husband says to ignore it but the man has no shame!"

"Aw, it's not so bad. Reminds me of my youth."

"Oh you're just teasing." Another tap to the wrist. "Anyone can see you're not involved in such things. You must come in and meet my husband. You can tell him about the Dobermans."

"No really, I'm expecting a phone call —"

"Nonsense, we're right next door." She leans over the doorknob, patiently fitting key to lock. When the door swings open a slight, white-haired man is crouched in the doorway clutching a cast iron skillet.

"Gracious Walter, you were right there! Why didn't you open the door?"

"I thought you were being robbed," he says sheepishly. The skillet slips from his hand and crashes to the floor between his feet.

"And what were you going to do, dear?" Mrs. Kelleher brushes past him. "Console me with an omelette?"

"Why no. I was going to leap to your defense."

"Oh Walter, you're just like that old man in the hijack movie. The heroic one, remember? Those terrorists swatted him like a fly."

Picone's not so sure. He has, in fact, been coldcocked by just such a skillet during an ill-advised burglary some years earlier. His attacker was in his eighties. He sets the groceries on the counter and steps away.

"I really should be going."

"You must stay for tea." Martha waves him away from the door. "Walter, this is the young man who was playing *The Valkyries* the other night. Our new neighbor, Lou Dorsey. Mr. Dorsey? Walter."

"Mr. Kelleher." Picone offers his hand. The old man steps over the skillet to take it.

"My boy, it's a pleasure to meet you. I hope you'll excuse the paranoia but it's not like Martha to bring a handsome young stranger home." Walter chuckles. "I don't know what I intended to do with that frying pan, but I'm sure it would have been a humiliation for all of us."

"Walter is a physical wreck," Martha explains, herding them along. "I'm surprised he made it all the way to the kitchen without his walker."

"She's making that up — the walker part anyway." Walter gives him a pat on the back. "Although I must admit I've seen better days."

"Oh, he could go anytime." Martha takes Picone by the arm.

In contrast to his place the Kellehers' apartment is crammed with furniture. Bookcases and curio cabinets line the walls. They make their way around armoires and davenports to a set of facing sofas. Walter and Picone each take a sofa. Martha hesitates for a second then settles next to her husband.

"Any pets, Mr. Dorsey?" Walter asks.

"No birds. I already checked," Martha answers. "Tell him what you said, Mr. Dorsey."

"Aw, I was just being a wise guy." Picone blushes.

"He said a bird would disturb his Dobermans."

Walter stifles a groan.

"He was only teasing." Martha slaps his thigh.

"Walter and I are from Holland originally. We eloped to America when I was eighteen. You know something, Lou? We never looked back." Martha nods emphatically. They are into their second round of brandies and Haydn is playing ever so softly above their conversation. Picone wonders what happened to the tea.

"You didn't like Holland?" he asks.

"It's a lovely country, but we were young and ambitious. Walter saw himself as a New York gadabout jumping in and out of taxis. I planned to spend my life shopping."

"You did dear," Walter reminds her. "You see, Lou, when people come here for the first time they generally assume we moved here from a large house. That would explain the abundance of furniture. This, however, is not the case. Our Manhattan apartment was smaller still. Martha sees a room as something to be filled."

"I was preparing for a real home someday, but alas . . ."

"I've never met a Hollander before," Picone tells them.

"The Dutch have a way of blending in," the old man gently corrects him. "You probably know dozens without realizing it."

"Did you live near the windmills?" Picone conjures his puzzle.

"As a matter of fact, we did." Martha scoots to the edge of the sofa. "Walter and I lived near the sea. His town was twelve miles from mine and every evening he would ride over on his bicycle, right past the windmills."

They replay the scene in their heads, smiling serenely. These two are a riot.

"What do you do, Lou?" Walter arches an eyebrow.

"I'm in restaurant supplies." Picone gives his standard response. It's a line of work he could see himself in if he wasn't boosting apartments or doing time. It's also something he can bullshit his way through in a pinch. His cousin Dom is in restaurant supply and all he does is bitch.

"That sounds dangerous." Martha tugs at the hem of her dress.

"Dangerous?"

"Well, the papers say the restaurant business is run by the Mafia. Those gangsters from Philadelphia."

"The papers say everything is run by the Mafia. It saves a lot of legwork," Picone quotes his cousin directly.

There's a painting lit by a brass lamp above Walter's head. A night scene — the shadow of an old barn set against a moonlit sky. From where Picone is sitting the moon appears luminescent. He gets up to take a closer look but the effect is the same from any distance.

"Cadmium." Walter pulls a pipe from a rack built into the sofa.

Picone leans in closer. "In the paint?"

"A popular but imprudent artistic experiment. The man who painted that picture is said to have died from toxic poisoning."

Picone backs away. Through a gap in the drapes he can see a slice of the city in the fading light. A skewed version of his own view. Behind the washstands, cabinets, and common wall lies another world. Picone's world. Empty and wasted. An enormous craving for furniture rises within him. Forty-eight years old and nary a couch. What does this say about him? Loser. Convict. Not a single lamp or painting. He lived in a flophouse for two years before moving here, but when he tries to envision his furnishings he gets only vague shapes and general locations.

"My grandparents came over from Palermo in 1924," he hears himself say.

"Well then they must have come through Ellis Island, as we did sixteen years later." Walter scrapes at the bowl of his pipe with some sort of instrument.

"My grandfather was a mortician. He worked on Dutch Schultz and Fiorello La Guardia."

Is he crazy? Why is he telling them this? The truth. His mother grew up in a house filled with stiffs. His grandfather worked into his nineties and toward the end his own deterioration did little to comfort the bereaved. Rather than follow in his in-laws' footsteps, his own father turned to crime. In the end the old man sold the business and gave his money to the church. The new owners kept the name. *Venuto's*. Picone feels a chill every time he passes the place.

"Walter and I have decided to be cremated when the time comes," Martha says. "Our daughter has agreed to keep our ashes on a particular shelf above the radiator in her den. Frankly, the idea of moldering away is very distasteful." She wrinkles her nose. "This old body has been good to me and to throw it in a hole when I'm done seems downright disrespectful, if not barbaric."

"The older you get the more funerals you're obliged to attend," Walter adds. "We've been to a dozen in the past two years and I must tell you, I always shudder when they lower that box into the ground."

"Yes. How can we do that to them?" Martha wonders.

"And I, for one, get no consolation from the fact that my flesh will provide nourishment to the lower life forms," Walter grumbles. "It may be natural but it lacks dignity."

"Twin Cloisonné urns for us, right Walter?"

"Dignified."

Martha opens a tin of shortbread cookies and offers them to Picone. As darkness falls she traverses the room, angling gracefully around secretary desks and uncornered corner cabinets to light assorted stained-glass lamps. The soft glow makes Picone want to kick off his shoes.

"My grandfather talked to the dead," he babbles on. "He would address them by name as he worked and if he asked them a question, he would pause long enough for them to answer." All true. "The living didn't really interest him. My grandmother actually ran the business."

"Ridding the world of its dead. A lucrative profession," Walter observes.

"But your poor mother, growing up in a mortuary. I don't see how that could be healthy." Martha clutches at her collar. Picone thinks back to intermittent periods of refuge in his grandfather's house. He never once saw a body, but he knew they were there, draped in shrouds in the basement. When Petey Falcone died of leukemia Picone's grandfather handled the embalming personally. In deference to the family he made Petey look better in death than he ever looked alive.

"The way I figure it, when you're dead it really doesn't matter what they do with the body." Picone shrugs. "It isn't you anymore. It's just meat. The thing you gotta remember about cremation is it takes a while. It's not like they just pop you in the oven. They gotta cook it for a couple of hours."

Martha winces. "Is that true Walter?"

"I suppose so, dear. It is rather a large . . . er, piece of meat."

"Well, I never imagined the exact procedure . . ." Her face clouds for a moment. "Oh, I don't care. It's not like you can feel it."

"Who's to say?"

"Stop that Walter. You know how anxious I am about this. Besides, I already bought the urns."

"Why doesn't that surprise me?"

"I'd take this a little more seriously if I were you, Walter. After all, you're the one who's hanging by a thread. Perhaps I'll just have *you* cremated and see how it goes."

"That would be the wise thing."

"You could always freeze him," Picone suggests.

"Heavens no!" Martha shudders at the thought. "The idea is to avoid the cold. We want to be comfortable, you see."

Walter fires up the pipe and for a moment his head disappears in a cloud of smoke.

"Spending eternity in an urn might prove tiresome," he points out.

"They're lined in satin. I used the lining from one of your old violin cases."

It turns out that Walter Kelleher was a violinist in the Philharmonic orchestra before arthritis forced him into a well-furnished retirement. For the next hour he reflects upon a life unknown to the likes of Picone. Travel, culture, the arts, the artists. He tells colorful anecdotes about symphony screwballs and society geezers and describes the world's great concert halls in vivid detail.

"You don't strike me as the Wagner type." He jabs his pipe in Picone's direction.

"It was just the radio."

"The man was a fascist. The most insufferable egomaniac ever to draw breath,"

"It was just the radio."

They have progressed to the scotch and Martha's cheeks have taken on a distinct glow. The old timers can really put it away. Picone knows he should leave but is unsure if he can even stand. Walter steps effortlessly over to a framed photograph and hands it to him. The picture shows a stately brick building with a young Martha poised at the top step.

"The Academy of Music in Philadelphia," he says. "On the evening this picture was taken Pinchas Zuckerman nearly lost an eye to a broken violin string. Martha and I had just moved here. And this" — he points to a slash of white tail fin at the picture's edge — "is my Caddy. For a time I was the automotive trendsetter in residence."

"How long ago was that?"

Walter lights a match and holds it to his pipe.

"Well, let's see. We moved here in 1968, so that would make it twenty-eight years. Of course the neighborhood has changed considerably. First the Asians and now the movers and shakers. They're thinking of turning the building into condos, you know."

"No, I didn't."

"Can you imagine taking out a mortgage at our age?" Martha rolls her eyes. "We've decided to move if they force us to buy. Of course moving will probably kill Walter."

"I think we should just sell off everything and sponge off the children for a few years." Walter replaces the photograph.

"Listen to him, a few years. And then what Walter?"

"Oh, I don't know. Retire to Alaska?"

"Alaska? The idea is to get away from the cold."

"That's when we're dead, dear. While I still live and breathe I intend to distance myself from my fellow geriatrics."

Picone marvels at their patter. Most of the old people he knows have outlived their sense of humor. He wants to hear more about Holland and the symphony and possibly a bit more about their daughter who is, judging from various photographs, a younger version of her mother. But just as he's slipping off his shoes he hears a telephone ring in his apartment.

"I'd better be going." He struggles to rise. Before he can straighten up the ringing stops. Half bent over he glances over, smiles, and settles back into the sofa. Walter chuckles and fusses with his pipe.

"You know, Lou, Walter still has that Cadillac." Martha breaks the silence. "It's been sitting in a garage for almost fifteen years."

"A classic overindulgence. I'm afraid we became very attached, the Caddy and I." Walter shakes his head. "I intended to have it completely restored, but the automatic transmission self-destructed and then, before I knew it, a decade had passed. Even now I envision Martha and me rolling across the desert to parts unknown."

"That's my husband for you." Martha sighs. "I don't drive and he's one Scotch away from cerebral hemorrhage. Did you have a particular desert in mind, dear?"

"As a matter of fact I was thinking of Death Valley. The wildflowers in springtime. It's the kind of place old men dream about when they realize their limitations."

"Take a green pill, Walter. It'll make you feel better."

It's nearly eleven when Picone drags himself away. Martha sees him to the door and rises on her toes to peck his cheek.

"Thank you so much, Lou," she whispers. "We get so little company these days. I haven't seen Walter this animated in years."

"I think I might know somebody who might want to buy that Cadillac, Mrs. Kelleher."

"Oh goodness, I don't think Walter would ever sell."

"This guy is crazy for Cadillacs. He'd pay top dollar, depending on the condition. Tell you what, why don't you give me the address where it's stored and I'll take a look at it."

Martha glances over her shoulder and steps into the hallway. "It's at 227 Walker Street," she tells him. "I'm afraid it wouldn't be worth much after all these years.

"You never know. This guy's loaded."

The moaner arrives at the pothead's an hour later. Through the peephole Picone sees her pacing and hears the impatient snap of chewing gum. The pothead answers the door in a burgundy kimono. A real piece of work, this guy. Picone returns to the Matterhorn, listening as they gush over each other. Their enthusiasm undermines his solitude and he finds himself losing interest, even as he fits the jagged peak in place. For lack of anything better to do he goes to the kitchen to fix a sandwich. As he bends to search for the mayo the tiny joint falls from his pocket and rolls beneath the refrigerator. He hesitates for a moment, then kneels to retrieve it.

From the window he can see the old marquee of the Strand Theater. He remembers riding in the car, listening to his father describe the old landmarks — the dancehall turned into a tire outlet, the dry cleaners where the cigar shop used to be. Old places gave way to new places in those days. Now there is nothing to replace the past. It stays to haunt you, crumbling in front of your eyes. The Strand has been boarded up for more years than it was open. The dry cleaners and tire outlet are long abandoned. Anchored to empty neighborhoods, they fade but refuse to fall. Picone has walked these streets at night, moving through the shadows like a ghost. When he was a kid he was always afraid, but now he just feels sorry for himself.

One time they broke into a building over on Fourth Street that turned out to be a lodge meeting hall. They found uniforms and funny hats and in a back room, wonder of wonders, a steamer trunk filled with gleaming sabers. For weeks they played pirates under the Baker Street bridge until Danny Burns's mother called the cops. The papers dubbed them the Baker Street Buccaneers and even ran a picture of Danny with the sword jutting from his belt. The old lodge burned down while he was in prison. Danny Burns retired from the police department ten years ago.

He watches a show about hydrocephalics. The narrator explains that the brain continues to function even when compressed against the rim of the skull. He has the computer graphics to prove it. Picone hangs on his every word. He switches to a program about alternative energy sources and marvels at the logic. The CNN business report makes perfect sense.

Stan drops by in the morning to check on him. He sees the puzzles through the doorway, pushes past Picone, and walks the narrow path to the center of the room.

"Un-fucking-believable! If I didn't see it with my own eyes I wouldn't think it was possible."

"Yeah well, I'm trying to get it out of my system." Picone scratches his head. "There isn't a hell of a lot to do here, Stan."

"What's this?" Stan points to a puzzle with his shoe. "I think I've seen this one before."

"That's Pompidou Center. It's like an art museum."

"Looks like somebody turned it inside out."

"It's in France."

"The thing is, this makes me very nervous, Lids. Here you're schmoozing with Dopey next door and now you're doing the place in wall-to-wall puzzles. Think you got enough fingerprints here?"

"What do you think, I'm gonna leave them behind?"

"I don't know what to think. Why not just spray-paint your name and address on the wall?"

"Hey Stan, don't get your bowels in an uproar. Just worry about your end, okay? I open an empty safe and you owe me big time."

Stanley moves over to the window, straddling the Roman Colosseum to look outside.

"This is like one of those stories you hear on the corner, Lids. You know, local bungler takes a fall. Don't forget I have my reputation to consider."

"So give me a grand and we forget the whole thing. It's all the same to me."

Stanley steps away from the window, edges his foot beneath the Colosseum's upper rim, and sends the pieces flying.

"It's a matter of professionalism. Understand what I'm saying?" He sidesteps over to the Grand Canyon. "Fraternizing with a mark is unprofessional. This" — he kicks the Canyon halfway to the ceiling — "is not professional."

Picone doesn't flinch. Stanley's capacity for violence is a matter of record. As the beefy ex-con begins demolition on the Acropolis, Picone settles in the corner to watch.

"As for forgetting about it, forget about it." Stanley flings whole sections of the temple his way. "Friday night you go to work. When you're finished you check into the airport Holiday Inn. I'll meet you there Saturday morning. It's a cakewalk, Lids, in and out. You do this right and we move on to bigger things."

"Anything else, boss?"

"Yeah, scrub the place down. Every handle, every door, every fucking thing. They lift a print outta here and I promise you you'll never make it back to Rahway."

"What's that supposed to mean?"

"Hey, it ain't just me, homeboy. I got partners. The only thing these guys like more than money is whacking guys like you."

"Partners? What do you think I'm going to find in there, Stan?"

"Whatever you find you grab it all. Hey . . ." Stanley crouches next to Picone, balancing on the balls of his feet. "Listen, Lids, we go back a long way. I know you're a stand-up guy, but you're a little flaky sometimes, know what I'm saying? I worry."

Picone rolls his head into the corner.

"If you got partners how come I gotta lay out eight bills?"

Stanley rises and tends to the crease in his pants.

"Think of it as an investment, Lids. Come Saturday and you'll have more money than you can count."

Walker Street is a walled-in cinderblock building rimmed in razor wire. Inside, a half dozen uniformed mechanics huddle over assorted dismantled vehicles. Picone approaches a wiry Asian with a cigarette dangling from his lower lip. The Asian directs him to a fat man with mutton chop sideburns.

"Kelleher?" the fat man looks him over. "You mean that piece of shit Caddy? You want it? I'll give it to you."

"I want to know how much it would cost to restore it."

"Kelleher. Jesus, he must be in his eighties by now. What's this, a second childhood thing?"

"He doesn't know about it. I want it to be a surprise."

"It's a surprise all right. I woulda junked that boat years ago but the old guy sends a check every month for storage."

"How much?"

"Sixty bucks. Okay, it's a little steep but it ain't like I hold a gun to his head."

"To fix it. How much?"

"Jesus, I'd have to check it out."

"Would ten grand do it?"

"Oh yeah, we could do a nice job for ten grand. Not mint, of course, but very nice. Say, who are you, his kid? Kid Kelleher? Hey, Lee . . ." he calls to the Asian. "You ever hear of Kid Kelleher?"

Lee mutters an obscenity without losing the ash on his cigarette.

"I'm just a friend," Picone says. "Is the Caddy here?"

"Yeah sure, it's in the back."

Picone follows the fat man to a back room — "the morgue," as he calls it. A handful of vintage gas guzzlers sit shrouded in dust. At the far end, the Caddy. No serious body damage, no rust.

"Say, uh . . ." Picone glances at the name above the fat man's pocket. "Vince. Let me ask you something. For fifteen grand can we roll this off the assembly line, or what?"

"Fifteen grand and you got yourself a cherry Cadillac, Mr. . . . ?"

"Dorsey. Lou Dorsey. So Vince, when do you think we could get started on this?"

The fat man shakes his head. "Well, I'll be honest with you. We're booked for a good two months. With all the hotshots moving in, I got my hands full."

Picone paces the length of the room, marking the silence with each step. He pauses at a gutted '57 Chevy, shoves his hands in his pockets, and heaves a dramatic sigh. When the tension has reached the proper level he turns to the fat man and cups his hands to his chest à la Corleone.

"Like you say, Vince, the problem here is Mr. Kelleher is getting on in years. Did I mention that I'll be paying cash?" He repockets his hands and retraces his steps until he is standing in front of the sweating fat man. "What would another grand get me, Vince?"

"Another grand would put you at the top of the list, Mr. Dorsey."

"I won't forget it." He takes the fat man's hand, squeezing just hard enough. "I'll be around Saturday morning. What time you open here, Vince?"

"Usually eight-thirty, quarter to nine."

"Nine it is. Vince? . . . Ciao."

*

Friday night.

Maurice arrives carrying a suitcase in lieu of the attaché. Nostrils flaring with greed, he nods to the pothead and leads him through the handshakes before stepping inside. Picone can barely hear them at first. Moving along the wall with the stethoscope he tracks them through the living room to the bedroom. More locks, a dropped key, mumbled curses, and then they're inside.

"Come on, let me look at it," the pothead sputters.

The snap of suitcase latches is followed by a muffled scream, then two muffled screams. Stanley has stepped in it this time.

"Put it away, put it away," Maurice squeals. "No, don't touch it, don't touch it." His unseen histrionics send the pothead into belly laughs.

"We're rich. We're freaking rich," they shriek in whispers.

Picone makes himself a sandwich while they blow off steam.

Midnight comes and goes. Sprawled on the carpet smoking one cigarette after another, Picone endures a litany of delusions and pipe dreams culminating in a Maurice island fiefdom crawling with nasty bitches. His prurient interests revived, the pothead calls a cab to take them to the Cabana Club. The whine of tumblers sets off a medley of keys, locks, and shrill giggles fading down the hallway and into the night. Picone waits for fifteen minutes, then heads to the closet for his tools.

On his knees he runs the box-cutter blade over the wallboard in a low arch. Deep, but not deep enough to be heard. He retraces the cut line again and again moving left to right. After twenty passes he changes the blade and reverses directions. Slowly, methodically. A thin layer of dust covers the carpet, the scattered puzzle pieces, and the tops of his shoes. By the second pack of blades the carved-out section begins to work loose. A dozen more strokes and the blade pierces the wall at the top. Straining to be quiet, he pulls out the hump of sheetrock in one piece. The inside studs are placed a foot apart. Plenty of room. Stuffing a blanket in the gap between walls, he uses the cross beam as a straight edge, cutting parallel lines in the inside wall, connecting the lines with a cut along the cross beam. He works in a catcher's crouch, bracing himself with his free hand. He's done this sort of thing before. Patience is the key.

When the cut line is paper thin, Picone rocks on his backside and kicks out a perfect rectangle. It lands in the pothead's bedroom with a soft thud. The safe is centered on the far wall in a square patch where a picture should be. A toy with a ten-digit tumbler. He wedges a crowbar in the seam and pops it open.

Stanley calls at 2 A.M. Picone can hear the screech of brakes on a passing bus.

"What's going on, Lids? I'm going nuts here."

"I'm just getting started. Our boys left about an hour ago."

"It's a cakewalk, Lids," Stanley insists. Picone fingers a wad of bills, picturing a frosted cake with Betty Boop legs.

"Go to bed, Stan."

"By this time tomorrow we'll be in Atlantic City. I can see us, Lids. I can see us so clearly it scares me. I don't know what it is, man, but whenever I get this close something always screws up. Tell me nothing is gonna screw up, Lids. I need you to tell me."

"It's a cakewalk, Stan. Just like you said."

"Jesus, I got heartburn like you wouldn't believe. I can't get comfortable, you know? It's like I wanna crawl out of my skin. Sometimes I think it was better inside, Lids. No pressure, you know?"

"You need to relax, Stan. Take a bath. Fix yourself a stiff drink and soak awhile. It works for me."

"Yeah right. If I try to do anything I'll forget to worry and then we're in trouble. I swear to God this stuff makes me nutso."

"You could always come over and help."

"I can't let anyone see me there. I shouldn't even be calling. You know how far I had to walk to find a phone booth that works?"

"Let me go to work Stan."

Picone runs his finger along the map from the expressway to the Turnpike, then west to the interstate. The names of the towns run together like a morning traffic report. He remembers a class trip to Valley Forge when he was a kid and the time his parents stopped at Hershey Park on their way to Ohio. Dayton. That was the name of the town. His single Dayton memory is of his father sideswiping a station wagon, then berating the driver as his mother pleaded. From Pittsburgh he can catch a flight to Frisco. Find a nice place with a view of the Golden Gate Bridge. Picone closes his eyes and pictures the furniture in his future — a roll-top desk with secret compartments and tiny keys. A solid mahogany chest of drawers.

On the way out he tapes a note to the pothead's door.

See Stanley, Black Lexus. Airport Holiday Inn. 8 A.M. Love Lou

"How do I look, dear?"

"Positively rakish!" Martha reaches over to smooth a silver side-burn. Rakish indeed. In his tweed cap and Ray-Bans Walter is the picture of senior chic. He conceded the white ascot and cigarette holder at Martha's insistence, but then Walter has long deferred to Martha's sense of style.

"You look like an older FDR," she tells him.

"I feel like a new man, by God. A rambling rogue full of spit and vinegar." He takes her hand and brings it to his lips. "I can only think it's a miracle. The angel Lou Dorsey sent to us in the eleventh hour."

"A bolt out of the blue."

"And the timing, Martha! The exquisite confluence of fate. I must confess, at first my euphoria was tempered with regret for the lost years."

"You sure had me fooled, leaping around like an old baboon."

"Now I see it as a fitting conclusion to lives well lived. A finale of the grandest sort."

"I just pray he's not in some sort of trouble."

"The boy's a pistol, Martha." Walter pounds the steering wheel for emphasis. "I didn't think they made them like that anymore."

They lose themselves in silence as the miles slip by. At the freeway interchange Walter bears to the left and heads the old Caddy into the sunset.

Low Tide

FROM *Flesh and Blood*

SHAY STUDIED the customer's driver's license. It had been issued by the State of California approximately two years before. It stated that the name of the woman standing across the counter was Noreen Waldman and that she'd been born eighteen years ago. Her photo indicated that in the period of time since she'd posed for the DMV Noreen had gone through a few changes. The brunet bangs and rosy cheeks had been traded in for a platinum rooster cut and a chalk-powdered face accentuated by jet eyebrows and purple-black lipstick. Instead of a pressed schoolgirl blouse, Noreen was wearing a boutique-tattered T-shirt over latticed black spandex tights.

The bank was located on LA's Sunset Strip, an area not known for its conservative style of dress, but the girl was pushing it, Shay thought. And her orchid musk was almost as toxic as sewer gas.

But she did have a body on her.

"That's a screamin' corsage," Noreen Waldman said, pointing a black fingernail at the violet flower pinned to Shay's blouse. "I'm going org just looking at it."

Shay responded with a brief, patronizing smile. She placed the ID on the marble counter and picked up the check Noreen Waldman wanted to cash. It was for the sum of fifteen hundred dollars and no cents from Aristo Escorts, Inc., made out to "Nasty Wald." Shay looked at the girl and raised a questioning eyebrow.

"Nom de business," the girl said.

Trying to ignore another blast of the orchid musk, Shay turned the check over. It was properly endorsed. "How would you like it?" she asked.

"In my hand."

"I mean, in what denominations, large or small?"

"Like my men, big and hard."

Shay felt the blood rising to her face. She glanced at her cash drawer and saw nothing larger than hundreds. The bank had a prescribed limit to the amount a teller was allowed to keep there. The big bills were in a drawer below, near the carpet. Shay bent down and retrieved three five-hundred-dollar notes.

Nasty stared at the bills on the marble counter. "Can't you find me a Grover down there?"

Trying to hide her annoyance, Shay drew back two of the bills and hunkered down again, exchanging them for a one-thousand-dollar note from the bottom drawer.

Nasty smiled at her, folded the crisp bills once, then twice. Watching Shay watching her, she slid them inside the front of her tights. "My bank box," she said. "Big bills keep it nice and smooth." She touched herself. "Wanna feel?"

Shay stared at her without expression or reply.

"Well, *c'est la vie*," Nasty said, and blew her an orchid-scented kiss.

Shay watched the girl strut to the door.

"You okay?"

Taylor, the security guard, was standing at the counter in his gray uniform, holstered pistol on his hip. His ordinary, almost handsome face registered concern.

"I'm fine," she said.

"Problem with Morticia?"

"Nope."

"Smells like a two-bit whore," Taylor said.

"She's a little more expensive than that," Shay said.

"Strictly low tide," Taylor said. When Shay didn't respond, he added, "You know, what's left on the beach after —"

"I got it," Shay said.

He made her nervous. She hadn't seen anything about it in the rule book, but she assumed the bitchy bank manager wouldn't be too crazy about tellers yakking it up with the bank guard during business hours.

"Flower looks better on you than it did on the vine," he said, pointing to the violet bud.

"It was sweet of you."

"It's called a Princess," he said. "You up for a taco at lunch?"

She'd been working at the Sunset branch for only eight days. Her second day, she'd made the mistake of letting Taylor share her table at the Mucho Taco down the block. She'd thought he might be able to bring her up to speed on gossip about her coworkers and the manager, Sylvia Berg. But Taylor, a stolid man in his mid-forties whose half-day security turn was supplementing a retirement check from the army, seemed totally indifferent to office politics.

He was one of those God-and-country guys, full of talk about honor and integrity and all that happy horseshit. But he apparently had a thing for her. That morning he'd brought her the flower. A proud part-time security guard. Jesus!

"No taco today, Taylor," she said.

"Tomorrow?"

"We'll see."

She was watching him reluctantly amble back to his position near the door when a considerably more appealing figure caught her eye. Young, wearing an expensive Italian-cut cocoa-brown suit, narrow in the waist, broad in the shoulders. Deep-tanned, with blond hair that, combed straight back, was long enough to whisk against the collar of his black silk shirt. His eyes were hidden behind very dark sunglasses so thin and smoothly curved they resembled a burglar's mask.

She was amused by the overall effect. Buccaneer businessman.

He was headed toward her when, suddenly, a rumpled, bearded figure plunged in front of him clutching a deposit slip and a wad of cash. The buccaneer businessman shrugged and moved to the teller on her right. Greg something. She could remember the teller's full name if she concentrated.

But her new customer wouldn't let her. He shoved his money and deposit slip at her. "Hurry it up, honey," he said. "Got things to see, people to do."

"Yes, sir," she said.

"Shay."

The teller, Greg whatever, was calling her. His face was pale. Silently he showed her a slip of notepaper. His customer, the buccaneer, was smiling at her.

"What part of 'hurry it up' don't you understand?" her customer asked nastily.

"Y-yes, sir. Just a second."

The neatly typed note read: "My partner is watching with gun.

Take two stacks of $500 bills from bottom drawer. Place on counter. No alarm, no harm."

Greg was at his bottom drawer, complying with the request.

Shay searched the room. Business as usual. Taylor stood beside the front door, pointing a customer toward the area known as the platform, where the bank's service reps sat. Sylvia, the manager, was absent. Probably in the alley catching a smoke. Great timing.

Shay bent down and found two stacks of five-hundred-dollar bills. Twenty-five to a stack, tightly wrapped. Twenty-five thousand dollars.

"Hey, honey," her customer said. "What the hell are you doin'? I said I'm in a hurry. Chop-chop."

Then there was a softer voice, almost a whisper. "One more peep out of that hairy mouth and my partner will shoot you in your fucking head. Dig? Good boy. Now, I'll take that off your hands."

Shay arose. The buccaneer businessman was standing next to her customer, his back hiding his actions from Taylor. No one else in the bank seemed to notice that a robbery was taking place. The bearded customer stood wide-eyed and frozen as the blond man added his bills to Shay's packs and slipped the combination into his inside coat pocket. Then he took a sideways step and retrieved Greg's packets.

"Thanks for your cooperation," he said quietly. "Stay chilled for five minutes. My partner will leave and nobody bleeds."

He turned and calmly walked toward the door. He stumbled on the way and Taylor grabbed him and helped him regain his balance. The blond man smiled gratefully and Shay could see his lips form the words "Thanks, Officer."

Then he was gone.

Shay, Greg, and the bearded customer stood like statues for about a minute, with the tension growing nearly unbearable. Then the bearded customer threw himself to the floor, shouting, "It's a robbery, goddammit!"

Faces turned their way. Taylor was the first to react, charging toward them, hand on holster. He scowled at the customer in the fetal position on the floor.

"It was the guy in the brown suit," Greg said in a rush. "With the shades."

"His partner's here with a gun," Shay said.

Taylor scanned the frightened and startled faces on the scattered customers. "Not likely. Hit the alarm."

"Done," Greg shouted at Taylor, who was racing to the front door. "And he's got a dye pack."

A dye pack. Shay couldn't believe it. She'd pegged Greg as a total wuss. But he'd had balls enough to slip the buccaneer a dye pack along with a stack of real bills. Two to three minutes after exposure to the microwave signal at the bank doors, the dye pack would explode, covering the buccaneer with red paint, dyeing that long blond hair, sending blinding tear gas past those expensive sunglasses, maybe even scorching that expensive suit.

Convinced that there was no longer any danger, the bearded customer rose to his feet just as the branch manager, Sylvia Berg, approached from the rear of the bank. "What's going on?" she demanded.

"We've been robbed, Sylvia," Shay said.

"Dammit." The bank manager wheeled around, looking at the startled customers. "Where's my security?"

"He ran off after the guy," Greg said.

Sylvia pursed her lips, then turned to Shay. "Your station?"

"And Greg's."

"How much?"

"Twenty-five thousand," Shay said.

"Twelve thousand five hundred," Greg said, adding smugly, "and a dye pack."

"You were carrying that much? You know the bank's policy —"

"The robber made us get it from the bottom drawer," Greg said.

"He knew about the bottom drawer? I have to call Mysner." Joseph Mysner was the bank's head of security.

The bearded customer said, "You in charge?"

"Yes, sir. I'm the branch manager, Sylvia Berg."

"Well, Sylvia, you're out another nine hundred bucks, too. That's what he took off me."

"The robber took your money, Mr. . . . . ?"

"Calusia. Chick Calusia. Yeah. He took my cash. And it's this broad's fault."

Sylvia's unblinking, birdlike green eyes shifted to Shay.

"My fault?"

"If you'd got off your ass and deposited my cash, I'd of been out of here."

"Shay?" Sylvia asked.

"I'm sorry. This 'gentleman' started to hand me his deposit — which was for only six hundred dollars, by the way — and that's when the robber —"

"Excuse me, sister. You move like you're being paid by the hour. I was standin' here for ten fucking minutes waiting for you to get it in gear. And the amount was nine hundred fucking dollars."

"Sylvia, that's not —"

"We'll discuss this in a —"

Sylvia was interrupted by the sound of gunfire from out on Sunset. All conversation stopped in the bank. People turned toward the front door, curious, afraid.

A young man with spiked hair and tattoo-covered arms banged against the door, backed up, and tried again. This time he got it open. "Call the cops," he shouted, ducking down, hands protecting the back of his partially shaved head. "There's a dude out in the street, wailin' with a gun. Crazy. Covered in red paint."

Shay's heart skipped a beat.

Ignoring Sylvia and the bearded man, she rushed to the teller gate, fumbled it open, and headed for the front door. She heard Sylvia calling her name. Screw her.

Shay stepped from the bank to a glare-bright, shockingly subdued Sunset Boulevard. Traffic had stopped. People were pressed against the sides of buildings. Everyone seemed to be staring at the red-dye-stained figure sitting in the middle of the street, keening in pain, hands pressed against his tearing eyes. His discarded gun was at his side.

It was the bank guard, Taylor.

Taylor's eyes stung so much his mind wasn't working. One side of his chest seemed to be aflame. His eyes felt like they'd been hit by acid. He knew he was down and in trouble. He just couldn't sort out what had happened. Had he been shot? Stabbed? Maybe he could start to figure it out if he opened his eyes. But they hurt so bad. What hurt even worse was that he'd fucked up, dishonored himself.

He was brought back to some semblance of reality by a woman calling his name. He recognized the voice. The beautiful teller. Shay.

"We've got to get you out of the street," she said.

Car horns began to blare.

He nodded.

She bent beside him, guided his arm around her shoulders. "Up we go."

Even through the pain and confusion he was vitally aware of her body rubbing against his as they struggled. Then he was up. Not quite balanced, but up. She hugged his waist, her firm breasts pressing against his arm as she walked him slowly toward the bank. His eyes were wet, still burning, but he was catching up to the situation. "My gun," he said.

"In the street. I'll get it in a second."

"Christ! Did I shoot anybody?" he asked.

"Not that I can see," she said, propping him against the front of the bank.

Blinking through the tears, he watched her blurred image run back into the street, bend down, and retrieve his gun. What a goddamned woman! And what a goddamned disgrace he was.

They fired his ass, of course.

Taylor's chest was tender from the dye pack, but the skin wasn't even broken. An optometrist from the neighboring discount glasses store checked his eyes and bathed them in some kind of fluid.

The burning had just about disappeared when the bank's head of security, Joseph Mysner, showed up with John Pinella, the head of American Guard Services, the guy Taylor worked for. Mysner looked like a college footballer gone to seed, big, balding, and red-faced. At about half his size, Pinella was a sleek, olive-complexioned man wearing a wrinkle-free pinstriped suit and a faintly amused smile.

Taylor sat quietly in the bank's conference room while Sylvia Berg and the two men discussed his pathetic response to the robbery. They all seemed to be on the same page: he'd fucked up royally. He couldn't disagree.

When the bank reps left to "confab" with the arriving FBI agents, Pinella sighed and shook his head. "You really fucked the duck, my boy."

Taylor looked down at the bright stains on his hands. He had them under his chin, too. "Guess that's why my face is so red, huh?"

"It's the gunplay I don't get," Pinella said. "That the way you did it in the MPs? Shoot first?"

The question shook Taylor. But there was no way Pinella could know about the way he did it in the MPs, no way anyone alive could. "I never took a dye pack to the chest and face before," he said. "I coulda sworn I'd been hit by incoming, Cap." Pinella liked his men to call him Cap.

"That's the other thing. You let the goddamned perp slip the pack into your jacket pocket."

Right. That's what really galled him. The son of a bitch had played him. Just like the towelhead had played him that night in Kuwait City. But he'd found the Arab scam artist again and regained some of his self-respect. He felt his fury rising, but this wasn't the place for it. He took some deep breaths and said, "You think I like being played for an asshole, Cap?"

Pinella's face softened a little. "Guess not," he said.

"It'd be nice to get out of here. Go to bed and nurse my wounds."

"Not gonna happen, guy. Not for a while. You got cops to talk to, and FiBIes, and paperwork like you've never seen. Lucky nobody got hurt."

"Except me," Taylor said. "Maybe I should check in with a lawyer."

Pinella frowned. "Don't piss me off, Taylor. You already put us in the soup. Be a good boy and we'll find you something to do. Night watchman. Something."

Key-ryst. Night goddamned watchman. If only he could get his hands on that fucking Mr. Slick, he'd . . . aw, what the hell!

Taylor staggered from the conference room in search of cops and/or feds. He desperately wanted to do what he had to and get the hell away from the bank, from the scene of his humiliation and failure.

He wasn't sure how he felt about seeing Shay, but he needn't have worried. She wasn't in the main room. Probably off somewhere being questioned. Debriefed. He hated jargon like that. It was one of the things he didn't miss from the MPs.

Shay had expected to stay the full day at the bank, but she was out and away by three in the afternoon. And once again at liberty.

She'd asked for it. There was about an hour in which she sat around waiting to give her deposition. And another hour, roughly, before the representatives of law and order were finished with her. At that point she and Sylvia got into a discussion about Chick Calusia and the amount of his deposit.

"Since the robber took Mr. Calusia's deposit slip with his money," Sylvia had told her, "it's your word against his."

"So?"

"So we're depositing nine hundred dollars into Mr. Calusia's account," Sylvia said. "And, to minimize the bank's exposure to possible legal action initiated by Mr. Calusia, you're going to personally apologize to him for any inconvenience or indignity he may have experienced."

"I don't think so," Shay said.

"This isn't a discussion. If you wish to continue working here at the bank —"

"Fuck the bank," Shay replied. "Fuck Mr. Calusia and, Sylvia, especially, fuck you."

Shay was feeling remarkably alive as she drove through the afternoon traffic. She was approaching the house when she recognized a woman driving past in a periwinkle-blue Miata convertible, her short platinum hair dancing in the wind.

It took a few seconds for Shay to weigh the odds of her crossing paths with Nasty Wald again that day. She didn't put much stock in coincidence.

Taylor was lying on his couch in his underwear watching TV when the door buzzer sounded. He'd been there for nearly an hour, sipping vodka from a half-gallon plastic jug and trying to get his mind off the humiliation he'd suffered. On the small screen a woman in a dress cut down to her pierced navel appeared to be singing while a shirtless stud, standing behind her, kissed her neck and ran a hand the size of a phone book down her firm thigh. Taylor had the sound turned down as far as it would go. He hated contemporary music. But he was a big fan of videos.

He'd seen this particular one before and he knew that as a result of the stud's rubbing, or something, the singer's nipples were about to burgeon under the gauzy gown. Whoever was at his door knocked.

Annoyed, he called out, "Go away."

"It's me. Shay."

Taylor grabbed the remote and clicked off the TV right in the middle of the nipple shot, then rolled off the couch. "Minute," he told her. He looked down and saw that he was poking out of his Skivvies. He staggered to the bedroom and grabbed a ratty striped bathrobe from the floor where he'd dropped it a couple of days ago. When he got to the front door, his fingers struggled with the slip lock before it came free.

Then she was standing in the doorway. Outlined by the dim lighting in the hall, she reminded him of the way women looked in movies when he was in the first throes of puberty. The Angie Dickinson kind of blonde — full-bodied, golden-haired, the back-light adding an irresistible air of streetlamp mystery.

She was wearing the same clothes she'd had on earlier at the bank. But her blouse had lost its press, its top buttons were undone, and her legs were bare under her skirt. "Okay if I come in?" she asked.

"Wha — oh sure. Yeah."

He was embarrassed by the place. It was a cheap furnished apartment in a lousy section of town. But she didn't seem to care about the surroundings, one way or another. "I was worried about you," she said.

"I'm okay." He kicked sections of the morning paper out of the way, opening a path to the couch. "Sit down. Can I, uh, get you something?"

"Maybe later," she said. "Right now, you should get dressed and come with me."

"What?"

"You stoned, Taylor?" she asked, not reprimanding him, merely curious.

"I'm okay," he said, a little defensively.

Her eyes dropped to his crotch and she smiled. "I guess you *are* glad to see me," she said. His dick was poking through the robe.

Mortified, he tucked himself away.

She moved closer and to his surprise and pleasure placed her hand on his erection. "That's some icebreaker," she said. Then she rose on tiptoe to kiss him. Her lips were soft and moist and he felt them part as her tongue slid past.

His battered body shivered as her pelvis rubbed against him, her tongue exploring his mouth. Then she pulled away, breathing heavily. "That was . . . good for openers," she said.

He reached for her, but she danced away. "Not just yet. There's something more important for us to take care of."

"I don't think so," Taylor said, reaching for her again.

"I know where he is," she said. "Right this minute."

Taylor's boozy, sex-revved mind couldn't take the shift. "He?"

"The man who robbed the bank."

He blinked. "You found him? How?"

"The freak-show girl who came in just before him. The one you called low tide. She drove by me a while ago and it got me to thinking. She made me open my bottom drawer. Then the crook showed and he knew where we keep the big bills. Anyway, she drove past and I followed her right to the bastard.

"I was going to call the police. But I got fired today, too. So I don't give a damn about the money or the bank. But I do give a damn about you, and I hate the way you've been fucked over. All your talk about honor and pride, I figured you for the kind of guy who'd rather do the job himself."

"You got that right," he said. Goddamn, but she was one of a kind! "Where are they?"

"Get dressed and I'll show you," she said.

It was at that moment that Taylor discovered something new about himself. He wanted her more than he wanted revenge. "They can wait," he said, pulling her to him.

"There's no time," she began. But her resistance was half-hearted. When they kissed, the fever he was feeling seemed to infect her, too. Her hand pushed his robe aside just as his went beneath her skirt.

The couch was only a few feet away, but they didn't get that far. They made love on the hard floor, the sheets of the discarded morning paper crackling and tearing beneath them. She wasn't wearing anything under the skirt. He slid right into her.

Taylor was nearly delirious with pleasure. When he thought about it later, he wondered if part of his euphoria wasn't due to the prospect of getting his hands on that smug fucking bank robber.

"What do we do if they're gone?" Shay said as Taylor's battered pea-green Chevy bounced along the freeway.

"Find 'em again," He liked having her with him, liked everything about her. But, in his postcoital mood, romance was losing its battle with revenge. Even with her hand on his lap.

The hand moved and he felt himself stirring. But it was the Beretta Centurion stuck behind his belt that she touched. "This isn't the same gun . . ."

"At the bank? Hell no. That one's in a bag in some evidence locker. This is something I picked up overseas."

"You ever . . . use it?"

"There was a time something happened, kinda like what went down at the bank. This Kuwaiti asshole set me up."

"What'd he do?"

"Tried to disgrace me, to make me less a man," Taylor said. He wasn't about to provide her with any of the details.

"Turn here," Shay said.

The canyon road took an abrupt upward angle. As they continued following the road, the dinner-hour traffic thinned to almost nothing. The higher they went, the fewer houses they passed. The occasional streetlights did a lousy job of chasing the night away.

Inside the car, there wasn't much conversation, until:

"There," Shay said, pointing to a shadowy two-story wooden house tucked into a notch in the canyon wall. A shiny black Porsche Boxster was parked near a wooden stairwell that led to an upper-level entrance. A light was on deep in the house.

Taylor gave the place a snapshot glance, then continued up the canyon just far enough to be out of view from the house. He hugged the canyon wall, leaving enough room for other cars to pass if the drivers were careful. "Only the Porsche," he said. "The girl's?"

"She was driving a Miata. He must be alone."

"Or they both left in her car."

"I don't think so," Shay said. "If they'd gone somewhere together, he'd have wanted to drive the Boxster, right? Mr. Macho."

"Probably," Taylor said. "Ill go see." He opened his door.

She slid over to get out, too. "No. You stay," he said. He pulled the Beretta from his belt.

"What's your plan?" she asked, eyes on the gun.

"That's why I want you to stay here," he said. "So you won't know."

He eased the car door shut. Shay's face looked pale in the moonlight. Pale and beautiful and troubled. He leaned through the open window and kissed her on the lips. It was a cool, almost passionless kiss.

"It'll be fine," he said.

He was expecting her to say something like "Be careful." Or maybe "Don't shoot unless you have to."

She said, "Any hint of trouble, honey, shoot the son of a bitch."

She was definitely one in a million.

The left side of the house came within inches of the canyon wall. On the other side a high wooden gate guarded what appeared to be a narrow path to the rear. The gate was locked. That left the door at the top of the stairs.

Taylor climbed the heavy wooden steps quickly and soundlessly. As he approached the front door, he could hear music. Samba, maybe. The door was cracked an inch or so. He used the gun barrel to push it open farther.

Light filtered through a glass wall at the rear of the house. There was enough of it to illuminate a room with a few pieces of cheap wicker furniture. A couple of chairs, a matching table, a sofa with cushions of a dark color that might have been black or midnight blue. The floor was unfinished; the walls bare. The only things that suggested human occupancy were the odors of the punk girl's cheap orchid perfume and something even more repellent.

Taylor moved cautiously and quietly across the concrete, stepping down into a sunken area that had no furniture at all. The glass wall looked out on a brightly lit patio with a wooden deck and a small dark pool constructed to resemble a lagoon. A stream flowed into it from a fake waterfall that seemed to extend from the canyon wall. The music was coming from a medium-sized boom box on the deck, between a couple of cheap lawn chairs. A beer bottle was on its side near the boom box.

Satisfied that the pool area was deserted, Taylor moved to the right, where a narrow hall led to a shadowy bedroom. The odors intensified. Decaying orchids and sex and overriding them both, the nearly toxic smell of feces and urine. Holding his breath, Taylor stood at the doorway to the bedroom, getting a quick fix on it before stepping in.

It, too, drew its light from the patio, through an open sliding glass door. It was the only room in the place that looked lived in.

Clothes were thrown around, men's and women's. A wastebasket overflowed with cleaner's bags and wrappers. The bed looked well used, with what appeared to be black silk sheets rumpled enough for the mattress to peek through. From his position, Taylor could see nothing to account for the terrible smell.

Near the foot of the bed was a pile of loose thousand-dollar bills and a packet of money that still had the bank seal attached. If the loot was still around . . .

Taylor took a step into the bedroom and immediately regretted it. His peripheral vision picked up a naked arm pointing a gun directly at him from a corner of the room.

Taylor froze, then slowly raised his hands, slipping his finger from the trigger guard of the gun but not dropping the weapon. He didn't know what else to do. He figured the robber would tell him. Or shoot him.

There was only silence.

He turned his head in what he hoped was a nonthreatening manner.

The man with the gun was the same one who'd robbed the bank and humiliated him. He wasn't looking so good. He was naked, huddled in the corner, his skin waxy and tinged with blue. His gun arm was propped on top of a wicker table. His head rested against a wall, unblinking eyes flat and cloudy, staring at the doorway without seeing it.

Taylor was reasonably sure the man was dead, but he still took a sideways step out of the line of fire. His eyes were watering from the stench, his stomach churning, as he cautiously approached the naked body. Blood, now crusted, had flowed from three holes in the bank robber's chest and stomach. He was seated in his own excrement, not that he minded the discomfort.

Taylor reached over the table and grabbed the barrel of the naked man's gun. But he couldn't pry it loose without breaking fingers. There was no pulse in the man's neck. He was definitely an ex-human. Let him keep the fucking gun if it meant so much to him.

Taylor felt a breeze against his neck and turned quickly.

Shay stood at the bedroom door, a handkerchief pressed to her nose. In her other hand she held a gun. Everybody had one these days, it seemed.

"I . . . was worried," she said, lowering the weapon. "Is he dead?"

"None deader," Taylor said.

"I didn't hear . . . You didn't . . . ?"

"Shoot him? No. This happened a while ago. He's already start-ing to stiffen up," he said, walking toward her. "Let's get out of here."

"The freak must have killed him."

"That's a good bet. C'mon. Before I toss."

"Look at all the money," Shay said behind the kerchief.

"Yeah. Stomach full of bullets and he still was able to scare her off before she could grab any of it."

"You think that's what happened?"

Taylor nodded. "Let's get out of here."

"Shame to leave all that money." She moved into the room. Shoving the handkerchief into a pocket, she grabbed a handful of the loose bills.

They'd been covering something small and violet.

Taylor blinked, but the violet object didn't go away. It was the Princess flower he'd given Shay that morning.

She saw it, too. "Well, shit," she said, and pointed her gun at him. It was a nice little Walther, he noticed. A good choice. "Better drop that piece of yours, huh, Taylor."

She threw the money back on the pile and picked up his Beretta, A gun in each hand, she said, "Let's take this out on the patio. It's getting a little close in here."

Shay followed Taylor out into a warm night and the sound of samba music and the gurgling of the fake waterfall. It was a relief to breathe, to clean some of the stench from her nostrils.

"Whoo-eee," she said, using her clothed elbow to slide the door shut behind them. "I always knew Del was full of shit, but c'mon now."

"What happened, Shay? You catch him with the punk bimbo?"

"You want to turn off that music?" she said. "I don't much feel like a mambo right now."

It took him a second to find the off button on the boom box.

"Now sit, Taylor," she said. "We have to talk."

"It won't do us any good if we're caught here with ol' Del," he said.

"This place is pretty isolated."

"Miss Low Tide might come back."

"I hope not," she said. "Three's a crowd. Sit."

The lawn chair scraped against the deck under his weight.

"Lie back," she said. "That way we can talk without me worrying about you making some stupid macho move." She perched on the edge of the remaining chair. "First off, I didn't kill Del. It must've been the psycho bitch. I saw her driving away."

"You Del's wife?"

"No way. We played around a little. That was about three years ago, when I was still an honest, underpaid teller at a bank in Arizona. Del picked me up in a bar. He fucked me and together we fucked the bank. Then we fucked more banks. Once I wised up a little, saw the kind of fella he was, I ended the romance. Too many deadly diseases out there. Del couldn't keep it in his pants and he didn't believe in rubbers. Since then, we've just been business partners, me getting jobs at banks and him robbing 'em."

"How does Miss Low Tide fit in?" Taylor asked.

She shrugged. "My guess is he picked her up today. It was just like him to be hustling tramps on the street in front of a bank he was about to rob."

"Why'd she shoot him? Lovers' quarrel?"

"Who the hell knows? Maybe she saw the money, tried to kill him but screwed up. He was able to get his own gun and chase her off."

He had his head cocked to one side, looking at her with an odd smile. She suspected he was wondering if she was bullshitting him, if she'd been the one who'd put the holes in Del. Was there something on her face for him to read? Maybe that she'd left the bank earlier than Del had expected and saw the crew-cut bitch driving away. That the goddamned house had been reeking of the stink of orchids and their lovemaking. That fucking Del hadn't even bothered to put his clothes back on or change the sheets.

Could he tell that Del, the insatiable bastard, had thrown her down on that still-damp bed and fucked her and then gone out to the patio for the beer that he'd been drinking? Could Taylor see it in her eyes that she'd put her clothes back on, found the money and one of Del's several guns, and called out sweetly for him to come back to the bedroom?

He'd been at the patio door, smug and with a hard-on, when she shot him twice. But the bastard didn't fall. He staggered toward her and she lost it. Dropped the money and shot him again. He fell on the bed and she thought that had to be the end of it. But as she moved toward the fallen loot, he rolled over on the bed. In his hand was his gun, the one he slept with.

She stumbled back without the cash, firing again as she ran from the room.

Breathless, she paused near the front door, considering the situation. She'd shot him what? Three, maybe four times? How long could it take for the blood to run out of him?

There was no sound from the bedroom. Just the fucking radio music out on the patio.

"Hey, Del," she called out. "How's it hanging?"

"Come on in and see, baby."

Shit. He didn't sound that weak. So what? She could outwait him. Then grab the loot and drift away. But . . . the cash was minimal, compared to the more than four hundred grand Del had stashed away in bank boxes across the state. He used to joke that he wasn't stealing the money, he was merely moving it around from one bank to another. She'd made it her business to keep track of the locations and the various fake names he'd used. And she could do a fair job of imitating his handwriting. But she couldn't stand in for him. She needed a man to front the deal.

That was when she'd thought of Taylor.

She was a little startled when he asked, "Why'd you come to my apartment, Shay? What am I doing here?"

"I'll level with you," she said. "At the bank I thought you were a nice enough guy, but there wasn't anything there for me. Then Del messed you up. When I saw you like that, blind and in pain, I felt . . . I'm not sure what I felt. But it was something . . . different. Intimate." The weird thing was that she wasn't lying, exactly.

"That's good?"

"Yeah. Intimacy. Something I've been missing."

"It'd help me to believe that," Taylor said, "if you put down the guns."

She hesitated, then thought, What the hell? She needed him, needed his cooperation. Considering the sort of lovesick way he was looking at her, she didn't think she needed the guns. She placed them on the deck. "Better?"

"Much." He leaned forward and picked up her Walther. Sniffed it and smiled. "Sorry, but I had to make sure."

"I know," she said. The gun she'd used, one of Del's many, was resting at the bottom of the canyon. She stood slowly. "Maybe we'd better collect my stuff, clean up a little, and get going."

"There's no hurry, like you said." He shifted his legs to make room for her.

She sat down, facing him. She felt a slight unease because she couldn't quite read his mood. But she was a firm believer in her sexual attraction. She was convinced she could seduce him into joining her in collecting Del's loot. She placed a hand on his arm. "After the . . . incident at the bank today," she said, "I wanted to stay with you while you were recovering. But Sylvia and that security guy insisted I go with them."

She tenderly touched one of the red splotches on his neck. He closed his eyes, apparently enjoying her touch. "What happened after you left the bank?" he asked.

"I drove here."

"Del was alive?"

"Yes. I told him I'd decided to end the partnership. He wasn't happy. I was packing a bag when he grabbed me and dragged me to the front of the house. He threw me out, told me never to come back. I said I wanted my things. He laughed at me. Slammed and locked the door. There wasn't much else I could do, so I drove away. When I reached the bottom of the drive, Little Miss Punk passed me driving up."

"Why didn't you tell me all this before?"

"I . . . didn't want you to know I was involved in the robbery." Was that true? Good lies always had a little truth hidden in them. She didn't want to lose him. Was it more than just the money? Maybe. "I was afraid you'd throw me out, too."

"I'd never do that," he said.

She pressed against him, resting her head on his chest. His arm went around her shoulders. "I love you, Taylor," she said. "It just might work, you and me."

His body relaxed. His hand moved a strand of her hair so that he could kiss her ear. "You and me," he whispered.

Something was definitely happening to her. She was no longer conning him. She was falling in love with him. Either that or she was conning herself.

"I don't want any secrets between us," he said.

"No secrets," she agreed, curious now as to where he was headed.

"You asked me about the Kuwaiti who screwed me over," he said. "Still want to hear the story?"

"If you want to share it," she said.

"Seven years ago in the Persian Gulf, during my last tour of duty, about eight o'clock at night, a pretty local girl waved down my jeep near this town of Kazimah. Her boyfriend had gotten pissed at her and left her out there on the road to hitch back to Kuwait City. She was a secretary for one of the oil companies, she said. The whole thing was a lie. A setup."

"A setup for what?" Shay asked.

"My partner, Jeb Cooley, and I were scheduled that night to guard an army warehouse. While the girl and I were . . . while we were at her place, her lover and some other guys bounced a lead pipe off of Jeb's skull and cleaned out the warehouse. Nothing crucial like arms or medicine. Just cases of whiskey, wine, beer, Coca-Cola, little foil pouches of macadamia nuts — crap like that — all of it about to be sent out to temporary officers' clubs throughout the area. Over a hundred grand in booze and snacks, worth three times that on the Kuwaiti black market."

"You must've got in terrible trouble."

"No. I told everybody I'd had a flat tire. They were suspicious, of course, and on my ass for a while, but since I wasn't really involved in the robbery, there was no way they could find any evidence. Still, the suspicion was there. Jeb, who'd been as close to me as a brother, put in for a new partner. And that was that for my military career."

"Why didn't you try to catch the real thieves?" she asked.

He smiled ruefully. "That was the beauty of it. If I'd brought in the Kuwaiti who planned the break-in, the story about me and the girl would have come out. I would have gotten off the hook for the theft, but I'd have been found guilty of dereliction of duty. By keeping the lie I could at least get an honorable discharge and collect a pension."

"So the guy who pulled the robbery walked away free and clear."

"Not exactly," Taylor said. "I found him and I beat him with my gun butt until my arm got tired. He never recovered."

"You killed him?" She seemed shocked.

"Don't you think he deserved it? He robbed me of my good name and my self-respect and he forced me to give up the only job I ever loved."

"Oh, honey," she said, hugging him. Then a question popped into her head. Without thinking, she began, "What happened to the g —" She censored herself.

But not soon enough. "The girl?" he asked. "What happened to her?"

"I guess. Did you ever see her again?"

"Once more," he said. "The guy — the one I pistol-whipped to death — there'd been nothing personal in what he did. I was just somebody in the way of his plan, so he had me removed. But the girl — she made it very personal. I had no choice. I did the only thing I could."

Shay was frowning now. She didn't really want to know, but she heard herself asking, "Wha-what did you do to her?"

"What I had to," Taylor said. "I did this." He pointed her own Walther against her taut stomach.

She barely got out the word "No" before he pulled the trigger.

Taylor rested Shay's body on the chair. Her cheek was still warm when he kissed it. He dabbed at his tears. Then he wiped the Walther clean. He wiped the power button of the boom box, too. He was glad the white-haired freak hadn't participated in the robbery, in his humiliation. Taking a human life gave him no pleasure.

He paused for one final look at Shay. "You and me," he said.

He reentered the dreadful bedroom and tossed Shay's Walther onto the roiled king-size. Holding his breath, he wiped his prints from the barrel of Del's pistol.

As he made his way to the door, he was stopped by the pile of cash. Over thirty-five thousand dollars. A nice bundle of found money. But it was stolen goods. Tainted. It offered no temptation to a man who prided himself on honor and integrity.

Taylor bent down and reached past the money to pick up the wilted violet flower. He took that away with him. He thought he'd get it laminated. Carry it in his wallet. Once the red dye and the burns wore off, it would give him something to remember Shay by.

RICHARD A. LUPOFF

The Incident of the Impecunious Chevalier

FROM *My Sherlock Holmes*

IT WAS NOT BY CHOICE but by necessity that I continued to read by oil lamp rather than arranging for the installation of the new gas lighting. In my wanderings throughout the metropolis I had been present at demonstrations of M. Lebon's wondrous invention and especially of the improved thorium and cerium mantle devised by Herr von Welsbach, and thought at length of the pleasure of this brilliant mode of illumination, but the undernourished condition of my purse forbade me to pursue such an alteration in the condition of my lodgings.

Even so, I took comfort of an evening in crouching beside the hearth in my lodgings, a small flame of dried driftwood flickering on the stones, a lamp at my elbow, and a volume in my lap. The pleasures of old age are few and small, nor did I anticipate to experience them for many more months before departing this planet and its life of travail. What fate my Maker might plan for me, once my eyes should close for the last time, I could only wonder and await. The priests might assert that a Day of Judgment awaited. The Theosophists might maintain that the doctrine of Karma would apply to all beings. As for me, the Parisian metropolis and its varied denizens were world enough indeed.

My attention had drifted from the printed page before me and my mind had wandered in the byways of philosophical musings to such an extent that the loud rapping upon my door induced a violent start within my nervous system. My fingers relaxed their grasp upon the book which they held, my eyes opened widely, and a loud moan escaped my lips.

With an effort I rose to my feet and made my way through my chill and darkened apartment to answer the summons at the door. I placed myself beside the portal, pulling at the draperies that I kept drawn by day against the inquiring gaze of strangers and by night against the moist chill of the Parisian winter. Outside my door I perceived an urchin, cap set at an uncouth angle upon his unshorn head, an object or scrap of material clutched in the hand which he was not using to set up his racket on my door.

Lifting an iron bar which I kept beside the door in case of need to defend myself from the invasion of ruffians and setting the latch chain to prevent the door from opening more than a hand's width, I turned the latch and drew the door open far enough to peer out.

The boy who stood upon my stoop could not have been more than ten years of age, ragged of clothing and filthy of visage. The meager light of the passage outside my apartment reflected from his eye, giving an impression of wary suspicion. We studied each other through the narrow opening for long seconds before either spoke. At length I demanded to know his reason for disturbing my musings. He ignored my question, responding to it by speaking my name.

"Yes," I responded, "it is indeed I. Again, I require to know the purpose of your visit."

"I've brought you a message, monsieur," the urchin stated.

"From whom?"

"I don't know the gentleman's name," he replied.

"Then what is the message?"

The boy held the object in his hand closer to the opening. I could see now that it was a letter, folded and sealed with wax, and crumpled and covered with grime. It struck me that the boy might have found the paper lying in a gutter and brought it to me as part of a devious scheme, but then I remembered that he had known my name, a feat not likely on the part of a wild street urchin.

"I can't read, monsieur," the child said. "The gentleman gave it me and directed me to your lodging. I know numbers, some, and was able to find your place, monsieur."

"Very well," I assented, "give me the paper."

"I've got to be paid first, monsieur."

The boy's demand was annoying, and yet he had performed a service and was, I suppose, entitled to his pay. Perhaps the mysterious gentleman who had dispatched him had already furnished him with payment, but this was a contingency beyond my ability to influence. Telling the child to await my return I closed the door, made my way to the place where I keep my small treasury, and extracted from it a sou coin.

At the doorway once more, I exchanged the coin for the paper and sent the child on his way. Returning to the dual illumination of hearth and oil lamp, I broke the seal that held the letter closed and unfolded the sheet of foolscap. The flickering firelight revealed to me the work of a familiar hand, albeit one I had not glimpsed for many years, and a message that was characteristically terse and demanding.

Come at once. A matter of urgency.

The message was signed with a single letter, the initial *D*.

I rocked back upon my heels, sinking into the old chair which I had used as my comfort and my retreat from the world through the passing decades. I was clad in slippers and robe, nightcap perched upon my head. It had been my plan, following a small meal, to spend an hour reading and then to retire to my narrow bed. Instead, I now garbed myself for the chill of the out-of-doors. Again I raided my own poor treasury and furnished myself with a small reserve of coins. In a short time I had left my apartment and stood upon my stoop, drawing behind me the doorway and turning my key in the lock.

No address had been given in the demanding message, nor was the messenger anywhere to be seen. I could only infer from the lack of information to the contrary that my old friend was still to be located at the lodgings we once had shared, long ago.

It was too far to travel on foot, so I hailed a passing cab, not without difficulty, and instructed the driver as to my destination. He looked at me with suspicion until I repeated the address, 33 Rue Dunôt in the Faubourg St-Germain. He held out his hand and refused to whip up until I had delivered the fare into his possession.

The streets of the metropolis were deserted at this hour, and mostly silent save for an occasional shout of anger or moan of despair — the sounds of the night after even revelers have retired to their homes or elsewhere.

As the cab drew up I exited from it and stood gazing at the old stone structure where the two of us had shared quarters for so long. Behind me I heard the driver grumble, then whip up, then pull away from number 33 with the creak of the wooden axle and the clatter of horse's hooves on cobblestones.

A light appeared in a window and I tried, without success, to espy the form of the person who held it. In a moment the light moved and I knew that my erstwhile friend was making his way to the door. I presented myself in time to hear the bar withdrawn and to see the door swing open.

Before me stood my old friend, the world's first and greatest consulting detective, the Chevalier C. Auguste Dupin. Yet though it was unquestionably he, I was shocked at the ravages that the years had worked upon his once sharp-featured visage and whip-thin frame. He had grown old. The flesh did not so much cover his bones as hang from them. I saw that he still wore the smoked-glass spectacles of an earlier age; when he raised them to peer at me his once ferretlike eyes were dim and his hands, once as hard and steady as iron rods, appeared fragile and tremulous.

"Do not stand there like a goose," Dupin commanded, "surely by this time you know the way."

He retreated a pace and I entered the apartment which had meant so much to me in those days of our companionship. Characteristically, Dupin uttered not another syllable, but instead led the way through my one-time home. I shut the door behind me, then threw the heavy iron bolt, mindful of the enemies known to seek Dupin's destruction in a former epoch. That any of them still survived was doubtful, that they remained capable of working mischief upon the great mind was close to what Dupin would have deemed "a nil possibility," but still I threw the bolt.

Dupin led the way to his book closet, and within moments it was almost as if the decades had slipped away. He seemed to regain his youthful vigor, and I my former enthusiasm. Not waiting for me to assume the sofa upon which I had so often reclined to peruse musty volumes in past decades, Dupin flung himself into his favorite seat. He seized a volume which he had laid face downward, its pages open, upon the arm of his chair.

"Have you seen this?" he demanded angrily, brandishing the volume.

I leaned forward, straining in the gloom to recognize the publication. "It bears no familiarity," I confessed. "It looks but newly ar-

rived, and my reading in recent years has been entirely of an anti-
quarian nature."

"Of course, of course," Dupin muttered. "I will tell you what it is.
I have been reading a volume translated from the English. Its title
in our own tongue is *Une étude en écarlate*. The author has divided
the work into chapters. I will read to you from a chapter which he
entitles ingenuously 'La Science de Déduction.'"

Knowing that there was no stopping Dupin once he was determined upon a course, I settled upon the sofa. The room was not
uncomfortable, I was in the company of my ancient friend, I was
content.

"I will omit the author's interpolations," Dupin prefaced his reading, "and present to you only the significant portions of his work.
Very well, then! 'Now, in my opinion, Dupin was a very inferior fellow. That trick of his of breaking in on his friends' thoughts with an
apropos remark after a quarter of an hour's silence is really very
showy and superficial. He had some analytical genius, no doubt;
but he was by no means such a phenomenon as Poe appeared to
imagine.'"

With a furious gesture he flung the slim volume across the room
against a shelf of volumes, where it struck, its pages fluttering, and
fell to the carpet. I knew that the Poe to whom the writer referred
was the American journalist who had visited Dupin and myself
from time to time, authoring reports of the several mysteries which
Dupin had unraveled with, I took pride in recalling, my own modest but not insubstantial assistance.

"What think you of that?" Dupin demanded.

"A cruel assessment," I ventured, "and an inaccurate one. Why,
on many occasions I can recall —"

"Indeed, my good friend, you can recall the occasions upon
which I interrupted your words to tell you your very thoughts."

"As you have just done," I averred. I awaited further words from
Dupin, but they were not at that moment forthcoming so I resumed my speech. "Who is the author of this scurrilous assessment?"

"The author's name matters not. It is the villain whom he quotes,
who is of significance."

"And who, may I inquire, might that person be?"

Dupin raised his eyes to the ceiling where smoke from the fireplace, draughty as ever, swirled menacingly. "He is one whom I met

some years ago, long after you had departed these quarters, *mon ami.* I had by then largely retired from my labors as a consulting detective, and of course my reputation had long since reached the islands of fools."

By this time I could see that Dupin was off on a tale, and I settled myself more thoroughly than ever upon the sofa, prepared to listen to the end:

Those were days of tumult in our nation (Dupin said) when danger lurked at every turning and the most ordinary of municipal services were not to be taken for granted. When I received a message from across the Channel I was of course intrigued.

The writer was a young man who professed admiration for my exploits and a desire to learn my methods that he might emulate them in the building of a reputation and a career for himself in his own land. I received many such communications in those days, responding to them uniformly that the entire science of detection was but a matter of observation and deduction, and that any man or even woman of ordinary intelligence could match my feats did he or she but apply those faculties with which we are all equipped to their full capacity. But the person who had written to me mentioned a particular case which he had been employed to resolve, and when he described the case my curiosity was piqued.

Your expression tells me that you, too, are aroused by the prospect of this case, and I will tell you what it concerned.

The young man's letter of application hinted only of a treasure of fabulous value, a cache of gold and gems lost some three centuries, that had become the subject of legend and of fanciful tales, but which he believed to exist in actuality and to be in France, nay, not merely in France but in the environs of Paris itself. Could he but find it he would be wealthy beyond the power of imagination, and if I would but assist him in his quest a portion of it would be mine.

As you know, while I am of good family I have long been of reduced means, and the prospect of restoring the fortunes of my forebears was an attractive one. My correspondent was reticent as to details in his letters, for I wrote back to him seeking further information but was unable to elicit useful data.

At length I permitted him to visit me — yes, in this very apartment. From the first his eccentric nature was manifest. He arrived at a late hour, as late I daresay as you have yourself arrived this night. It was the night before that of the full moon. The air was clear and the sky filled with celestial objects whose illumination, added to that of the moon, approached that of the day.

He sat upon the very sofa where you recline at this moment. No, there is no need to rise and examine the furnishing. You do make me smile, old friend. There is nothing to be learned from that old sofa.

The young man, an Englishman, was of tall and muscular build with a hawklike visage, sharp features, and a sharp, observant mien. His clothing bore the strong odor of tobacco. His hollow eyes suggested his habituation to some stronger stimulant. His movements suggested one who has trained in the boxing ring; more, one who has at least familiarized himself with the Japanese art of *baritsu,* a subtle form of combat but recently introduced in a few secretive salons in Paris and Berlin, in London, and even in the city of Baltimore in Maryland.

It took me but moments to realize that this was a person of unusual talent, potentially a practitioner of the craft of detection to approach my own level of proficiency. It was obvious to me as we conversed on this topic and that, the politics of our respective nations, the growing incidence of crime which respects neither border nor sea, the advances of science and literature among the Gallic and Anglic races, that he was watching me closely, attempting to draw my measure even as I was, his.

At length, feeling that I had seen all that he would reveal of himself, and growing impatient with his avoidance of the topic that had drawn him to my apartments, I demanded once and for all that he describe that which he sought and in the recovery of which he desired my guidance, or else depart from my lodging, having provided me with an hour's diversion and no more.

"Very well, sir," he replied, "I will tell you that I am in search of a bird."

Upon his making this statement I burst into laughter, only to be shocked back to sobriety by the stern expression upon the face of my visitor. "Surely, sir," I exclaimed, "you did not brave the stormy waters of the Channel in search of a grouse or guinea hen."

"No, sir," he replied, "I have come in search of a plain black bird, a bird variously described in the literature as a raven or, more likely, a hawk."

"The feathers of hawks are not black," I replied.

"Indeed, sir, you are correct. The feathers of hawks are not black, nor has this hawk feathers of any color, but the color of this hawk is golden."

"You insult me, sir," I stated angrily.

My visitor raised his eyebrows. "Why say you so?"

"You come to me and speak only in riddles, as if you were humoring a playful child. A hawk that is black but has no feathers and yet is golden. If you do not make yourself more clear you must leave my apartments, and I wish you a speedy return to your country."

He raised a hand placatingly. "I did not wish to offend you, sir, nor to speak in conundrums. Pray, bear with me for a little longer and I will make clear the nature and history of the odd bird which I seek."

I permitted him to continue.

"This was the representation of a bird," quoth he, "the creation of a group of talented metalworkers and gemsmiths, Turkish slaves employed by the Grand Master Villiers de l'Isle d'Adam, of the Order of the Knights of Rhodes. It was crafted in the year 1530, and dispatched by galley from the Isle of Rhodes to Spain, where it was to be presented to the Emperor Charles the Fifth. Its height was as the length of your forearm. It was of solid gold, in the form of a standing hawk or raven, and it was crusted over with gems of the greatest variety and finest quality. Its value even at the time was immense. Today it would be incalculable!"

He paused, a look in his eyes as if he could envision the fantastic sight of a golden falcon, emeralds for its eyes and rubies for its claws, circling the chamber. Then he resumed his narrative.

He then did something which seemed, at the moment, very peculiar but which, I would come to realize, was in truth to have been expected of a man such as he. He leaped from his seat upon the cushion and began pacing restlessly around the chamber. At once I inquired as to what had caused such an abrupt alteration in his manner and demeanor, whereupon he turned upon me a visage transformed. The muscles of his face were drawn, his lips were pulled back to expose gleaming teeth, and his eyes, by heaven, his eyes glittered like the eyes of a wild leopard.

"I must visit an apothecary at once," he exclaimed.

In response to this demand I remonstrated with him. "Sir, there is an excellent apothecary shop upon the Rue Dunôt, an easy walk from here, but what is the urgency? A moment ago you were calmly describing a most extraordinary bird. Now you demand directions to the establishment of a chemist."

"It will pass," he responded, most puzzlingly, "it will pass."

He sank once more to his former position upon the sofa and, pressing the heels of his hands to his deep-sunken eyes, paused to draw a deep breath.

"Do you wish to continue?" I inquired.

"Yes, yes. But if you would be so kind, monsieur, as to furnish me with a glass of wine, I would be most grateful."

I rose and proceeded to the wine cupboard, from which I drew a dust-coated bottle of my second-best vintage. In those days as in these, as you are of course aware, I saw fit to maintain my own household, without benefit of servant or staff. I poured a glass for my guest and he tossed it off as one would a draught of water, extending the emptied goblet for a second portion, which I forthwith poured. This he studied, lifted to his lips and sipped, then placed carefully upon the taboret before him.

"Do you wish to continue your narration?" I inquired.

"If you please," he responded, "I beg your indulgence for my outburst. I am not, I must confess, entirely well."

"Should the need arise," I assured him, "M. Konstantinides, the chemist, is qualified to provide specifics for all known illnesses. The hour is late and he would by now have closed his establishment for the night and retired to his chamber, but I could rouse him in your behalf."

"You are gracious, sir. I trust that will prove unnecessary, but I am nonetheless grateful." Once more he paused as if to gather his thoughts, then launched upon a further exposition. "I will not trouble you with every detail of the peregrinations of the golden falcon, save to point out that within our own generation it had passed into the possession of the Carlist movement in Spain."

To this statement I nodded. "Wars of succession are tiresome, but it seems they will be with us always, does it not? I was struck by the recent surrender of Señor Maroto's Basque followers after their lengthy and strenuous resistance."

"You are well informed, sir! If you are familiar with the fate of the

Basque Carlists, then you would know that Señor Ramón Cabrera has continued the struggle in Catalonia."

"He is also in dire straits, is he not?"

"Yes, it appears that Her Majesty Isabella the Second is at last about to reap the harvest of the Salic Law invoked by her royal father. But I fear I am boring you, M. Dupin."

"Not so much boring as stimulating my curiosity. Surely, sir, you did not travel here from London merely to relate the saga of a fabulous bird and then digress upon the politics of the Spanish succession. How are these things related, for surely that must be the case? If you would be so kind as to come to the point, then."

"Indeed." He bowed his head, then raised it once more. "You are aware, surely, that Don Carlos has sympathizers here in France. You were perhaps not aware that Señor Cabrera had sent an agent on a dangerous and secretive mission, to traverse the passes of the Pyrenees and make his way to the château of a French sympathizer, no less a personage than the Duc de Lagny."

"I am familiar with Lagny," I confessed. "I have had the pleasure of being introduced to His Grace and to Her Grace the Duchess. Their château is of noteworthy architecture. But of the Duke's Carlist sympathies I must confess profound ignorance."

"That is not surprising, sir. The Duke is known, if I may make a small play on words, for his reclusiveness."

He paused to sip once more at his, or perhaps I should say, my, wine. "Regarding the golden bird as an omen and token of majesty, and sensing the imminent defeat of the Carlist cause, Señor Cabrera had sent the bird to Lagny rather than have it fall into the hands of his niece's followers."

"And you wish me to assist you in retrieving the bird from the château of the Duc de Lagny?" I asked.

"That is my mission."

"You are in the employ of Her Majesty Isabella?"

"I am in the employ of one whose identity I am not at liberty to disclose." He rose to his feet. "If you will assist me — for my knowledge of the French countryside and culture is limited — you will receive, shall I say, sir, a reward of royal proportions."

"You wish me to accompany you to the château of the Duke," I objected, "there to obtain from his custody the fabled bird. What causes you to believe that he will relinquish it?"

"You have my assurance, monsieur, the Duke will be eager to part with that which he safeguards upon receiving proof of the identity of my employers."

"You have such proof with you?" I demanded.

"I have, sir," he insisted. "Upon this fact I give you my solemn assurance."

Unable to deny an interest in obtaining a share of the lucre to which he referred, and perhaps attracted to an extent by the lure of the romantic story he had spun, I agreed, at the least, to accompany him to Lagny. I have told you already that the hour of my guest's arrival was an unconventionally late one, and his disquisitive manner of speech had caused the hours to pass before our bargain, such as it might be, was struck.

At length I excused myself and proceeded to the front parlor of my apartment. The act of drawing back the draperies confirmed that which I had already suspected, namely, that dawn had broken and a new day was upon us. Feeling impelled to violate my custom and venture forth from my lodgings in the light of day, I urged my visitor to the stoop, drew shut the door behind us, and locked it. We set out on foot to the apothecary shop of M. Konstantinides. Here my guest purchased a preparation and introduced it into his own system.

I was by no means unfamiliar with the effects of various stimulants and depressants upon the human organism, but even so I will own that I was startled at the strength and portion taken by this nearly skeletal Englishman. At once his air of distress left him and his visage assumed an altogether more friendly and optimistic appearance than had previously been the case. He paid M. Konstantinides his fee, adding a generous overage thereto, and then, turning to me, suggested that we set out for Lagny.

Our journey was not a difficult one. We hired a hackney carriage and negotiated a fare all the way to the village of Lagny, the sum being paid from my guest's purse, and proceeded eastward from the capital. It was necessary to pause but once at an inn, where we procured a loaf, a cheese, and bottle, my English guest and I dining in democratic fashion with the hackman.

The sun drew low in the sky behind us as we approached Lagny. I was able, by drawing upon my memory of earlier days, to direct the hackman past the village to the château of the Duke. It was a tall and rambling structure of ancient Gothic construction; as we

neared the château the sun's guttering rays painted its walls as if
with a palette of flame. We debouched from the carriage and instructed the hackman to return to the village and to return for us
in the morning.

He asked in his rude yet charmingly colorful way, "And who's to
pay for me sups and me snooze, ye two toffs?"

"We shall indeed," my English guest responded, dropping a handful of coins onto the coach box, upon which the hackman whipped
up and departed.

The Château de Lagny, if I may so describe it, radiated an air of
age and decadence. As my guest and I stood gazing at its façade he
turned to me and asked a peculiar question. "What do you hear, my
dear Dupin?"

Perhaps I ought to have taken offense at this unwonted familiarity, but instead I chose to deal with his query. I cocked an ear, gave
list carefully to whatever sounds there might be emanating from
the chateau, then made my reply. "I hear nothing."

"Precisely!" the Englishman exclaimed.

"And what, sir, is the object of this schoolmasterly exchange?" I
inquired.

"Sir" — he smiled — "would one not expect to hear the bustle of
life in such a setting as this? The neigh of horses from the stables,
the cry of servants and workers, mayhap the sound of revelers?
None of this, I repeat, none of it do we hear. Only a silence, M.
Dupin, only an eerie, deathlike silence."

For once I was forced to concede that my visitor had scored a
point upon me. I acknowledged as much, to which he perhaps
grudgingly conceded that I was yet the master and he the eager pupil. He refrained from commenting upon the looming day when
the pupil might outstrip the master in achievement, nor was I prepared to do so.

Arm in arm we approached the main entryway of the château.
We carried, of course, walking sticks, and I permitted my companion to raise his and strike heavily upon the great wooden door. To
my astonishment no servant appeared to grant us entry. Instead,
the door swung slowly open and the two of us set foot upon the
flagging on the château's foyer.

At first nothing appeared out of the way, but in moments our
nostrils were assailed by the unmistakable odor of decomposition.

Exchanging glances but not a word, we drew kerchiefs from our respective pockets and knotted them over our nostrils and mouths. I turned toward my companion and observed him, hatted and masked like a highwayman. Full well I knew that my own appearance was as sinister as his.

The first cadaver we encountered was that of a liveried footman. First instructing my guest to maintain careful watch lest violence appear from within the château, I knelt over the still form. Had the stench not been evidence enough of death, the condition of the footman's body would have fully convinced the veriest of laymen. He had been struck down from behind. He lay upon his face, the back of his head crushed, the pooled gore already beginning to crawl with insects.

Turning aside to draw a breath of clear air, or at any rate of air more clear than that surrounding the cadaver, I examined the clothing of the deceased in search of a clue as to the motive for his murder, but discovered nothing.

Proceeding through the house my associate and I found, in turn, the remains of maids, cooks, laundresses, and an elderly male servant whom we took to be the majordomo of the establishment. But what had happened, and where was the master of the château?

Him we found in the stables behind the château. Surrounded by stablemen lay M. le Duc. The hearty nobleman whose company I had enjoyed more than once had been treated disgustingly. It was obvious from the condition of the remains that the Duke had been tortured. His hands were bound behind his back and his face showed the discolorations caused by the application of a heated implement. Surely the intention had been to force from him the location of the fabled golden bird. Marks upon his torso were enough to sicken the viewer, while the final, fatal attack had come in the form of a sharpened blade drawn across his belly, exposing his vital organs and inducing the ultimate exsanguination.

Her Grace the Duchess had been treated in similar fashion. I will not describe the indignities which had been visited upon her. One prayed only that her more delicate frame had reached its limits and that she had been granted the mercy of a death more rapid and less agonizing that that of her husband.

Horses and dogs, like the human inhabitants of the estate, lay at random, slaughtered every one.

"Is this the work of Señor Cabrera and his men?" I asked.

"More likely of the servants of Isabella," my guest replied. "The deaths of these unfortunate persons and their beasts are to be regretted, but of immediate concern is the whereabouts of the bird." He stood over first one cadaver, then another, studying them as would a student of medicine the dissected remains of a beast.

"It appears unlikely that the secret was divulged," he suggested at length. "Obviously the Duke was tortured and dispatched first, for such a nobleman as he would not have permitted his lady to be treated as we see her to have been. Nor, I would infer, did the Duchess know the whereabouts of the bird, for once her husband was deceased, she would have had no reason to protect the secret. On the contrary, having presumably seen her attackers, she would have sought to survive in order to exact revenge for the murder of her husband."

His callous attitude toward the carnage we had only just beheld was appalling, but then the English are known to be a cold-blooded race, and it may be that this Englishman felt a degree of sympathy and outrage that he did not show. Very well, then. When the hackman returned for us on the morrow, I would inform the mayor of the village of Lagny of our terrible discovery. The brutal criminals responsible would be sought and, one hoped, brought to face their fate beneath the guillotine in due course. But my guest was right, at least to the extent that our own presence at the Château de Lagny had been brought about by the report of the presence of the bird.

We would seek it, and if it was here, I knew that we would find it.

"Let us proceed to locate the golden bird," I announced to my guest. "So splendid an object should be conspicuous to the eye of anyone save a blind man."

"Perhaps not," the Englishman demurred. "I will confess, my dear Dupin, that I have withheld from you one item in the history and description of the bird."

I demanded that he enlighten me at once, and in what for him passed for a direct response, he complied. "You have doubtless noticed that in my descriptions of the bird I have referred to it both as golden and as black."

"I have done so, sir. You may in fact recall my bringing this discrepancy to your attention, and your pledge to reconcile the conflicting descriptions. If you please, this would seem an excellent time to do so."

"Very well, then. The bird as originally created by the captive Turkish craftsmen, of solid gold virtually encrusted with precious stones, was considered too attractive a target. At some point in its history — I confess to ignorance of the exact date — it was coated in a black substance, a thick, tarry pigment, so that it now resembles nothing more than a sculpture of ebony in the form of a standing hawk."

"What leads you to believe that the bird is still in the château? Even if the Duke and Duchess died without revealing the secret of its hiding place to their enemies, those villains might still have searched the château until they found the bird. But look about you, sir, and you will see that we are surrounded by a scene not merely of carnage, but of despoliation. It is obvious that the château has been ransacked. You did not yourself know of the bird's hiding place? Your employers did not inform you?"

"My employers did not themselves know the hiding place. It was the Duke himself who chose that, after the messengers had left."

"Then for all we know, the bird has flown."

"No, sir." The Englishman shook his head. "By the condition of the bodies, even in winter, this horror occurred at least four days ago, before I left London. I would have received word, had the villains succeeded. They have committed these horrendous crimes in vain. You may rest assured that the bird is still here. But where?"

"Let us consider," I suggested. "The interior of the château and even, to the extent that we have searched, the outbuildings, have been torn apart. Furniture is demolished, pictures and tapestries torn from walls. The Duke's library has been despoiled, his priceless collection of ancient manuscripts and rare volumes reduced to worthless rubble. Even a suit of ancient armor has been thrown from its stand so that it lies in pieces upon the flagging. The invaders of the château may be monsters, but they are not unintelligent nor yet are they lacking in thoroughness."

I paused, awaiting further comment by the Englishman, but none was forthcoming. I observed him closely and perceived that he was perspiring freely and that he alternately clenched and loosened his fists almost as one suffering a fit.

"If the bird is still on the estate," I resumed, "yet it is not within the château or its outbuildings, logic dictates its location to us. Consider this, young man. We have eliminated the partial contents

of our list of possibilities. Having done so, we are drawn irresistibly
to the conclusion that the remaining possibilities must contain the
solution to our puzzle. Do you follow the thread of ratiocination
which I have laid before you?"

He seemed to relax, as if the fit had passed. He drew a cloth from
a pocket of his costume and wiped the perspiration from his brow.
He acknowledged the irrefutable nature of my argument.

"But," he continued, "I fail to see the next step in your procedure."

"You disappoint me," I uttered. "Very well. If you will please follow me."

I retreated to the main entry hall of the château, and thence to
the terrace outside. I proceeded still farther, my boots leaving a
trail behind me in the heavy dew that had accumulated upon the
lush lawn surrounding the château. The moon had attained full-
ness, and the sky above Lagny was even more impressive than that
above the metropolis had been.

"Do you look upon the château," I instructed my pupil, for I had
so come to regard the Englishman.

He stood beside me and gazed at the structure, its stone pedi-
ments rendered in pale chiaroscuro by the light streaming from
the heavens. "What see you?" I asked him.

"Why, the Château de Lagny," he replied at once.

"Indeed. What else do you see?"

The young Englishman pursed his lips with the appearance of
impatience. "Only that, sir. The stable and other outbuildings are
concealed by the bulk of the château."

"Indeed," I nodded. I spoke no more, awaiting further comment
by the other. There ensued a lengthy silence.

Finally, in a tone of impatience, my student spoke once more.
"The lawn before the château. The woods which surround us. The
moon, the stars. A tiny cloud in the southwest."

I nodded. "Very good. More."

"For the love of God, Dupin, what more is there to see?"

"Only that which is vital to our mission," I replied.

As I watched, the Englishman raised his eyes once more, then
froze. "I see a row of birds perched upon the parapet of the château."

"My good fellow!" I exclaimed. "It appears now possible that you
may have the makings of a detective. Further, I urge you, do not sat-

isfy yourself with merely seeing, but observe, observe, observe, and report!"

He stood silent and motionless for some time, then took an action which won my admiration. Although we stood ankle-deep in the dew-soaked grass before the château, there was nearby a driveway used by carriages approaching and departing the estate. Our own cabman had followed this path, and it was my expectation that he would utilize it once more upon his return for us in the morning.

The Englishman strode to the driveway, bent, and lifted a handful of gravel. He threw back his cape so as to free his arm and flung the gravel at the birds perched upon the parapet. I was impressed by the strength and accuracy of his arm.

With an angry outcry several of the birds flew from their perch. They were silhouetted against the night sky, their forms limned in a drab black against the glittering stars and clear darkness of the heavens. One of them passed across the face of the full, brilliant moon, its widespread wings and the shining disk behind it creating the illusion that the bird was as large as the legendary Pegasus.

My student and I remained motionless, observing the behavior of the aerial creatures. They were more annoyed than frightened by the clattering pebbles, or so I inferred, for it took mere moments for the plurality of the creatures to return to their former places, midst an audible flapping of feathery wings and grumbling calls.

The Englishman bent and lifted another handful of gravel, drew back his arm, and flung the stones at the birds. Once more his action evoked an angry response, most of the birds crying out in annoyance and flapping away from their perch. By now the solution to the mystery of the missing hawk was apparent.

"Good work," I congratulated my student. "It is clear that you have grasped the difference between observing and merely seeing, and have observed that which is necessary to locate your prey."

A small indication of pleasure made itself visible upon his face, the momentary upward twitching of the corners of his mouth by a few millimeters. Without uttering a word he seated himself upon the grass and proceeded to remove his boots and stockings. I watched in equal silence as he strode to the outer wall of the château.

It had been my expectation that he would return to the interior of the structure and seek access to the roof by means of interior staircases. Instead, to my amazement, after studying the wall with its closely fitted stones and creeping ivy, he proceeded to climb the exterior of the château, using his powerful fingers and almost orangutan-like toes to assure his grasp. As he advanced his cape flapped about his form like two huge wings.

As he approached the parapet he called out to the winged creatures perched there, making a peculiar sound unlike any I had previously heard. Without preliminary, the avians watching his advance extended their wings and rose from the château, disappearing into the blackness that surrounded them. All save one. A single bird remained stationary, silhouetted against the starry domain.

The strange, almost inhuman, being into which my erstwhile visitor had transformed himself, perched now beside the sole remaining avian, so high above the earth that a single slip, I could see, would plunge him to a certain doom. Yet no sound reached me from this strange personage, nor any indication of fear.

He lifted the unmoving bird from its place and in a moment it disappeared beneath his cloak. I could only infer that he had come prepared with an extra section of leather belting or rope, concealed until now by his outer garments.

Then as I stood aghast he lowered himself to lie flat upon the parapet, then reached over its edge to gain a handhold on the stone wall, then slid from his safe perch and proceeded to climb down the wall of the château, headfirst, the bird secured beneath his clothing. His appearance, for all the world, was that of a gigantic bat.

When he reached the greensward he righted himself and drew the bird from beneath his cape. "I thank you, my dear Dupin, for the lessons you have given me, equally in observation and in deduction. Our prey is recovered."

So saying he held the black bird toward me. Even through its black coating I could make out the shape of its feathers, its claws, its beak, and its eyes. It was clearly a magnificent example of the sculptor's art. My student asked me to hold the figurine while he once more donned his stockings and boots. The weight of the black bird was so great that I felt even greater astonishment at his ability to descend the wall of the château with it strapped beneath his clothing.

We spent what little remained of the night exploring the interior of the château, utilizing torches which remained from that sad structure's happier era. The only clues that we uncovered were further evidence of the brutality of the invaders who had slaughtered the Duke and Duchess as well as their retainers, all in a futile attempt to learn the whereabouts of the treasure which my pupil and I now possessed.

With morning our hackman arrived, somewhat the worse for wear and, one inferred, for the consumption of excessive amounts of spirit. I instructed him to take us to the village of Lagny, where we concealed the bird inside the boot of the hack, promising the hackman a generous tip in exchange for his silence. We thereupon made a full report of our gory findings at the château, making no mention of the bird. The reason we gave for our visit to the château was the truthful one that I was an old acquaintance of the Duke and Duchess and had been eager to introduce to them my visitor from England.

The mayor of the village of Lagny and the *chef des gendarmes* were duly horrified by our descriptions, but permitted us to depart for Paris upon our pledge to provide what information and assistance we could, should these be called for at a later stage of their investigation.

In due course the hack pulled up at my lodgings in the Faubourg St-Germain. A light snow had fallen in the metropolis, and I picked my way carefully to my door lest I slip and fall to the stones. Exhausted by the activities of the past day and night, I turned my key in the lock of my lodgings and pushed the door open so that my guest and I might enter. When we did so we were confronted by an unanticipated sight. My quarters had been ransacked. Furniture was overturned, drawers were pulled from their places and inverted upon the floor. The carpeting had been torn up and rolled back to permit a search for trapdoors or loosened boards.

Every picture was pulled from the wall and thrown to the floor, including that of my friend and idol the great Vidocq. Shocked and offended by the invasion of my quarters I proceeded to examine their contents, assessing the damage and grieving for the destruction of precious mementos of a long career. I clutched my head and expostulated my outrage.

Drawing myself together at length and hoping in some manner

to mitigate the harm which had been done, I turned to confer with my visitor, only to find that he had disappeared without a trace.

I flew to the doorway and exited my premises. The hack had of course departed long since, but a row of dark footprints showed in the fresh snow. Following without heed to the risk of falling I dashed the length of the Rue Dunôt. At length I found myself standing upon the doorstep of the establishment of M. Konstantinides. I sounded the bell repeatedly but without response, then pounded upon the door. Neither light nor movement could be seen from within the shop, nor was there response of any sort to my summons.

At once the meaning of these events burst upon my tortured brain. The Englishman was a dope fiend, the Greek apothecary the supplier of his evil: chemicals. How Konstantinides had obtained knowledge of the bird was unfathomable, but it was at his behest rather than that of either the Carlists or the Bourbons that I had been recruited.

Konstantinides had ransacked my lodgings merely as a distraction, to hold my attention while the Englishman brought the bird to his shop. By now, even though mere minutes had passed, it was a certainty that both the Englishman and the Greek, along with the black bird, were gone from the Faubourg and would not be found within the environs of Paris.

What would become of the bird, of the English detective, of the Greek chemist, were mysteries for the years to come. And now at last (Dupin completed his narrative) I learn of the further career of my student, and of the scorn with which he repays my guidance.

As I sat, mortified by my friend and mentor's humiliation, I saw him clutching the small volume from which he had read the cruel words as if it were a dagger with which he planned to take his own life. All the while he had been telling his tale I had been carried away by the narrative, to another time and place, a time and place when Dupin was young and in his prime. But now I had returned to the present and saw before me a man enfeebled by the passage of the years and the exigencies of a cruel existence.

"What became of the bird?" I inquired. "Did it disappear entirely?"

Dupin shook his head. "The apothecary shop of the Greek

Konstantinides was reopened by a nephew. Of the elder Konstantinides nothing was ever again heard, or if it was, it was held inviolate in the bosom of the family. I attempted to learn from the nephew the whereabouts of his uncle and of the Englishman, as well as of the bird itself, but the younger Konstantinides pled ignorance of the fate of the two men, as well as that of the bird. For two generations now the shop has remained in the family, and the secret, if secret there is, remains sealed in their bosom."

I nodded my understanding. "And so you never again heard of your pupil, the strange Englishman?"

Dupin waved the book at me. "You see, old friend? He has become, as it were, the new Dupin. His fame spreads across the seas and around the globe. Did he but make the meanest acknowledgment of his debt to me, I would be satisfied. My material needs are met by the small pension arranged by our old friend G — of the Metropolitan Police Force. My memories are mine, and your own writings have given me my small share of fame."

"The very least I could do, Dupin, I assure you."

There followed a melancholy silence during which I contemplated the sad state to which my friend had fallen. At length he heaved a sigh pregnant with despair. "Perhaps," he began, then lapsed, then again began, "perhaps it would be of interest to the discerning few to learn of a few of my other undertakings."

Shaking my head I responded, "Already have I recorded them, Dupin. There was the case of the murders in the Rue Morgue, that of the purloined letter, and even your brilliant solution of the mystery of Marie Roget."

"Those are not the cases to which I refer," Dupin demurred.

"I know of no others, save, of course that which you have narrated to me this night."

Upon hearing my words, Dupin permitted himself one of the rare smiles which I have ever seen upon his countenance. "There have been many others, dear friend," he informed me, "many indeed."

Astonished, I begged him to enumerate a few such.

"There were the puzzle of the Tsaritsa's false emerald, the adventure of Wade the American gunrunner, the mystery of the Algerian herbs, the incident of the Bahamian fugitive and the runaway hot-air balloon, and of course the tragedy of the pharaoh's jackal."

"I shall be eager to record these, Dupin. Is the list thus complete?"

"By no means, old friend. That is merely the beginning. Such reports may in some small way assuage the pain of being aged and forgotten, replaced on the stage of detection by a newer generation of sleuths. And, I suspect, the few coins which your reports may add to your purse will not be unwelcome."

"They will not," I was forced to concede.

"But this" — Dupin waved the book once more — "this affront strikes to my heart. As bitter as wormwood and as sharp as a two-edged sword, so sayeth the proverb."

"Dupin," I said, "you will not be forgotten. This English prig has clearly copied your methods, even to the degree of enlisting an assistant and amanuensis who bears a certain resemblance to myself. Surely justice forbids that the world forget the Chevalier C. Auguste Dupin!"

"Not forget?" my friend mumbled. "Not forget? The pupil will live in fame forever while the master becomes but a footnote to the history of detection. Ah, my friend, my dear, dear friend, but the world in which we live is unjust."

"It was ever thus, Dupin," I concurred, "it was ever thus."

JOYCE CAROL OATES

Doll: A Romance of the Mississippi

FROM *The Gettysburg Review*

WHAT HAPPENED between Ira Early and his (step)daughter Doll is a secret between them of long standing. What has happened to *x* number of men as a result of this secret is more public.

Is Doll your actual name? (Doll is frequently asked.)
   Doll is trained to say, Yes.
   Yes but you may call me anything you wish. If calling me by another girl's name is what you wish. (Doll giggles. Doll nibbles at the end of one of her pigtails, winningly positioned over her slender shoulder.)

In fact: Doll is not her name but what she is called. Doll has difficulty remembering her baptismal name as she has difficulty remembering the years before she turned eleven. Now Doll has been eleven for so long, it's like trying to remember an old TV movie you hadn't paid much attention to when you saw it. You can remember but only in patches. And why?

Doll is not a worrier. Doll leaves worrying to her (step)father, Ira Early.
   And Mr. Early is a worrier. Complaining how first there were individual gray hairs in his thick dark hair that proudly swooped from his brow like a rooster's comb, then swaths of gray, a kind of ugly tarnished gray, now this kind of piss-tinged white, and a bald spot at the crown of his head big as a grapefruit, as a result of Doll's unpredictable behavior. When Doll swerves from the script and gets down-dirty *mean.*

Mr. Early sighs, shudders. Runs a hand through his thinning hair, strokes his bristly beard. Plays the role of the addle-brained old coot, granddaddy or bachelor uncle, in a TV family sitcom of the 1950s. As if he, a reasonable man, a man another man can trust, can't control his daughter in these down-dirty *mean moods*.

(*Is Doll in such a mood tonight?* Mr. Early worries. It has been how many weeks since Doll's last mean mood; he's counting on his fingers one, two, three . . . and a half? Not a good sign.)

In the cushioned interior of the stately old La Salle Luxury sedan, Mr. Early, awaiting Doll's return, pours himself a much-needed drink from his chilled thermos. A martini prepared exactly to Mr. Early's taste, very dry. Tiny cocktail onions bob in the liquid; he scoops them out deftly in the crook of his little finger. Doll sneers at her (step)daddy for exhibiting what Doll believes to be incipient alcoholism, some notion Doll has picked up from afternoon TV, but Mr. Early knows better.

Mr. Early drinks and nods. Ah yes. Much needed.

A fierce December wind rocks the stately old relic of an automobile. A battalion of storm clouds like clotted intestines blows high overhead, in and out of the moon's ghastly light. Mr. Early shivers. What city is this? East or west of the Mississippi?

(Doll has some childish notion, doesn't like to stray too far from the great American river. Ask why she'll pucker her snippy little face and say, Who wants to know? *You?* Which is an answer Doll has begun to give often, when she doesn't like Mr. Early questioning her.)

(Who are you to judge *us?* What right do you have to believe yourself superior to *us?* So Ira Early fantasizes defending himself in some public place. Blinding lights in his eyes, possibly he's handcuffed, legs shackled.)

Doll appears! Doll has been with a Mr. *X* (prepaid) and has subsequently fetched late supper for her Daddy and herself. In knee-high white leather boots that grip her slender legs like pythons, in stiletto heels that add several inches to her diminutive height, Doll makes her way with childish carelessness across patches of icy pavement. Her plaited pigtailed milkweed hair bobs winningly about her small head. Mr. Early calls out the window: Doll, damn! Don't slip and fall.

For Doll is a beautiful little girl, but breakable.

Yessir we have money saved from our travels. It has been years now. Two or three days in a city then move on. Sometimes, and just possibly this will be one of those times, I will behave badly, and we'll have to move swiftly on, not even staying the night and getting a little rest. Mostly we straddle the Mississippi River. You'd have to ask Daddy what his investments are.

At first Doll can hardly see her (step)daddy in the back of the La Salle where he's waiting in the shadows. That ample belly, a fat old spider. Oh Dad-*dy!* Surprise.

Doll is bringing Mr. Early his seafood sushi (ugh!) and her (yummy) taco burger with home fries, cole slaw, giant Pepsi in a waxed container. Oh Daddy, open the damn door. Expect me to do goddamn *everything?*

Of course, Mr. Early has the door open, quick.

This child just enjoys being bossy. (Like her late mother.)

Mr. Early sure doesn't approve of Doll's eating habits. Bad as a taco burger is, and deep-fried fries, Doll can devour even worse food. Her nervous metabolism burns calories away at the present time, she's just a child, but what about later? Years to come? Mr. Early's face crinkles in worry envisioning a fattish Doll. The nougat-creamy skin puffed and bloated and certain to attract a less discerning, less well-bred category of admirer.

A wild windy river-smelling wind. A weekday night in Anonymous Metropolis, USA.

Yes we are on the Web. Daddy hooked on, it's been a long time now. Like shrewd financial investments. Daddy looks like a dear old cuddly-cosy fat thing, but Daddy is *wired.*

There's a pleasure in food when you're hungry as there's a pleasure in drink when you're thirsty. Ira Early and his (step)daughter Doll devour their take-out suppers, sip and swallow their precious drinks, even as, less than two miles away in room twenty-two of the E-Z Economy Motel, the next friend (prepaid) stares at himself in a scummy mirror. He's faded-red-haired with a maggoty pale skin even his doting (now deceased) mother dismayed over. He's a man of conscience or wants to think so. Staring at his reflection murmuring, Sicko! Now we know.

The phone on the burn-scarred bedside table rings.

Ira Early watches Doll's rapid fingers, pointy bloody-red manicured nails, as she punches numbers in the cell phone, an absurdly small gizmo (to Mr. Early's bifocaled eye, most "new" electronic gadgets are gizmos you halfway expect to explode in your face) that never ceases to surprise him; it actually works. Like a regular phone.

Doll laughs at Daddy. Of course it works like a *regular phone,* silly. It *is* a regular phone.

(But isn't a cell phone actually a radio? Some kind of miniature radio? Ira Early knows better than to argue with a moody daughter.)

Mr. Early takes the gizmo from Doll after she has dialed the number he's told her. (His fingers are too big for the task.) Clears his throat, assumes his formal frown, elocution.

Hel-lo! Sir, this is —

Doll doesn't pay much attention as her (step)daddy confirms with Mr. *X.* Place, time, duration. Doll has heard it all before, numberless times. (Hundreds?) Already in this old midwestern city on the river they've had good luck, and you have the feeling there's more to come. Yesterday, today, now this evening. Mr. Early has planned a third day of appointments before moving on. Doll yawns into her hand that smells of taco burger.

No. Doll isn't yawning, Doll is wiping her greasy mouth. That barracuda flash in Doll's glassy dilated eyes. Mr. Early, fumbling to turn off the phone, happens to see. Or thinks he sees.

Doll? You're going to be good tonight, yes?

Pouty Doll shrugs. Wriggles that little Doll-shiver that can mean yes for sure or just the reverse.

Mr. Early fumbles now with the remains of his sushi. Doll jeers at him for using chopsticks. Chopsticks! Damn, Dad, we're *Americans.* Raw tuna glop and crumbling rice that looks to Doll like dried-out brown ants drop into his crotch. Doll tosses him a soiled paper napkin with a snort of derision.

Ira Early is a worrier because he's a perfectionist. He's a perfectionist because he's scared as hell of things going wrong. He's scared as hell of things going wrong because he has long witnessed, and witnesses almost daily, things going wrong for other people. Sometimes seriously wrong. (Mr. Early can't know how wrong things will go for Mr. *X* in room twenty-two of the E-Z Economy Motel except, having caught a glimpse of Doll's barracuda eyes, he has an uneasy premonition.)

Still, there's the solace of the Do Not Touch policy. This, implemented by Ira Early from the start of his and Doll's travels, is a shrewd piece of strategy. Do Not Touch (DNT on the Web) guarantees a discerning class of admirers. Also the age, eleven: young, prepubescent, but not too young. A higher class of (male) individuals of varied ages but tending to the educated middle/upper-middle income levels. Rarely less than college degrees, predominantly liberal arts. DNT among such individuals is an enticement, a novelty, and a relief.

Doll, you navigate. We'd best be on our way.

Doll whines, Oh Dad-dy! I'm not finished with my supper, you know I can't eat fast as you.

Read off the directions, dear. We have only fifteen minutes.

He'll wait. Geez!

It's nearly 11 P.M. The moon has shifted conspicuously in the sky, like a protracted wink.

Driving south, or what seems to Mr. Early south, into the hive of the inner city. Maze of Exit Only lanes, exit ramps, cloverleafs, glaring lights. He hates expressways but has no choice. Beside him Doll balances her giant Pepsi between her knees and reads off directions from a sheet of paper. For a girl so clever and canny as Doll she has difficulty with words of more than a single syllable or containing unfamiliar consonants.

Kway top of the ramp. Exit right.

What's that?

Kway —

Key you mean. Q-u-a-y pronounced *Key.*

Doll turns sullen. How the hell would I know that, home-schooled like I am?

Unknown to old-fart Daddy I have my neat little razor hidden in my boot. Wrapped in aluminum foil for safety. Maybe yes maybe no is what I'm thinking.

Since St. Louis it's been a long time on the road.

Saying to Daddy, Know what? I want ostrich boots for Christmas. I want some sun in New Orleans.

At the E-Z Economy Motel he washes face, forearms, underarms, and hands. Though he isn't (swears he isn't!) going to touch the girl. His maggoty skin aflame as if peppered with acne. Thirty-seven years old, not seventeen, still has pimples, something must be wrong with his basal metabolism.

Now he's out, on parole, should check this out.

When Mr. Early and his (step)daughter Doll, known then as Margaret Ann, were living at what authorities called a Fixed Address, up to two years ago, in fact in Mr. Early's late wife's family home in a dignified old historic district in Minneapolis, there were problems in their domestic life that going on the road has largely solved.

Hated to take this bright questing child out of school. My solace is, she's scrupulously homeschooled. Hardly a day passes we don't visit natural history museums, butterfly houses, pioneer villages. Planetariums.

Ira Early, long ago a student of Latin, mathematics, and world history at the Cincinnati Academy for Boys, is one to prowl second-hand bookstores and flea markets. The trunk of the La Salle is crammed with random volumes of the *Encyclopaedia Britannica, Webster's Unabridged Dictionary, Reader's Digest Condensed Books.* Doll has, or used to have, a photographic memory and can still entertain enraptured Mr. Xs by reciting in a breathless schoolgirl voice the American presidents and their little-known vice presidents, summaries of economic theories (Kondratieff long wave cycle, econometrics, monetarism, neo-Keynesianism), major wars of Europe from the One Hundred Years to World War II. Also, major cranial nerves and arteries.

What's my favorite? The carotid.

We tried! We did. But domestic life on Mount Curve Avenue was not for us.

Doll's Mummy departed this world when Doll was, let's see, two or three years old. At least it's believed that Mrs. Early departed this world, in fact her remains have never been found. Doll has said

indignantly that she *does not* believe "allegations" that her Daddy
murdered his wife/her mother, dismembered her corpse, and scattered the pieces along forty miles of the Mississippi south of Minneapolis, weighed down with rocks and never to surface, no Doll
does not.

Doll says, It was a long-ago time before cable TV and cell phones.
I know my Daddy's heart and he would never harm a hair on anyone's head who did not deserve it.

When one of Them asked me, Does your father mistreat you,
showing me silly naked rubber dolls, I said, No no not I and
hummed loudly to myself and rocked from side to side.

I love my Daddy. (It's true; Ira Early is Doll's biological father.
Not her [step]father as they tell associates and Mr. Xs. Even among
Mr. Early's widespread contacts there exists the principle of *drawing the line* at certain forms of behavior, and this principle, if you're
in business for yourself, it's wise to respect.)

(The long-ago time? Some say it was in the early 1970s, and some
say it was 1953, but still others argue that Ira Early and his (step)-
daughter Doll began their travels in 1930, after the crash. Doll is
perplexed by this notion — she's been eleven years old for more
than seventy years?)

How old are you, Doll, Mr. X will surely inquire. If Mr. X in room
twenty-two of the E-Z Economy Motel is any kin to Mr. X of the
other motels scattered along the Mississippi. That question I've
been hearing all my life, getting so it seriously pisses me off.

Daddy says, Humor 'em. They are a priceless (because inex-
haustible) commodity.

Daddy says, Play the script. See, they'd recoil from *ten*.

They don't want to hear *twelve*, either. Still less *thirteen*. There's a
kind of consensus.

DNT has worked out really well. Or almost.

On Mount Curve we tried. There was even a Grandma with a with-
ered cherry face and Jell-O eyes, Mummy's mother, Doll tried hard
to love but failed. Sniffing in the old woman's arms holding her
breath as long as she could then gagging and pushing free. And
Daddy who was a youngish widower bearing his grief stoically one

day tugged at his then-dark goatee and said, Margaret Ann you're my daughter, aren't you! And nothing of hers. My genes are your destiny, darling. Gravely shaken Daddy was, he'd not realized father-love until that instant.

Still we tried for (how many?) years to lead "normal" — "average" — "approved-of" — lives. Even went to Mummy's old church, sometimes.

For all the good it did us.

Always motels or "cabins." (Yes, there are still "motor cabins" in the rural American Midwest.) Never hotels with lobbies. (Though Mr. Early and Doll sometimes check into Marriots on the expressways, father and daughter traveling under a variety of names and guises.) If Mr. *X*, Mr. *Y*, Mr. *Z* journeys to meet them in Anonymous Metropolis, if he wishes to stay at a good hotel, he will have to take a room at a motel too, like the E-Z Economy. Best for Doll not to appear in any populous brightly lit lobby in her high-heeled white leather stiletto-heel boots, purple suede jacket, plaited pigtailed milkweed-hair bobbing about her exquisite Doll head.

Parentless eleven-year-old with painted eyes, luscious peachy lips, and blusher on her cheeks. Oh, no.

They fled Minneapolis for a good reason. Hounded out, you could say. Persecuted. That terrible day the "public health" inspector arrived uninvited, unexpected, at the house. An officer with the fascist power to "report" Ira Early to the authorities and to threaten him with arrest for Parental Negligence.

Well, possibly there'd been warnings. Registered letters from Margaret Ann's school addressed to Ira Early, importunate telephone calls from the principal of Mount Curve Elementary he failed to take seriously. Margaret Ann Early, who is enrolled in sixth grade, where is she? Why is she so frequently absent from classes? Why, when she's in school, does she fall asleep at her desk? Why are her grades so poor, her deportment so rebellious?

Examined for Signs of Abuse. There were none.

In room twenty-two of the E-Z Economy Motel the man known variously as Mr. *X* and (as mischievous Doll is shortly to call him) Mr. Radish gazes at himself in a scummy bathroom mirror. Runs his hands through his thinning faded-red hair, observes liquidy despair and mad exulting desire in his otherwise ordinary, mildly bloodshot, eyes. Thinking it isn't too late, he could call this off. Could just walk out.

He's a decent guy, really. He's made mistakes he will never make again. (He believes.)

His groin is throbbing, a pleasurable sensation that fills him with disgust. Do. Not. Touch.

He flushes the toilet to make sure it's flushed and reenters the other room, smooths the soiled rust-colored corduroy bedspread with both his hands. It's 11 P.M.; maybe the child won't be delivered?

It's 11 P.M., true. But Ira Early can't be coerced into speeding even by his own wish. In fact, he has an exasperating habit of driving ten miles below the speed limit. In the restored 1953 relic he drives with the fussiness of an elder who disdains contemporary life. It's part of Mr. Early's gentlemanly style. It's part of why you trust him. In his suits with vests, neckties from another era, rimless bifocals riding the bridge of his slightly pudgy nose. His white hair and whiskers give him an appealing Santa Claus look, or maybe it's that kooky genius Albert Einstein you're made to think of. Ira Early's cold shrewd eyes sparkling behind the bifocals like a school teacher's and that vague smile, lips tight over big chunky carnivore teeth. Bartenders, motel managers, the majority of Mr. Early's colleagues and associates persist in the error, *This old fart is no threat.*

After Quay, what?

Looks like — City Center? Exit left.

This Anonymous Metropolis is a maze of ugly streets that should be familiar to Ira Early; he's been here before, and Doll has been here before, who knows when. You will have noticed that the Inner City is the same city throughout the Midwest. Endlessly repeated Decaying Inner City of a Once-Thriving City. It's like a suction tube, drawing them in. Like bloody water swirling gaily down a drain just slightly clogged with hairs.

(Why is Doll thinking such a wicked thought? Snaky little pink tongue wetting her crimson lips.)

Exit *left*, I said, Dad-dy! You're headed right.

You said left. I mean, you said right.

I said fucking *left,* Dad-dy.

Just watch that mouth, miss.

And I'm hungry, too, Doll says loudly. After this I want some ice cream. Fucking fudge ripple.

I said, miss, watch that mouth.

Watch your own mouth, Dad-dy. You're the wicked ol' pre-vert.

(Doll is slipping into a mean mood. The taco burger was mostly cheese. She's thinking possibly she won't go for just the carotid; that's too easy. That was St. Louis. It's been eight months at least since she did the other; that's more challenging. And brought back a certain rubbery goody for Dad-dy.)

(Who pretends to be horrified, sickened. But for sure Mr. Early keeps these Mementos of Adventure like any honest pre-vert.)

Front Street. See it, Daddy?

Of course. I'm not blind.

In the E-Z parking lot, Doll repairs her makeup. For an impatient spoiled girl she's surprisingly deft at painting her face, the eyes especially. As Mr. *X* nervously strokes his flushed face, turns his head from side to side staring at himself in the mirror.

But is that me? Or some sicko who has dragged me here?

Mr. Early escorts Doll to room twenty-two (which is lighted within, shades drawn). But Mr. Early discreetly steps back into the shadows of a dumpster when Doll knocks on the door and the door swings open.

Silently mouthing the words *God be with you, dear.*

And your Daddy close by, standing watch.

(Should he have forced his moody prepubescent daughter to show him the contents of her handbag? Her jacket pockets? Her sexy leather boots? Damn, he'd meant to but forgot.)

The door is opened warily. Doll is invited inside. Biting her lower lip to stifle a nervous giggle. Why, Doll isn't fearful of this individual she has never glimpsed before — is she?

Not Ira Early's (step)daughter. Not Doll.

This guy reminds Doll of an upright radish. Mr. Radish!

He's nervous of her, too. He's excited. He's just standing there. Fingers twitching and a sickly oily glow to his face. Like he has

never seen anything like Doll before. Like he's trying to decide
what to make of her. But he has enough presence of mind to shut,
lock, double-lock the door.

Trying to smile. Licking his wormy lips.

D-Doll. That's your . . . actual name?

Doll shrugs. Maybe yes maybe no.

And you're — Mr. Radish has a stammer? — elev-elev-ven years
old?

Doll shrugs and mumbles what might be Yessir. She's a fascinating mix of mute, shy, sly, naughty-girl, fluttery eyelashes, and something sullen beneath, like the beat of hard rock. Mr. Radish is enraptured, gaping and smiling and flexing his long fingers.

Saying, stumbling with the words, You l-look older than eleven I
guess . . . but you're v-very beautiful, Doll. Whoever you are.

Doll mumbles, Um, thanks mister. Shrugs off her purple leather
jacket, lets it fall onto the bed like this is the most natural gesture in
the world. Shakes out her bristly plaited pigtails seeing in the corner of her eye how ol' Mr. Radish stares.

Long as the policy is Do Not Touch, what's it matter?

Oh he's feeling morose, melancholy.

Maybe this isn't the right life; sometimes you wonder. The moon
so vivid, like the eye of God. Seeing all and forgiving? Maybe not.

Ira Early has emptied the thermos of its contents, decides to
drop by the Kismet Lounge he'd noticed a block from the E-Z
on Front Street. Doll won't know; be gone just a few minutes, sweetheart.

This Mr. X, junior high school teacher, Mr. Early has been assured wouldn't hurt, wouldn't so much as touch, a flea.

Where's the TV remote? Doll's eyes scan the grungy room.

Mr. Radish just wants to talk. Well, fine. Except Doll can't be expected to answer his meandering questions or even to listen. She's
done her part; she's wound up like a mechanical doll, one-two-
three-four, the usual. But it sure looks spontaneous! Facial movements, fluttering eyelashes, more of the smile, variants of the smile,
sweet lowered gaze, snaky pink tongue moistening her lips, simula-
tion of a blush, if Doll could blush. She's a little pissed at this guy,
saying she looks older than eleven. Fuck that. Obviously she looks
older than eleven, but not that much older! Doll's thinking she has

been insulted; she'll slash this asshole's carotid artery, watch him bleed out like the last one. Except this time, for sure, Doll won't get blood splatters. Bad enough on your clothes, but in your pigtailed hair it's a bummer.

Bum night, sort of sad-making says the graying balding ponytailed bartender like he's wanting to converse with Ira Early, the joint is so dead. Mr. Early runs his fingers through his white hair and beard like the rakings of conscience. Yes, says Mr. Early with biblical intonation, it is sad indeed. Mankind's lot.

The ponytailed bartender, you can imagine was a flower child in the previous century, says eagerly, Tragic, d'you think?

Mr. Early gazes into his drink. Frank truth resides there.

Well, maybe just sad, my friend. *Tragic* is big league.

Mr. Radish manages a coughing sort of laugh. Bad as clearing his throat. Saying, like an upright corpse flirting, Doll you say you're c-called Doll . . . meaning your name is something else?

Doll bounces on the bed, stinky old corduroy cover, softly squealing, giggling, in the manner of a six year-old, since this is expected. Mr. Radish is an ideal audience, gaping and gazing with mouth slightly ajar as if he has fallen asleep on his feet.

Doll shrugs. Maybe yes maybe no.

You can tell me, Doll. Your name.

Doll has located the TV remote, half-hidden beneath *USA Today* on the bedside table. Graceful as a child ballerina she leaps from the bed to snatch it up.

My n-name is . . .

Doll isn't listening. Doll sees this guy is no threat. Homely as a broken-down shoe, faded-red hair like an old brush, those blinking doggy eyes. Almost you'd feel sorry for this creep. (Almost.) He's no age Doll could judge, but then Doll is no judge of adult ages: anyone not a kid is "old" — "old bag" — "old fart." Mr. Radish she sees is wearing a white shirt, sleeves rolled up to reveal hairy forearms, but hairy in patches like he has the mange. Trousers that look like he's been sleeping in them. Ugly old lace-up shoes. Mr. Radish is flabby, slope-shouldered, otherwise he'd be tall as Ira Early. But lacking what you'd call dignity, stature. And Mr. Radish smells.

Ugh. That boring odor of an excited male. Plus anxiety and

shame. An odor Doll has been smelling in rooms like this for a long
long time since leaving Mount Curve, Minneapolis.

It's TV time. But Mr. Radish keeps pacing in nervous half circles
around Doll, making asshole small talk in this hoarse crackling
voice like something you'd want to mash beneath your stiletto heel.

Saying, D-Doll? Who are your people?

Ummm. Dunno.

Is that man who . . . that man who spoke with me on the phone
. . . really your stepfather?

Doll drawls, Stepdaddy.

Why, that's terrible!

Doll switches on the TV. Doll drawls some answer that sounds
right.

Your own stepfather? Has done this to you?

(Fudge ripple is what Doll wants. Damn, she deserves it.)

(This guy. Not worth his throat cut; he's just a sad jerk. Or the
thing between his legs, assuming he has one, sawn off. Not tonight.)

But, dear . . . how has this . . . your life . . . happened?

Doll drawls, Dunno, sir. Just happened.

Do you go to school, Doll? I mean . . . are you being educated?

Mr. Radish has shoved his fidgety hands deep into his trouser
pockets, stands staring at Doll on the bed and breathing like something wounded.

Doll says, a little sniff of pride, I'm homeschooled.

Homeschooled! Mr. Radish laughs like someone has grabbed
him and squeezed between the legs.

In the mostly deserted dark of the Kismet Lounge, Mr. Early is
nursing a second martini. Down-in-the-dumps, he'd better be careful he isn't losing track of time; he'd meant to return to the E-Z
after a ten-minute break, but more minutes have passed.

Frankly Ira Early has been hurt. His own (step)daughter he
adores called him a wicked ol' pre-vert. That's unfair.

Wicked ol' pre-vert, she'd said. And laughed.

Well, maybe there is something to this: Those mementos Doll
has given Mr. Early — consequences of Doll's mean mood in one
or another E-Z motel — he has not discarded in haste like you'd
expect. For some reason, he can't. These goodies, as Doll calls

them, are signs. Symbols. Hard to say what they mean. But they do mean something.

See, Dad-dy? What you made me do.

Better them than me, girl.

An old-fart nervous type would "dispose of" such evidence in case of police intervention, but Ira Early is a unique personality. More unique, you might say, than the legendary Doll.

Chronicles of Midwestern crime will never plumb the depths of Ira Early. Even those who'd met Ira Early and his (step)daughter Doll will not know how to speak of them.

These mementos Mr. Early stores in jug bottles, in formaldehyde. He has five, six . . . seven? . . . scattered in rental lockers as far north as Mille Lacs, Minnesota, and as far south as Greenville, Mississippi. Under various names, not a one of them "Early." Some kind of sentimental record maybe he'll look back on one day when Doll is finally too mature to be Doll. Now Mr. Early is feeling maudlin.

Refresh your drink, mister? inquires the ponytailed bartender.

Mr. Early shakes his Santa Claus head no, better not, hears himself say, Well. If you insist.

Doll, sprawled provocatively on the bed, hasn't removed the sexy white knee-high boots; her black satin miniskirt rides up her lovely thighs. Her spaghetti-strap top is crushed-velvet gold, and there's a teasing suggestion of little-girl breasts, or padding, at her bosom. Those bristly pigtails sprout from her small head with a look like, if you touched them, they'd give you a shock. (Mr. Radish's wickedest dream come true. Maybe he should rape-murder, or murder-rape, this exquisite child, get it over with in a burst of passion, and then murder himself? But how, practically speaking, is a man like Mr. Radish going to murder himself? He's not made for heroics.)

Doll is watching a TV game show. Looks like *Millionaire*. Squeals and applause and that sappy emcee who bears a resemblance to Ira Early, in fact. Bored, Doll switches to another channel. She's gotten too restless, these months and years of traveling with her (step)Daddy, to watch any TV program more than three or four minutes, likes to surf the channels from one to ninety-nine and back again like a merry-go-round. If Mr. Early is present, he'll take the remote from Doll's fingers firmly no matter how she protests.

TV is just plain bad for the brain, Mr. Early believes. But Mr. Early is not here, just Mr. Radish, who seems to adore her and will not touch her. Staring as Doll aims the remote at the TV like a wand.

Doll hates commercials, but she's staring at this one for PMS. That is, for the prevention of. Premenstrual stress. Doll whispers these mysterious words aloud. Her Daddy has assured her this will never happen to her. He gives her pills daily, and there are other ways of keeping Doll from that ugly phenomenon called *pubescence.*

Switches the channel to *Funniest Animal Videos.* There's a mournful-looking basset hound and a bald oblong-headed baby sharing an orange Popsicle as family members look on howling, tears running down their cheeks. Doll laughs too, but in disgust. Yuck! Everyone knows dogs' mouths are cesspools of germs.

Mr. Radish has tugged his shirt open, revealing a patchily red-haired pimply chest Doll doesn't wish to see. Mr. Radish is still chattering excitedly; maybe he's drunk or high on painkillers. Doll seems to recall Mr. Early mentioning this Mr. *X* at the E-Z is something like a junior high teacher, an educator, and an idealist.

Saying, swallowing hard, D-Doll, are you listening? I'm real ashamed of myself, for this. You're a beautiful child. I just know you have a b-beautiful soul. It's shitty what your own stepfather has done to you. You deserve a whole lot better than . . . this.

Doll shrugs. Uh-hmm?

Frozen-faced Doll ignores this bullshit. Staring fiercely at the TV screen as she clicks through the channels rapid as a lizard scaling a wall. Her Cleopatra eyes have the glassy-hungry TV look of a child rushing through the channels, certain that something special is waiting. In a cold fury she's thinking maybe she'll not only saw open Mr. Radish's bulgy carotid artery, she'll gouge out one of his bulgy eyes. That time she surprised Mr. Early with a coin-sized slab of flesh containing the belly button of some crude Ozark trucker, the old humbug had been truly amazed. Doll: this goes beyond my DNA, I swear.

Wish I could, Mr. Radish says, oh God wish I could save you. Beautiful little girl like you.

Mister thanks, but I'm *saved.*

(Doll checks the time: Oh God not even 11:30 P.M.)

I could p-pray for us. The power of prayer is awesome.

Mister thanks, it's okay.

A man like that stepfather of yours, Mr. Radish is panting, should be cast down in fire and brimstone forever. Should be turned in to the police, at least.

Doll pretends she hasn't heard this. Though she has heard it.

Well. Let Mr. Radish say what he wishes — that's part of the fee — and he can do what he wishes, to himself exclusively; Doll won't so much as glance around at him. If this creep strangles in his own spit, if his face turns the color of boils, she won't glance at him.

But she might say, if the urge comes upon her, Oh mister is it time for Doll's bath?

Or, smiling the naughty-little-girl smile, batting her eyelashes like butterfly wings, Doll wants her bath. It's time!

In the Kismet Lounge, Mr. Early sees suddenly to his horror it's 11:46 P.M. He's been in this place far longer than he'd planned, and he's had more to drink than he'd planned. Shame! What if, back at the E-Z, his little girl is crying piteously for him?

Nothing like that has happened yet, exactly. Not since an unfortunate night in El Dorado, Arkansas, when Ira Early and his (step)daughter Doll were new and naive in their adventures.

Are you nek-ked, mister? Don't peek.

From inside the steamy bathroom, Mr. Radish croaks out, Yes.

Doll, naked too, biting her lower lip to keep from giggling, pushes open the door. Looks like Mr. Radish has done as she requested.

The last twenty minutes of Mr. Radish are going to be a game.

Mr. Radish has been told it is a bath. Doll has another game in mind.

(Seems that, that morning, I'd done the bad thing. Prepared a fresh razor blade on a ballpoint pen from one of the motels, fixed with that Crazy Glue that can't ever be pried off, as my Daddy had forbidden after St. Louis. Oh, this blade is *sharp*.)

Doll is slender and small-boned as an actual doll might be, of some long-ago time. Doll has tiny breasts with warm brown flowerlet nipples and no more hairs at the fork of her legs than the down on the back of her neck. Her legs are long, like they could spring into action and run her out of your reach, just make the wrong move. In the humid bathroom air, Doll's creamy nougat skin is slightly flushed, and her big eyes shine with anticipation. Doll's bristly pigtails are pinned up neatly onto her head and covered with a cheap plastic shower cap provided by the E-Z Motel. Must be in one of her mean moods, as Mr. Early would say, but in fact Doll is laughing.

Like an actual eleven-year-old might cry, breathless, Is that bath water nice and hot?

It's hot, Doll. It . . . is.

Mr. Radish, obeying the rules of the game not to peek, splashes the water with his cupped hands. Doll sees a wedge of sickly pale chest and a swath of faded-red hair. It isn't too hot, mister, is it?

No! It's just right.

I don't want to be burned, see. But I like a hot bath.

D-Doll, it's just right. You can stick a t-toe in.

Is there some nice soap, mister? I want lots and lots of suds.

There's a real nice soap here. Big as the palm of my hand, see?

Don't peek! I can see.

It smells real nice, too. Ivory.

Doll says, chiding, as if Mr. Radish had naughtily begun to peek over his shoulder at her, Mister! Turn your head and shut your eyes too.

I am, Doll. I am.

Poor Mr. Radish quivering and shivering in the bathwater in that grimy tub and the tattered shower curtain like a stage curtain pulled back to reveal him to jeering eyes. Doll summons forth her Doll-rage. Doll is holding the razor-on-the-stick just behind her right buttock, along the smooth curve of her warm flesh. Seeing naked hairy knees drawn up to a collapsed-looking chest reminds her of Ira Early and that look of a man who, in his clothes, looks solid, but without his clothes is flaccid and lumpy and you just want to slash-slash-slash.

Doll's eyes are revealed a sharp glassy-green, like reflectors.

Mister? Pro-mise? Don't look till I'm in the tub?

Back in the bedroom the TV is turned up loud but not too loud. The E-Z is that kind of reliable motel; people mind their own damned business. The time, Doll has shrewdly noted, is 11:48 P.M. A practical time. If her weak-willed Daddy has drifted down the street for a drink or two, by this time he's back. Mr. Radish croaks out a final reply, yes he p-promises not to l-look, and Doll tiptoes to

the tub to where the naked man awaits her trembling in anticipation, and she strikes unerringly with the razor one! two! three! in
the sawing technique she has perfected, and a four! and five! for
good measure with such deadly force (city homicide detectives will
marvel) that the victim's head is nearly decapitated from his body.

Softly Doll murmurs, See?

Oh, God, it's after midnight. Mr. Early pulls into the parking lot
panting and repentant. Where is Doll? Hasn't Doll left the motel
room yet? He'd had a premonition something bad might happen;
he'll never forgive himself if it's his own daughter it happened to.

Seeing how the moon has slid halfway down the sky behind the
E-Z Economy Motel and when you glance up, shreds of cloud like
broken cobweb are dragging across its surface.

Dad-dy. I'm not mad at *you*.

Departing this city south on I-55 thirty-six hours earlier than Ira
Early planned. He's speechless in indignation and worry, and Doll
just laughs at him. Tossing a small wad of bills onto his lap when
she'd climbed into the car, no credit cards. Ira Early never swipes
credit cards; that's how you get caught. Doll is humming to herself,
unplaiting her pigtails. Oh, her scalp hurts, the roots of her hairs
and every hair. And she's hungry.

Across the state line in Missouri they stop at a twenty-four-hour
diner. Sliding into a corner booth not wanting to be noticed. Mr.
Early is wearing a coal miner's cap meant to hide his hair, but there
isn't much he can do about the Santa Claus whiskers. Orders a
beer; he's damned thirsty. But too upset to eat. Doll shamelessly de-
vours a fudge ripple sundae. Wiping her prim little mouth to say
finally, knowing how Mr. Early has been frantic to hear, Well, Daddy. Could be I have something for you.

Oh, Doll. No.

A good-y. For Dad-dy.

Giggling, passing to him beneath the table the aluminum-
wrapped thing out of her purple leather jacket from Gap. Mr. Early
would shove it back onto her knees in disgust except his fingers
grasp it instead, groping. He wonders what it might be, something
soft and fleshy still warm inside its wrapper? You ol' pre-vert, Doll
giggles. All for you.

It's our reputation I'm worried about, Doll. Our livelihood in the world.

Oh *grump!* Nothing's gonna stop *us.*

Is this true? Ira Early, stroking his bristly beard, wants to think so.

Before they leave the diner, Mr. Early takes out the revered AAA map, much creased from their travels, and smooths it open on the tabletop. Doll gets to choose their next destination, though sometimes, in the interests of business pragmatism, Mr. Early intervenes. Doll's pointy red-painted nail hovering over the map. Where next?

JACK O'CONNELL

The Swag from Doc Hawthorne's

FROM *The Magazine of Fantasy & Science Fiction*

YUK TANG LIKES TO THINK of himself as Darcey's partner. Darcey would choke if he knew this. He works with Yuk Tang because everyone else he knows has moved west or south. And because Yuk Tang is connected with more than one guy in Little Asia who can move anything — TVs and jewelry right down to paintings and rare stamps and precious metals — in less than a week. And because Yuk Tang agrees to a sixty-forty split, with Darcey hugging the sixty end.

Though Darcey dislikes Yuk Tang on instinct, he admitted to himself last week, while sober and bored, that they work well together. They work the way he dreams about, like they had one smart brain and six fast hands. Yuk Tang has this innate talent for smelling dogs. He can take one whiff, any room of any house, halfway in the window, and give the thumbs down. Darcey has never known Yuk Tang to be careless or unpredictable. He'd walk away from an open jewelry box without flinching if the fifteen-minute buzzer on his watch went off.

For his part, Darcey thinks of himself as smart and in control. And it's *his* friends who know whether someone's enjoying a week in the Bahamas or just doing three hours at a funeral. Darcey's generous with these friends. He gives them money and as much time as he can spare. There's the guy whose sister is a groomer at a ridiculously expensive kennel. There's the kid who works for the award-winning landscaper. And there's Scalley, a new electrician for a hot local burglar and fire alarm company.

Darcey pays close attention to these people. He studies them the way he'd study a hotel poker game. He knows, without exception, what it is they respond to, what it takes to cement their trust in his friendship. He bought himself a pager so he can return their calls immediately. He knows their favorite restaurants and reserves good tables monthly. He takes them to terrible movies and manages to discuss the films afterward over coffee. He spent a serious chunk of money recently on Scalley's dental restoration.

All of this has paid off like you read about. Without getting sloppy or greedy, Yuk Tang and Darcey have put away a barrel of money. Yuk Tang has shipped a wad to less fortunate family members back in the homeland. Darcey has filled more than one closet suitcase with respectable dollars. It's a happy time. They're not logging a lot of hours and they're rarely losing any sleep. And most importantly, the worry is minimal. Their timing, their attention to detail and planning, has meant few close calls and no sudden trips out of town.

Darcey would hate to have to leave Quinsigamond again. He's done it in the past and it breaks his heart. Even when the trip has been to Miami or Bermuda. He's spent hours on clean beaches, ninety degrees and a breeze, dreaming about the coffee and the smell of the meatloaf at the Miss Q Diner. What he'd really like to do, and what he keeps hidden from everyone, is let some time pass and then launch into a legitimate business. A bar or, more exactly, a club. Something with style and subtlety, where people dress up and it never gets too loud. Sometimes, while on the phone with Scalley, Darcey doodles pictures of the club. Ceiling fans. A long bar. An office for himself, in an upstairs loft, with a one-way mirror for a wall.

Yuk Tang has some of his own plans that he keeps to himself. They're vague, but they also involve the entrepreneurial arts. He's thought about opening a restaurant. Or maybe a video-rental franchise that specializes in martial arts films. What he'd like most is an import clothing store. Women's satin dresses and silk scarves. The mark-up could be tremendous. Because of relations in need, he hasn't managed to pile up as much ready cash as Darcey. And though he doesn't resent this, he is unhappy with the sixty-forty split. But his options are limited and he knows he'd have a hell of a time finding a reliable and intelligent partner who'd work with an Asian immigrant who can't drive.

They both hold irritating part-time jobs, though at this point there's no need to do so. They had these jobs before things got lucrative and, because of a fear they don't understand, they haven't quit. They know that seeing someone go off to work on a regular schedule keeps any neighbors from being too interested and the routine keeps their minds calm and occupied for the few days before any gig.

Yuk Tang works as an aide in an old-age home out on Main South. Darcey drives a shuttle van for the Foundation for Experimental Biochemistry. Yuk Tang pushes around a cart twenty hours a week, placing tiny cups of ginger ale and apple juice into palsied hands. He pulls lit cigarettes out of sleeping mouths and helps pick up people who have slid out of chairs to the floor. Darcey drives a two-year-old silver Ford van back and forth, every twenty minutes, down the same boring stretch of tree-lined road, dropping off and picking up people who, for all he knows, could be world famous. They all carry large manila envelopes and ask about the weather. They're condescending without meaning to be. About ninety percent of them are Asian, which amuses and annoys Darcey at the same time. It makes him look funny at Yuk Tang sometimes, even in the middle of a job.

Lately though, Yuk and Darcey's luck won't let up. It's good and it's steady. It's like they can do no wrong. Storm windows are missing from the shrubbery side of the house. Rolex watches are left out on the bathroom vanity. Ten hundred-dollar bills, all brand new and banded together, are found by accident underneath a thirteen-inch Trinitron when they move it off its stand. Street lights are out. Dogs have died or been shipped down to Florida. It's getting scary, it's so damned easy.

Then there's a moment in this lawyer's place up in Windsor Hills. Because things have been so sweet, Darcey and Yuk Tang have been pushing it up in the Hills. They've talked about setting a monthly limit on jobs in the Hills. They kicked numbers back and forth on the way to this lawyer's house. Yuk Tang wanted to play it simple, a given number of houses in the area in any thirty-day period. Darcey, thinking of his club, figured it would be better to work up until they hit an agreed gross. They decided nothing and drove the last block to the job in silence.

They'd been given the word on the house two days before. Attorney and Mrs. Bennett stopped at the Avondale Animal Hotel on their way to the airport. Darcey drove past the Bennett home after work and filled out his checklist. He drove by again with Yuk Tang and they spent a few minutes discussing it over a small dinner plate at the Grille. Though neither one will acknowledge it, they know they didn't give this gig the attention it requires. But it's hard when things have been coming so easy. It's like they're working with the guardian angel of thieves and he doesn't want a cut.

Then, in the midst of lifting a Toshiba receiver out of its slot in an enormous media wall, Darcey's beeper goes off. He nearly has a coronary and drops the receiver and it breaks on the hardwood floor. Yuk Tang runs down from the bedrooms, glares at him in the doorway, and motions a thumb outside. They leave with half the potential take. In the car — a semi-restored MG — Yuk Tang, ever the minimalist, says only, "You're not thinking," and Darcey comes back with a loud "Screw you, Bruce Lee. Find me a phone booth."

There's a tension that grows in the quiet. Yuk Tang only recently confided in Darcey that Bruce Lee was a real spiritual hero to him, that at night he said what Darcey might consider prayers to Bruce Lee. Darcey, in the driver's seat, knows he's screwed up for the first time since their streak began. It's no big problem. No one is hurt or pinched. But the stupidity of bringing the pager on a job has brought him next door to panic. He knows what to do on a job like he knows his own name. Like he knows how to breathe.

Darcey swings into a drugstore lot and uses the phone outside. The page turns out to be from Scalley, who's excited and confused: He's got some information. He's not sure Darcey's interested. He's talking second-hand tip here. He needs a few dollars. He hasn't eaten in two days. He thinks he has a fever. He's leaving tonight on a plane for Ensenada or Buenos Aires.

Darcey has to scream into the phone to get him to quiet down. He tells Scalley to be at the Menard Diner in twenty minutes, jumps back in the car, and starts to head for the Menard without consulting Yuk Tang. Yuk Tang, not normally a hateful or violent man, daydreams as they drive, too fast, to the meeting. He imagines Bruce Lee holding Darcey above his head, Darcey's terrified body parallel with the ground, Bruce Lee's arms expanding with muscle and tension, waiting to snap this careless thief in two.

The Menard is one of the best of the many diners in Quinsigamond, always clean and almost never crowded. They sit in the wooden booth near the exit for close to an hour, getting wired on too many coffees. Darcey would like to talk, but thinks Yuk Tang might take this as an apology and a sign of weakness. A kind of peace gets made when Darcey orders a veal cutlet sandwich and Yuk Tang puts half the money on the table and says, "I don't think your friend is coming."

Darcey nods and pushes the money back at Yuk Tang.

"I don't think we would have wanted what he had to offer," says Yuk Tang.

"Little hard to say at this point," Darcey says, cracking his knuckles and immediately regretting it. "I didn't think you ate meat."

"I'm a flexible man," Yuk Tang says.

Darcey nods again, readies himself, and says, "About the crap with the pager . . ."

"I don't think we need to talk about that," says Yuk Tang. "Am I right?"

"You're right," Darcey says, and he slides out of their booth and up to the counter to hurry along the sandwich.

At the end of the counter, on the last seat on the left, sits an elderly man that he hadn't noticed before. As he looks at the man, he thinks the guy might be blind. The man's eyes have that rigid, unmoving stare. The man holds a full soup spoon an inch from his lips but doesn't blow on it or sip at it.

The fry-boy hauls up the cutlet from the grease and Darcey's tongue goes a little wet. He's about to ask for two large milks when the blind man, the old man he thinks is blind, says, "Would you be Mr. Darcey?" in a quiet voice you'd use to talk to someone next to you. The voice contains an accent that gives the man away as a foreigner, but won't get more specific.

Darcey looks over his shoulder to Yuk Tang, who holds out his right hand, palm down, like this were some signal between the two of them. Darcey turns back to the old man and, like he's been called before the Pope, he walks down the aisle and slides onto the stool next to him.

"That's right. I'm Darcey," he says.

"I'm George Lewis," the old man says and sinks his spoonful of soup back in his bowl, uneaten. The name doesn't sound foreign and as he turns his head, Darcey wonders why he had the impression this guy was blind.

"Do I know you, Mr. Lewis?" Darcey asks.

"You do look familiar," Lewis says, "but I really doubt we know each other. I haven't been in Quinsigamond in years. Actually, I'm just passing through tonight."

He looks at Darcey's face and decides to continue. "I'm really just an accidental messenger," he says and pulls a long white envelope from the pocket of his raincoat.

"From a friend of yours, I assume," he says, "a Mr. Scalley. He asked me to say that he had to leave and to give you this."

The envelope has been folded over and *Darce* is written across it in what looks like a child's handwriting.

"I've been here awhile," Darcey says, even but firm.

Lewis stirs his thick orange soup and after a minute says, "Yes, well, you don't look a bit like your friend described you."

The night's not going well. Darcey wishes he'd just remembered to leave the damn pager on his bureau. He feels as if forgetting about the pager is the first domino in a long row, just falling over. Scalley would be number two. George Lewis, with his eyes and his voice, he might be three.

Darcey nods to George Lewis and mouths the word *thanks*. He walks backward, pulling money out of his pocket and placing it on the counter to his right. Yuk Tang slips out of their booth, mixes his money with Darcey's, and thanks the fry-boy. He lifts the sandwich off the plate, one half in each hand and tomato sauce oozing down the sides, and follows Darcey out of the Menard.

In the car, they sit for a moment, both a little shaken. To calm himself, Yuk Tang begins arranging the sandwiches on the glove box door like this was a formal banquet. He finds napkins from various drive-through restaurants, packets of salt and pepper, tubes of ketchup and mustard. When he comes across a container of duck sauce, he eases it out the window.

Darcey opens the envelope, reads it once, looks at Yuk Tang without expression, and hands the letter over. Yuk Tang sucks tomato sauce off his thumb and reads:

Darce,
     I'm screwed. Sorry I can't get that 200 to you. I know you'll understand. You and Bruce Lee go easy. I got no time. I'm heading south. You know what to say when you get the calls on me. Thanks for your time and

my new teeth. I'm glad I could show you all those horror movies you
would have missed otherwise. Go easy.

Scalley

P.S.

Here's something better than the 200 bucks: 99 Usher. Up in Windsor.
A doctor and his wife. No dog. They're doing some cruise. Cheap
bastards. Discount store alarms (batteries are prob. dead already).
Could be a good haul. Look close for specialty items. Sorry.

Yuk Tang hands the letter back to Darcey as if it were evidence in
a trial. It ends up with a red tomato stain despite his attempt to be
careful. Darcey folds the letter several times, lifts his behind off his
seat, and crams the paper into a back pocket.

They sit in silence, watching cars run down Orbis Ave. until
Darcey says, "What the hell you figure got into the little bastard?"

Yuk Tang stares forward, takes a breath, and says, "I think we
know what got into your friend. I think we should discuss retirement."

Darcey reaches over and pulls his half of the veal cutlet off the
glove box door. He decides to ignore Yuk Tang and says aloud to
himself, "And how the hell did he get to the Menard before me?
The little shmuck is late for everything. He gets there, writes a half-
assed note, gives it to some weird old fart at the counter, and gets
on the road before I pull in?"

In an attempt to be taken seriously, Yuk Tang's voice drops to
a whisper. He says, "You can ignore me. This is fine, ignore me.
But we both know there's a problem here. Something scared your
friend Scalley enough to make him run. Do you really want to wait
around and find out what it is?"

Darcey licks across the front of his lips, swallows hard, and says
to Yuk Tang, "First of all, stop calling the little bastard my friend.
I hate it when you do that. My friend. Jesus. And second, you little
wuss, you don't cut and run because some half-retarded scumbag gets a tough question and decides to tour South America.
Goddammit."

"We could vacation," says Yuk Tang. "Just for a little while."

Darcey turns, mouth bulging with veal and bread, and says, "It's
this pager crap, isn't it? You're spooked because of this pager crap.
Christ Almighty."

They chew in the dark, watch lights go on and off in the apartments over the storefronts. When he finishes his sandwich, as if

he's decided to give in to things he can't change or understand, Yuk Tang says, meekly, "So you want to do this Usher job?"

Darcey, unsure if this is a challenge or not, says, "You're damn right."

The quiet comes again. At one point they turn at the same moment, and look in the windows of the Menard Diner. Neither one says a word. George Lewis has left his soup and his stool and walked out of the diner.

At the Mother of Angels Home, Yuk Tang is having a confusing day. He's followed two move-patient memos and found the wrong people in the rooms. A new carton of ammonia bottles was missing from the supply closet. Though he looked everywhere for Mr. Bernard Cooper from 319, the new nurse swears that Mr. Cooper did *not* die overnight. Yuk has put down six Extra-Strength Tylenol, but his headache seems to be getting worse. His stomach's off and he can't bear the thought of macaroni and cheese for lunch. He's got more than one bad feeling about tonight.

Passing out ancient paperbacks in the dayroom — a Zane Grey for Mr. Ash, a Harlequin for Mrs. Wiclif — he thinks about jumping on a train after work. No call to Darcey. No explanation. But as he sits to read the first page of *Tex Buckley's Ambush* to Mr. Kerrigan, he puts the thought out of his mind. As always, he'll do the honorable thing. He'll work tonight and let things happen. He'll do the Usher job and give over to fate.

Yuk Tang finds the nurses' lounge empty so he stops for a minute to rest and make a cup of tea. He closes the door and takes a few deep breaths. He wishes they had a couple of days to confirm some information. To double-check a few facts and drive through Windsor Hills with a stopwatch and a clipboard. But if the Usher job is going to happen, it has to be tonight. For a lot of reasons, one of them being their mutual diminishing nerve.

There's an old metal coat rack in the corner, next to the table that holds Mister Coffee. Hooked on it are three or four nurses' uniforms, simple white dresses that end at the knee. He guesses that they're Doreen's. They're fresh from the dry cleaners, starched and looking perfect on separate wire hangers covered with cellophane. Yuk Tang lifts the sleeve of the top uniform and pulls up the cellophane. He holds it close to his nose and breathes in the fresh laundry smell. He takes it off the coat rack hook and looks to the neck for the size. He presses the uniform against the front of his body and holds out his arm and the sleeve, comparing lengths.

And that's when he's engulfed in the pleasing smell of pipe tobacco. He turns around and sees, in the doorway, standing rigid and staring, a tall man with a dark complexion. The man is dressed in a well-tailored business suit. It's impossible to tell his age. Though he seems fit and agile and in command of himself, something makes Yuk Tang want to estimate that the guy is as old as anyone in the Mother of Angels. He's clean-shaven. In one hand he cradles the pipe. It's white, maybe ivory, and carved into a shape that Yuk Tang can't make out.

Yuk Tang puts the uniform back on the hook and, forgetting his normal politeness, says, "You really shouldn't be in here."

In his left hand, the man holds a leather suitcase that makes Yuk Tang suspect he's a pharmaceutical salesman trying to catch Dr. Brophy. Though the case looks heavy, the man keeps it in his hand, at his side. He takes several steps into the lounge and says, "Would you be Mr. Tang?"

Without thinking, Yuk Tang reaches into his smock pocket for a Tylenol, but finds none. He repeats, "You really shouldn't be in here. Is there someone I can help you find?"

The man eases into one of the blue plastic seats opposite Yuk Tang and says, "I'm Mr. Estrada. I believe you're expecting me?"

Yuk Tang's stomach heaves. He clenches his back molars and shakes his head "no."

Mr. Estrada is undisturbed. He says, "No matter," and for the first time, looks around the lounge. His eyes end up back on Yuk Tang and he says, "I'm glad we can finally get together. I've come to you about a purchase."

Yuk Tang stays quiet and Mr. Estrada reaches to his back pocket and takes out a handkerchief. He dabs at his forehead and says, "Could you tell me when we might be ready to make the transaction?"

Yuk Tang repeats, "Transaction."

Mr. Estrada closes his eyes and pinches the bridge of his nose between his forefinger and thumb. His eyes open and he seems on the verge of being angry. He says, "I assure you I'm fluid. And

I'm not attempting to negotiate at this late date. You people have my word, three times the estimated book value with the payout in equal parts diamonds, bullion, and your choice of currency, though my people asked me to propose to you the option of paying the final third in dinar, for the obvious reasons of speed and convenience. You can trust that I forewarned them that, most likely, this would not be acceptable."

Yuk Tang has no idea what to say. He wishes the nurses would file in laughing, having put this drug salesman up to a practical joke. He says, "I'm sorry, sir, you have me a little confused."

Mr. Estrada's face goes rigid. Then his mouth broadens into a smile and he gives out a short bark of a laugh. "Business is booming, I see," he says and Yuk Tang laughs with him, relieved but just as confused.

Mr. Estrada folds his hands on the table and says softly, "Obviously we have a few missed connections here. I'm very sorry. My party is interested specifically in the Belgrano volume."

"Belgrano," Yuk Tang says.

"Yes. The Belgrano volume," Mr. Estrada says. "Though it has been mentioned, and I shouldn't be telling you this, but it has been mentioned that if things work out suitably here, there could be a future commission arrangement for yourself and Mr. Darcey."

Darcey's name hits him like a slap. He says, "I think you've confused me with someone else." He's on the verge of being giddy with fear.

Mr. Estrada doesn't react immediately. Then he stands, nods, and whispers, "I understand." He takes a business card from his suitcoat pocket and slides it across the table toward Yuk Tang. He turns precisely and moves out of the lounge.

Yuk Tang takes the card. It's white and blank. He flips it over. Hand-printed in tiny block letters, it reads: *Belgrano 552–7263.*

With persistence and careful planning, Darcey has used the past month to turn his day job into an intricate and compulsive game. He found this necessary because of the boredom factor inherent in the constant five-minute, twenty-mile-an-hour van runs between the various labs of the Foundation. There were start-up expenses right off the bat to get the game under way — a Discman and a huge assortment of CDs (mostly 1950s collections from the discount bins), some stationery supplies, and, though it really wasn't necessary, a thick rock 'n' roll encyclopedia.

Darcey makes thirty sweeps a day around the Foundation's grounds. On the last sweep of his day, he often says, "Last call for the ovens," and lets the doctors wonder. The doctors could easily walk the short route between the labs. The grounds are beautiful and there are paths lined by flowerbeds. But the shuttle van supposedly saves precious time and there was money allotted for it. Darcey's not about to complain. He loves the job. He's come to rely on the monotony. The monotony gave birth to his game and the game has come into its own. It has started to grow and expand and take advantage of a number of possibilities.

The game originally used a basic point system and three testing categories. Category One involved beginning and ending the short drive at five-minute intervals exactly, points being deducted for seconds off, either fast or slow. Category Two involved knowing the exact wording of all the lyrics on any given CD, picked at random from a paper bag. Darcey started with a Sam Cooke disc and got hooked, so he stayed with the artist for two weeks and called it preseason exhibition. Category Three — Darcey's personal favorite — involved how many times in a day he could speed off, just as a passenger was about to catch the shuttle. Last month he began awarding himself bonus points for random and spur-of-the-moment achievements. And lately, things have gotten completely out of hand. There are now subcategories and half-points, challenges that involve the Ford's tire pressure and the number of miles driven per gallon of gas. The scoring has gotten algebraic. Days of the week and times of the day have new and complex meanings. Darcey has begun keeping the long and complicated scores and results and ratings in a fat, spiral notebook. At the end of his shift, he leaves it in the van under the driver's seat.

Today, after he clears out everyone on the last stop at the ovens and spends a few minutes jotting down the scores from his last round, he pops Sam Cooke into the player and cranks the volume. He sings along to "Chain Gang" at the top of his lungs on the drive to the Foundation's garage. He parks before the song is over and so leaves the motor idling while he and Sam Cooke finish out the number. Then he turns off the key and as he reaches around to lock the sliding back door, a man in the far back seat says, "Good afternoon, Mr. Darcey."

Darcey's arm smashes into the steering wheel and the horn sounds.

"Jesus Christ," he yells.

The man is apologetic. He holds an arm out before him and says, "I'm sorry, I . . . ," but Darcey again says, "Jesus Christ."

They sit in silence for a second and Darcey catches his breath and finally lifts his head and says, "You stupid bastard, you nearly gave me a goddamn heart attack."

The man tries, "Again, I'm sorry," his voice strange and calming.

Darcey's angry and embarrassed. He says, "What the hell are you doing in here? I thought I dropped everyone at the ovens."

"The ovens?" the man asks.

Darcey wipes at his face and begins to settle himself.

"Goddamn," he says. "You almost took me out."

They look at each other over the distance of the van. The man is dressed for rain in a heavy trench coat. It's fully buttoned and he has the collar turned up. Darcey suddenly thinks that the guy might have fallen asleep. He decides to sit, look menacing, and wait for an explanation.

"I apologize for startling you," the man says. He accents some of his words in the wrong places. "I thought it was in our mutual interest to speak alone. I had thought you might be expecting me. I'm Mr. Rochelle."

Darcey stays quiet, looks out into the garage, and tries to think. Finally he says, "Yeah, well, I'm sorry I jumped. I was listening to the music. You spooked me." He pauses and squints at Mr. Rochelle. "So, I'm locking up now."

Rochelle gives no indication that he intends to leave the van. It's as if he's made it his home and he won't be evicted. He says, "I have people who are extremely interested in a recent acquisition of yours." He doesn't appear angry, just intent.

Darcey thinks about jumping out of the van, but instead he says, "I'm afraid I don't understand you. Do you want me to drive you back to the labs? Did you fall asleep?"

Mr. Rochelle looks confused. He glances down at his shoes and then back up at Darcey and says, "Mr. Darcey, are we not alone? Is there a problem?"

Darcey can't help getting edgy. He says, "I think you've got the problem, friend. We don't know each other."

Mr. Rochelle breaks in with an easy "Of course not."

Darcey says, "Well, I've got to go. You want to spend the night in the van, that's fine with me." He pulls up on the door handle. The ceiling light snaps on.

Mr. Rochelle doesn't flinch. He stares at Darcey for a minute and then reaches into a coat pocket and removes something. His hands are so large they cover the entire object. Darcey feels a little nauseated. Mr. Rochelle looks into his hand at a note card or picture, then replaces it. He sighs and smiles and says, "Mr. Darcey, this is not professional behavior on your part. Please sit."

Darcey closes the van door.

"Is this a problem with money, Mr. Darcey?" Mr. Rochelle asks. "You should know better than that. My people are not interested in bargains. They are not looking for a . . . " His eyes turn to the side as if he'll spot the word he's searching for out the window. They turn back on Darcey and he says, carefully, "flea market."

He smiles, pleased with himself. "I'm sure you are aware of the extent to which they will go," he says. "Within reason, of course."

Darcey repeats, "Of course."

Mr. Rochelle continues, "Very simply, my people mean to acquire, from you and Mr. Tang, the Bikaner volume you recently removed from Dr. Hawthorne's residence."

Darcey's breath starts coming hard. He hates the idea that he and Yuk Tang have been mentioned in the same sentence. He'd bet both their lives that this has to do with that scumbag Scalley and his note in the Menard. And then he remembers the note. Word for word.

> 99 Usher
> Up in Windsor
> A doctor and his wife.

Goddamn Scalley, he thinks. And goddamn that phone-pager.

Darcey wants to leave, to be out of the van and the garage. Out of Quinsigamond. He says, "I have to discuss a few things with my partner."

Mr. Rochelle sighs again, then says, "Very well," and moves to the front of the van. He presses a small card into Darcey's hand. He climbs out the side door and into the darkness of the garage.

Usher Drive is a cul-de-sac. It branches off from Cromwell and bends, like a short, twisted arm of civilization interrupting Kingstown Woods. Kingstown Woods is a well-tended preserve that borders Windsor Hills, ropes it off from everything around it, as if nature gave the Hill's residents their own buffer zone as a gift.

Usher Drive is the most remote and isolated street in the Hills, but it's still entirely part of Windsor. It fulfills all the requirements. For a house to be part of Windsor Hills, it has to have a certain privileged and stable look. The homes are all oversized Colonials. Solid brick, a lot of them with ivy running up the walls. Five bedrooms and up. Three- and four-car garages. Long and curving brick or flagstone walks and perfect lawns that roll into a lake of mulch.

Darcey and Yuk Tang wait in the rented Jaguar down below the Hills. Once they break over the line and drive up, that's it — head for the job, hit it, and get out. Time, during Windsor Hills jobs, becomes even more of an important factor than it normally is. Time becomes everything.

They've left the MG behind, an unusual move and one that bothers Darcey. Though he doesn't doubt the speed and performance of the Jaguar, he's intimate with the MG. He knows how and when to push it. There's a cushion of instinct when he has the MG. But, as Yuk Tang found out — and Darcey will admit it's a worthy idea — Dr. Hawthorne's out-of-town son drives an olive green Jaguar. An olive green Jaguar has parked often in the Hawthorne driveway, so it wouldn't jar any neighbors' eyes.

Darcey and Yuk Tang sit below the Hills, both wishing they were someplace else. They wish they were sitting on fat, foreign bank books and studying difficult languages on a beach with white sand. They're having trouble concentrating. They've lost all the calmness that once came so naturally.

Yuk Tang did some checking with a few normally reliable people. He runs it down for Darcey: The guy's a surgeon. Due for retirement. Comes from old money — his old man was a surgeon. Married forever. They've got one kid, a son, who's doing a residency at Johns Hopkins. The old man's got a houseful of awards. He's a world traveler with a big interest in the Middle East. He's tight about weird stuff — won't eat in the better restaurants, wears the same clothes forever, and, bingo, the one that counts, won't spend the money for an alarm system.

But there's not a word about Dr. Hawthorne being any kind of collector. Even when Yuk Tang put out some dollars. Not a word about antiques, paintings, coins or stamps, wine. Nothing. So, they're going in cold, no idea what to look for or where to start looking. That, combined with the time factor, does not make for an easy night. They know going in that they can't be as neat and careful and professional as they'd like.

The Hawthorne house sits near the end of Usher. Because of the age of the houses in Windsor, the lots are only a half-acre. That doesn't give them the best border protection. They'll have to be frugal with noise and light. They've decided on mid-to-early evening, nine o'clock, because of the rented Jaguar/visiting-son angle.

The house is number six. Mid-sized. Brick with black shutters. A standard, moneyed Yankee estate. Darcey would've bet the owner was a doctor or a judge. Classy but subtle. A huge front door with a golden eagle above it. Fake "alarm protected" certificates pasted into the corners of the front windows. It's like they put out a neon sign that they're on vacation. Took a commuter-time ad on a popular radio station. There isn't a light left on and the drapes are pulled tight across all the windows. The place looks like a tomb.

They pull slowly into the driveway and cut the engine. Yuk Tang moves into the entryway, takes a stack of banded mail out of the mailbox, and stands, easily and patiently shuffling through it. He wears latex gloves and tries to ignore the feeling they give him. Several letters have foreign postmarks, and on one the return address is in another language. Arabic, he thinks.

Darcey moves fast to the most hidden side of the house. He finds some good protection behind an out-of-control shrub. He cuts the screen out of the storm window frame and lays the mesh against the bush. He takes a diaper from beneath his jersey, lays it against the window. Takes a flashlight from his waist and smashes in the pane, then reaches in and up carefully and grabs the plastic alarm box that rests on the lip of the casing. He muffles the momentary honk against his body, then dumps the battery and box beneath the bush. He enters into the dining room, takes a breath, and calms himself and lets his eyes adjust to the darkness.

He finds his way to the living room and the front door, but tenses up when he discovers that it's locked with a dead bolt. He can feel Yuk Tang's nerves beginning to fray on the other side of the door. On instinct, Darcey lifts a cushion on a cane-back child's chair, positioned by a coat rack to the side of the door. He finds the key, a thick Yale, turns off and removes the alarm box that's hanging from the doorknob by a plastic strap, and lets Yuk Tang in.

They stare at each other in the dim foyer, both waiting for the other to flinch, to move back out the door and into the Jaguar. Finally, Yuk Tang looks to the floor and Darcey clears his throat. They've made a vague plan about splitting up once inside and taking different rooms, but now the plan seems useless.

"All right, let's get at it," says Darcey, and Yuk Tang moves instantly out of the room and up the stairs in the hallway. Darcey thinks Yuk Tang is being a fool. Instinct tells him that they'll find what they're after on the first floor of the house. He steps into the living room and snaps on a dim light on a side table by a huge leather chair. He guesses the bulb is about forty watts and laughs to himself at cheap Doc Hawthorne. He imagines the old surgeon suddenly at a desk somewhere in the house, scribbling on the backs of grocery lists his wife tried to throw out, squinting under the forty watts of illumination and figuring how many gall bladders or tonsils he has to chop out to equal the year's electric bill.

Trying not to think about what he's doing, Darcey eases himself into the leather chair. He sits back and lifts his legs onto the matching ottoman. It's a comfortable chair. He could sleep or eat in it. He can hear Yuk Tang upstairs going through drawers. He knows he should be up and moving, thinking on his feet, but he tells himself this is a new approach. He'll sit and think about the best single place to look for *specialty items*. He doesn't care that his new approach is most likely brought on by panic or that he hasn't felt panic on a job, even in the worst of situations, in five or six years.

He loves the leather chair and regrets that he can't take it with him. He can picture the perfect spot in his apartment for it. Something made of glass falls and breaks upstairs and Darcey knows Yuk Tang is just as rattled.

Darcey takes a long look around the room. Everything appears normal. There's a fireplace, sofa, framed portraits, floor lamps, small tables covered with bells and photographs and small crystal figurines. There's a small upright piano across the room, pushed against a wall, and Darcey would bet that no one in the house can play it well. There are dozens of things, right here around him, in easy reach, that he could pocket and turn over in a day. But none of them are what he came for.

He wonders if he could live here. In Doc Hawthorne's house. He wonders what it feels like to be Doc Hawthorne's son. Does the kid call the old man up and ask technical questions about tough cases? He can picture them, the cheap bastards, both sitting in dark rooms, late in the evening when the rates are low, talking about people they've cut open and the things they've found inside.

The thought pumps Darcey up. He pulls himself out of the chair and bounces on the balls of his feet, looking around the room. He takes a Swiss Army knife out of his pocket, opens a blade, and slashes across the seat of the chair. He's never done anything like this on a job. He's never even tracked mud into a house or dropped a cigarette. He feels flighty and unsure of himself. He hops up and down in place, tosses the army knife up and down in his hand. He turns and spits on a family portrait hanging on the wall. He picks up two figurines and smacks them together like cars on a wet highway. On an end table he finds a pair of reading glasses and tries them on. The room seems to bend. He takes them off, squats, and places them on the carpet, then stomps, shatters the glass, snaps the arms, grinds the mess under the toe of his boot.

He waits to hear Yuk Tang's voice from upstairs, but he hears only movement, drawers being opened, things hitting the floor. Darcey walks to the piano and opens the key cover, sits on the stool as if he were about to play. He looks over the keys, then barely rests some fingers on them. No note sounds. He thinks about pressing down on the keys again, but hesitates. And then a thought hits him. He gets up from the stool and moves to the side of the piano. He tries to raise the top to look in, but it won't budge. When he tries again, harder, his side of the piano swings away from the wall. The opposite side is hinged to the wall, making the entire thing a huge, bulky door.

Darcey puts his hand over his mouth and tries to think. What he wants to do is to grab Yuk Tang and start driving south. Secondary highways. Drive-through food. Dump the Jaguar in some thick southern forest, and pick up something common but fast. For rea-

sons he doesn't understand just now, he'd like to get hold of
Scalley and break all of his straight new teeth.

Behind the piano is a hole in the wall. There's imitation walnut
molding that makes it look like a weird low window frame. It's
roughly three feet by three feet and it's too dark to see what's on
the other side.

Darcey feels as if time is slipping away from him. He feels incapable of making small decisions. Suddenly, he can't recall the layout
of the downstairs of the house. Wasn't there an open hallway on
the other side of the living room wall? It's like his brain is punish-
ing him for lack of sleep. He would bet serious dollars that *specialty
items* are through this door, this window. He wishes there were a
stranger here to give him direction. He wishes Mr. Rochelle would
speak to him harshly. Throw money at him and order him through
the hole.

And, as if he has received orders, he scrambles. He throws himself, off balance, onto the floor and through the opening. As if he
were diving into freezing waters and couldn't get an idea of depth.
He stays on his hands and knees, wishing his heart would stop racing, but it's no use. He's so aware of the possibilities that lie in the
next few minutes that there's no chance of keeping calm and unimpressed. The trick here, he thinks, might be to avoid any exten-
sive thought, to operate like some determined animal or tremen-
dously reliable machine. The trick, most likely, is to avoid thinking
about why or how he has come to be in this position.

He pulls his flashlight from his pocket and thumbs it on.

He sees books.

He is in a small compartment, a vault maybe, loaded with books.
He shoots the light up and down the walls rapidly and sees shelf after shelf of books. His breath comes slowly as he turns, on his
knees, in a circle. The room is about a six-by-six square box, lined
on all sides by thick metal shelves. And the shelves are completely
covered. Volume after volume. Most of them look very old and the
words that he sees on some spines are written in foreign languages.
He expects to smell a musty odor but there's none. He moves into a
sitting position and stays still, his legs tucked in as if he were about
to meditate.

He knows he should get Yuk Tang but decides against it. He
looks around trying to get comfortable with the vault, trying to

notice as much as possible. Beyond books, there are a few other items: a golden bowl, or at least a bowl that once looked gold but now is tarnished and junky. It's filled with letters and postcards and a magnifying glass. His flashlight reflects back at him and his heart pounds and when he follows the beam to a corner where the wall meets the ceiling, he sees a tiny window, no bigger than a half-dollar, and round. He stands carefully to look. The ceiling is only an inch or two above his head. The round thick pane has a syrupy look to it. Darcey puts his eye to the glass and can see the night sky, stars and light from the moon.

He knows he's going to have to decide what to take soon and this bothers him. How can he know? He sits again in front of the gold bowl and notices, for the first time, candles on either side of it, secured in elaborate gold candlesticks. Automatically, he pulls out a butane lighter from his pocket and sparks the candles. The vault gets brighter. He starts to relax a little, then is startled by the idea of flames so close to all these books. But he can't bring himself to blow out the candles.

He stares without really focusing at a wall of books. Darcey would never describe himself as a reader to anyone. Now and then he goes on a binge with the crossword puzzle books, tears through them with no problem, word after word and page after page. And occasionally he'll read one of those Louis L'Amour westerns. Sometimes, a mystery. Espionage stuff. A fact that Darcey understands now is that he has never thought a great deal about books. He has never considered them a movable property. He always thought stamps and wine were as weird as it got.

He reaches to a close shelf and starts taking down volumes and piling them next to his legs. They're all heavy. Much heavier than he'd have bet. They don't feel like normal books that he sees around. There are no illustrations on the covers. No pictures of the authors on the back. The bindings are all smooth and cold as if the vault were a refrigerator. He picks the books up, holds them, runs his hands over them, and reads the titles, when he can, off the spines.

There are two short, slim white volumes — *Vortigern and Rowena* and *Henry II*. There's a pamphlet sealed in plastic called *The Diagnosis and Treatment of Bibliophagia*. Darcey thinks about breaking open the seal and taking a look. He thinks there'd be some great pictures in that one. He picks up *The Courier's Tragedy and Other Jaco-bean Revenge Plays* and puts it down. Glances at *More Astronomical Studies, R. A. Locke & S. John Herschel; Rappaccini's Other Daughter* by Auberpiner; *The Life and Death of Og of Bason; Recipes and Cocktails for a New State* by Ernst Toller. His eyes linger on *Travels in North America: Quinsigamond* by Chesterton, then he throws it to the side. He pulls a thick and tall volume called *A History of Bitic Literature, Vol. 1,* into his lap. He judges its weight and lets it slide to the floor. He tosses on top of it *The Babel Catalogue: Argentina Ed., 1899.* He breathes deeply and feels confused and nauseated.

Darcey can find no order or category to the books. They're published in different years, in different languages. There are plays and medical texts, histories and cookbooks, atlases and bibles. He begins to have hateful and destructive thoughts. Like torching this goddamn vault. Torching Doc Hawthorne's whole house. Driving the rented Jaguar off the Havelock Cliffs. Maybe with Yuk Tang locked in the trunk.

He decides to pocket the magnifying glass that's in the gold bowl. As he reaches for it, he notices, underneath the thick stack of bulging envelopes, the top of a package wrapped in brown paper. He pulls it out. It looks like a large brown brick. It's addressed to Doc Hawthorne and it hasn't been opened. Darcey rips off layers of brown wrapper. He pulls and tears at the paper, getting frustrated and tense, but finally uncovering a book. Another book. It's old, not in great shape, and bound in cloth. The front is blank, but on the spine are the words *Holy Writ* and beneath them, *Bombay.*

Darcey's not sure why he's excited. He moves closer to the two candles and licks his lips. As he begins to open the volume, a cough explodes behind him and his heart and lungs collapse for a second. He falls to the side and awkwardly turns his body. The book stays in his hand, shaking.

In front of him, in the opening to the vault, shoulders hunched and on his knees, is Yuk Tang. Darcey has lost his voice. Yuk Tang lets his head fall to the side and in the dim light, Darcey gets a better look: Yuk Tang's face is completely made up. He looks like a rodeo clown. He has on lipstick, rouge, mascara, false eyelashes. There are long, dangling diamond earrings hanging from his earlobes and around his shoulders is some kind of fur stole.

Yuk Tang leans into the vault. Darcey begins to rise and Yuk Tang swings his arm forward and catches Darcey solidly above the eye.

Darcey falls backward. He has no idea what has hit him. Something heavy and metal. A wide and fast stream of blood is making its way from Darcey's skull down his face. He tries to move and falls back against a shelf of books. He watches with one eye as Yuk Tang withdraws from the vault. The light from the living room closes out and he hears a metallic click as the piano comes flush against the wall.

Now two streams of blood make their way in a slow race down Darcey's right cheek and past the corner of his mouth. His tongue comes out and licks at his own blood, hesitantly at first, and then furiously. The tongue twists and stabs, trying for the thick lines of red. There is an ache that takes over his skull, obliterates everything else for a time, and then eases off, leaves just a dizzying and constant echo of pain and confusion. Darcey thinks he hears his own voice and gets startled, sits up to listen, but gets dizzy and falls back to the floor.

He rests his head against books and time goes by. He dozes and wakes, dreams quickly and mumbles to himself. His eyes blink open and closed, one continually bathed in a fresh wash of blood. He has confusing, rapidly changing nightmares: Yuk Tang and Darcey, buried alive in a cave. Yuk Tang and Darcey buried alive in a rented, olive green Jaguar. Buried alive in the Menard Diner, an earthquake or avalanche throwing walls of mud and rock up on the roof and against the stained glass windows, sealing them in. And himself, alone and helpless, all energy run out a hole in his body, being carried into a raging ocean in the arms of George Lewis, carried like a sleeping child into deafening surf, and the ocean changes form, becomes a heaving sea of books, encyclopedias and dictionaries, ebbing and banking, swallowing broken Darcey under an endless wave.

His good eye opens then closes. It opens again. He forces vision. The vault seems to be getting darker, the flame from the candles seems to be shrinking, flickering. He looks up the wall of books opposite him, to the half-dollar window in the corner, and he thinks he sees blue and white lights revolving, lighting the circle of sky and then leaving it.

He would bet something will happen soon. In his lap is the *Holy Writ* from *Bombay*. He opens the cover and several pages slide under his fingers. He tilts his head and tries to focus his eye and makes a ridiculous effort to read. An almost perfect way of killing time.

FREDERICK WATERMAN

Best Man Wins

FROM *Hemispheres: The Magazine of United Airlines*

I WALKED ONBOARD FLIGHT 587 from Paris to New York, showed my ticket to the flight attendant, then walked through first class, where I usually sat, and continued back to coach. At Row 22, I stopped and looked down at the man sitting in Seat A, the man who I knew would be there, the man who had been having an affair with my wife for the past four months.

I sat down in Seat B.

Jean-Louis Vachon did not look up from the pages of *Le Monde*, for he was not a man to be bothered with nods of hello to other travelers. I have known him for nine years, but I wasn't sure how I'd react this time. Five days ago, a computer at home malfunctioned, restoring a hundred deleted files. My wife's words to Vachon left no room for doubt.

What did I feel? Rage, bitterness, bewilderment, and sick despair each took their turns with me. I have not told her that I know, but each day I struggle to hide my anger, while every night my best and sweetest memories of love are turned into nightmares — with the Frenchman in my place.

I'm trying to think clearly now, trying to get back to who I am. I want to know whom to blame. Her? Him? Probably both. Revenge is tempting, but I'm going to solve this problem for good.

The wedding ring on my left hand still looks new. Our impulsive, romantic marriage took place three years ago, in a small stone chapel outside of Paris. At the post-wedding dinner, I remember my best man, Jean-Louis Vachon, saying how envious he was, for I was marrying "the most beautiful woman in the world." I didn't know how deep his envy ran.

I glanced at Vachon. If I waited too long to greet him, my presence would seem ominous, and he would guess that our seat assignments were not by chance.

I took a deep breath. "Jean-Louis! Is that you behind the newspaper?"

He turned to me. "Edward, my friend! They have given you this seat? How lucky for me!" His charming smile was now in place, but I had seen a flicker — not of guilt, for Vachon would have none of that — but animal alertness.

"It's wonderful to see you, Jean-Louis. It's been too long."

What, I'd asked myself last night, should a cuckold sound like when he's sitting next to his wife's lover? I would try for one part happy, two parts ignorant, with a thin coating of fool.

"How are the Vachon vines?" I asked cheerfully. "Provence is getting good weather this summer, and I've heard two vintners say they are dreaming of another year like 2000."

"We are all dreaming of another 2000, though it may not come in our lifetime." Vachon's English was perfect, but his words still rode a French cadence. "Men who grow grapes are always at nature's mercy."

I smiled at the man I hated. "Jean-Louis, at Les Mirettes my customers don't even look at the wine list anymore. They only want to know if I have 'Vachon.' I might as well take the rest of the wine cellar and throw it into the East River."

"Let me know the day, and I'll help you. I'm always glad to get rid of my competition. But, Edward, as a wonderful chef, you will never have that problem. You have no competition."

Vachon, I thought, you are playing a little game with your words — you are my competition, and you know it. But I let no recognition come into my face while the Frenchman enjoyed his private double-entendre.

The last, breathless passengers arrived on Flight 587. The usual announcements were made as we taxied across the tarmac, and the plane barely paused at the head of the runway before accelerating, lifting off, and angling upward.

Vachon traveled frequently to the United States and often came to my restaurant, though not in the past four months. Now I knew why.

"Jean-Louis, it's been too long since you've been to Les Mirettes," I said, with a cuckold's amiability. "I can't tell you how much Carolyn enjoys seeing you."

Vachon studied my innocent face and relaxed completely. He was safe.

"You are a lucky man, Edward, being married to Carolyn. If you ever get tired of her, give me a call."

And there was the problem: I wasn't tired of her.

Four years ago, blond, blue-eyed Carolyn, whose face had looked out from a hundred magazine covers, came to my restaurant with a group that I knew. They invited me to join them for a drink, and I sat next to her. As we talked, I remembered her pictures because her eyes had an intelligence that, through the makeup and poses, seemed to say, "Isn't this silly?"

She treated her beauty like an inheritance — unearned, but appreciated. Of all the models who came into Les Mirettes, Carolyn was the only one whom I never saw glance at herself in the long mirrors.

She was from South Dakota; I grew up in Brooklyn. We were country and city, but from that first evening, the chemistry was good. The following night, at my invitation, she returned to the restaurant alone. And the next night, she ended up eating in the kitchen, talking and laughing with my crew, who threatened to quit en masse if I let her get away.

I was thirty-four when we made that impetuous marriage trip to France, and Carolyn was twenty-four — young enough to make the age difference interesting.

There is one invaluable skill that I think comes easier when you are from a city: the ability to talk to anyone, and a successful restaurant owner must know how to work both the stove and the crowd. But how do you handle seven hours with your wife's lover? What do you say — "What's new? How's your business? How's my wi . . ."

Stop it! I told myself. But the anger, so alive it had a voice, whispered to me, "He's right next to you! One punch! Do it now!" At this range, I could knock Vachon out with a single blow. Afterward, I would quietly tell the flight attendants, "Shhhh, he's sleeping." And if he started to come around? I could hit him again. What husband would not be tempted?

It is impossible not to compare myself to Vachon, to ask: Who is truly the best man? I will concede right now that he is far better-looking. Vachon is handsome in a sleek, self-aware way and possesses an almost courtly demeanor. "Half-prince, half-tennis pro" is how someone once described him. Vachon looks like men wish they did; I look like they do. I look like the man who comes to fix the washing machine.

But there are similarities between us. We are both driven men who have become rich because people will pay well to satisfy the whims of their taste.

Fifteen years ago, Vachon inherited the vineyard from his father. He understood how good the wine was and how underpriced it had been, so he canceled the vineyard's long-standing European contracts, came to the United States, and began selling only to restaurants — at ten times his father's old price. And he made a killing.

"Vachon vines" now have cachet and are one of the standards by which the top restaurants distinguish themselves from the second tier. Vachon has made his name famous — and I know how much that pleases him.

High above the Atlantic, the brilliant August sun turned the white clouds below into an ethereal wonderland. I was not in the mood for beauty.

"Jean-Louis," I said, idly turning the wedding band on my finger, "I'm surprised to find you here, flying in coach." In fact, I'd been astonished when my travel agent located the Frenchman's reservation.

He responded with a "What can you do?" shrug. "I had a meeting this morning in Montrouge that could not be changed, and I must be in New York tonight. This is the only flight that fit into my schedule, and first class is sold out. And what is your excuse, Edward?"

"A last-minute reservation," I answered, and it was true — somewhat.

Yesterday, the owner of Les Tifs mentioned Vachon's arrival from Paris. I called my sous-chef, told him he was running the kitchen that night, and gave him a list of instructions. Four hours later, I left for Paris — for the sole purpose of taking this flight back, in this seat.

Why, I've asked myself a thousand times, did the affair happen? Carolyn and I had fought no fights, had suffered no silences. I had not cheated on her, nor, I thought, she on me.

For the first two years of our marriage, Carolyn only went on one-day photo shoots. But, I was rarely home, my life was at the restaurant. During the past year, she went back to a full schedule, includ-

ing location shoots in Bali, Tangiers, and Rio, and runway work at
the fashion shows in Milan and Paris. There was too much distance,
too many nights apart. Either you're together or you're not; it's
one of the basics, and both of us had missed it.

A salesman doesn't sell a product, he sells himself, and Vachon
never stops selling. How can a woman tell which whispered words
of love are real, for winning a woman's heart is the greatest sales
pitch of all.

"Jean-Louis, my friend," I said, "you are remarkable. Who else
could make his wine the most popular one in the United States
without ever hiring a salesman there?"

"I worked hard those first two years," he said, "taking the wine
myself from restaurant to restaurant. That was before the dinners,
of course."

Among restaurateurs, an invitation to a Vachon dinner is as prized
as an invitation to the White House. Every April, Vachon gives eight
dinners: four on the East Coast, two in California, one in Chicago,
and one in Texas. His guests are the men and women who own the
finest restaurants in the United States. We are each asked to invite
someone else, and we always do, for every meal is an epicure's
feast, and every course is designed to complement the Frenchman's wine.

At the dinners, Vachon, always wearing a dark, European-cut
business suit, listens intently to every owner's words, flirts just the
right amount with every woman, and never mentions the business
of wine — not once. But, a week later, one of his staff will call from
Provence and ask if the restaurant is interested in placing an order.
Once, an owner said "no," and he never received another call from
Provence, nor an invitation to dinner. No one is sure if the story is
true, but no one will take the chance that it isn't.

It was at one of these dinners that Carolyn first met Vachon, and
there was no connection, no chemistry between them. After Carolyn and I sat down, with a mischievous smile she began whispering
interesting possibilities into my ear. New love is a fine and imaginative thing.

At the following year's dinner, after we'd been married, I saw
Carolyn looking at Vachon, appraising him. Later, when the three
of us were talking, I noticed that her arms were crossed in front of
her — a barrier in body-language terms.

This spring, after dinner, while I spoke with three other restau-

rant owners, Carolyn talked with Vachon, and this time there
were no crossed arms. Twice, my wife touched his shoulder as she
laughed; I knew that gesture, and its touch. Afterward, in the taxi,
Carolyn never mentioned Vachon, but she talked a little faster and
her words came out a little brighter. That's what she does when
she's trying to hide her thoughts. I've never brought this flaw to
her attention.

In the past four months, I heard that extra animation in her
voice a dozen times, but I always ascribed it to the wrong things: to
a gift, to a birthday, to the moment. I never reached for the larger
answer. I never thought the unthinkable.

In summer, the time difference between Paris and New York is
six hours. Flight 587 left at 12:55 P.M. and would arrive just before
three o'clock. The timing would be perfect.

I worked the conversation with Vachon until we were talking like
brothers, discussing his business, my business, the latest strikes in
Paris, and a dozen other things. I marveled at how cool he was, joking and laughing with the man whose wife he was bedding.

The in-flight movie was a thriller and, to my relief, a long one. Afterward, I again talked with Vachon about every subject that would
interest him — but one — until the plane touched down at Kennedy International at 2:59 P.M.

"Jean-Louis," I said as we walked off the flight, "it's nine o'clock
in Paris, we're both hungry, and New York has a thousand restaurants. Let's find a good one and have a great meal."

"Ahh, my friend, I like the way you think. You make time for life's
pleasures. How fortunate that we share the same tastes." His words
were filled with self-amusement.

A car and driver were waiting for Vachon and, during the ride
into the city, we discussed our restaurant options. We each suggested a dozen names and considered Bartolo's, Sierra Leone, and
Jacquie M. before Vachon finally offered the compliment I was
waiting for: "Edward, your restaurant is better than any of those."

"Then it's decided," I said. "I will make the food, and we will
drink Vachon wine."

"The perfect meal," he agreed.

I leaned forward and told the driver, "Fifty-fourth and Lexington,
please."

When we walked into Les Mirettes, I was reminded again how
much a restaurant, in its off-hours, feels like an empty theatrical

set, waiting for the actors to arrive. Here, it would have been per-
formers in a French play, for the restaurant's high ceilings, tall
paintings, and cream-colored walls with gilt touches have elicited
more than one mention of Versailles.

It was not yet four o'clock; even the earliest dinner customers
wouldn't arrive for another two hours. One of my instructions was
for the kitchen staff to complete today's prep work by three-thirty,
then take a break away from the restaurant — mandatory.

Vachon followed me from the luxury of eighteenth-century France
into the stainless-steel, operating-room cleanliness of the kitchen,
where pots hung overhead, the floor was easy-on-the-feet rubber,
and the refrigerators and freezers hummed together.

I exchanged my clothes for chef's whites, then from the tempera-
ture-controlled wine cellar at the back of the kitchen took out a
bottle of Vachon wine. While the original owner opened it, I set up
two wineglasses on the metal counter between us.

From the walk-in refrigerator, I took a flat, plastic Lexan box that
had two loops of clear tape around it. My name was written in block
letters on a piece of paper that I crumpled and put into my pocket.
I sliced the tape, appreciative of how well my sous-chef followed
orders.

"Jean-Louis," I said, "have you ever tried amontillado?"

Vachon did not look up from the glass he was pouring. "That little sherry from Spain? I choked a glass down once because the silly
woman who gave it to me was pretty. Why do you ask?"

"I remember reading about it once," I said, "but I've never tried it."

I took the glass of Syrah that Vachon handed me, swirled the
wine in the small bowl, then brought the glass up to my nose. The
aromas of fruit and earth triggered my salivary glands; I was tasting
the wine before it reached my mouth.

"Outstanding," I acknowledged, enjoying the wine's long finish.
I took a second sip, savored its three distinct stages of taste, then
put the glass aside. From the Lexan bin, I removed several smaller,
plastic containers and a package wrapped in wax paper.

"Jean-Louis," I said, "you've always succeeded in enjoying life to
the fullest."

"Life is for the living," he replied, holding the glass of wine up to
the overhead light and studying its reddish-plum color. "I want to
die with a smile on my face."

I'd be surprised if you did, I thought.

"But, Edward," Vachon continued, "you, too, are living well. After all, you are the best chef in America. What did that food critic write? That you cook like someone who 'knows twelve languages and can mix the words together into a new language that only he can speak, but everyone can understand'? With you, every meal is like a trip around the world."

Vachon, the master complimenter, I thought. And so I stole his tactic.

"Jean-Louis," I said, "sometimes I think that before people sit down to dinner, they should be required to sing at least a chorus of 'La Marseillaise.'"

Vachon's eyebrows rose in question.

"After all, it is France that gave us all the great sauces, pastries, bouillons, and stocks. And, after doing that, France gave us the best wines to go with every dish. Without your country, there would be no great food." Someone once told me you'd probably get physically sick before the recipient of a compliment thought you were being too effusive.

"Ah, Edward, what can I say?" Vachon replied, as if my praise had been given directly to him, instead of three centuries of chefs and vintners. "The French just know how to live. We appreciate the best things in life."

While Vachon talked about his country's magnificence, I began cooking. I opened one container, poured the pork and noodle broth, with shrimp, into a saucepan and turned the stove's burner to a low heat.

The second container held leeks and mushrooms. I stripped the leaves off a sprig of thyme, mixed it with ground mustard seed and Szechuan peppercorns, then added these seasonings. I put the completed dish into a saucepan and set the heat at simmer.

From overhead, I took down a low, wide pan, put in olive oil and turned on the flame. I prepared and added, in order, garlic, onions, bell peppers, eggplant, zucchini, tomatoes, herbs, saffron, and finally pignoli. Vachon nodded in approval. "Ratatouille," he said. "Provence's other great export."

I pulled out a knife, checked the sharpness of its point and edge, unwrapped the wax-paper package, and took out the wide, flat fish. I sliced off the head and tail and dropped them into the shiny trash bin below the cutting board. I gutted, skinned, filleted, and pan-seared the fish, brushed on a hot-ginger glaze, and put it into the oven for a few minutes to caramelize.

From the shelves near the dining-room doors, I took two large plates, two soup bowls, two linen napkins, and a handful of silverware. I served the broth, then the food. The aromas were as good as I knew they'd be.

Vachon took his first taste of the soup, closed his eyes, and said, "Amazing!" After another few spoonfuls, he could not wait any longer for the food. With almost gluttonous speed, Vachon picked up a fork and tried the fish, then moved on to the leeks and mushrooms, and finally the ratatouille. He was torn between savoring each bite and hurrying to the next one. I enjoy watching people eat what I've prepared; this time more than ever.

In just a few minutes, Vachon was halfway through each dish. That would be enough.

"You know, Jean-Louis," I said, as if a thought had just come to mind, "a beautiful woman is a remarkable creation, and there is nothing like the effect she has on a man."

Vachon, between bites, grinned at me.

"After all," I continued, "that's why you're still a bachelor, because of all the beautiful women. Every man who marries wants to marry a beautiful woman — but he forgets that after he walks his wife out of the church, she's still beautiful to other men, and jealousy is a terrible thing."

An uneasiness entered Vachon's eyes.

"In fact, I've wondered what's at the core of that emotion for men, and I think that jealousy goes back to something very basic."

I paused, considering for a moment whether Vachon would ever love any woman enough to be jealous.

"And what is the reason for men's jealousy?" Vachon was trying for a casual, amused tone, but his voice had moved up half an octave.

"Over the centuries, before the scientists and their laboratories, how many men looked into their children's faces, searching for any resemblance, wanting to ask, 'Are you mine?'"

I now had Vachon's full attention. He had forgotten about the fork that his right hand was still holding.

"Now, if a husband found out that his wife was having an affair, I wonder how he'd react," I said. "First, he might ask himself whose fault it was. Who was the pursuer, the wife or the lover? Or was the lover the kind of man for whom women were just a game? Could he make any woman feel beautiful and desired — make her feel as if she had found the perfect, romantic lover?

"Then, what would the husband do? Get angry? Get quiet? Want to talk it out? We'd all react a little differently, but some would decide to solve the problem — permanently. And, how they'd go about it would probably depend on what they knew.

"A carpenter, for example, would own a nail gun, and the next time he was pouring cement into a building's foundation, he'd have his problem solved. And a fisherman? Well, he'd probably take his wife's lover on a boat trip, along with a rope, a rock, and a net." I paused. "But a chef? I wonder what a chef would do?"

I looked at Vachon, who was now incapable of speech.

"I think a chef would look into all his cookbooks and find all the foods that had warnings; he would then invite his wife's lover to share a meal." I looked at the bowl and plate in front of Vachon. "For example, maybe he makes the soup with an extra ingredient — the botulism bacillus; then he might serve Death Cap mushrooms with the white ridge around their stems, and complete the menu with a Japanese delicacy — the poisonous fish fugu, which is delicious, but will kill you if it's not gutted just right. And maybe a very angry husband would serve all three to his wife's lover, just to make sure the job was done right."

I smiled amiably at Vachon. "But, I don't have to worry about you, Jean-Louis, my good friend, my best man. You would never do a thing like that — not with Carolyn. Now, as the chef who made this meal, I want you to know how much pleasure it gives me to watch you eat."

Vachon stared at me, frozen with fear.

"Eat up," I said, holding my smile. "Otherwise, Jean-Louis, I will start to wonder if there might be something between you and my wife. Go on."

Vachon dropped his eyes to my plate and saw that my fish, leeks and mushrooms, and soup were all untouched. The ratatouille was the only thing I'd eaten. He suddenly noticed the fork in his right hand, a piece of fish speared on its four tines. Vachon started to lift the fork to his mouth, but his hand only moved a few inches. The fork dropped to his plate.

"I'm not hungry," he said, his French accent suddenly thick.

"I understand," I said. "A man can suddenly lose his appetite; it happens. So, let us just sit here for a while and enjoy your good wine. It will help you digest your meal that much faster."

Vachon was a broken man. He stood up and smiled a ghastly smile. "I must go," he said. "I just remembered an appointment." And the Frenchman shot out of the kitchen. I heard the heavy front door close.

The nearest hospital was Bellevue. I guessed that Vachon would be there in about ten minutes. I've never had my stomach pumped, but I've heard it's a miserable experience.

I looked down at the plate of food in front of me and realized that my appetite was back. I picked up a fork, cut a large piece of fish, and tasted it. Excellent. I've always enjoyed the puffer fish, a safe, distant cousin to the famous fugu.

The dining-room door swung open. I glanced up at the clock — 5 P.M. exactly. My wife is a wonderfully prompt woman.

"Edward! I just saw Jean-Louis jump into a taxi. He was screaming to be taken to a hospital. What happened?"

"He thinks that someone poisoned him," I said, and took a sip of wine.

"But who would do that?"

"I would," I said, "if I thought he was having an affair with my wife."

Awareness came into her eyes, and, I think, a bit of relief. Sometimes, the hardest part of a mistake is ending it. Carolyn looked at me for a long moment, then sat on the stool where my old friend had been. She looked down at the half-eaten meal.

"Do you have a plate for me?" she asked quietly.

I shook my head.

"I deserve it," she said.

"You probably do," I replied.

I raised my left hand, took off my gold wedding band, and put it on the metal counter between us, next to the bottle of Vachon wine. Carolyn stared down at the ring that, in three years, she'd never seen off my finger.

"Your choice," I said. "What will it be?"

Carolyn looked up at me, then down at the ring and the bottle of wine. Without hesitation, she picked up the Vachon, and my heart sank. So it hadn't been just an affair.

"There's no choice," she said, and turned away from me. With a flick of her wrist, she tossed the dark bottle ten feet into the trash bin below the cutting board.

Carolyn turned back to me. "Do you have another bottle of wine that you could open? Something American — something that goes well with confession?"

I studied my wife's face, the face that I wanted to see every day for the rest of my life.

"I'm sure I do," I said. "Red or white?"

TIMOTHY WILLIAMS

Something About Teddy

FROM *Plots with Guns*

HALFWAY BETWEEN DAYTON AND CINCINNATI, snow spit-
ting and slush gathering on I-75, Tom Lennox regretted telling
Teddy his secret. Teddy, nineteen or twenty with greasy blond hair
smashed to his forehead by a sock cap and the tattoos and
piercings that even nice kids his age had these days, wanted to
make it a game.

"What about her?" he asked when they passed a woman in a
Honda Civic. "How would you kill her?" Teddy propped his feet on
the dash, licked his bottom lip. "You'd play with her first though,
wouldn't you? Do her before you did her."

Lennox checked his rearview mirror and measured a car-length
distance before he glided the Buick back into the right lane.
Twenty-seven years on the road as a sales rep for Lindite Bowling
Balls had made him a lot of things — twenty pounds overweight,
enough money to support his wife's addiction to Home Shopping,
a few friends, and a cautious driver. Once the Buick had settled
into its lane, he glanced at Teddy's filthy Reeboks on the dash and
fought the urge to slap him.

The boy was crude. That was his wife's term for boys like Teddy.
Muriel taught geometry in their hometown of Port Huron, Michigan, and she said most of her students were crude these days. She
was thankful that they had never had children. Lennox wasn't sure.
Maybe children would have changed things, would have given him
a reason to come home from the road. Muriel's womb had been
the source of their problems. It still was. This afternoon she had an
appointment with an oncologist who would confirm what both
Muriel and Tom knew. She was beyond treatment. The fact that

Muriel had insisted that he continue his sales route instead of coming home to accompany her to the doctor both angered and frightened him.

"Get your shoes off my dash," Lennox said.

Teddy dropped his feet to the floor, sucked air between his teeth, and grinned. "Hey, you'd pop her before you popped her. Right?"

"I wouldn't rape her."

"Sure you wouldn't," Teddy said. "In a pig's eye."

"I've never raped anyone."

Teddy leaned forward and took a last look through the rearview mirror. "I'd do her," he said. "A lot of women like that. I read it in a book once."

Lennox quickened his wipers against the snow and shifted his weight behind the wheel to give his hemorrhoids relief. He reached for a pack of Camel Lights, told himself he could wait ten more miles before he smoked another, and then lit it anyway. He'd been trying to quit for months but nothing worked. Not the patches or the gum or even the fear he felt when he climbed a flight of stairs and felt fluttering in his chest. He was forty-nine, a big, balding man carrying too much weight in his upper stomach, with high blood pressure and an even higher cholesterol count thanks to a lifetime of eating in diners and truck stops from Saginaw, Michigan, to Valdosta, Georgia — the endless ribbon of I-75 that he'd traversed for decades. Sooner or later, a half-clogged artery would clog completely or a platelet would burst free and hit his heart and Tom Lennox, excellent salesman, competent Canasta player, mediocre husband, would be a lump of dead weight for a maid to discover. There were nights when he lay in bed at a Motel 6 in Ohio or a Comfort Inn in Kentucky or a Ramada in Tennessee and prayed for sooner rather than later. He couldn't imagine life at home without Muriel. The three-bedroom ranch house would be quiet and empty and there would be nothing but the sound of the television for company while he ate and drank alone. It would be exactly like being on the road.

Lennox took a hard drag from his cigarette and thought of the .22 stuffed beneath the front seat. He imagined pressing the barrel to Teddy's left ear and squeezing the trigger and knew that doing it would push away the worry, the same way saying his prayers before bedtime had kept nightmares at bay when he was a boy.

"What about Fred and Wilma?" Teddy asked as they pulled even with a minivan and a fat, dark-haired man and his redheaded wife. "Gut shoot them, right? Make them suffer a little bit."

"It's not about making people suffer," Lennox said. "I'm not disturbed."

Teddy cocked his eyebrow and slouched back against the seat. Lennox snubbed his cigarette. He didn't know how to make the kid understand or see the order and self-control of his murders. Lennox wasn't a sadist, and he wasn't excessive. One a year. Twenty-four murders so far, the first a vagrant who slept behind a liquor store in Lexington, Kentucky, the last a seventeen-year-old runaway who solicited travelers at a Waffle House in Dalton, Georgia. Lennox had been so discreet in choosing his victims and so cautious in his methods that the police had never guessed all of the murders were connected.

"You make them beg?" Teddy asked.

The boy would never understand. Lennox wasn't sure he understood it. Occasionally, he tried to figure out why he'd started killing, but he'd never come up with a satisfactory answer. Sometimes, he thought it was just the road. Years of driving the same, unchanging highway and staring at the same billboards and same cityscapes and the patches of pine trees and grass that were always the same whether the signs told you that you were in northern Ohio or southern Georgia and eating in the same restaurants and diners and listening to the same songs on a dozen different radio stations and vomiting the same spiel a dozen times a day to bored Bowl-A-Rama managers made life as meaningless as the fragments of graffiti he read on overpasses and bathroom walls — Jesus Saves or Sandra's a Slut, perhaps. One murder a year gave him a reason for his life on the road. The boy would never understand. With his endless chatter and his crudeness, Teddy was making even murder seem meaningless.

"Sure you do," Teddy said. "You make them beg. I bet you get off on it."

"Shut up," Lennox said, surprising even himself with his anger.

Teddy blinked his bright blue eyes. "You don't have to get pissy," he said. "I was just talking."

"That's the problem."

Teddy pretended to be fascinated by the billboards advertising Cincinnati FM stations and Budweiser. Lennox shouldn't have told the boy about the murders and wasn't sure why he did other than there was something about Teddy that drew Lennox to him. He'd felt it when he spotted the boy hanging around a payphone at a rest area just south of Toledo, and the feeling had been so strong that Lennox had broken his own rule and offered the boy a ride, telling himself it was because in his baggy jeans, windbreaker, and sock cap Teddy was likely to freeze on a snowy January day but knowing that he didn't want to be alone today, not when the world was as gray and cold as Muriel would be under the hospital's fluorescent lights.

He'd regretted it five minutes after Teddy got in the car when the boy leered at him, scooted across the seat, and offered to give him a blowjob. Lennox had recoiled, threatened to put him out on the side of the road. He told Teddy that one thing Tom Lennox was not was a faggot. Didn't he see the wedding ring on his finger? Teddy had shrugged and said there was no reason to get angry. A lot of straight guys wouldn't turn down a blowjob, and he'd just wanted to say thanks for the ride. Ten miles later, Teddy launched into a long discourse on why he always wore a sock cap. He said if you took your cap off your heat leaked out, which was bad, but sometimes your soul went with it and then where the hell were you, walking around without a soul? That was crazy talk, and it scared Lennox. But Teddy had just smiled as if the whole thing were a joke, and Lennox couldn't decide if the boy was putting him on or if he was really crazy. Twenty minutes later, Teddy told Lennox that he'd served five years in a juvenile home for armed robbery and that while he was there he'd knifed two boys, but no one had been able to prove it so he walked away free as a bird. Something about Teddy was like a key turning inside Lennox's mind, and when the boy finished his story, Lennox told his own. Now, Lennox looked at Teddy slumped against the door and felt guilty for the way he'd spoken to him. He wasn't sure why, just that indefinable something.

"I'm sorry," Lennox said. "Never mind what I said."

Teddy's head popped up, and he reached for a cigarette without asking. "You're probably just tense," he said. "You sure you don't want me to blow you?"

Lennox squinted through the snow at the high rises and bridges that marked the beginnings of Cincinnati. "I told you I'm not a homosexual."

Teddy blew a smoke ring. "Me neither. I mean not really. But I don't mind doing a guy a favor."

Then Teddy said he had a great idea. Why didn't they kill some- one. Make it a special occasion. If they killed somebody together, Lennox would know his secret was safe. The only other way to guar- antee it was if Lennox killed him.

"And I don't meant to be offensive or anything," he said. "But I'm pretty sure I could take you."

Lennox told him to stop talking. Traffic was picking up, the road was icy, and he needed to concentrate. They headed south through Cincinnati. With its snow tires and steady wipers, the Buick glided through traffic as anonymous as the first wayward cells of cancer.

They stopped at a Ramada just south of Richmond, Kentucky, and Lennox had Teddy lie across the front seat while he registered. Except for his diet and his smoking, Lennox was cautious in all things. If anything went wrong tonight, he wanted no one to be able to connect him with Teddy.

The sky was stained a molded gray, and snow swirled in a whip- ping wind that whistled from the foothills outside of town. Three- quarters of the parking lot was already full and yellow lights glowed from dozens of steamed windows.

"Nice room," Teddy said when Lennox unlocked the door.

It was just a motel room — worn carpet, heavy green drapes, a paisley bedspread on a hard, queen-size bed, a couple of vinyl chairs, a burn-scarred writing table, and a television bolted to a stand on the dresser. Lennox unpacked while Teddy paced the room, turning the faucet on and off, bouncing on the bed, flipping through channels on the television.

Lennox pulled off his sweater, uncomfortably aware of the way his gut sagged over his Dockers. It was five-thirty EST, which meant Muriel should be home from the doctor. Lennox pulled a pint of Jack Daniel's from the side pocket of his suitcase, broke the seal, and poured a double shot into a plastic cup and then offered Teddy the bottle.

"I never drink the stuff," he said. "A beer now and then, but that's it. That junk will kill you. You don't believe me ask my old man."

Lennox downed his whiskey. He poured another two fingers into his cup.

"Don't get soused," Teddy said.

"I can handle my whiskey."

Teddy fiddled with his sock cap. "I'm not preaching or anything."

Lennox drank, refilled his cup, and told Teddy to keep quiet while he called home. Then he sat on the bed and dialed the number and was surprised that his hands weren't shaking. The phone rang four times before the answering machine kicked on.

"Pick up," Lennox said. "It's me, babe. Pick up, okay?"

The phone beeped to let him know his time was over. He hung up, wondering if Muriel was there, alone in the living room with the lights off, terrified by the certainty of her dying. He dialed home again.

"It's okay, babe," he told the machine. "Things will be all right. Just pick up."

Maybe she'd sent him on the road because she knew what the doctor would say and knew what she was going to do about it. He could see her lying across their king-size bed, her eyes closed, an empty pill bottle on the nightstand.

"Goddamn it," he said.

Lennox slammed the receiver on the hook and then dialed again.

"Muriel, please answer," he said. "Let me help you."

Still no answer. Lennox had another idea that was as horrible as the first. Maybe she'd sent him on the road because there was someone else she wanted to comfort her.

"Okay," he said. "I'll be home tomorrow night. We'll talk then." He held the phone, and then just before his time ended, he remembered to say, "I love you."

He was as tired as he'd ever been in his life. He unlaced his shoes and pulled his shirt from his trousers and lay back on the bed and closed his eyes.

"Trouble at home?" Teddy asked, his voice soft and concerned.

Lennox sat up on the edge of the bed. He told Teddy his story. When he finished, it was as if his body was a balloon that lost its air. His shoulders sagged, his muscles quivered, and he flopped back on the bed, his eyes burning as if the effort of staying open was too much for them. He didn't think he was crying, but maybe he was.

"Just take it easy," Teddy said. "Rest awhile."

Teddy helped him beneath the covers. Then Teddy stood and

stretched, took off his windbreaker and tennis shoes. Lennox wasn't surprised when Teddy slipped in beside him. But then Teddy moved closer and laid an arm over his shoulders, and Lennox stiffened.

"Don't touch me," he said.

Teddy put his mouth close to Lennox's ear. "Don't push me away," he said. "Just let me stay here with you."

Lennox shut his eyes. The whiskey still buzzed through his head, and he felt as if the world were disappearing down a long, narrow tunnel. A few minutes later, he rolled onto his back and told himself it was because his shoulder was aching. When Teddy's hand moved under the cover, Lennox didn't stop him.

"I'm not gay," Lennox whispered.

"Relax," Teddy said. "You don't always got to put labels on everything."

Then Teddy pulled the covers away. Lennox lay still and let the boy do what he wanted and told himself that the moaning in the room was coming from the wind rushing at the windows.

Afterward, Lennox dozed and woke later when he heard the door closing. He sat up, blinking stupidly, and then rushed to the window in time to see the Buick's taillights easing from the parking lot. His mouth was dry with panic. The boy had stolen his car and probably his wallet and how in God's name would he explain why he'd picked up a hitchhiker and what they were doing in a motel room with one bed.

"Little queer," Lennox said. "Goddamn hustler."

He went for a drink and found the note that Teddy had placed beneath the whiskey. Teddy had "borrowed" a hundred bucks from his wallet and was gone after supplies. Lennox took a shot of the whiskey and lit a cigarette and swore to himself that his relief came from not having to offer an explanation about what happened and not from his fear that he'd never see Teddy again.

Lennox finished his drink and went to the bathroom, stood staring in the mirror at his fat face with bloodshot eyes and broken capillaries on his cheeks. The self-loathing started slowly like water heating on an electric stove. It began with the sight of the bags under his eyes and moved to his hairy gut and then to the shriveled old prick that had stiffened at the touch of another man.

"Faggot," he said to the mirror.

His disgust passed. He hadn't touched Teddy. Not once. That proved that he wasn't gay. A gay guy would have touched back, wouldn't he? By the time Lennox sat back on the bed with another cup of whiskey, he was sure that almost anyone would have done the same thing under the circumstances. Tonight, they would find a victim, kill him or her together, and say goodbye in the morning. It would be as if none of this had ever happened, and the pain he felt in his chest at the thought of parting with Teddy was just heartburn brought on by too many cigarettes and too much whiskey.

Lennox followed Teddy's directions. After a lifetime of Michigan winters, he drove expertly in the snow, guiding the Buick around snowdrifts and ice patches while the glowing lights of the fast food joints and strip malls faded and gave way to rolling hills and stretches of field broken only by the occasional farmhouse. Teddy was hyperactive, his hands moving constantly to light a cigarette or pick at the insulated hunting vest he'd bought with Lennox's money or adjust the sock cap on his head.

"A good time," he said every few minutes. "This is just too cool."

Lennox grunted his response and scanned the side of the road for deer. Teddy had been saying the same thing since he came back to the motel with a Wal-Mart bag loaded with a hunting knife, his new jacket, duct tape, and a flashlight. He'd spread their supplies on the bed like a kid showing off his toys on Christmas morning and told Lennox that he'd taken a drive and spotted a target, a house far enough outside of town to give them privacy and yet not too far from the main road to make getting out quickly a problem. Then he stood with his hands in his pocket and waited for Lennox to offer his approval.

"Next right," Teddy said now.

Lennox took the turn. The snowdrifts were higher here, the road curving and narrow.

"That's it," Teddy said.

A small farmhouse sat back from the highway, the last home before a crossroads, and Lennox guessed the nearest neighbor was at least a quarter of a mile away. Teddy had chosen well. Lennox cut his headlights and eased into the drive and killed the engine. His throat was dry and his temples pounded. Teddy was grinning, rubbing his hands together, his eyes wide and manic. Lennox had the urge to let Teddy step out of the car and then lock the door and drive away. He was no stranger to the nerves that came before a killing, but this was different. Teddy was a wild card. Lennox had made him promise that they would play by the rules — they would not be brutal; they would try to terrorize the people as little as possible; when they finished they would slip away, taking nothing with them. Teddy had promised, but now his eyes gleamed and his muscles quivered with anticipation.

"Just do what I tell you," Lennox said as they started up the drive. "You're the expert."

Teddy slid into the shadows, moving quickly and easily in the dark to the side of the front door just outside the glow of the porch lights. Lennox trudged straight to the door, out of breath, the snow swirling in his eyes. He kept one hand in his pocket on the butt of the .22 pistol. The ruse was simple. He was a stranger lost in the storm, having car trouble. Just his luck that his cell phone had gone out the first time he really needed it and would they be kind enough to allow him to call Triple A? When they invited him in, Teddy would follow.

He knocked once, waited five seconds, and then knocked again. A thin, thirtyish man with horn-rimmed glasses and a UK sweatshirt opened the door.

"Sorry to bother you," Lennox said. "But I guess I'm lost and my car's quit running."

The man frowned at the intrusion. Then a woman in the background asked who it was. Before the man could answer, Teddy jumped from the shadows, pushed Lennox aside, and rammed his shoulder hard into the door, knocking the thin man off balance.

"Wait!" Lennox shouted.

The thin man brought up his arm, but it was too late. Teddy jabbed the knife hard into the guy's leg and then hit him in the chin with a right cross that sent him to the knees. A vaguely pretty blond in a bathrobe dropped a bag of microwave popcorn and started screaming. Teddy smiled at her and kicked her husband in the face.

"Please," the woman said.

She seemed to realize what was happening and broke for a cordless phone on the coffee table. Lennox had no choice. He pulled his gun and told her if she took another step he'd shoot her. Then Teddy hit her.

"Way too cool," Teddy said when the woman brought her hand to her bloody mouth and stopped screaming.

Half an hour later, Lennox sat on the sofa and smoked a cigarette while Teddy paced the room and brandished his knife and talked incessantly about zombies and vampires and bogeymen. This was ugly and disorderly, but Lennox was too tired to stop it.

The couple looked at him with pleading eyes, but Lennox shook his head and smoked his cigarette. They were gagged and duct taped to straight-back kitchen chairs. Both of them were bleeding — the husband more profusely than the wife and Lennox figured before long the man would go into shock, since it looked as if Teddy's knife had nicked an artery — and Lennox just kept thinking, "Thank God they don't have children."

Teddy went into the kitchen, came back with a bottle of Budweiser and a roll of salami. "This is a good fucking time, man."

He downed the beer and pitched the bottle through a mirror over the mantel. Then he tilted his head and let out a grating yell, a poor imitation of Carol Burnett's imitation of Tarzan. Lennox gave the woman the embarrassed, uneasy smile of an indulgent parent trying to explain the behavior of a toddler. Then he touched the .22 in his lap. He could put an end to it now. All he had to do was lift the gun, aim at the man's head and then the woman's. Their suffering would be over. But he couldn't find the energy to do it.

"It wasn't supposed to happen like this," Lennox said.

Teddy took a bite of the salami. "Relax. You're too uptight, man." He chewed with his mouth open. "It's all rock 'n' roll, baby."

Lennox stared at the television. They'd interrupted the couple's Blockbuster night. On screen a frightened little boy told Bruce Willis that he saw dead people. Teddy picked up the remote and clicked off the movie.

"I saw that a couple of years ago," he said. "It's spooky shit. Gave me nightmares."

Then Teddy plopped down on the sofa beside Lennox and pointed the knife at the husband. "How long until he bleeds to death?"

Lennox didn't answer. Teddy said maybe the next one would be in the gut to sort of speed the process along. Then he cocked his head to the side and smiled at the woman and licked his lips.

"What do you think about her?" he asked.

What Lennox thought but wouldn't admit was that there was

something about her hair and the line of her jaw that reminded him of Muriel. He told Teddy to leave her alone.

Teddy smirked. "Don't get jealous, pop. We could share her." His smirk spread into a leer. "I mean both at the same time. That's a real big fantasy for a lot of girls." He leaned forward and pointed his knife at the woman. "You ever thought about it, hon? Two guys doing you together?"

The woman's eyes widened, and she began to cry and shake her head. Lennox felt sick to his stomach.

Then Teddy crossed the room. He whispered something in the man's ear that made him thrash his head and strain against the tape. Lennox didn't want to watch, so he stared at his fingernails and thought how they needed cutting. When he looked up again, the woman's robe gaped open, and Teddy stood smiling and whistling his admiration for her body.

"How'd a geek like you get a babe like this?" he said to the man. Then he slapped the guy's shoulder. "This is some fucking party." He came back to Lennox and flopped on the couch. "Let's do her man," he said. "That would be too much."

Lennox shut his eyes and shook his head. He felt ridiculous, like a little boy refusing to eat his peas or carrots. Then Teddy laughed, a deep, knowing laugh that Lennox found repulsive.

"Suit yourself," he said. "Tell you what. I'll do her and you can watch." His hand found Lennox's lap and squeezed. "Then I'll take care of you the way you really like it."

Lennox willed himself to not respond to Teddy's touch, but he couldn't help it. When Teddy massaged his erection right in front of the man and woman, Lennox felt ashamed and filthy. Teddy let him go and went for the woman. He cut the tape from her arms and legs and dragged her from the chair by her hair. She struggled and thrashed, but Teddy hit her once and put the knife to her throat, and she stopped fighting. The husband stomped his feet on the floor and thrashed his head and came close to tipping over.

"Come on, honey," Teddy told the woman. "You know you'll like it."

Instead of leading her to the bedroom, he pushed her to the floor and ripped her robe away and told her to get on all fours. The woman kept shaking her head but she did as he told her.

"Doggy style!" Teddy said. "That's the way uh huh uh huh I like it."

He ripped her panties and pushed his jeans down and wrapped

his arm around her neck to hold her head in place. The woman didn't move. She just held still and waited for the inevitable.

Teddy craned his neck and grinned at Lennox. "You change your mind you can have sloppy seconds."

When Teddy turned to mount the woman, Lennox raised the pistol, aimed slowly, and then squeezed the trigger. Blood splattered the husband, who stopped struggling and stared at Lennox in disbelief. Teddy fell forward and his weight drove the woman to the floor. Then Teddy struggled to get back to his knees. He'd almost made it when Lennox shot him again. Teddy fell on top of the wife, and she bucked her hips until he rolled off onto the floor.

"It wasn't right," he said.

Lennox nodded his head as if agreeing with himself. He'd repeat that as long as he needed to make himself believe it. If that didn't work, he'd swear he shot Teddy because the woman reminded him of Muriel. Under no circumstance would he ever believe that a second before he pulled the trigger, he'd thought, "The son of a bitch is cheating on me."

"It just wasn't right," he said again.

Lennox helped the woman to her feet and set her in the chair and grabbed the duct tape to secure her. Then he went to the front window and squinted outside. It was still snowing.

"I'm sorry," he told them when he turned around.

He pulled the pint of Jack Daniel's from his overcoat's pocket and sat on the couch and took a long pull from the bottle. He lit a cigarette and leaned forward with his elbows on his knees, searching for the words to tell his story. He wasn't sure where to begin, but he knew he wanted them to hear all of it — the years on the road with nothing but miles in front of and behind him; the times he'd awakened alone and frightened and certain that he was dying; how he'd first met Muriel at a skating rink in Ohio; the absurd rituals they'd followed in an effort to conceive a baby; the way she'd turned away from him now that she was dying and didn't want him with her and wouldn't answer the phone. Afterward, he'd have to decide what to do with them. Would he kill them and move on down the road, or was this the night to put an end to his useless traveling? He took a deep breath and glanced back at the window. He made a bet with himself, a traveling game that he'd played a hundred times to decide meaningless decisions — if he'd eat at

McDonald's or Denny's, stay on the interstate or break up the drive by taking a state road, stop for a drink or wait until he checked into his motel. If it was still snowing when he finished his story, he'd cut them loose, take one last swallow of bourbon, and put the barrel of the gun in his mouth. If it was clear, he'd make their deaths as quick and as painless as possible and get back on the road.

Lennox smiled at them and then glanced at the dead boy lying on the floor. He knew where his story would begin.

When he finished, Lennox went to the window to discover the future.

SCOTT WOLVEN

El Rey

FROM *Lost in Front*

BEFORE THE LOGGING OPERATION in Maine closed, Bill drove a big rig and generally got paid more than I did. I ran a saw. I drank quite a bit. It ate into my wallet. We kicked around in Maine. I was in good shape from working so much and in a bar outside Houlton I managed to sneak a right hand in and knocked a guy out for two hundred dollars. I thought I was a boxer.

We finally ended up at Bill's mother's house in Saint Johnsbury, Vermont. On the way there, we stopped at a reservation and picked up some tax-free cigarettes for her. She didn't seem happy or sad to see us when we pulled up. She didn't hug Bill, but she did take the cigarettes. "Are these for Mother's Day?" she asked Bill when he gave her the cigarettes. "They are now," he said. "You don't have to pay me for them." Hard times had made that love, for the two of them.

In the morning, I walked down to Thompson's wood lot and fifteen minutes later, I was working. When I first started in late May, my back took a month to come into its own. I was lucky I was in decent shape to start with, or I couldn't have done it at all. I hurt so bad some nights after work that I slept on the hardwood floor. My hands hummed from running the chain saw all day. My spine rusted tight. I didn't think I'd be able to raise myself out of a bed to walk to work in the morning.

Bill started to cash a check, driving a log truck down from Quebec for a big outfit and then an accident got him, crushed him against the steering wheel. He sat totally paralyzed in a wheelchair at the house. He could look out the window and see me at the wood lot, and I would wave up to him, give him the high sign.

Nurses from the county came in to feed him. His mother made sure the door was open so people could get in. A buddy of his, Tom Kennedy, came to see him once in a while. His voice still worked, and I imagine he gave those county people hell for the hour they were there. He hated being paralyzed. Beyond hate, really.

I ran the chain saw most days, filling firewood orders as they came in and trying to stay ahead, as people got ready for winter. We had as many as fifteen orders a day, mixed cords and half-cords. Gary worked with me, a wiry little local with a mustache and a tattoo on his arm that said AMBER inside a hand-drawn heart. Gary ran the hydraulic splitter and packed the cut cords into the rusted dump truck. He was a good worker. We managed eight cords a day, ten if nobody drank heavy the night before. The heat would drive it out of you anyway, sending you behind the shed to puke before eleven o'clock in the morning. We all did it, kicked sawdust over it, and kept right on working. The log trucks made the turn off the road down into the main yard and the French-Canadian drivers would hop up into their cherry pickers and unload themselves right onto the big stacks, and then walk over to the pay shed where Harold sat, answering the phone and paying cash for any decent load of logs that happened to come his way. He didn't care where the logs came from or whose property they were. The log business can depend a lot on timing. You leave a load on the ground in the forest too long and bugs can get at the wood and ruin things quick. Or maybe somebody crossed a property line on a clear cut and had to get rid of some wood fast. Once the wood found its way into Harold's yard, it was his, and the exchange rate being what it was, the French-Canadians made sure plenty of wood always managed to show up. Bill watched all day from his bedroom and we'd talk about my day at the woodlot when I got home.

"Better than television," he said. I always knew if Tom had stopped by because Bill would be drunk. Tom left beer and sometimes whole bottles for Bill. "He keeps me in the juice," Bill said. Then I'd join him for a drink in his room and look out the window at the woodlot where I worked all day.

Whether it was the heat or the work or the booze, I don't know, but the job made everybody pretty mean. In the beginning of August, somebody made a comment at lunch about Gary's pregnant girlfriend and the next day, Gary came in and took a swing at this new guy who was standing near the barn and came back to work the splitter with a bloody nose and the beginnings of a black eye. About two weeks later, a log truck pulled in and unloaded and while the driver walked across the yard, I looked at him through my goggles for a minute with the chain saw still running. He gave me the middle finger as he walked into the shed, and I started to move fast. I shut the saw down and took off my Kevlar chaps, headphones, plugs, and helmet, tossed my goggles into the sawdust, and met him as he came out the shed door. I hit him right in the face and then again and he fell to one knee and I picked up an ax handle that was leaning against the shed and started beating him on the shoulders and ribs and back. I hit him so hard that the ax handle stung my hand to the bone. As he lay in the sawdust, I reached into his right front pocket and took the money he'd just earned from the log delivery. Somebody helped him back to his truck and he sat there for a while and then drove out. Later that night, I counted five hundred dollars with my hurt right hand and then I went out and walked to the corner Gas Mart and treated myself to a twenty-four pack of cold beer. I drank three of them before I made it back to my sweltering attic room of Bill Doyle's house. Bill was howling, laughing upstairs when I came in.

"You gave it to that frog," he called down to me. The door to his mother's room was closed with light coming out underneath. I walked upstairs. Bill's face always looked tight and windburned, from all those years driving a truck. "That's what I feel like doing, every day. Jumping out of this fucking chair and giving it to somebody."

I poked my head in his room. "I hurt my hand doing it," I said.

"You've got another one, don't worry about it," he said. "I wish Tom could have seen that."

"Tell him about it," I said. Bill talked about Tom Kennedy so much, I felt like a big deal to be mentioned in the same company.

"I will," Bill said. "He loves a good fight."

I came home from work one day and called up into the empty house from the bottom of the stairs like I always did and there was no answer. I went up to Bill's room and opened the door and got sick. Bill really wasn't there anymore; he'd sprayed most of his head onto the wall with a shotgun blast. A faint blue haze hung close to the ceiling. The wheelchair was there with the headless

torso slumped in it and the shotgun on the floor. A bunch of beer
bottles and a liquor bottle, cheap whiskey. Empty. For so much violence in such a small room, you'd have expected to hear noise, an
echo, something. But it was silent. His mom left after the funeral,
went to Florida to live with her sister, and I moved out too, got a
new room in another house for an apartment.

In the last week of August, two shiny black four-by-fours with
tinted windows and New York plates pulled off the highway and
down into the main yard. I assumed they were new homeowners,
maybe up from New York City, looking to fill a wood order for winter or with some land they wanted clear. I was wrong.

The man who got out of the first truck was a dapper-looking Hispanic, with the whole outfit on. The sunglasses, the gold chains.
Shirt open a couple of buttons. The creased black dress pants,
black pointy shoes. He spoke with a thick accent. Harold, his gut
hanging out of his denim coveralls, walked out of the pay shack
and shook hands with the Hispanic man. The rest of us stopped
working, wandered over, and listened.

"Hello," he said to us. "I am Melvin Martinez and we are looking
for strong men to spar with." His accent was so thick I could barely
understand him. Several more Hispanic men got out of the trucks.
Young, muscular, with black hair, all in blue warm-up suits.

Harold looked over at the men standing by the trucks. "Where'd
you last fight, up in Quebec?"

"Yes," said Melvin. "We started in a logging camp up there and
are working our way back down to New York City." He pointed at
one young man wearing red boxing trunks. "That is El Rey," he
said. "We're preparing him for the pros."

"Did he win?" asked Harold. He took a kerchief out of his back
pocket and wiped the sweat off his forehead and neck.

"El Rey has not lost," Melvin said. The gold chains around his
neck caught the sun. He wore a thick gold bracelet on his left wrist,
along with a gold watch and some rings.

Harold considered this a minute. "What weight class are you
looking for?" he said.

"El Rey will fight anyone, he doesn't care, as long as there are
gloves and a ring and timed rounds. No headgear. No kicking. Regular boxing."

Harold nodded and his beard moved. "Well, usually before a

fight, there's another match, there's more than one fight on the card. Got anybody else who wants to fight?"

"Yes," Melvin said. He turned to the men who had come out of the trucks. "Hector will fight. He is El Rey's sparring partner." One of the men raised his hand and began to take off his warm-up jacket.

"Fine," Harold said. "That's fine. We'll get something going here, just give me a minute." He turned around and pointed at Gary. "Take a sledge and a tape and some of those long iron stakes by the shed and make me a ring here." Harold turned to Melvin. "How big do you want?"

"Twenty feet is good," Melvin said. "We've got gloves with us, sixteen ounces, for better protection. Do you need them?"

"Yeah," Harold said. "I don't have any boxing gloves sitting around."

Gary held a stake as I pounded the top of it with a sledgehammer. The sawdust jumped around the base as it went into the ground. We used the tape to measure out twenty feet for the next stake, and snapped a plumb line to make sure the thing was square. The blue chalk dust hung in the hot air after the line drew taut. We drove in all four stakes this way and tied a white rope all the way around.

Harold and Melvin held a private conference on the hood of the closest four-by-four and then Harold came back over to us. Everybody was standing near the pay shack, looking at the ring. Harold ran a hand through his hair and spoke as he walked toward us.

"I put two hundred fifty dollars on it, so let's see what happens," he said. "If you want to bet, go give it to him." He pointed at Melvin. "No odds, just straight win by time or knockout." A couple of guys walked over and gave Melvin some money, but I wanted to wait.

Harold turned to George Hack. George was a big man, a drinker and a bar brawler. He generally ran the skidder if we were in the woods and he always worked on the big saws on any cutting job. He played football for Saint Jay High School and still talked frequently about it, although it was years ago and I'd seen him knock the daylights out of Jimmy Conrad, the bouncer over at Suedon's Bar on Main Street. We prepped the ring area with a rake, and George went into shed and came out without a shirt on, just a pair of jeans, his work boots, and the sixteen-ounce boxing gloves on his hands.

Some of his flab hung over his jeans. Hector was smaller than George, but there was no fat there. Hector had on boxing trunks and shoes laced up to his knees. His gloves. Melvin agreed to take the first round as referee. He wore a white towel around his neck.

The bell rang and both men came out of their corners toward the middle of the sawdust ring. George took a wild swing that hit nothing. He almost slipped. He was already sweating. Hector set him up fast. Two quick left-handed jabs, one to the face, one to the body, and all the time, the right fist was waiting, held back, the pressure building, as George's hands chased Hector's up then down, still back, the bombsight zeroed in on George's left ear, then boom! Right on George's ear, clean, solid, through, and George's knees buckled and his head bounced when it hit the sawdust. George wasn't even conscious and yet, tears were coming out of his eyes. Two guys jumped into the ring and pulled George into the back of a pickup truck. As they turned him over, sawdust stuck to his chest and his face and his crotch, which was soaked. He'd wet himself from the shot to the head.

Harold suddenly pulled me off to one side, behind the pay shack. "Go get me Tom Kennedy," he said in a low voice. He handed me a hundred-dollar bill. "Tell him there's more to go with that."

"Let me fight El Rey," I said.

Harold shook his head. "I want to win," he said. "You can't take an ax handle out there in the ring with you." He talked out of the side of his mouth and then turned toward me. "Besides," he looked straight at me, "you don't have the life in front of you that Tom does."

I took the money and walked along the stream that made the back border of the wood lot. It brought me out at the end of Langmore Street and Kennedy lived one over, on Hartsel Avenue. I walked down the cracked sidewalk, full of frost heaves.

Tom Kennedy was Harold's main tree climber, for any residential job that went up over a hundred feet. At least, that's what everyone at the wood lot would say, but I'd only seen him at the woodlot once. I heard more about him through Bill than anything else. In reality, Tom Kennedy managed to collect weekly pay from Harold just for staying away from the wood lot. His temper and drinking were two of the things I first heard about when I came to Saint Jay. Tom Kennedy was also a local fighting legend. I'd heard stories about him from Bill, and the last I'd seen him at the wood lot, he'd yelled at Harold like I'd never heard anybody do, ever. You could tell he was a mean drunk just from the force of his words. Told Harold to suck it, then stood there and waited for Harold to say something. Harold didn't say anything. I was nervous going to get Tom Kennedy.

He sat on the wood porch of his big house, drinking a beer. Bill told me Tom's father had been the first Irish cop to leave Boston and tried to bring some big-city justice to the force here in Saint Johnsbury. Tom had tried to be a cop too, for a little while, but something went wrong and after a short time, he simply wasn't a cop anymore. He didn't wear the uniform and he didn't drive the car anymore; he just faded out of that life into another.

There were kids running around, some his, some his girlfriend's. Some belonged to other people and I thought that ten years from now, those same kids wouldn't even hang out with anyone named Kennedy. Tom sat there on the front porch, drinking a beer. I walked up the sidewalk to the bottom step of the porch.

"Hi, Tom," I said.

"Hi yourself," he said. "What does Harold need done?" He tilted his head back and drained his beer, tossing the can on the porch. His reddish hair looked bronze in the sun.

I took the hundred-dollar bill out of my pocket and handed it to him. "There are some men from New York City over at the wood lot, looking to fight." I indicated the money. "Harold says there's more after that."

"What type of men?" he asked. "Niggers?"

"No," I said. "Hispanic men. From New York City."

Tom made a noise I took as a laugh. "They aren't from here," he said. "They're not local. There's no Spanish Vermonters." He looked at me. "How tough are they?" He touched his own cheek. "Some black guys got hard faces, their faces can break your hands. And they take people's crap all the time, so they can get pretty mean. Hispanic guys aren't like that."

"The one guy just sent George Hack to the hospital," I said. "Hurt bad."

"George Hack?" he said. "George Hack couldn't fight my sister."

"Well he went down pretty hard," I said. I thought of the tears coming out of Hack's eyes, that he pissed himself.

"Did you think George Hack was tough?" he asked. He started lacing up his work boots.

"Maybe," I allowed.

"George Hack was a fat slob," Tom said. "I should go over to the hospital and beat him in his bed just for losing so bad." He pushed on his right ear with the flat of his hand and I heard the cartilage crack. "He couldn't box," he said.

"He got hurt," I said.

"How big is this guy I'm fighting?" he asked.

"Big," I said. "Probably two-twenty, maybe more."

"You know what they say?" he asked.

"No, what's that?" I asked.

"It isn't the size of the dog in the fight, but the size of the fight in the dog," he said.

"Oh," I said. Tom stood and stretched his arms out. He sat again. "Thanks for looking in on Bill those days." I appreciated Tom buying Bill's booze.

"We went back a long way," Tom said. "Used to be good friends, he knew my father when my father was still alive. I made sure his mother got around in the snow sometimes." He waved it off. "Just friends, that's all."

"Thanks," I said.

He pointed toward the woodlot. "Think I can beat him?" he asked.

I took a minute to answer. "No," I said. "I don't think you can. If he's better than that guy who fought George Hack, no way."

"Is he mean?" Tom asked.

"I don't know," I said.

"Oh, you'd know," he said. "Heard you beat some frog with an ax handle a while back. Bill told me."

"Yeah," I said.

"Sorry about Bill," he said. "But he's better off. He wasn't living much. Not that any of us are but at least we can still walk."

"Yeah," I said.

"You should learn to use your fists," he said. "Learn to box."

"I know how to box," I said.

He snorted. "I'd have shoved that ax handle so far up your ass you'd have coughed splinters," he said. "You want to see boxing? Come watch me right now. I'll show you boxing." He stood and stretched. He looked at one of the little kids running in the street. "A plastic helmet and toy gun don't make a soldier."

"You should've seen what this guy did to George Hack," I repeated.

"Did he piss his pants?" he asked.

"Yeah," I said. "How'd you know?"

"I been around," he said. He showed me his right hand. There was a raised scar between his first and second knuckles. "I hit a man so hard his front tooth was lodged in there." He pointed at the scar with his left hand. "All the way to my bone," he said. "That's what happens when you put that torque on your punches. I'm not just talking about a brawl. I'm talking about boxing, like my old man taught me." We walked down the sidewalk in silence and as we turned, I stole a glance at his right hand again and at the massive scar between his knuckles.

We walked back the way I'd come over and by the time we got there, there were probably fifty people crowding around, looking at the little ring and staring at El Rey, who sat on a stool in the corner with his back to the four-by-fours. He and Hector were talking in Spanish, along with Melvin.

Harold came over to us as soon as we walked onto the lot. He went to shake hands with Tom, but Tom brushed him away.

"Two hundred dollars besides what you already gave me," Tom said.

"Done," Harold said. He reached into his coveralls and pulled out two damp hundred-dollar bills and gave them to Tom.

Tom stripped to a pair of shorts and sneakers, no shirt. On his back, along the right shoulder blade, he had a half-finished tattoo that looked like a shroud with a scythe and the words GRIM REAPER in shaky script. It was the color of mold. Tom got into the ring and sat in his corner. He looked over at El Rey.

Melvin and Harold both got into the ring and after looking at each other, Melvin clapped his hands. Everyone was quiet.

"Ladies and gentlemen, this is going to be a twelve-round fight with two-minute rounds," he said. Melvin pointed at El Rey. "And in this corner, wearing the red trunks, the Hispanic Panic, undefeated in his career, weighing two hundred and twenty-one pounds, the King of Knockout, from the Bronx, New York New York, El Rey!" The other Hispanic men whistled and clapped and El Rey stood up and shadowboxed for a minute, finished up with a flurry of short punches, then remained standing, dancing on his feet, loose. Melvin stepped out of the ring and Harold cleared his throat and pointed to Tom Kennedy.

"In this corner," he said, "weighing one hundred eighty-five pounds, the Pride Of Saint Jay, Tom Kennedy!"

And when his name was called, Kennedy got off his stool and danced for a minute, bobbed and weaved and threw a few light punches and we all cheered him, really cheered him, and he remained standing too, moving and ready.

Harold motioned for both guys to touch gloves and they did and Melvin hit the bell. El Rey came out fast, moved up to Tom and swung and missed, and Tom made two quick jabs at his ribs and backed off, his hands held at an almost awkward angle, his feet always moving. They moved together and El Rey jabbed with his left, pulling his right hand back, jabbed again, and swung full with the right, but Tom wasn't there anymore, he moved back and to the side and then in again and bang! bang! two fast rights to El Rey's head and the bell rang.

Tom came over to the corner and sat on the stool, and I gave him some water, which he spit into the sawdust. Melvin and Hector were in El Rey's corner, talking loud in Spanish. Tom spit his white rubber mouth guard into his right glove and spoke.

"Watch me now, and learn about those fists," he said. He popped his mouth guard back in and stared across at El Rey's corner. The bell rang and he stood, and I grabbed the stool out of the ring.

He and El Rey met in the middle of the ring and El Rey juked left with his head, then right, swung, but Tom ducked under, and one two! Shots to the body and one two! again, one to the solar plexus. I saw the look on El Rey's face, I knew it, and as he brought his hands down to cover himself, Tom slammed the right side of his head with the glove, hard, and again, and there was blood flying, and I thought for sure Tom would step back, but he stepped forward, closer, almost hitting down on his target and bang! a strong left hand to El Rey's nose and the bell rang.

Tom sat on the stool. He was breathing heavily, sweat all over his body, and we toweled him down and they were screaming in Spanish in the other corner. Tom popped his mouth guard out. He didn't say anything. He looked mad. He stared across at El Rey's corner and put his mouth guard back in. The bell rang and Tom came off the stool like a rocket. He threw a couple of light punches, and El Rey took a step back and Tom stepped up, closer again. Then he swung twice, fast, and it was like punching bullet holes in a paper target — El Rey didn't feel the shock until the punches were through him.

I didn't know exactly what happened next because Tom moved so fast and his back shielded me from seeing the punches directly. All I could watch were his shoulder blades, moving with each punch, over and over and all to the body of El Rey and El Rey's face looking at me over Tom's shoulder, trying to stay alert, and now Tom was on El Rey's head, he found the range, it was a right, another right and a right and El Rey fell to his knees hard and Tom kept hitting him, blood coming out of El Rey's ear onto the sawdust, and El Rey went down face first, the sawdust jumping up as his head hit the ground, his eyes closed, and it was silent. The Hispanic men jumped in the ring and popped amyl nitrate capsules under El Rey's nose and he didn't move, and Tom just sat there on the stool, with blood on his chest, as they picked El Rey up and carted him back to the trucks and presumably the hospital.

It stayed quiet as men collected their money from Melvin and came over to congratulate Tom. He was still sweating, still trying to catch his breath. A bruise was starting on his face from a punch I hadn't even seen. The marks on his chest seemed to glow red. Slowly, he took his gloves off with his teeth.

"You want some help?" I asked.

"No," he said. "I'm just taking my time." He put a shirt on after a while and he and Harold talked and then I watched him walk back the same way we'd come over, along the stream toward the house.

I have a different job now, handling shipping and packages for a company near Montpelier. Every time I drive past Thompson's wood lot and see the men working there, I'm glad it's not me. Last night, I was up late — my wife had already taken off to her mother's house, she lives just down the block — had a couple of beers, and turned on ESPN. The late-night fight card had El Rey on it. He looked bulked up. I decided to walk to the corner store for some more beer and snacks. It was mid-November and snowing pretty hard.

Tom Kennedy was at the store. He smelled like beer. He was in the back, looking at the coolers full of beer.

"Hey, Tom Kennedy," I said. "The Pride of Saint Jay."

He turned and stared at me. Sometimes when people drink a lot, they have a certain look about them, a fog they have to get through before the world reaches them, and Tom's gaze had retreated into that phase. He didn't know who I was.

"Hey, mister," he said. His jeans were ripped and he wore an old flannel shirt.

"I've got El Rey on ESPN over at the house," I said. "Want to come over and watch?"

"What?" Kennedy said.

"You know, El Rey," I said. "That guy you fought over at Thompson's." His hearing seemed a little weak too.

"I haven't been in a fight," he said.

"No," I said. "Three years ago."

He looked at me. "Three years ago? What the hell's three years ago got to do with today?"

The question hung there in the air. I had the luxury of thinking about three years ago, of a TV, or having a fight with my wife. "Nothing," I said. "Just thought you might be interested."

"I'm interested in getting some fucking beer, but that asshole won't sell it to me." He pointed at the high school kid behind the counter. "Says I'm already drunk. Right?" Tom Kennedy gave him a deadly stare.

"I'll call the cops if you don't leave the store," the kid said. "I've done it before on him," the kid continued. "He makes me." A phone hung on the wall behind him. Tom Kennedy headed back to the beer cooler. He grabbed a six-pack of bottles and ran out of the store, into the snow. I tossed a ten-dollar bill on the counter and ran after him. He was already headed down the sidewalk.

"Hey, Tom," I called. "Wait up."

He turned fast. His face seemed to come clear out of the snow and I knew that he remembered me.

"I shot him," he said. "He begged me to do it, and if you had been a good friend to him, you'd have done it."

"What?" I said.

"I blew his head right off," he said. "What was the point of him living if he didn't want to live?"

"What?" I said. "You mean Bill?"

"That's right," Tom said. "But it should have been you. To pull the trigger."

He hit me in the side of the head with a full bottle of beer. I lay there in the snow and went in and out of it. I heard a police siren going through the night, a sound you don't hear very often in Saint Johnsbury, through the quiet streets and houses, echoing out into the huge forest of the Northeast Kingdom and beyond.

ANGELA ZEMAN

Green Heat

FROM *A Hot and Sultry Night for Crime*

TYREE GARCIA ARRIVED LATE in the afternoon. For the last
twenty miles he'd ridden State Highway 6 all alone and so felt free
to indulge in a leisurely survey of Rushing River Hollow by riding
the brakes of his black Cherokee van down the final hill. At a Mobil
station, by all appearances the official western border of the town,
he pulled over and rolled to a stop next to a gas pump. According
to tattered and faded ads pasted across the office's windows, the
Mobil supplied repair services, gas, tires, beer, sodas, cigarettes,
and tobacco in chewable form. Tyree guessed the strips of paper
served to shade the Mobil's glass-walled office from the merciless
sun as much as to list the services offered.

The narrow asphalt highway flattened out and disappeared into
the town's main street, which was as neatly obscured beneath a
layer of dirt as if deliberately coated. While he sat massaging sleep-
deprived eyes, he noticed the occasional pedestrian scuff down the
middle of the street, raising dust that obscured his or her feet in little dun-colored clouds.

He wondered if avoiding the sidewalks was a local habit. His was
the only vehicle in sight. For all he knew, the tourist trade infused
the Hollow with bustling life in spring and fall, and maybe even
winter, but the intense summer heat drove them away — if this was
a normal summer. Was this brain-sizzling heat unusual for the Hollow? Like a drought? He didn't know that either. Country, especially genuine country like Rushing River Hollow, baffled him, was
beyond his experience. Heat waves shimmered up from the concrete slab sidewalks bordering each side of the road. Maybe the
thick layer of dirt was kinder to tender feet than roasted cement.

He just didn't know.

To a Chicago kid born and raised in and devoted to its crowded neighborhoods, West Virginia looked like a foreign kingdom of crystalline creeks and river rapids and green, softly rounded mountains. An occasional ramshackle cabin propped up on a webbing of raw, unpainted four-by-fours dotted the steep slopes. A paradise — unspoiled, vast, and rich — which accounted for the sprawling luxury resort hotel he knew from his AAA map occupied the other end of this dirt-crusted road. Pinebrook Resort offered — if one paid outrageous fees — hunting, golf, tennis, skeet and trap shooting, river rafting, nature hikes, even lessons in falconry. He'd picked up a travel agency brochure before driving all the way down here. He wondered if the privileged lives of the guests — outsiders — invited jealousy and comparison to the obviously scratch-scrabble lives of the residents.

Tyree finally swung his long, stiffened legs to the ground and began a series of stretches. He was a tall man, heavily muscled, and moved without haste.

As he reached for the fuel pump handle, he noticed a small sign propped against the second of the Mobil station's two pumps (one for diesel fuel, but he'd happened to park beside the one dispensing gas: a sign he interpreted as a favorable omen; in his profession, he constantly looked for favorable omens). The sign, weatherbeaten almost to illegibility, said Rushin River Hollow, Population: the 421 was crossed out, 303 crossed out, 112 crossed out, then 427. A graph of the town's fortunes. Had the millennium brought about a baby boom here?

Suddenly, a short, thick man with roughened skin so red his neck and face resembled a turkey's wattle rushed up and grabbed the pump handle from Tyree's grasp and inserted the nozzle into the Cherokee. "High test, I'd say, right?" He moved fast but talked slow.

Tyree nodded. The man punched a square plastic button on the pump, then turned on the juice. He apologized that he'd been "out back," his slight flinch telling Tyree that "out back" meant the men's rest room, then introduced himself as Emil Powers.

"Tyree Garcia," Tyree said politely, nodding down at the top of the little man's head. He saw no reason to lie about his name; nobody would've heard of him in this wilderness.

For no reason other than to open a conversation, Tyree asked what had happened to the *g* in *Rushing* on the population sign. The gap from its loss was obvious.

"Aw," said Emil, sounding deeply distressed, "if'n you don't mind a long story?"

Tyree shook his head, eyebrows lifted.

"Ya see, it ain't in truth Rush-*ing* River. It's *Rooshion* River. Like the Rooshions that come from Moscow. And somehow, 'cause we do a lot of business river rafting, y'know from the hotel, it got mangled over the years inta Rush-*ing* River. By the tourists, I guess." He shrugged his narrow shoulders, jiggling the gas pump handle. "We need them tourists. So we jes' didn't know, should we change it legally or what, or did it even matter? So when the sun bleached the *g* off'n the sign, we left it. I got maps in the office, legal ones from the gov'ment, *they* even call us Rushing River Hollow now. How they got aholt of the wrong name, nobody knows, or gives a hoot. Well, except for the Rooshions what established the town. They's pissed. But," he waved his free hand, dismissing them, "just Joey and Eban left, and they's ninety something. Be gone by the time we decide anything. So we're kind of relaxed about it. Now the sign itself, though —"

To Tyree's amazement, he took a deep breath. Then, with a stiff dignity obviously meant to disguise personal embarrassment, confessed that he'd promised the Chamber of Commerce last spring he'd make a new sign, but jes' hadn't got to it. But he will. He will! He promised Tyree as fervently as if Tyree were an important Chamber member to be placated, a color-blind attitude that amazed Tyree. He'd anticipated some anxiety or even obstruction because of the color of his skin. After all, West Virginia was not known for high standards of education, an aspect that usually coincided with prejudice. Suddenly Tyree thought of the extreme heat and the deserted street. Possibly the color blindness meant only that in a roasting August barren of tourists, his color was green: income on the hoof.

A companionable silence set in between the two men as the gas slowly filled the Cherokee's immense tank. Tyree nearly grinned as he watched Emil struggle not to peer too obviously into the darkened side and back windows, curious about what might be in there. He would see nothing, Tyree knew, of his altered shotgun, his semiautomatic 9mm and .357 Magnum with extra clips, a red-dot laser scope on the .357, and the Archangel holster Tyree favored for its fast-draw design. His laptop, connected wireless phone, and portable printer were packed neatly in shockproof canvas carriers. His monocular night-vision headgear, an air taser (stun gun), and a Dazer he used for protection against guard dogs; mace in various sizes and canister shapes; and a digital camera with special lenses were all nested, like the laptop, in specially designed carriers. As was his Game Finder scope for detecting body heat behind walls. Tyree's Cherokee was also designed with special features, one of which kept his equipment from prying eyes. And just as well. No need to panic the populace. Yet.

Emil sighed and gave up his covert peeking without resorting to the rudeness of trying to pry info from Tyree. Tyree liked him for that sigh; it revealed an easygoing nature. Tyree liked laid-back attitudes. They worked so much better for him when he was on a job.

Soot-blackened buildings dotted both sides of the street, reminders of the town's coal-mining history. Edna's Gift Shop leaned, bricks crumbling, against the timbered stones of Willem's Pizza, which looked sturdy. The tall-pillared, red brick U.S. Post Office, which despite its height was about as wide as a cubicle, shared a wall with Mick's rakish wood-paneled Railroader's Pub. Across the road, Janna's Coal Miner's Daughter Clothing Boutique had been a similar wooden shack before being amateurishly slathered with a coating of infelicitous yellow stucco now flaking into a blotchy mess. A cracked cement sidewalk fronted these places of business, tilting along with the fortunes of those who'd hung on through both good and bad years.

"Where ya from?" asked Emil.

"Chicago," murmured Tyree absently, studying the town. "Tourist trade the big industry here?" he asked his new friend Emil.

"Only industry, now the coal's played out." Emil tossed a hand to direct Tyree's gaze down the length of the street. "They do what they can to brighten up the storefronts." Emil shook his head sadly. "Order stuff from Sears catalogues or haul fancy goods in from Richmond or from Charleston, our capital, and then tell people it's local handicraft. That's big here, handicrafts. Not to criticize."

Tyree nodded.

Elaborate Victorian wood lace and railings festooned porches that hadn't worn such finery since their birth at the turn of the century. Log cabin–style benches had been sprinkled about, nestled near cedar tubs that Tyree guessed normally overflowed with pansies or geraniums or whatever grew here in cooler weather. He was no gardener, either. Flowers, in his experience, were just bright things hung in great lush balls from light poles lining Lake Shore Drive or the Miracle Mile. The tubs here were barren, filled only with tangles of sun-roasted brown moss. The stables near some derelict railroad tracks had been transformed into a hardware store, but the owner had scattered old horse tack and hay bales around to contribute to the desirable "charm."

Suddenly Emil volunteered, "Talk's going around about making a public park on the east end, just afore you get to the hotel grounds. Everybody hopes Miz Doree Zendall will donate her family's Civil War iron cannons and cannonballs, now she's widowed and no kids. Three generations of her husband's family owned 'em. What good're they to Doree? They'd make a center of interest for the park. Half rust, but still, it's history. Lotta history here. And *that's* genuine!"

Tyree nodded, tiring of his new friend. He checked the revolving numbers on the pump. He breathed deeply for patience and prepared to ask if there was a place to stay here other than the hotel, but Emil jumped in again.

"That woman! City council tried to bribe her with a white-painted gazebo, her name on it on a brass plaque. Only Doree's cannons and the street lamps on Main Street here are for real; ever'thing else is like I said, from a Sears catalogue or hauled in. But Doree thinks her cannons ought to fetch her more 'n' a plaque."

Tyree jumped in as Emil took a breath. "You know a place I could stay? That hotel of yours is too rich for my wallet."

Emil shrugged a bony shoulder. "We gots a couple B and Bs, if you don't mind sharing bathrooms."

Tyree frowned. He did mind. "No."

"Oh, wait now. Doree's place is huge. One of the rooms she rents gots its own bath. I'm sure it's empty. Hell, whole damn town's empty lately. Except she talks a lot, if you can stand it. What'd you say you here for?"

Tyree understood and didn't hold it against the little man. Curiosity was a tough urge to control. "Vacation. No hunting yet, right?"

"Out of season right now."

"Good. I don't care for shooting." It was true. He didn't. "I'll need directions."

Tyree got the directions, climbed back into his Cherokee, and devoutly wished for a soft bed. If Rushing River aimed for historical accuracy, then the bed should sport a feather mattress. Of course, the blacks all slept out back in those historical days, too. He hoped Ms. Doree Zendall would be greedy enough to see his color as green, as Emil had.

He rolled slowly down the street, still taking in the sights, noticing a few side roads, unpaved paths, really, not visible from Emil's station. He also noted a small, slightly built old man sweeping the sidewalk in front of a store. Suddenly the man looked straight at Tyree, shouted, "Ho! What's up?" Tyree looked again, taken aback. The man hastily ducked inside the Little Bear Market's screen door, banging his broom on the stone steps as he dragged it in behind him.

Later. First get a place to park his car and his aching body.

Ms. Doree Zendall's tiny raisin eyes narrowed, taking a long, silent moment to catalog the price of his black tee belted neatly within his black silk-and-linen-blend slacks, and the subtly expensive sleek black sneakers. Tyree congratulated himself for leaving behind his gold chain, bracelet, ear stud, and rings; he didn't like to fit into a cliché of a typical big city black. The word *hood* usually attached itself to the end of that description. Now he was gold-free, and his watch stainless steel, although it included a few features he doubted Ms. Zendall would understand. Finally, she nodded. She tucked a stray strand of coarse hair into the ratty gray ball that rested on the roll of fat behind her neck and led the way to his new home for the next few days. As she hauled herself up the stairs, she began a rambling stream-of-consciousness monologue that Tyree listened to carefully in case he could use any of the info.

She was short and very heavy, a fireplug of a woman. Huffs appeared between her words as she struggled to talk and climb stairs simultaneously. *Emil had it right,* Tyree thought. Her house was massive and empty. The winding stair seemed endless. Her face reddened until sweat coursed down her round cheeks to plop like rain on her heaving bosom. When they finally gained the top landing of the wide, curving stairs, painted white but carpeted thickly in plush deep maroon, she abruptly finished with, "Breakfast is extra, how do you like your eggs?" The sudden cessation of sound as she waited for his answer woke Tyree from the mesmerizing flow of words. He'd almost fallen asleep on the stairway behind her.

He blinked, then registered the question. "Four eggs, easy over medium. You got whole wheat toast?"

"Muffins are better."

"Toast," he said firmly. "Whole wheat. No butter. And fresh juice?"

"Well sure, fresh!" she bristled. "Seven sharp."

Tyree nodded, then handed her the agreed in-advance fee in cash. One shrewd glance at the interior of his wallet, and she wheeled smartly to leave him standing before the open door of a room more appropriate for a debutante than Tyree Garcia. The bed was a double, with an overlarge white lace coverlet that drifted to the varnished wood floor all around, the corners puddled like piles of snowflakes. It felt scratchy to his skin. He bundled it onto an overstuffed boudoir chair and dropped onto the crisp sheets, careful to let his feet hang off the side, too tired to remove his sneakers. The two corner windows were open, but no breeze stirred the sheer white curtains to cool the stagnant air.

The next hour passed in a luxurious haze of drifting between sleep and a blissful physical consciousness of the soft mattress cradling his weary body. When his conscience demanded he pull himself erect to get to work, it was a wrench. He wasn't here to laze away the day after driving eighteen straight hours, racing newspaper or TV reports that might complicate his errand.

An early dinner, he decided. Coffee with sugar for the jolt, although he rarely drank coffee. Then get to it.

With little trouble he found a diner, the only source of food within sight, which helped narrow his choice, slid into the red plastic–covered bench seat, and just avoided propping his elbows in a pool of syrup left by a former customer. A battered window AC unit manfully refrigerated the air, although it hampered conversation with its metallic death rattles. Tyree basked in the chill.

After an agonizing attempt to swallow the larded slab of meatloaf floating in a lake of ketchup, he gave it up and asked for the freshest pie in the place. The waitress, a moon-faced teen, studied him like a science specimen, then brought him a large plate of banana cream pie. It was fresh, fragrant, and tasted like heaven. He got a second piece, making a mental note to ask for her recommendations if his job lasted long enough to force him to eat here again, swilled down the burnt coffee, and left her a 50 percent tip.

He strolled back toward the main part of town, suddenly aware that he, like the others he'd watched, was walking down the middle of the dirt-covered asphalt. After a small laugh at himself, he focused on looking for more conversationalists like Emil and Ms. Zendall. A small group had gathered in front of Edna's Gift Shop, so he shifted his direction to end up there, but he moved slowly.

Give them all a chance to look him over, take in the details, like Ms. Zendall. He hoped his color would again be judged green. Helped a hell of a lot.

Again a good omen: Emil was there, holding court, telling the saga of Tyree's arrival. Tyree stepped up on the sidewalk and smiled warmly at Emil, nodded hello. Bristling with pride, Emil greeted Tyree like a cousin, made introductions. Told his name and that he had come from Chicago, and didn't have any interest in hunting. Just liked the peace of the area, "That right, Tyree?" he asked. Tyree nodded.

The nervous sidewalk sweeper was there, head bobbing. Again he declared in a booming voice, "Ho, what's up!" then shyly backed away, tangling his broom between his own legs, nearly falling. His head hung as if ashamed of himself.

Emil said, "That's Frankie. Says that to everybody. Sweeps sidewalks for the town. Gotta do something. 'Sides, it's awful dusty this time o' year. Good thing to do."

Tyree nodded. Close up, he could see that Frankie was much younger than his wizened features indicated. An impaired young man who looked sixty. "Good job, Frankie," he said. He held out his hand to him. Frankie went totally still. Despite his lowered head, his eyes went up to Tyree's, holding there for a second. Then he grasped Tyree's hand and squeezed, grinning. "Hey!" he said.

"Hey," Tyree answered. Frankie's hand was bony and fragile, with skin like leather. Then Emil introduced him to an older woman, nearly as fat as Ms. Zendall but taller. "This is Mrs. Barstow, Lisle. And her beautiful Wendy-girl. Wendy married Rudy Stern a whiles back. Rudy's on late duty today. At the hotel," he confided. "Desk clerk. Good future!"

Tyree nodded, smiling. "Congratulations," he said. The girl could not possibly be older than seventeen or eighteen and looked many months pregnant, although Tyree was careful not to mention this in case he was wrong. The women he'd met so far in this town had a tendency to corpulence, and he couldn't afford to offend quite yet.

He turned to the girl's mother and tipped his head. "You couldn't possibly be old enough to be this young lady's mother!" *An oldie but goodie,* he sighed to himself. Women. But to his surprise, Mrs. Barstow didn't do the normal simper and denial that usually followed the compliment. She just gazed at him with a puzzled look on her face.

She blurted, "You rent that car? Don't look like no rental. Rentals don't normally black out their windows like that. But it's got a West Virginia plate on it."

Tyree nodded. "Yeah, I thought that odd myself, the dark windows. But I'm fond of vans. Roomy. I'm a big guy, long legs." He shrugged at the mysteries of rental car companies, put an earnest but puzzled expression on his face. But Mrs. Barstow's eyes chilled as she took in his explanation, studied his face. Calculating. *Shit,* he thought. He habitually changed the plates every time he crossed state lines to stay inconspicuous, but weariness had led him to reveal to the town crier, Emil, that he'd come from Chicago. Might as well've put a blue chicken on the roof for Mrs. Barstow to point out.

"You drive here from the airport?" she asked.

He nodded.

"Which one?"

"Well, hell, Lisle. Give the man a vacation, will ya?" Emil rescued Tyree, who silently blessed the man. "Obviously he drove in from the capital. Look at the dust on the thing."

"He could've flown in to the Greenville airport," she said defensively. "It's closer. And lotsa straight flights come there from big cities, 'cause of the hotel."

"C'mon, Lisle. Then he woulda driv in from the opposite direction. I saw him myself hit town back thataway," Emil exclaimed in exasperation, pointing toward the Mobil station. "Obviously he came by way of Charleston!"

"Well his car's so filthy looks like he drove here all the way from Chicago!" she demanded. "And where's the rental car sticker?"

Tyree rapidly reassessed the intelligence of Rushing River's population. No detail too small to notice. "They don't mark rental cars anymore, since the tourist shootings in Florida," he said, crossing mental fingers that West Virginia had subscribed to that policy, too. He groaned, wondering what else he'd screwed up. Better get in, do it, get out. This is what allowing himself too little sleep got him.

"There now, happy, Lisle?" started Emil, gathering wind to begin a good long rebuke.

"You know what made me think of coming here?" Tyree said to divert attention from his car. "I had a buddy. Moved to this area, around, oh, twenty years ago."

"Colored like you?" asked Mrs. Barstow innocently.

He distrusted her innocence. "No. White like you," he said, trying to restrain his annoyance.

"What's his name? You been in touch, know where he lives exactly?"

"Not exactly."

She tilted her head, looking up at him with opaque pale eyes, same color as a blued gun barrel, he thought. She continued, full of attitude: "But twenty years pass, you think, hell, he probably hasn't moved in all those years. I'll just look up my old buddy an see how the fish'er jumpin', is that it? What's his name? You didn't say."

"Jeeze, Lisle. What's your britches in a hitch for?" asked Emil plaintively.

Yeah, Lisle, Tyree asked himself, his interest in her sharpening with each passing second. "My friend's mother died. And he didn't come to the funeral, her only child. Didn't seem natural. Wonderful woman, awfully good to me over the years, and she mentioned he was still here shortly before she died. That's what brought me. I'd been working hard, had some time off coming to me. Thought, well, I'd see what was up with him and get some R and R same time." Don't explain so much, he reminded himself. Too much detail could trap a man like a web of steel. He shrugged. "No big deal if he's not here anymore." He gazed around the green mountains surrounding the dusty town and said, "Beautiful," his voice quiet with appreciation. Sunset had begun, streaks of brilliant coral and mauve tinting the rows of small shops and even his new friends' faces a reddish gold. He figured the time to be about eight or eight-thirty. Darkness might not come until nine-thirty or after, this late in the summer. He sighed inwardly. He was tired, but no rest waited for him tonight.

"Whatcha do for a livin', Mr. Tyree?" asked a new voice softly. "In Chicago?"

He looked down at the area near his right elbow. A pixie stood there in baggy overalls, yellow work boots, and a white sleeveless man's ribbed undershirt.

"Hey, Tyree, this's one o' our Master Wilderness Guides. Miss Amy Bearclaw." Emil's voice lifted with pride.

The dusky-skinned pixie smiled, but like Mrs. Lisle Barstow, her greenish eyes had a metallic glint. With the experience of a lifetime of observation, he saw she was the product of some sort of mixed marriage. Bearclaw? Sounded Indian. Her dark hair was cut like a boy's, and she obviously ignored makeup, but nothing could make this little woman look like a boy.

"Master Wilderness Guide?" he repeated.

She nodded. "My pa and I have an exclusive contract with Pine-brook, because we're the best. And the hotel believes in maintaining the highest standards."

Obviously she had no objection to self-promotion, thought Tyree, amused. "Do you ever take on outsiders, people not guests at the resort? I wouldn't mind a tour of a mountain or two. Maybe a river ride."

Her eyelashes lowered to half-mast as she considered him. "Your city ways shine through you like a lamp, although you'd be good in a fight, I'd bet."

"It's been said," he agreed, wondering why she didn't talk as much like a hick as the others in the group. "Fights happen in a city. In the country, too?"

She ignored this query, her expression labeling it stupid, as it was, he admitted to himself, and asked him if he'd had his dinner.

"At the diner," said Mrs. Barstow. He looked at her. "I saw you in the window," she said, shrugging.

"The pie was fantastic," he said.

"That was the banana cream, right?" asked Emil with authority.

Tyree nodded, beginning to feel hemmed in.

The pixie said, "My mom made it. She bakes for the hotel, too. And grows vegetables so they can offer organic dishes. You couldn'ta liked anything else there, though. Somebody big as you needs to eat. Want to come home with me for dinner?"

Dazed, Tyree threw all plans to the wind and just nodded yes.

The pixie wheeled to tromp down the middle of the street. Automatically, he hastened to follow. She would've made a natural military drill sergeant, was his first thought. It took a stunned second before he remembered his manners and turned to wave good-bye to Emil and the others. Frankie boomed out, "Ho, what's up?" but also waved good-bye. Mrs. Barstow just turned and strode away, pulling her daughter along by her plump arm as if otherwise the girl might run off. To Tyree's amusement, all moved to the middle of the deserted street before taking to their individual directions.

Dinner took on dimensions he hadn't expected, but by now he'd learned not to let anything surprise him. This place was too far beyond his experience.

Mrs. Bearclaw was a beautiful woman, slender and graceful and tall, her hair silky and pale and twisted back out of her face. And she was blind. Probably not completely, he judged. Legally blind. Although he'd offered to help, at Amy's command he instead sat quietly on a small painted wooden chair in the kitchen and watched as Mrs. Bearclaw kept track of several operations going on simultaneously on a modern commercial stove with three ovens that took up at least half the space in the kitchen. The smells seductively drove away all memory of the diner's meatloaf. As if drawn home by the aromas, Mr. Bearclaw soon arrived, a small lanky man with ropy muscles, obviously Amy's father and the source of her miniature dusky version of her mother's beauty. They shook hands, and he was invited to call Amy's father David, her mother Lydia. When the food finally reached the table, Amy nodded he could start eating.

He tried to restrain himself, knowing a belly too full of food would work against him that night, but Lydia Bearclaw's talents overcame him. When he finally sat back with a sated sigh, Lydia spoke. In a cultured East Coast voice, she asked who he was after.

Tyree lowered his head and shook it. "Is every person in this Hollow psychic?"

Amy tilted back on the hind two legs of her wooden chair, thumbs hooked in her overalls pockets. She grinned. "You think we're so danged dumb we ain't never ran up against bounty hunters before?"

"Don't say *ain't*," reproved her mother.

Amy ignored her. "Look around. Are we overflowing with cops,

DEA? Feds? We got no sheriff, even. Half the world has tried to hide here: Colombian drug dealers, punks from Atlanta, kneecap men from New Orleans. I mean, we're so nowheres, we're ripe for disappearances — or so these types think before they get to know the locals. Besides, it's pretty here. People like it."

Tyree stared at her.

As if patiently explaining the obvious to a halfwit, Amy finished, "You saw our town's population numbers if you was at the Mobil. You know how in each other's pockets neighbors get in a place this size? Nothin' else to do." She held up her hands as if to say, *Well duh!*

She finished, "So who you after?"

He stared at her father, who just shrugged, then her mother. Lydia sat quietly, sipping her coffee.

Tyree squirmed, which is what he suspected Amy had intended him to do. "What's with the jump in population, then? From 112 to 427 in the last year. Or did I read it wrong?"

David Bearclaw nodded, his mouth screwed tight as if suppressing anger. "You read right. The hotel. Sells plots now, fancy houses all squashed together like fleas, in sections tucked between the three golf courses they got. Word is they're building another golf course just for the residents. Pools, all that."

Tyree asked, "Vacation homes or permanent?"

David eyed him. "What's the difference?"

"Permanent means schools," said Tyree. "Post offices, restaurants, sewers, service roads. And eventually some type of industry to employ them. Lotta extras come with permanent residents. Money for the Hollow, though." He lifted an eyebrow in question.

David shook his head. "Don't need, don't want that kind of prosperity."

Tyree frowned. "You got no police at all?"

Amy grinned. "Didn't say that. We got Kizzy."

David said quietly, "My mother. One of the remaining full-blooded Cherokees from the Trail of Tears. Descended from those who hid so the soldiers missed them in the roundup."

Tyree considered. "Didn't I read that about a third of the Indians force-marched to the reservations out West died on the trail?"

David nodded, looked aside.

Amy grunted. "That's why the name, Trail of Tears."

Tyree folded his arms, said to David, "So your ma, Amy's grandma, is the law here?"

Lydia smiled.

Amy grinned. "She's a Wise Woman. She sees and knows it all. Nobody can get away with a dang thing. She nails somebody, they're nailed for good. Who needs a pushy cop shooting up innocent bystanders? She's teaching me to take her place someday. She can't die until I take over from her."

Tyree slid his eyes sideways to examine the half-pint-size girl so smug, so *big* for such a pixie. Tried to keep the flummoxed look off his face. He finally sighed. "I believe you. You asked about my mark: Don't know his name. I know what *used* to be his name. Edgar Fallon."

Silence.

"What'd he do?" rumbled David Bearclaw at last. "In Chicago, was it?"

"Oh, Dad. Drugs and beatin' up women, you can guess that much."

Tyree lifted his hands. "Holy shit. You sure Captain Sabinski didn't just mail you the guy's jacket?"

Lydia Bearclaw smiled. "It's hard to get used to, I know. Like jungle drums. Kizzy is a . . . a natural force, like a tornado. Amy, too. *She's* just not as disciplined or schooled. Yet."

"And where'd *you* come from?" Tyree asked. "The Upper East Side of Manhattan?"

"Very good," she said, still smiling.

He thought a minute. "So you were running, too, when you got here. From what?" He studied her, brow furrowed in thought. "Were you blind before you got here? From birth? Or from —"

"Not nice, Mr. Tyree," said Lydia Bearclaw. "Mind your manners. I know you have some. And I know you're used to minding them, because you've restrained yourself amazingly ever since you arrived in Rushing River."

Tyree nodded. "You read me right. Sorry, ma'am. Sir," he said to her husband, who just faintly smiled and shrugged. *Not a talker,* thought Tyree.

"So now what?" he said, more to himself than to his hosts.

"Tell us the whole thing," insisted Amy. "I don't get the twenty years ago part."

Tyree looked at her ruefully. "Twenty-*four* years ago, to be exact. This kid lied about his age — he was seventeen then — so he could marry a twenty-year-old dumb Polack girl in Chicago. He'd knocked — he'd gotten her pregnant. Too innocent, no family. A pretty blonde. So she works hard in a local diner while he's supposedly driving a cab, and she thinks they're socking away every penny so they can escape the projects with their baby, but he's depositing it all into his veins. But she trusts him. The sweet little girl has her beautiful baby boy, goes right back to work. He switches to nights to watch the kid during the day. Next thing she knows, stuff starts missing from the apartment. See, his addiction's growing beyond their joint income. So she reports the thefts to the precinct, but they're all petty. I mean, what do they have to steal? The local beat cop, after one look at the husband, guesses the truth, tries to tell her, but she won't listen. Until one day she catches hubby snitching her paycheck from her purse. Big fight, lots of screaming, and then silence. Some hours pass, but the silence bothers one neighbor who really cares about the poor girl, who finally decides to check on her. He pushes open the door, finds the girl in the kitchen, bloody and out cold on the floor next to her baby. Baby's head is smashed flat on one side. The woman's physically OK. The blood is all the baby's."

"Jesus wept," murmured David Bearclaw.

"The cops went for the husband at his place of work, found out he'd been fired a few weeks before. His former dispatcher confirmed Eddie was supporting a monster habit and unable to hold a job. He had to be getting desperate for cash. Dealers don't extend credit." His mouth twisted wryly. "Cops figured, with nerves raggedy from too long off the juice, his wife catching him in his theft — screaming wife, screaming baby — he popped. Then either he slam-dunked the child to shut it up, an accidental murder, or he just flat murdered it. Luckily a chop to his wife's head knocked her cold, or the cops figured she'd be dead, too. No Eddie. And when she woke up, she'd lost herself. Catatonic."

Mrs. Bearclaw asked gently, "That makes it twenty-three years ago, then. So why are you here? And why now?"

"Because after twenty-three years of institutionalization, therapy, and whatever they do to help poor souls like that sweet girl — woman now — she regained her mind and memory. The doctors say she not only recovered, although still frail, but can be believed.

And she told what happened. The cops had the story nailed pretty much correctly."

"But you're no cop," said Amy. "Doesn't sound like there's a bounty on the guy. Why are *you* here?"

Tyree sighed. "'Cause I had the misfortune of going through elementary, then junior high, then high school with a good buddy who's now Captain Lee Sabinski of Homicide in Chicago. And over the years, he's kept track of our running balance of favors. I owe him big right now, and bounty hunters don't suffer from a need for search warrants, extradition paperwork, and that stuff." He looked Amy in the eye, man to man, so to speak. His sharp cheekbones bunched up into his own grin. "Plus, I'm good at my job. The cops had nothing then, and Sabinski's men found the same nothing now. They aren't even sure he ever left Illinois. But I work with a rather special computer information expert — a genius in his own way. Probably should meet your Grandma Kizzy. He decided to start with Eddie's car. Even if he ditched it fast, in that first flight away from his own house, we figure he used his own car. In the projects, he was one of the few who *had* a car.

"So my man patiently traced from car to car to car, all but a few of them stolen, natch, but the ones that he didn't steal: he changed his name just a little with each transaction. And two patterns emerged: a trail that never went beyond West Virginia, and a name that by now we figure might somewhat resemble Roy Barso."

Amy settled her chair back down on all four of its feet and gazed levelly at her father. Her father shook his head, then stood to take the used dishes from the table to the sink.

Tyree jumped to his feet, grabbed his dirty dishes. Lydia patted the air. "Never mind, Tyree. Amy, better lead Mr. Tryee back to his car."

"If it's still there," Amy agreed. David nodded and started squirting dish soap in a large metal sink.

"Better run on," David said, taking the dishes Tyree held.

"What?" said Tyree.

"C'mon," said Amy. "Gotta chore to help you with, then you can bed down in comfort until tomorrow."

"No, not tomorrow. Tonight. Sabinski and I both know the newspapers're onto this. We have to nail him before he's warned. He could run again and be smarter about it by now."

Lydia shrugged, her back turned to him.

Tyree let out the breath he'd been holding, and a puzzled anger started to rise. Amy grabbed his large hand and tugged. "C'mon, we might be too late as it is."

Tyree went.

When they reached the car, pulled into the deep shadow beneath a golden rain tree, Amy chided, "You parked under a rain tree? You've got crap all over your car from the tree droppings now. Worse than sitting under a caged polecat."

She was right. Yellowish green bits covered his black car all over. "I bet your mom wouldn't like you to say *crap*."

"I know. I do my best around her."

Tyree felt like saying worse than *crap* as he tried to brush the sticky yellow stuff off and it only rolled in the dust already coating his Cherokee.

"There." She pointed at the back window of his car. Or actually, at the black hole where the window had been. He didn't need his key to open the door. Swearing fluently but as quietly as possible under his breath to keep from corrupting his accomplice, he stuck his head inside the Cherokee to view — nothing.

He swung in fury to face Amy. "You knew!"

Amy shrugged, absolutely unintimidated. "Guessed. Might as well go on in and get a night's sleep."

He glared at the pixie, his eyes slits. Then he relaxed. "Good advice. See you in the morning." He wheeled and strode his way up the broad white stairs to Ms. Doree's back door. Finding it unlocked, he let himself in. As soon as he reached his room, he turned on the light, moved around here and there, sure Amy must still be down there watching, then extinguished the light. He rolled around on the bed for a few seconds, pulling back the covers, ruffling the sheets. For an instant, his body sank into fatigue like a warm bath, but he didn't allow himself to stay there. He rolled sideways off the bed, crawled to the window, looked down. No sign of Amy. He couldn't even see his car in the darkness, and he noticed the moon cast hardly any shadow. A good night for hunting. A frail sliver of moon slid from behind a cloud, confirming his assessment. He sat down and thought. Hunt with what? He held up his hands. Well-trained weapons. He preferred them to guns anyway. He hadn't lost everything after all.

He let his back rest against the wall under the window. An hour's rest. Sitting up. He didn't trust the soft bed he longed for. One hour. Then go.

The hour passed, he lunged to his feet, did a few limbering stretches, then like a black cat crept down the stairs to let himself out the back door. It still wasn't locked, at which he tsked, until he remembered he was in the land of Kizzy and Amy.

He took the side paths one by one, figuring that with many of the four hundred population tucked cozily up by the hotel, he could scan from house to house for a forty-year-old man without it taking all night. He had a detail he hadn't shared with Amy. The man had a tattoo of a knife etched onto the back of his left hand. A jailhouse tattoo, which meant it was blue and homemade fuzzy, probably nearly invisible after so many years. The point of the knife aimed at the fugitive's left middle finger, recording a knifing he'd done in Juvenile many years ago, his way of refusing a jailhouse romance. A matter of pride for a punk kid, to have killed an enemy and gotten away with it. For no proof had ever pointed to Edgar Fallon except that he'd never shown up in the clinic with a torn-up ass, and then the sudden appearance of the tattoo. Health and a tattoo were proof of nothing in court, although crystal-clear evidence inside. And Edgar was left-handed.

Keeping his head down and low, wishing fervently for his monocular night vision headgear and the Game Finder scope, he made do with his own eyes and crept through the Hollow. At both cabins and houses, going slow, he found that the Hollow residents had an uncommon love for dogs. One cabin even had pigs roaming free. He'd read that pigs were smarter and even more vicious than dogs, so he skirted this place nervously. Finally, the sky lightened and made his stealth ineffective. Not having gotten even close to one cabin, one bedroom window, or one man of the right age, he turned to creep home, then said, "Fuck it," and straightening himself, scuffed like a native directly down the middle of the street.

In his room, he threw himself onto the soft bed and totally disgusted, fell into an intense, dreamless sleep. As the sun moved high enough to enter his window, he woke long enough to remember breakfast, then fell asleep again.

In the early evening he finally came to. His dusty sweat had dirtied the sheets, a detail he knew would anger the formidable Ms. Doree Zendall. He peeled himself off the hot bed and climbed

naked into the curvy tub with legs and a shower nozzle like a
sunflower. The shower curtain, a daisy-covered film of plastic,
glued itself to his thighs as he stood in the hot downflow of water.
Washing away his sins, he thought to himself with a snort. His stupidity in thinking all people were the same, all methods would
work the same everywhere. He should've farmed out this chore to a
fellow skip tracer from a nearby area, one used to country ways.

He put on clean clothes and descended the stairs. Ms. Zendall
stood waiting, a stony expression on her flushed face as she
watched him descend. He felt like he was approaching doom, not a
landlady. He wondered if the glistening coat of sweat on her brow
was from the heat or anger at him for missing breakfast.

"I'll pay for —" he started, but she chopped off his words with a
jab of a fat hand.

"Ms. Bearclaw is waiting to talk to you. Her and Amy." She
wheeled and marched away, her errand fulfilled.

Eyebrows high, Tyree whistled away the ghosts of last night's failure as he strode easily down the middle of the road again, aimed
for the path to the Bearclaw home.

Again seated in the kitchen, Tyree waited. Amy clearly had some
things to say. Eyeing him with amusement, Amy asked, "Any luck
last night?"

"You know the answer to that."

She tapped her foot on the linoleum floor. "Ready to meet Kizzy
now?"

He thought about it. "Whyn't you offer this meeting last night?"

"'Cause you weren't in any mind to listen to anybody. You knew
what you wanted, and what you wanted was no interference. Now.
Ready to meet Kizzy?"

He sighed. "Sure."

In minutes he found himself climbing a hill along a path he
doubted he'd have found without Amy's guidance. A small, square
cabin sat up high, tucked among the treetops and wedged into the
hillside. With no knock, Amy opened the screen door and waved
him through. The front door was in direct line with a back screen
door, and as a result, a slight breeze cooled the small house, and
the air felt pleasant to his baked skin. Amy pointed to a scoop-
shaped bench of a sofa, padded with patterned Indian blankets, so
he sat. The blankets smelled of sweet chamomile.

An old woman of an age he couldn't guess, using a stick to

lean on, was ushered into the room by Amy and helped to lower herself into a rocking chair padded so thickly it looked like a catcher's mitt. Her balding head was outlined against the sun coming through the back door, and her hair looked like wiry fuzz in shadow. He stood to be polite, but she patted the air, motioning him to sit down.

"I'm Kizzy, hon. Amy's told me about you and said she told you about me, so that starts us both off square."

Tyree blinked. "Yes, ma'am."

"Amy told you to rest yourself last night; you shoulda taken her advice. But you didn't."

"Ah, no ma'am."

"Wasted yourself, din'tcha, son."

Tyree settled back into the sofa with a sigh.

"I understand your feelings," Kizzy said. "Now fill me in about this boy you're after."

Tyree told her all he knew. And this time included the tattoo and the left-handedness.

Amy frowned. "You held back on me."

Tyree shrugged. "Sorry."

Kizzy tapped her stick on the floor twice, turned to Amy, said, "Fetch 'im, hon. Hurry up afore he takes off."

Amy said, "I kept watch on Elroy all night. He's still here, but not much longer."

Kizzy nodded and waved Amy away. "So run, then." Amy darted for the door and was soon out of sight.

"You tellin' me this little girl is going to fetch my perpetrator to me while I sit here?"

"Rather be bit by a pig?"

Tyree shut his mouth, shifted his broad shoulders within his T-shirt.

Kizzy smiled.

Despite slamming the flimsy screen door of Barstow's Dry Goods store in her haste, then her boots tromping loudly on the wood slat floor, Amy composed her face in a pleasant, hopefully sociable smile. "How ya doin', Mrs. Barstow?"

Mrs. Barstow nervously fingered a bolt of flowered cotton material still draped across her counter from some earlier customer. "Just fine, Amy. 'N' you?"

"Oh, good, good." Amy lounged against the counter to show her worry-free state.

Mrs. Barstow tugged the material from beneath Amy's forearm. "You're dusty, hon," she said apologetically.

"Your hubby round back like usual?" asked Amy.

Mrs. Barstow firmly eyed the material as she wound it back onto the bolt. "I 'spect. Always doin' the books; don't know why it takes him so long. Why?"

"Got a question for him, ma'am. You mind?"

Mrs. Barstow looked at Amy for a long moment. Then she looked again at the bolt of material and took a deep breath. She shook her head and turned her back on Amy.

Amy pulled reluctantly away from the counter. "Gonna be okay?" she asked.

Mrs. Barstow glanced over her shoulder at Amy, eyes glistening. "Was fine before. Got Wendy now. 'N' the grandbaby's comin' soon. I'll be fine again." Amy squeezed the woman's round arm quickly, then rushed for the back door. Mr. Barstow wasn't there, but the outside door stood ajar, so she pulled it open. Mr. Barstow was in his old brown Buick, slowly edging it backward, spinning the big steering wheel to back and turn the huge car down the alley toward the road.

Amy just walked over and stood in front of the old car's front bumper. He turned his head to put the gear into forward, then saw her. Mr. Barstow slammed on brakes. They looked at each other. Amy could see his left hand, high on the steering wheel, illumined in a glare of sun through the windshield. A big scar disfigured the hand. A scar that ended in a point over his middle finger. Amy'd known about the scar for years, never thought a thing about it before. Lots of people have scars. Of all kinds.

Amy pointed. Mr. Barstow, without a word or nod, rolled the car back into its parking place. The back seat was piled with boxes and clothes wadded into bundles. *Not a good packer,* Amy thought. A black, rectangular nylon case poked up through some shirts. Tyree's goods might've pawned into enough to stake a man to a modest new start in life.

When he opened the Buick's door, it creaked. Dust and old age had worn down the hinges. He slowly emerged from behind the wheel. Amy took his right hand in hers. "Kizzy wants to see you."

He nodded.

Contributors' Notes

Jeff Abbott has written seven novels of mystery and suspense. He is a three-time nominee for the Edgar Allan Poe Award (including a Best Short Story nomination for "Bet on Red") and a two-time nominee for the Anthony Award. His first novel, *Do Unto Others,* won both the Agatha and the Macavity Award for Best First Novel. He is the author of the Whit Mosley suspense series (*A Kiss Gone Bad* and *Black Jack Point*); his latest novel is *Cut and Run.* He lives in Austin, Texas, with his wife and two sons.

▪ When I was approached to write a gambling-themed short story, I wanted to draw on the hip mythos of Las Vegas: cool criminals, beautiful and world-wise women, and enormous stakes that go way beyond what's being wagered at the tables. I also wanted to bring that feeling of high-stakes staredown to the relationship between Sean and Red, to lead up to a moment between them where one of them must blink and change a life forever. From the opening line, I wanted to create the feeling for the reader of watching a roulette ball in an extended spin: anticipating that delicious yet awful moment when the ball tumbles to rest and someone wins and someone loses. Sudden reversals in fortune are the engine for both gambling addictions and suspense stories. That was the central idea I wanted to explore in "Bet on Red" — what happens if an unexpected downturn in our fortunes creates a new and dangerous opportunity. And mostly, I wanted to entertain the reader. I had a great deal of fun writing "Bet on Red," and I'm adapting it into a screenplay for a short film.

Jeffrey Robert Bowman was born in 1979 and raised in Atlanta, Georgia. After attending Tufts University for three years, he graduated with a B.A. in literature and history. Currently, he divides his time between the United States and South America, where he works as a freelance writer and English teacher.

▪ "Stonewalls" has remained a favorite of mine ever since I first conceived of the idea ages ago. While I do not consider the story a classic mystery story in the tradition of Chesterton or Doyle, there is a certain element to the tone I associate with my having read far too much Poe in too short a period of time. Poe was, to a great degree, the creator of the mystery genre, and it is his influence to which I am indebted for "Stonewalls."

William J. Carroll, Jr., was born in Marlboro, Massachusetts, in 1947. He served in the army in Vietnam, Thailand, and Korea, and settled in Hawaii. He has a B.S. from Chaminade University, and an M.A. and Ph.D. from the University of Hawaii. He lives and works in Honolulu.

▪ The Virginiak stories, of which "Height Advantage" is one, were born of my military service, a love of the northwest, where many of the stories are situated, and a lifelong need to write. They also emerge from a desire to emulate the styles of the American greats of mystery fiction, Hammett and Chandler in particular; but, as Ross Macdonald accomplished in his long, wonderful Archer series, they are also born of a need to project what I consider the best of us — qualities of value — into a character who faces stressful, trying, and desperate circumstances. Which makes Virginiak not me by any means, despite the first-person narrative, but he is the best of me, mirroring qualities I like about myself and others; and seeing those qualities personified and under challenge is the real kick of this whole thing.

Benjamin Cavell was born in Boston and is a graduate of Harvard College, where he was a boxer and an editor for the *Crimson*. His first book, *Rumble, Young Man, Rumble,* a collection of stories in which "Evolution" appears, was published by Knopf and named an *Esquire Magazine* Best Book of 2003.

▪ I don't like to tell stories. I'm sure this is not a proper thing for a writer to admit, but I'm annoyed when I read interviews with novelists in which they say, "I write because I want to tell stories," or (worse), "I just had a story that needed to be told." I resent feeling obligated to make something happen. I'd rather just have my characters yap at each other.

I've always been attracted to the idea of writing mysteries, in part because a mystery supplies its own momentum. I think part of the reason I've never really been *able* to write a mystery is that I can't figure out how to do it without forcing my characters into situations they would never put themselves in, which in turn shakes my conviction in the reality of the story and makes everything feel false. My first attempts at writing (when I was eleven, twelve years old) were super-hardboiled detective stories that featured hip, wisecracking, Marlowe-style narrators who talked out of the sides of their mouths. My problem, even then, was that I couldn't quite make myself believe in the world I was creating.

While I was writing "Evolution," I never thought of it as a mystery (in fact, I'm still not sure that it is). I wrote it from beginning to end, without jumping around, without ever really knowing what was going to happen until it happened. Looking at it now, three years after I wrote it, I see a few things that bother me, things I might do differently if I were writing the story today. But I'm happy to see that the writing is not safe or polite, is in fact right where I want it — on the brink of out-of-control, pulling the story behind it toward the edge of the cliff.

Christopher Coake was born in Indiana, and raised there and in Colorado. He lives in Columbus, Ohio, where he has just finished an M.F.A. at the Ohio State University; prior to that he received an M.A. in creative writing at Miami University of Ohio. Chris's short fiction has appeared in the *Journal;* the late, lamented *Central Ohio Writing;* the *Gettysburg Review;* and *Epoch.* His first book, a collection of stories entitled *We're in Trouble,* is forthcoming from Harcourt in the spring of 2005. In January 2005 Chris will begin teaching creative writing at the University of Nevada-Reno; in the meantime he's hard at work on a novel.

• I've always been attracted to, and at the same time appalled by, true crime books and television shows — a conflict I let Patricia and Larry argue for me in "All Through the House." A couple of years ago I read two books that affected me particularly. The first — which has left my possession, and whose title I can't recall — was a biography of Charles Whitman, the University of Texas sniper. Whitman killed his wife and mother the night before his shooting spree, and the book included photos of these murder scenes with the bodies entirely blacked out — an odd touch that disturbed me more deeply than other books' lurid gore. Not long afterward I read a book called *Shadowed Ground,* by Kenneth E. Foote (a professor at UT; his book examines Whitman too), which is about the ways people either memorialize or erase the sites of murders and tragedies. From it I learned that the vacant farmhouse of serial killer Ed Gein had become, after his arrest, a twisted kind of tourist attraction, and that it was destroyed by an anonymous arsonist just before it was to be sold at auction. The idea of telling a story that melded both image and vignette — a story that was at once the history of a place *and* of the people who had been deleted from it — seemed pretty potent to me. I knew from the start I wanted to move backward; the metaphor I used for this process, which I realize is not 100 percent accurate, was that of an archaeological excavation. If I kept digging in the same place, what would I find?

I finished a draft of the story during my first year at Ohio State, and I was sure it was an incomprehensible failure. But Lee K. Abbott, who is (don't tell anyone) not quite the curmudgeon he claims to be, explained its worth to me during his workshop. Then he spent months badgering me to finish my revisions and submit the story to journals. Finally he grabbed it out of my hands and gave it to the good people at the *Gettysburg Review* himself. That a writer of his caliber could champion any work of mine continues to awe me . . . so my deepest thanks, Lee, yet again.

Patrick Michael Finn was born in Joliet, Illinois, in 1973, and was raised there and in rural southern California. He graduated magna cum laude from the University of California, Riverside, and completed his M.F.A. at the University of Arizona, where he was a Dean Charles Tatum Teaching Fellow. A winner of many fiction prizes, including the Associated Writing Programs' Intro Award and the 2004 *Third Coast* Fiction Award, his stories have appeared in *Quarterly West, Ploughshares,* the *Richmond Review,* and *Third Coast.*

▪ I wrote "Where Beautiful Ladies Dance for You" during my last semester of graduate school, when I was studying with Elizabeth Evans and Jonathan Penner, two terrific writing teachers who cultivated my imagination and productivity. The story began with only a vague sense of Ray Dwyer. I pictured a big Joliet guy who worked in the quarries, but I didn't really know what to do with him, which obviously meant I didn't know what to do with the story. And then one night while I was pacing and biting my nails, I remembered a young man I went to high school with — I hadn't thought of him for years — who was the son of Greek immigrants who owned a restaurant in nearby Tinley Park. His father actually had hired a belly dancer once or twice to entertain the customers; the city told him to stop, and that was the end of it. At the high school, we joked with his son about it. "Hey, Sam," we'd say. "How are your dad's belly dancers?" Anyway, once my memory dug up that information, I knew exactly where Ray Dwyer belonged. Thank you, Susan Straight, for believing that my story belonged somewhere as well.

Rob Kantner (www.RobKantner.com) has published, in addition to nine mystery novels featuring ex–union enforcer Ben Perkins, some four dozen short stories and novellas in the realms of crime, suspense, and the supernatural (and, in a single instance, romance), plus three nonfiction books and many articles and essays. He lives with his wife, Deanna, on their rural Michigan farm.

▪ As a writer I've always loved to tinker with point of view. As a person I'm intrigued by the idea that seemingly random events may be, unbeknownst to the participants, linked in a domino-game chain of cause and effect. In a sense, "Wendy" is a merger of these interests. The point of view is handed off like a baton from one mini-protagonist to the next, and the story is really a chain of vignettes depicting busy, messy lives linking for brief moments in a dance of cause and effect, ending with a positive outcome for the title character, whom we never really meet. I began it as an experiment and finished it because it refused to let me go. It was fun to write, and also about drove me nuts.

Jonathon King was born in Lansing, Michigan. His first novel, *The Blue Edge of Midnight*, introduced P. I. Max Freeman and won the Edgar Award for Best First Novel by an American Author in 2002. He has been a street reporter for newspapers since 1980 and has won awards from the Society of Professional Journalists (the Green Eyeshade award), the National Association of Black Journalists, and the American Association of Sunday and Features Editors. His third Max Freeman novel, *Shadow Men*, was published this year. He has lived in Florida for the past twenty years and continues to work as a senior writer for the South Florida *Sun-Sentinel*.

• I'd been spinning the storyline of "Snake Eyes" since 1999 when I wrote a series for my newspaper on the last one hundred years of South Florida. The foundations are historical. Men were hired in the 1920s to clear diamondback rattlesnakes from the scrubland where Hialeah Race Track was eventually built. Colonel E. R. Bradley ran an illegal casino for the rich and famous visitors to the City of Palm Beach for forty-eight years, starting in early 1898, and bragged that he had never been robbed. When a friend of mine first read the story, he commented that he thought it well written "but the hero is a thief!" To which I replied: "Yes?"

Stephen King was born in Portland, Maine, and raised in Durham, a nostoplight town twenty miles north of that city. He graduated *cum laude* from the University of Maine (known by some New England wits as the University of Cow) in 1970. He's written a lot of novels and short stories since then. Some aren't too bad, and a couple really kick ass.

• One night in early 2003, I woke from a terrible nightmare. In it, my wife and I were in our kitchen and I was making our breakfast while she read the newspaper. The telephone rang. She answered it, then held it out and said, "It's for you." But I didn't want to answer it, because I knew — positively *knew*, the way you sometimes do in dreams — that someone wanted to tell me one of our children was dead. I went directly from my bed to the word processor and wrote "Harvey's Dream" at a single go. All I really needed to do to make it work was to subtract the love that still powers the marriage I share with my wife, and change the point of view from the man to the woman. There's no explaining why these things work; you just know they will, and you do them.

Michael Knight is the author of a novel, *Divining Rod*, and two collections of short fiction, *Dogfight and Other Stories* and *Goodnight, Nobody*. His stories have appeared, among other places, in *Esquire*, *The New Yorker*,

StoryQuarterly, and the *Virginia Quarterly Review.* He teaches creative writing at the University of Tennessee.

▪ Every semester I assign my students some variety of an exercise on writing dialogue and scene. Often they ask for sample scenarios to help get them started. I borrowed this one, years ago, from Josip Novakovich: *Write a probing dialogue between a police officer and a burglar who pretends to live in the apartment from which he's stealing.* I mixed it in with a few others, some cribbed from teaching texts, others of my own devising. To my surprise, the vast majority of the class picked the cop/burglar scene to write. So did the next class. And the next one. And so on, with mixed results, until I quit using it. I included this particular scenario to allow for some room for comedy, but it always struck me as too ridiculous to generate anything of substance. Anyway, I decided, at last, to have a go at it myself. The final draft of "Smash and Grab" veers pretty far from the original source, but it does prove that my students are right about most things and I'm usually well served if I shut up and pay attention.

Richard Lange's stories have appeared in the *Sun,* the *Southern Review,* the *Iowa Review,* and other publications. He lives in Los Angeles and is currently working on a novel.

▪ Things weren't going so well for me when I wrote "Bank of America." I was angry and broke. I had a bad job and felt humiliated every day. I began to fantasize about ways out of my situation, and, living in the bank robbery capital of the world and all, those fantasies took on criminal overtones. The first drafts of this piece were too full of fire and ranting. I had to step back and let the characters do their stuff. It was a good lesson in corralling raw emotion. I'm doing okay now. I got a new job, a better one; I quit smoking. But I'm still angry.

It's important that I thank Marie Hayes and the other good people at *StoryQuarterly* for originally printing this piece. Without them, I wouldn't be here.

Tom Larsen lives in Lambertville, New Jersey, with his wife, Andree, and Langley the cat. His work has appeared in *Newsday, Cottonwood, Mixed Bag,* and *Christopher Street Magazine.* "Lids" first appeared in *New Millennium Writing* in the spring of 2003. "Straight Life," his latest story, is included in the current issue of *New Millennium Writing,* and his short story "What's Marvin Gaye Got to Do with It?" has been nominated for a Pushcart Prize by *Lynx Eye* magazine in Los Angeles.

▪ I first got the idea for "Lids" while living in an apartment in the Berkeley flatlands. The tenant next door ran a small-time drug operation and his customers included several local rockers who were poised on, but would never quite topple over, the brink of stardom. Mike, the tenant, never slept and rarely left the apartment. Traffic was horrendous and I was initially torn between calling the cops and stealing his stash. I settled, instead, on becoming his most reliable customer.

The character "Lids" came from thirty years of watching Robert Mitchum movies.

The location is an amalgam of every place I have ever lived.

The rest I made up.

New Orleans–born **Dick Lochte** worked for a detective agency, managed a travel company, and promoted and wrote film reviews for a world-famous magazine for men before moving to southern California and a career as a journalist, screenwriter, and author. His first novel, *Sleeping Dog,* a *New York Times* Notable Book, was nominated for the Edgar, the Shamus, and the Anthony Awards and won the Nero Wolfe Award. Lochte is the author of a short story collection, *Lucky Dog,* and eight novels, the most recent being the legal thriller *Lawless,* written with attorney Christopher Darden.

- It was inevitable that I write a story about bank robbers. Not only do I live in what the FBI considers to be the bank robbery capital of the world, I was able to do my research for "Low Tide" at the dinner table. My wife is the president of a nationwide organization of licensed psychologists specializing in caring for the victims of workplace trauma. The trauma is usually the result of bank robberies. My robber, who'd probably be nicknamed the Movie Star Bandit, is a direct descendant of a long line of genuine perps such as the Yankee Bandit, the Plaid Shirt Bandit, and (because he carried his gun in his tummy-pack) the Kangaroo Bandit. The other characters — bank employees, customers, lawmen, et al. — are pure fiction. As are the details of the robber's modus operandi, which, readers with larceny in their hearts should note, may not work as smoothly in real life.

Richard A. Lupoff has written more than fifty books spanning the worlds of crime, science fiction, horror, fantasy, and mainstream fiction. He is best known in the mystery field for his eight-volume arc of novels about insurance investigator Hobart Lindsey and homicide detective Marvia Plum. The series stalled, unfortunately, after seven entries, but Lupoff has sworn to complete the as-yet fragmentary eighth volume in the pretty near future.

- When I was a schoolboy we were taught history as a memorization exercise: the names of kings, generals, politicians, and inventors; the dates of battles and elections. Such dry stuff was horribly boring and turned me away from history for many years. Then I discovered, chiefly through observing the world around me, that history is, in fact, a *story,* and a fascinating one. This realization has informed my novels, short stories, and works of nonfiction.

Writers of crime, suspense, and mystery are best described as haunted by the genre, and **Joyce Carol Oates** is one of these. Born and raised in upstate New York, she received degrees at Syracuse University and the University of Wisconsin, and has been a professor of humanities at Princeton University since 1978. She is a recipient of the National Book Award and, in 2003, the Common Wealth Award for Distinguished Achievement in Literature. She is the author most recently of the novella *Rape: A Love Story* and *I Am No One You Know*, a collection of short stories on crime-related themes.

- "Doll: A Romance of the Mississippi" is about a subject that has always fascinated me: the conjunction of the familial and the murderous. That individuals who are devoted to blood relatives can be utterly heartless to nonrelatives; that individuals whom we might find attractive, even charismatic, if encountered in the right circumstances, can be monstrous in other circumstances where to encounter them would be lethal.

In what we call real life, as distinct from fiction, there are very few girls like Doll Early, who prey upon sexual predators. Young girls exploited in the flourishing sex trade are not likely to be empowered to avenge themselves upon their clients. But "Doll: A Romance of the Mississippi" is a romance, and Doll and her father, Mr. Early, are figures of romance. I meant them to have an American mythic aura, outlaws who in another era might be the subjects of ballad.

Jack O'Connell is the author of the novels *Box Nine*, *Wireless*, *The Skin Palace*, and *Word Made Flesh*. He lives with his wife and children in Worcester, Massachusetts, where he is currently at work on a new "Quinsigamond" book.

- In general, and from the start, I've preferred the long form. But every now and then, a notion for a short story arrives unexpectedly and pecks away at me until I heed it. "The Swag from Doc Hawthorne's" is a good example of this occasional ambush. The story began with an image from my misspent youth: I once lasted a week doing Darcey's job — driving a shuttle van from early morning until late afternoon around the same brief and circular route of a research institute. Such employment will breed stories or psychosis. In this instance, I bloomed a story about impossible stories. And though the future looks ambiguous, at best, for our two ill-suited partners in crime, I'm not at all convinced we've seen the last of Yuk Tang and Darcey.

Frederick Waterman is a former journalist and sportswriter who worked for newspapers in Connecticut and New Hampshire and for United Press

International. His assignments included coverage of murder trials, presidential campaigns, the Olympics, the Super Bowl, and Wimbledon. He also worked as a drama critic in New York and Boston. "Best Man Wins" is the sixteenth story in the "Row 22, Seats A & B" short-story series, which appears in United Air Lines' in-flight magazine, *Hemispheres,* and at Row22.com.

> • When I read a short story, I want it to be compelling from the start, so that I *must* know what happens. I want the writing to be clean and clear, I want the writer to have a voice that is so distinct I can almost hear the words being spoken out loud, and those words should have a rhythm and cadence that seem to carry the reader along. I want the story to have themes that I will find myself thinking about later and characters I'd recognize if they walked into the room — not because of their appearance, but because I'd understand who they are and why. Those are the things I admire in a good short story, and that is what I sought in "Best Man Wins."

Timothy Williams is a native Kentuckian and a graduate of the M.F.A. program at Southern Illinois University Carbondale. His fiction has appeared in the *Greensboro, Colorado, Cimarron,* and *Texas Reviews* and in several other literary quarterlies. A short story collection and a crime novel are now with his agent and should be landing on editorial desks soon. He currently lives in Murray, Kentucky, with his wife, Sherraine, and two children, Carson and Madelyn, and teaches creative writing and humanities at Murray State University.

> • "Something About Teddy" was inspired by a long, monotonous drive on an interstate with my wife. During the trip, she decided to pass the time by analyzing my personality. Her diagnosis? Being married to me is like being married to two men — one who craves order and meaning, another who thrives on chaos. That was enough to spark my imagination, and I began to wonder what would happen if you locked the two into a car and put murder on their agenda. Somewhere along the line, I realized that theirs was a love story with an inevitable ending. I'd also like to thank Neil Smith at *Plots with Guns* both for publishing my story and for providing a place on the Web where hardboiled and noir fans like myself can indulge our passion.

Scott Wolven is the author of *Controlled Burn,* a collection of short stories published by Scribner. Wolven's appearance in the 2004 edition marks the third consecutive year his stories have been selected for *The Best American Mystery Stories* series. He has taught creative writing at Binghamton University (SUNY) and attended graduate school at Columbia University.

> • "El Rey" is about hard work, boxing, and murder — a real action story. I grew up in Catskill, New York, so boxing and boxers were all around, in-

cluding the Champ, Mike Tyson. I read once that "action can be inscrutable . . . and desperately concealing. As we understand the story better, it is likely that the mystery does not necessarily decrease," but grows. Eudora Welty wrote that (along with her own fine stories), and she was a Ross Macdonald fan. So she knew about the increase of mystery through action, especially around dangerous characters like Tom Kennedy, and I thought about it as I wrote the story. In fairness to the setting, if you're ever in the real St. Johnsbury, Vermont, visit the St. Johnsbury Athenaeum, on Main Street. A true American treasure.

This story is dedicated to Tom Sahagian, the straight shooter. To all the men and women in our armed forces. Special thanks to Randy Duax at lostinfront.com, Denise Baton at Mysterical-E, Susan Strehle, Ruth Stanek, Stefanie Czebiniak, Jaimee Wriston Colbert, Colin Harrison, Sloan Harris, Ray Morrison, Alex Cussen, M & DW, and the super team at WSBW.

Angela Zeman was born in Corpus Christi, Texas, where her widowed mother brought her up mostly within the public library. She attended various colleges, the most distinguished being the Heron School of Art in Indiana. Having loved books all her life, she decided to learn to write at the age of thirty-five. Since then, as per the exasperated observation of her beloved friend and writing mentor, the late Gary Provost — "Like me, you want to write everything" — she began writing her first short story to distract her mind during a two-day car trip home from a Florida vacation. The car was full of children, some not her own. The car's driver was an unstable and violent man who had just discovered her secret: that she intended to divorce him. Potboiler indeed.

• Years later, Cathleen Jordan phoned from *Alfred Hitchcock's Mystery Magazine* to buy that story, "The Witch and the Fishmonger's Wife." My first sale! That story, however, was not my first attempt at writing. My earliest effort had been a novel about a female assassin-for-hire who only murdered husbands. (Are you detecting something here?) Although my protagonist did a superior job of eliminating nine, for some reason no one would buy that book. Thankfully, I've since sold many short stories and a different novel. That unsold book, however, began my fascination with a theme I seem compelled to explore in all my fiction, including this anthology's "Green Heat." Not that husbands are evil; I adore my current one. But that any relationship — among family or with the most vile stranger — can lead to terror, unexpected tenderness, or even a laugh. We humans, the planet's most imaginative connivers, endlessly validate my theory that we had no business living in the Garden of Eden in the first place.

Other Distinguished Mystery Stories of 2003

HOWARD, CLARK
The Mask of St. Peter. *Ellery Queen's Mystery Magazine,* April
HOWLAND, JACK
Hoover's Dad. *The Mississippi Review,* April
KNADLER, DAVID
Nobody's Business. *Ellery Queen's Mystery Magazine,* November
KRIEGLER, ELLIOT
My Only Jew. *Michigan Quarterly Review,* Winter
LIMON, MARTIN
The Filial Wife. *Alfred Hitchcock's Mystery Magazine,* March
MATHEWS, JAMES
Roar. *Northwest Review*
MINOT, STEPHEN
Venetian Rites. *StoryQuarterly,* #38
POE, DAVID R.
Wilson's Last Gardener. *StoryQuarterly,* #38
ROGERS, STEPHEN D.
Rousted. *Plots with Guns,* January/February
RUSCH, KRISTINE KATHRYN
Cowboy Grace. *The Silver Gryphon,* ed. Gary Turner and Marty Halpern
(Golden Gryphon Press)
SCHNEIDER, LON
The Chief Inspector. *The New Orphic Review,* Fall
SCHWARTZ, STEVEN
Seiza. *The Mammoth Book of Future Cops,* ed. Maxim Jacubowski and M.
Christian (Carroll & Graf)
SELLERS, PETER
In the Hole. *Ellery Queen's Mystery Magazine,* September/October
SMITH, CURTIS
Murder. *Cutbank,* Fall
WHEELER, GERALD R.
Signs. *North American Review,* January/February
WORKING, RUSSELL
The Irish Martyr. *Zoetrope: All-Story,* Fall

THE BEST AMERICAN SHORT STORIES® 2004

Lorrie Moore, guest editor, Katrina Kenison, series editor. "Story for story, readers can't beat *The Best American Short Stories* series" (*Chicago Tribune*). This year's most beloved short fiction anthology is edited by the critically acclaimed author Lorrie Moore and includes stories by Annie Proulx, Sherman Alexie, Paula Fox, Thomas McGuane, and Alice Munro, among others.

0-618-19735-4 PA $14.00 / 0-618-19734-6 CL $27.50
0-618-30046-5 CASS $26.00 / 0-618-29965-3 CD $30.00

THE BEST AMERICAN ESSAYS® 2004

Louis Menand, guest editor, Robert Atwan, series editor. Since 1986, *The Best American Essays* series has gathered the best nonfiction writing of the year and established itself as the best anthology of its kind. Edited by Louis Menand, author of *The Metaphysical Club* and staff writer for *The New Yorker*, this year's volume features writing by Kathryn Chetkovich, Jonathan Franzen, Kyoko Mori, Cynthia Zarin, and others.

0-618-35709-2 PA $14.00 / 0-618-35706-8 CL $27.50

THE BEST AMERICAN MYSTERY STORIES™ 2004

Nelson DeMille, guest editor, Otto Penzler, series editor. This perennially popular anthology is a favorite of mystery buffs and general readers alike. This year's volume is edited by the best-selling suspense author Nelson DeMille and offers pieces by Stephen King, Joyce Carol Oates, Jonathon King, Jeff Abbott, Scott Wolven, and others.

0-618-32967-6 PA $14.00 / 0-618-32968-4 CL $27.50 / 0-618-49742-0 CD $30.00

THE BEST AMERICAN SPORTS WRITING™ 2004

Richard Ben Cramer, guest editor, Glenn Stout, series editor. This series has garnered wide acclaim for its stellar sports writing and topnotch editors. Now Richard Ben Cramer, the Pulitzer Prize–winning journalist and author of the best-selling *Joe DiMaggio*, continues that tradition with pieces by Ira Berkow, Susan Orlean, William Nack, Charles P. Pierce, Rick Telander, and others.

0-618-25139-1 PA $14.00 / 0-618-25134-0 CL $27.50

THE BEST AMERICAN TRAVEL WRITING 2004

Pico Iyer, guest editor, Jason Wilson, series editor. *The Best American Travel Writing 2004* is edited by Pico Iyer, the author of *Video Night in Kathmandu* and *Sun After*

Dark. Giving new life to armchair travel this year are Roger Angell, Joan Didion, John McPhee, Adam Gopnik, and many others.

0-618-34126-9 PA $14.00 / 0-618-34125-0 CL $27.50

THE BEST AMERICAN SCIENCE AND NATURE WRITING 2004

Steven Pinker, guest editor, Tim Folger, series editor. This year's edition promises to be another "eclectic, provocative collection" (*Entertainment Weekly*). Edited by Steven Pinker, author of *The Blank Slate* and *The Language Instinct*, it features work by Gregg Easterbrook, Atul Gawande, Peggy Orenstein, Jonathan Rauch, Chet Raymo, Nicholas Wade, and others.

0-618-24698-3 PA $14.00 / 0-618-24697-5 CL $27.50

THE BEST AMERICAN RECIPES 2004–2005

Edited by Fran McCullough and Molly Stevens. "Give this book to any cook who is looking for the newest, latest recipes and the stories behind them" (*Chicago Tribune*). Offering the very best of what America is cooking, as well as the latest trends, timesaving tips, and techniques, this year's edition includes a foreword by the renowned chef Bobby Flay.

0-618-45506-X CL $26.00

THE BEST AMERICAN NONREQUIRED READING 2004

Edited by Dave Eggers, Introduction by Viggo Mortensen. Edited by the best-selling author Dave Eggers, this genre-busting volume draws the finest, most interesting, and least expected fiction, nonfiction, humor, alternative comics, and more from publications large, small, and on-line. This year's collection features writing by David Sedaris, Daniel Alarcón, David Mamet, Thom Jones, and others.

0-618-34123-4 PA $14.00 / 0-618-34122-6 CL $27.50 / 0-618-49743-9 CD $26.00

THE BEST AMERICAN SPIRITUAL WRITING 2004

Edited by Philip Zaleski, Introduction by Jack Miles. The latest addition to the acclaimed Best American series, *The Best American Spiritual Writing 2004* brings the year's finest writing about faith and spirituality to all readers. With an introduction by the best-selling author Jack Miles, this year's volume represents a wide range of perspectives and features pieces by Robert Coles, Bill McKibben, Oliver Sacks, Pico Iyer, and many others.

0-618-44303-7 PA $14.00 / 0-618-44302-9 CL $27.50

HOUGHTON MIFFLIN COMPANY www.houghtonmifflinbooks.com